Killing Tom

The places and characters in this story are fictitious and any similarity to, or apparent connection with, actual persons, whether alive or dead, is purely coincidental.

ISBN-13: 978-1530200474

ISBN-10: 1530200474

This book uses British English

PETER HILL is an internationally published author with 'The Staunton and Wyndsor Series' and 'The Commander Allan Dice Books' published by major publishing houses in both hard and paperback editions in the 1970s.

He has had a successful career in television drama as a writer, script editor and producer in the UK and New Zealand where he now lives.

Returning to novel writing *Killing Tomorrow* is the first of a new series, EVOLUTION'S PATH, set in the near future. The second book in the series is *The Ladies' Game,* and the third is *Procreation*.

All three are available as eBooks at most major online retailers and as paperbacks.

Find out more about Peter and his books by visiting his website:

peterjohneyershill.com

***

Principal Characters

Wenna Cavendish. A senior MI5 officer.

Charles Lovatt. Head of MI5.

Fleur Nichols. A high-profile TV journalist.

Joe Kendry. American documentary maker. Her lover.

Dr Simone Gofre. An internationally renowned virologist dying of cancer.

Auriol Preston. Her lover.

Walter Bloom. Head of news and current affairs at the BBC.

Phil Rogers. Joe Kendry's cameraman.

Colin Burcastle. Simone Gofre's boss.

Don Costello. Head of a secretive American counter-intelligence unit.

Alex Jones. A mid-rank MI5 agent.

Callum West. A New Zealand SIS officer.

Syed Siddiqi. A Pakistani secret service agent.

Salah Al- Rashidi. A senior terrorist. Top of the American hit list.

Detective Inspector Robert Purau. New Zealand police.

April Grosse. Fleur's agent.

PROLOGUE

'Do you love America?'

She is looking at him with interest, leaning forward as she withdraws the syringe of blood from his arm. Her head is tilted to one side; a thin lock of her straight jet-black hair has escaped its restraints and fallen slightly across her face. She is Hispanic, perhaps in her late twenties, of slim build with a pretty face and innocent wide brown eyes. The arthritic ceiling fan wafts her disturbingly attractive body scent towards him.

He does not know her and she hardly seems threatening but he is instantly alert. It's not the kind of question a nurse would be expected to ask a patient. It's precisely the sort of warning sign he had been told to beware of.

But this is routine, his annual free medical in the unit hospital. Just to keep an eye on his general health and especially the stomach ulcers that have been plaguing him for years. One of the perks of the job. He holds his breath for a moment, desperate to bring his heart rate under control, aware her eyes are fixed on him. She looks the part and she had seemed professional when she took the blood samples but was she really a nurse? Were those innocent eyes not so innocent after all, had she seen through his deception where others had not? No. Not possible. It is vital for him to regain his composure.

He is perched uncomfortably on the edge of a hospital bed in a curtained cubicle, dressed only in an open-backed surgical gown; his thin brown legs hang short of the floor. He feels vulnerable and alone. He forces a slight smile and drops his head to one side enquiringly, mimicking the way she is looking at him. There is nothing to fear except his own fear, he tells himself. So she's a bit strange; he mentally shrugs, he has been in the US long enough to know that sometimes first generation immigrants can be more patriotic than the native-born. He can handle this. The main thing is to make eye contact and not react in a way that incites suspicion.

'Of course you don't,' she says, before he has time to reply. 'You're a traitor.'

It is a cold, disinterested statement of fact and, as intended, it psychologically disables him. He is unable to make sense of what is happening. His mind is blank; fear unmans him, holds him immobile and dumb when he needs to make some response, anything rather than this stunned silence that screams guilt. Without further comment she turns her back on him and walks out of the cubicle with an angry swish of the curtains.

A tall, well-built man with greying hair replaces her. He is immaculately dressed and carries himself with the innate confidence that comes naturally to those of education, status and power. He is smiling gently but his snake eyes betray him. They are blank, without any hint of humanity or empathy, and now those eyes fix on him as if he were prey.

He shivers uncontrollably, clamping his teeth together to stop them chattering. No mercy can be expected from a man like this.

'I'm disappointed. You've let us down.'

As he hears the words, his stomach roils and he feels warm liquid soil the bed he is sitting on. He has been frightened many times in his life but has never experienced anything like the extreme terror this man induces in him. He is expecting vicious interrogation, beatings, maybe water-boarding; perhaps the torture chambers of a rat-infested prison in some East European state beyond the reach of Western law. He's been told this happens; if it happens to him he knows he will break; tell them whatever they want to know. He is a man of technical expertise, not a fighter.

But despite his powerful presence the man offers no threats. Instead he says, 'I think you should get dressed, don't you?'

***

In the days and weeks that followed there was no torture and barely any interrogation. They detained him in a motel-like suite within the complex and told his compliant wife that he was away on urgent business and out of contact. They left him alone for long periods to worry about how they had uncovered him, how much they knew of his activities and what his fate was to be. From the little they said to him it seemed that anything he could have told them they already knew. He was treated with unsettling courtesy bordering on comradeship. It was a careful and practised campaign of psychological grooming which left him physically unmarked but mentally dependent. When they thought he was ready, they made him an offer many stronger men than he would have willingly accepted. When he agreed, they clapped him on the back and the tall man gave him a manly hug and said he was one of them now.

He should have known that was never possible.

And because he was a painfully inexperienced player in the Great Game, it never occurred to him that once he had done as they asked he would have vital information that was tradable, and that would make him a threat to his new friends. A threat and an unacceptable risk.

***

In all his twenty-eight years he had never experienced such a buoyant sense of wellbeing. He had a new name, a completely new identity and he was free of the stress of duty and obligation that religion, ethnicity and family ties had placed upon him.

They had been informed of his exceptional programming talent when he was in his mid-teens. They were patient people, prepared to invest the necessary time and money to ensure this asset achieved its potential. An 'uncle' had offered him and his devout parents the dream of free further education in return for nothing more than accepting career advice and doing his duty to Allah and country. Thereafter he became totally immersed in his studies and later his marriage and the prestigious computer-programming job they found for him with an American-owned data protection company in Islamabad. At no point through these years did it occur to him that he had been recruited. Until that is, as his star was rising within the company, a visiting American Vice President sought him out and made an unexpected offer.

When told of his good fortune, his 'uncle' had hugged him close and praised Allah. Then he was told to whom he owed his dramatic good fortune; who owned him and what they expected of him. From that time on, fear had stalked his every waking moment.

Now those old ties had been severed. He had never been completely comfortable doing their bidding since, soon after he left Pakistan, an indiscriminate car bombing in a busy public market had killed his parents and dozens of other innocents, leaving him a vulnerable immigrant, working in IT for the American military; living in fear as he drip-fed what he learned to his deeply frightening terrorist controller.

Now he was a new person, with a new name, no longer Pakistani but a native-born American citizen, and he and his dutiful wife had birth certificates, passports and all the other necessary documents to attest to their new identities. Thrilled at his success she had accepted without question that these immense privileges were in return for the important computer work he did for the government. And he could just manage to convince himself that, although he no longer fed them information, all this had been achieved without any betrayal of his old masters.

The car he was driving was a new acquisition, provided as part of the deal, a somewhat nondescript but gas-miserly hybrid compact that fitted his inclination and new persona. His wife was beside him, now and then adjusting her seat belt to ease her discomfort as the child moved inside her. All their worldly goods had gone on ahead, the move arranged for them, like everything else, with dispatch and impeccable efficiency. It was late evening, dull and overcast with drifting misty rain that clouded the windscreen. He had the wipers on intermittent and headlights dipped. He kept to the inside lane in light traffic, driving well below the speed limit, conscious of the dangers posed by the conditions. For all his high excitement at the new life that awaited, he was a naturally careful and conservative man.

Ahead of him the four-lane freeway curved to his left and crossed high over rail tracks and a bleak industrial area that had been cleared for re-development. He had noticed the black SUV with the tinted windows behind them for some while; it was a rarity, there were few of these old gas-guzzlers on the road these days. When it pulled out to overtake him, spraying water up from its oversize tyres, he gave it no more than a casual glance.

It drew up alongside and hung there for a moment, holding position. He felt a moment's unease, but it pulled ahead and he relaxed. It was then, just before the corner above the rail tracks, that the steering wheel locked and the engine raced, thrusting his car forward in a sudden burst of uncontrollable speed. His instinctive reaction was to hit the brakes and knock the engine out of gear but the gearshift would not move and he lacked the strength to slow the vehicle against the full force of the racing engine. The car smashed through and over the side barrier and for a brief moment, supported by its momentum, hesitated above the void, headlights searching the leaden sky as if for celestial aid, before dipping suddenly as it plunged down onto the deserted lot below.

In the final seconds before he died he was still fighting desperately with the controls of the vehicle. To the last he did not understand that he had been betrayed.

KILLING TOMORROW

It could have got her killed, a simple error like that. She would hardly be the first celebrity to be hunted down for the trophy of her fame. Fleur Nichols was a determinedly private person but a very public figure and by all accounts an exceptionally bright lady.

Yet she trafficked her calls through her Hub and used her own name. No firewalls or alternate defences worth the mention. The tinkerbell boys could have hacked into it in their sleep. It was amazing how so many smart people sometimes did seriously dumb things.

Just in case she had missed some crucial element, Wenna indicated to her Hub to replay the extract. After the recorded message the number rang several times before pick-up. Then the conversation ran thus:

'Hi, this is Joe.' A male voice, light, with a hint of an American accent.

'Put her on, Joe.' A mature voice, heavy with authority.

'Who's calling?' Blandly unwelcoming.

'You know damn well who it is.' A blunt statement of fact from a man unused to being questioned.

'I'll find her.'

A reluctant sigh and a slight click as the mute is applied, then the room mike picks up the conversation.

'It's God again. Doesn't he ever give up?'

'Don't be grumpy, Joe, he's a lovely man.' The mute is clicked off. 'Daddy, how are you?'

'Could be a lot better, princess.'

'You work too hard.'

'Somebody has to.'

'Look, I promise, I am considering it.'

'I'm beginning to think it'll take a ton of Semtex to get you out of that love nest of yours.'

'That's very unfair, I needed a break.'

'So you've had one. Look, talk to me soon, okay?'

'I'll call you before the weekend. Promise.'

'Hmm. I'll hold you to that. Bye.'

'Bye.'

Wenna cancelled the replay, removed her earpiece and sat back in her chair, mulling things over. In the two months since the watch had been authorised, there had been only a handful of items flagged. The MI5 intercept software was primed to identify a long but carefully chosen list of words that might have some security application and when it did, SysLink forwarded the recording direct to the designated file officer to validate, analyse and assess the 'product'. So far, in the week since Charles had passed the file to her, none of the product had required action.

This time an idle word from Fleur's father had been enough to trigger the software and there was nothing else in the recording of interest. She wondered if she was missing something here. Why had Charles Lovatt allocated Fleur's intercept file to her? She was a Senior Intelligence Officer, Head of the Asian Desk, and on the face of it any of Wenna's junior agents could easily have handled it.

Nothing in the file gave any clear indication as to why Fleur Nichols was a surveillance target, so what had triggered interest in her? She had not been briefed on that or any other aspect of the case. Now she came to think about it, how had Charles persuaded the watchful powers-that-be to let him run an expensive 24/7 on Fleur, given it had such potential for a major PR embarrassment if knowledge of it ever became public. Invasions of privacy didn't come more blatant than this. If it all went pear-shaped then her head would be on the block as well as his.

Charles was a perennially busy man; had he really had the chance to think through the risk/benefit ratio of this particular project as he normally would? Maybe that was what he wanted her to do with the file, but he had not said so. Unless, for some devious reason of his own, there was a whole lot he was not telling her. Absolutely possible. She trusted him, of course she did, he was her mentor and she owed him a lot, but the more she thought about it the more uneasy she felt. It would hardly be politic to question him outright but maybe she could suggest a re-assessment and see what his reaction was.

Around her in the open plan office there was the ubiquitous murmur of Hubs and quiet background conversation. She said 'NFA' to the enquiring Hub screen in front of her, waited for the acknowledgement, flicked a finger for the next message, then hesitated. Something was not quite right. As Wenna recalled, Fleur had no close living relatives let alone a doting father. She returned to the Nichols file, ordered a trace on the call and sat back to wait.

Stuck on the side of her triple bank of monitors was a printed reminder pad. It read:

In secret offices across the land,
with whisper carpet
and cool humming air,
there walk the mighty and the grand.

Wenna Cavendish grimaced and stretched to relieve the stress in her shoulders. The anonymous doggerel had simply appeared one day. She looked around the room, taking in the eclectic mix of gender and ethnic origins of her staff. Which one was the poet? She knew the CV and file details of each and every one pretty much by heart and she had her suspicions, but did she know any of them well enough to identify the humourist with certainty? Probably not.

She was aware that some of her colleagues considered her too distant and aloof by far. The mild social rebuke the brief poem contained rather amused her, so she had left it there as a minor antidote to her recent ennui. Right at that moment she certainly did not feel mighty and, despite a bloodline more English than the parvenu royals, had never considered herself in the least grand.

The Hub identified the call. It had originated in the office of Walter Bloom. Well, that made sense. But intercepting the calls of the Head of News and Current Affairs at the British Broadcasting Company, who was unsurprisingly hypersensitive about phone hacking within the media or without, was akin to poking a starving tiger with a short stick. Not a game for the faint-hearted.

2

Fleur woke with her usual suddenness and was instantly aware of him. She breathed in the night scent of his body, deep draughts of aphrodisiac that worked their usual magic, sending twists of pleasure deep into her. She could sense he was slowly wakening.

She slid herself over him and butterfly-kissed his cheek with her eyelashes as she waited for him to rise to her. His eyes flicked open and he smiled.

Later they showered together, holding each other close under the spray, soaping and rinsing then stepping out to gently towel each other dry, all for the sheer tactile pleasure of it. They dressed, and Joe prepared coffee whilst Fleur, as she habitually did, walked through to the open-plan sitting room and pulled back the heavy curtains that had locked out the night. The outlook offered was uninspiring: a facing corner of the adjacent apartment block and a restricted three-quarter view of old man Thames. It did not matter to Fleur; she found it comforting in its familiarity.

The morning was dull; the sky obscured by low iron-grey cloud. A blustery, scurrying wind scattered whitecaps across the river and flicked spray up a set of stone steps on the far bank. She stood for a contented moment watching a police launch patrolling slowly up river, plugging determinedly into a low chop, passing an anchored barge. In the background there was the distant hum of the city traffic and the insistent wail of an ambulance demanding preference through the morning snarl.

She turned back into the room, content that her world had undergone no dramatic change overnight. The apartment had been hers long before he appeared so unexpectedly in her life and had an indefinable feminine feel on which his presence had had no discernable impact. Looking round the apartment, it would have been difficult to deduce with certainty what either did for a living or what their specific personal interests were. What hints there were could be found in the overflowing, ceiling-high bookcase, its library an eclectic mix of subject matter that filled half of one wall. Or perhaps the professional-standard multi-media Hub, clustered on a desk in one corner.

There were no family photographs, no framed diplomas, no awards or trophies or travel memorabilia. It was not that such things did not exist, rather that Fleur had elected not to have them on display. Nor did she have her own website or subscribe to any social networks. Such things belonged to the outside world and she had never wanted that world to intrude in here. This was her home, her haven, and now it was a place of safety for Joe as well.

Somehow, without the necessity for lengthy discussion, a mutually agreeable division of routine functions had been established over the year they had been together, a division that disposed of the duties of the day in a way that left them the maximum amount of time to themselves and never required them to be more than one room apart. They did not entertain. Joe's family were in the US, busy with their own lives, and somewhere along the line friends and acquaintances of both had fallen by the wayside, not brutally discarded but quietly put aside, not required on this voyage.

During that London winter, which had been long and hard but had seemed so short to them, they had spent their days at home, talking, listening to music or reading; seated in opposing armchairs so they could look up now and then and reassure themselves the other was still there.

Sometimes they read to each other, their selection a diverse mix of classic and modern literature. They followed the news on a variety of channels and talked at length of world events and social, religious and political issues – but always in the abstract, such things were of business and intellectual interest but no longer impacted on their daily lives.

Some days they made short darting forays into the retail world to stock up with essentials and sometimes they would walk the riverside paths shoulder-to-shoulder, hands clasped, oblivious to the wind-blown grime and the faintly nauseating waft of bio diesel from the exhausts of the city transport. They were never gone long; they had become reclusive, ever eager to retreat from a worrisome world of which they both had considerable experience, but had put aside for now. They were innocents playing house, loved-up and blind to the concerns and duties of maturity.

This selfish, self-absorbed and introverted life could not realistically last forever. Over recent days that disturbing understanding had come to both of them. They had talked about it briefly once or twice but had put the matter aside, the very thought was an unpleasant intrusion into their lives. But the problem would not go away, they were no more immune from the necessity to earn a living than any other couple and a year of idleness had taken its financial toll.

They finished a continental breakfast in companionable silence, disturbed only by the gentle background hum of the heating unit, and then wandered through to the sitting area with a final cup of coffee, putting off the evil hour.

They followed the pattern that habit dictated: Joe put his cup down on the coffee table and walked to the window, staring out at the grey morning and sluggish river traffic, hands deep in the pockets of his slacks, whilst Fleur flicked on the Hub screen.

She watched him as she took her usual seat and not for the first time wondered at her luck. Joe was somewhat over average height with the long and lithe body of a swimmer, a fact that owed much to his genetic inheritance and little to physical industry. His hair had grown unfashionably long over the winter months and was still tousled from his shower, almost reaching down to the collar of his favourite old rugby shirt, a tattered relic of his days at Cambridge. He should have felt cold, dressed in so little but, as she well knew, he generated a surprising amount of internal heat.

The Hub pinged discreetly in the background. Fleur could see the priority message on the screen without moving from her seat. It said 'Talk to me.' It was unsigned. Joe turned to look at it then resumed his perusal of the river.

She wanted to see his face so she said, 'Your coffee's getting cold.'

He turned slowly, reluctantly, with a shrug of the shoulders. Fleur's eyes were fixed on him. He looked at her with a wry, slightly sad smile. They both knew full well who the message was from; it was some days since Walter Bloom's last call. Joe came and sat opposite her as she put her cup and saucer down.

'Honey, we have to decide,' he said eventually.

'I know,' Fleur replied, reluctantly.

'But not Afghanistan.'

'There's nothing else on offer at the moment.'

'The place has been a near-permanent war zone ever since the West pulled their troops out and everybody knows it's so bloody dangerous they don't even bother to issue travel warnings anymore.'

'Only in parts and anyway, that's where foreign correspondents get sent,' she said gently.

'No, that's where war correspondents get sent.'

'These days that's a fine distinction.'

'Then let them send some guy with a death wish and no close relatives.'

Fleur grinned at him. 'Okay, we stay in our garret and live on baked beans. Except that sooner or later we'd be evicted for non-payment of the mortgage or the rates. There's not much the banks and local councils in this country don't know about legalised extortion.'

'I'm serious. What's the average lifespan of a journalist out there, a few days?'

'Oh come on, Joe, it's been over a year since... Anyway, you know perfectly well I don't want to go at all but if I keep on turning down work, sooner or later they'll stop offering. You know what the business is like.'

'Can't you get an office job at the Beeb? You could be their consultant on Arab affairs, resident expert on terrorism, that sort of thing.'

'They can buy an academic to do that, bring someone down from St. Andrews. There's a whole nest of terrorism experts up there. I think they breed them in Scotland. But you can't send an academic to do my job. You know that.'

Joe sighed and slumped back in his chair, pushing his untouched cup away. 'You're a damn adrenaline junkie and you miss it like hell, don't you?' he said, resigned.

'Yes. No. Well, not half as much as I'd miss you. I haven't missed it for the last year. Face up to it, Joe, we both have careers with a built-in risk factor. But look, Walter takes care of his people. I'd have a couple of ex-SAS minders to protect me and a chartered chopper in and out. Besides, I'd be looking into allegations the local terrorists are making. They're convinced America – no surprise there – is using biological warfare against their people. Sounds like they've been smoking too much of the local product but they invited me and they'll want me on their side, not dead in a ditch.'

'Great. So why don't I feel reassured? Okay, you miss it. I get that. I can hear you making a case to yourself to go and I understand, but these people are unpredictable, dangerous zealots.'

'Depends whose side you're on,' Fleur commented.

Joe stood up suddenly, taking short agitated steps back and forth, keeping his eyes fixed on her face, 'You know I don't normally talk like that but dead is dead, sweetheart. The Afghan government is not going to want you there. You'll have no protection. So how do you get in, tourist visa?'

'Not exactly…'

Joe was not listening. 'Suppose it's an AQE set-up to get a high profile target in there? Suppose they want a media hostage? You know these guys as well as anyone; to them you're an infidel, utterly expendable, they'd happily slit your throat in front of a camera knowing damn well they'll get headlines round the world. Plus, these people have a serious gender attitude problem. To them you'd be at best a second-class citizen, just a chattel, and I can't see you reacting well to that.'

'I can handle it, Joe.'

'What is the Beeb thinking anyway, asking a woman to go in there?'

Fleur raised her eyebrows. 'Er, pardon me?'

Joe waved the point away. 'I know I'm being sexist but I don't care. This is you. And suppose they're right and there really is some mutant bug on the loose, that's even worse – you'd be walking straight into danger.'

Fleur stood up and took his hands in hers. 'Joe, just calm down. I know what I'm doing and so does Walter. I've got a good nose for danger. And anyway, what happened to your well-honed liberal values?'

'You're trying to dodge the issue again. I'm dead serious. We're not that desperate.'

Fleur shook his hands. 'Being the control freak is my job,' she said, smiling.

Joe raised her hands to his lips and kissed them. 'I don't want to stop you working, honey, I know we can't always be joined at the hip but if you can't go in-house maybe they can send you somewhere safe.'

'Somewhere safe doesn't have any stories.'

'Then there's only one thing for it.' He dropped back into his seat as if the discussion were over. 'I'll take the UN job.'

'No!'

‘It’s the only thing that makes sense.’

‘Joe, it makes no sense at all. In Pakistan the NGO’s are under regular attack. The Taleban kill doctors and nurses just for providing polio vaccinations for God’s sake. And it’s bang in the middle of the Travel Warning Zone... No. Definitely not.’ Her face was set in grim determination.

Joe spread his hands in a placating gesture. ‘What can I tell you? Sure there’s some element of risk from random attacks but I’ll be on the move all the time. And I wouldn’t even be allowed into areas of a confirmed viral outbreak. Life goes on in these places, honey.’

‘No! It’s like you said, the risk’s too high.’

They were both on their feet again, Joe pacing.

‘So, boot’s on the other foot now, is it? You can put your life on the line but I can’t take the same level of risk? Pakistan, Afghanistan, exactly the same risk profile. Less in my case because it’s not as if I’d be actually meeting the enemy or investigating anything that has to do with the epidemic, is it?’

‘How would I know? You just told me you’d turned down a gig in Pakistan, not what it was about. You didn’t seem interested.’

‘I wasn’t. Then. But it’s better than you taking dumb chances.’

‘So you take dumb chances instead? I’m in love with an idiot.’

‘You’re not being reasonable about this,’ Joe protested.

‘I don’t do reasonable when your life’s at stake.’

‘Same.’

There was a long moment of unusually awkward silence before they resumed their seats.

‘So tell me about the project,’ Fleur said eventually.

‘You agree I should go then...’

She smiled sweetly at him. ‘Don’t push your luck, my darling. Just answer the question.’

Joe capitulated. ‘Okay, it’s a simple little UN-funded doco, the sort of thing I could do in my sleep.

‘Yes. And…?’

‘Okay. Reading between the lines, I’d say the UN wants to run a check on the Third World Two+One project, see what impact it’s had on the women who took the money, see if sterilisation after the third child not only reduced the population but improved their lives the way it was meant to. It’s not exactly that they don’t trust their people on the ground but they probably want an independent assessment and they want it on film. It's basically a PR exercise. At the moment there's no broadcaster involved, so it may never see the light of day. I'm a shoo-in to get it if I want it.'

'Is that Siggy talking?'

'Yeah, he said they asked for me. I only have to say yes.'

'Two+One has always been controversial. There's going to be a lot of heat around this,' Fleur commented.

'Okay, there's been religious opposition. Who would have thought Islam, the Catholic Church and the Bible Belt would agree about anything? But apparently the world doesn't have a population problem, and three children aren't enough for anyone. That aside, the main argument was about using an ACV instead of Quinacrine to sterilise the women. The usual stuff about the dangers of genetically engineered viruses. But I think the opposition's quietened down lately.'

'So you're being asked to make a doco that no-one outside the UN may see, about a subject that has no current news value.'

'Right. They're calling it a doco but it's more like a corporate video. How easy is that?'

'How long will it take to shoot what you want?'

'Two weeks. Maybe less.'

'Two weeks. And if the UN bean-counters are true to form they'll be paying peanuts for your trouble and risk no doubt.'

'No way. You may be the one with the BAFTA but I do have some standing in the business. Siggy would never let this monkey work for nuts.'

'Sorry, didn't mean it the way it sounded. I was just thinking. Not only will you be working in a TW Zone, you may be targeted because you're American, or because you may seem to be supporting Two+One.'

'Honey, I'll be in an uptown four-star hotel, not a backstreet dosshouse. My risk is nothing compared to what you were proposing to do.'

'But what about…'

'People live out their lives in those places and never get sick,' Joe interrupted. 'Besides, half the world is vaccinated with Roflu and I'll have a top up before I go.'

‘Hmm. Roflu’s not a hundred per cent. CNN had a report the other day saying the next mutation is overdue. It’ll be H5N50 or something.’

‘If it happens.’

‘It may already have happened, how would we know?’

‘Okay, it’s a big, bad, ugly world out there, but I’m just as likely to catch something on the Tube. So, are we agreed?’

Fleur sighed. ‘We’ve got to be adult and professional about this, haven’t we. Both of us.’

Joe shrugged. ‘Yes, but that doesn’t mean you...’

‘I still don’t like it. I want you in and out of there as fast as possible.’

He relaxed. ‘Sure.’

‘But I’m not going to sit here twiddling my thumbs until you get back. I’m going to Afghanistan. We’ll arrange it so we’re both away at the same time.’

‘Like hell!’ Joe exploded.

And for a while he actually believed it was an argument he could win.

3

Simone Gofre systematically removed her specialised work clothing piece by piece until she was naked. She bundled the items together and dropped them in the sterilising bin. Tiredness slowed her movements; in the last few months she had suffered frequent headaches and minor chest pains and often felt tired, putting it down to overwork and disturbed sleep, refusing to accept any more serious prognosis. She was critical of the body she saw in the cubicle mirror; it was not as it had once been.

Even so, few other women of forty-two would have complained at what she saw. She was tall and slim, her hair trimmed short and swept back, now showing a flick of grey here and there. She wore no makeup. Frown lines on her forehead gave the impression of permanent deep thought. She had long legs, a flat stomach and small, neatly pointed breasts that many a teenager would have envied. It was a body ageing slowly and with grace, undamaged by the trauma of childbirth.

That was not as Simone saw it however. Of late, little in her life had pleased her. Except for her work, and Auriol of course. Yet, if she had been put to the question, she could not have said what changes would have improved her lot. She knew that many would say she was fortunate indeed, with a loving relationship and a hugely important and fulfilling job. Despite this, lately she seemed destined to sip from a cup that was permanently half empty. She had no idea why she felt her life to be so grey and shadowed. She couldn't identify what, if anything, was wrong. Yet that dark feeling was real and because she did not understand it herself, that reality was the one thing she could not share with Auriol.

Simone showered, towelled and blow-dried her hair, combing it roughly into place with her fingers, then dressed in her street clothes before stepping through the double air lock of the PC4 facility. Fat Annie was on duty in the vestibule outside and greeted her with a cheery, double-chinned grin.

'Evenin', Doctor Gofre.'

'Good evening, Annie.'

Simone submitted to the security officer's body scan with what good humour she could manage, then stepped up to the security console to register her ID implant, retinal image and swab the inside of her cheek for a DNA check. All scientists in the PC4 unit went through the same process on entering and leaving. Genphree Biotics took their security responsibilities very seriously indeed.

'Computer's green,' Annie announced a few seconds later, beaming at Simone as if she had just won a Nobel Prize. 'Enjoy yer evenin' doctor,' she said, handing over Simone's identity tag, allowing her access through the rest of the facility.

Simone collected her handbag from her locker. She felt, as she always did when Annie beamed at her with such undemanding good will, an odd sense of intellectual *noblesse oblige*: the duty owed by the able and highly intelligent, who bore the worries of the world, to the carefree proletariat. It was, she acknowledged to herself, elitist, even arrogant, but it was real and to deny it was dishonest. The Annies of this world did not deserve to be visited with the indifference, let alone the ill humour, of those with letters after their name. So she managed a broad smile of friendship and sisterly equality.

Annie watched the scientist go. She felt sorry for Simone, who had not seemed herself in recent months. These days even her smile seemed manufactured, pock-marked with insincerity.

Naturally empathetic, Annie saw the handful of scientists with access to the PC4 unit as her special responsibility and she had a genuine concern for them. There was also the security aspect. Annie did not know exactly what was in that laboratory but she sure as hell knew it was vital it stayed behind the airlock. So Annie kept a sympathetic eye on Simone Gofre. If any of the scientists were ever likely to take their eye off the ball it was she, Annie considered. After all, the poor woman was, you know, one of them, and who knew what that would do to your mind?

4

Simone's swipe card let her into and out of the secure car park attached to the facility. For once she had left work after a mere eight-hour day. She had been nursing a serious headache since mid-afternoon and felt her concentration was slipping. Not even aspirin got through the security check and she was unwilling to countenance any errors of judgement, however minor.

She drove home through the Oxfordshire countryside with her usual care, welcoming the near silence of the late model hybrid; a recent indulgence that Auriol had hoped would cheer her up. It was early spring and a weak, late sun glanced across fields that had been uniformly tractored into submission.

The village of Wenham Major could not be described as picturesque. It had grown piecemeal over the centuries, originally owing its existence to its location at the crossing of two well-used cart tracks, and the good fortune of being a handy day's ride from Oxford on what was then the main route west. Long since bypassed by modern traffic, it had enjoyed a resurgence of popularity in recent years as the English middle class increasingly gave up the hive living of the over-populated cities and larger towns, joining a lemming-like rush to the supposed rural bliss of the countryside.

Simone Gofre and Auriol Preston had rented out Auriol's Oxford flat and bought a house together six years before. It was a late-Victorian stone and slate estate workers' cottage that they had spent time and a considerable amount of money modernising. It was still squat and ugly but inside it was warm and comfortable.

It was just after six when Simone parked in the drive in her usual place underneath the overhanging apple tree, away from the elderly garage, which was a barely serviceable conversion from an even older shed. Simone had refused to park her new car in it, convinced that one day a strong gust of wind would blow it down.

Auriol was in the kitchen preparing the evening meal, busy washing herbs from the garden, her back to the door. She flapped the herbs at a bluebottle that was taking a persistent interest in the cooking smells, inadvertently spraying water around the kitchen. The Aga's hot plates spat annoyance as spots of water landed on them. Simone smiled for the first time that day. That was Auriol, act first and clear up afterwards.

'Hello, you, I'm home,' Simone said.

'Oh, I didn't hear the car.' Auriol dropped the herbs on the worktop and turned with an eager smile on her flushed face.

She was half a head shorter than Simone, a year or two younger and of similar build, with an engaging grin that lit up an otherwise unexceptional face. They were just sufficiently alike to have been taken for sisters, a fact they had played upon for a time in the early days when, for a brief period, the opinion of others still mattered to them.

Auriol abandoned the wet herbs on the bench top and they greeted each other, as they always did, with a brief kiss and a hug. As with any couple, routine had taken over even these moments of tactile affection.

They had met at a 'Women in Science' seminar at Lady Margaret Hall eight years before. Simone, already a noted biochemist and virologist, had been one of the headline speakers and Auriol, a university administrator, had been on the organising panel. Within a month they were living together in Auriol's cramped little flat in Oxford and six months later they were married.

At first there were the frantic days of endless kissing, a time when no closeness was close enough, when every sudden blush was an invitation. Then, after those first hectic weeks, unhurried discovery took over and passions, although undiminished, slowed in unison with the tempo of everyday. In those times it had seemed that bliss was theirs forever.

In recent months however, an unacknowledged and unwelcome emotional distance had entered the relationship and in their own minds neither could quite say why.

'Glass of white?' Auriol asked, heading to the fridge in anticipation.

'No. Think I'll just have an aspirin and rest until dinner.'

Auriol wasn't sure she should say anything and stood irresolute, twisting her wedding ring nervously round and round on her finger as she watched Simone head for the door. 'More headaches?' she asked eventually, unable to keep quiet.

Simone was irritated at being questioned; irritated by Auriol's nervous fiddling with her ring; irritated by her loving concern; irritated by her constant need for reassurance; irritated by Auriol who, she had come to know, was prone to neurotic reactions and had to be placated frequently to avoid draining emotional explosions. But in fairness to her lover, she had to say something. She took a breath before answering and felt the now-familiar pain beneath her left armpit.

'I've seen Jennifer,' she said as calmly as she could manage.

'What did she say?'

'You know Jen, always over-cautious. She referred me to a specialist in London.'

'A specialist! Oh my God, what sort of specialist?'

'Oh, sort of neurologist, pain management, you know,' Simone lied. Auriol would not know of course and Simone had no intention of enlightening her.

'You work too hard, that's the problem. When's your appointment?'

'I saw him last week. Look, I had every kind of scan and test known to medical science so stop fretting.'

'Why didn't you tell me?'

'You would've panicked for no reason.'

'So, what did he say?'

'Nothing. Wait for the results to come back. They never commit themselves in advance. I'm sure it's nothing much.' It was difficult to inject any conviction into her voice.

'But he doesn't know...'

'I'm seeing him tomorrow, okay?'

Auriol ran to her and hugged her. 'You mustn't keep secrets from me, Sim. You know how upset I get if there's anything wrong with you.'

Simone sighed. 'Just relax and let me get myself an aspirin.'

'I'll get it...'

Simone could no longer contain her annoyance. 'No! I'll get it myself. Stop pestering me,' she said harshly and turned and walked out into the hallway, heading for the bathroom.

Auriol was devastated. There was a solid cold lump in her chest and she felt sick. It was the first time Simone had ever spoken to her in that tone of voice. As if she hated her.

5

They were in Charles Lovatt's spartan but highly functional fourth-floor office in Thames House on Millbank. Wenna Cavendish had just played back the audio intercept from Fleur Nichol's apartment. So far it had not elicited the slightest reaction from him.

Charles was in his early fifties, tall, sturdily built and impeccably groomed, with the look of a slightly world-weary patrician, which Wenna suspected he deliberately cultivated. He spoke quietly, asked seemingly simple questions and could have been mistaken for a well-educated lightweight. But probably only once. Charles Lovatt was a man who could have held down any number of high profile positions. In fact he was the Director of International Counter-Terrorism, Counter-Proliferation and Counter-Espionage at MI5, and hotly tipped to replace Margaret Morton-Grace when she retired as Director General in a few months' time.

Wenna broke the silence when it threatened to become awkward. 'Obviously it's another blank. I wouldn't have troubled you with this, but I understand you authorised this intercept personally.'

Charles's response, when it came, was bland. 'And what do you think of that decision?'

Wenna hesitated. You never quite knew where you stood with this man. He was adept at the oblique response, at putting people off their stroke and doing it in such an avuncular and gentlemanly way that it was difficult to take offence. Once again a simple question had put her on the spot. Well, two could play at that game.

'My problem is, there's no indication as to why you instigated the intercept in the first place and the ongoing purpose of the file is not clear. What sparked our interest? And most importantly, what now? Are we protecting her, proposing to run her or just fishing? Perhaps I should have asked before this.'

'Why did you not?'

Wenna breathed in slowly, seeking calm. She was thirty-four years of age and yet, despite her experience, education and status, he had already managed to make her feel like a six-year-old hauled out in front of class for some minor breach of school rules.

'I saw your encryption on the file and that was enough for me.'

'Was. But no longer is.'

Wenna could cheerfully have hit him. 'I simply make the observation that to date we have not derived any useful product from an intercept that has stratospheric potential for embarrassment if it went wrong,' she said, tight-lipped.

'You think we have learned nothing?' The question was delivered with a look of concerned interest.

What did he mean by that? Could she possibly have missed something? She did not believe it. He was simply displaying his usual exasperating verbal deviousness. 'That would be my assessment,' she said firmly. 'Unless of course you have information I am not privy to.'

Charles ignored the last riposte. 'Your assessment is based on what, exactly?'

'Based on my review of two months' worth of data from multi-point audio intercepts, plus the week since you passed the file to me, all of which has produced nothing of value, just background chatter.'

'You didn't think this latest conversation…' he pointed an elegant finger at his Hub, 'told us anything?'

'It told us she has done no work for a year since this guy moved in and at least one of her employers is not best pleased. Apart from his flip remark about Semtex the software would never have picked it up.'

'What can you tell me about Fleur Nichols?'

Wenna drew breath before answering. If she had been a gambler she would have bet a month's salary that there was little she could tell Charles Lovatt about Fleur that he did not already know.

'We can call up her bio,' Wenna suggested with an edge to her voice.

'No, just give me your impression of her.'

Wenna thought for a second. She had never met Fleur and was reliant on the information in her file, on the audios and on Fleur's recorded television appearances.

'She is a high profile freelance foreign correspondent with a string of awards behind her. Has worked a lot for the BBC. Speaks Arabic and is something of an expert on Middle Eastern affairs. She is highly intelligent, well read, undoubtedly a very capable and determined woman.'

'And in some quarters is thought to be sympathetic to Arab causes in general, I believe,' Charles said mildly.

'It's on file that she's done work for Arab news outlets but there's no hard evidence as to her socio-political beliefs. It would probably be fair to describe her as an urban liberal. As to ethnic allegiances, she's obviously interested in Arab matters in an intellectual and business sense but in her personal life, if Joe Kendry is anything to go by, her preferences are definitely Western,' Wenna replied.

Charles looked thoughtful. 'There also seems little doubt that she is something of an expert, albeit amateur, on international terrorism in general and allied syndicates in particular. When we looked through her hard drive some interesting names on the fringes of Islamic terrorism cropped up.'

'I think you and I could both name half a dozen academics you could say the same about,' Wenna said, a little more sharply than she intended. 'Those contacts are all historic and consistent with her work profile. As an Arab-speaking foreign correspondent it would be surprising if it were otherwise I would have thought. There's nothing recent and certainly nothing to raise our CT hackles.'

Charles leant forward on his desk, making eye contact. 'Would you not agree that in general her area of work has a certain crossover potential with your Desk?'

‘Yes of course.’ A sudden thought occurred to Wenna. ‘Have the Cousins any interest in this?’

‘Only in the most general sense.’

‘So I’m not running this one on behalf?’

‘No, if that had been the case I would have told you.’

‘The chat line was totally your idea?’

Wenna knew she was sailing close to the wind but Charles simply nodded as if he expected no less from her.

‘Exclusively,’ he confirmed. ‘Call it instinct.’

‘A co-production, then? Is someone else in the loop?’

‘No. This is our show. Mea culpa. Fleur Nichols just seems to me an interesting person in an interesting line of work. Don’t you agree?’

‘Absolutely,’ Wenna said. ‘Interesting, but that’s all. She has a public profile and her boyfriend makes earnest and seriously boring PBS documentaries. Neither of them is on anybody’s watch list. So how can we justify ongoing surveillance in the face of a complete absence of product?’

Wenna was aware that what she had just said was sailing dangerously close to the wind. Charles, however, gave no sign of being offended.

‘I admire your persistence, Wenna’ Charles said amiably. ‘However, I must ask you to bear with me on this one.’

Wenna knew she had been gently put in her place. She was flushing and fervently hoped it was not too obvious. Truly the man could be infuriating at times. He was smiling at her encouragingly, as if she were a promising pupil caught in a minor error of judgement and he the senior tutor anxious for her early rehabilitation.

Then he seemed to relent. ‘Some might say we are casting too wide a net,’ he admitted, ‘gambling with resources; and of course there is undoubtedly an element of risk...’, a slight shrug of the shoulders, ‘but then, there nearly always is when we play the long game. I particularly want you to keep an eye on this file, just in case it goes active. If it does, it’s likely to land on your desk anyway. If nothing further happens, come back with it in a month’s time. Would you do that for me?’

The question was patently rhetorical. He nodded acceptance of his own decision and stood up, an indication that the meeting was over.

Wenna eased herself to her feet. 'Of course,' she said, in a carbon copy of his earlier bland tone.

Much as she liked and respected Charles, she strongly suspected he was still being less than completely open with her. Well, she hoped he had good reason.

'Just one small thing,' Charles said. 'The caller was....'

'I know,' Wenna said, trying hard to keep the smugness out of her voice. 'It's his nickname. Everyone calls him Daddy. Just not usually to his face.'

Charles inclined his head in acceptance. 'And being who he is, I had to give the file to someone I could trust absolutely,' he said.

6

After several abortive attempts, Joe Kendry gave up trying to contact his agent in New York personally and settled for dealing with one of the office girls. It was a clear indication of the value Siggy placed on this particular UN contract and probably, Joe thought wryly, of Joe's position in the pecking order of his clients. In this business you are either hot or you are not and after a year of inactivity he had obviously slipped in the rankings.

The reply had come back quickly however, suggesting Siggy had been pretty sure he would take the job in the end. Either that or they could not find anyone else to take it, which was not a thought to inflate the ego. The instructions were short and to the point: 'Meet Rose Petchek, Executive Producer, ConSept Productions International, Fulham Palace Road, London, England, for briefing. 8.30am Monday next. DO NOT DISCUSS YOUR FEE! We will sign contracts on your behalf as per our agreement.'

That was vintage Siggy. He liked to keep the finances under tight control. Joe was slightly annoyed that he was not being given the opportunity to produce the doco himself – that way he could have pocketed the production fee – but he did not rate his chances of winning that argument.

He had never heard of Rose Petchek but that did not surprise him, execs came and went in the industry and, like the companies that employed them, often their fall was as meteoric as their rise. Typist today, Executive Producer tomorrow and when, through ignorance and lack of talent, they stuff up, blame the creatives. He found he did not care who she was or how big her ego was or how limited her abilities were. All that mattered was that she delivered what he needed to do the job and kept out of his hair while he did it. He could rely on Siggy to make sure he was paid.

When the money was in the bank and he and Fleur were safely back together, then there would be time to think about a project they could do together. A natural history series maybe, Fleur had all the contacts after all. Fleur. He felt her absence like a nagging pain in the side. He looked at his watch as he had every ten minutes or so since she had left, and tried to imagine where she was at that moment. He knew where she should be. He had insisted she take a cab. It was not that long since the last in a sporadic series of bombings had targeted Nelson's column in Trafalgar Square, a strike at England's martial pride.

He tried hard to put thoughts of Fleur and her safety aside. For the first time in a year he had work to do.

7

'We need to discuss the fee,' she said.

Fleur and April Grosse, her agent, were in Walter Bloom's modest office at the BBC Centre in Shepherds Bush. Walter, his portly frame squeezed into a well-worn executive chair, had outlined the background to the project and his concept of the way the shoot might go. As presenter and de facto director, the detail was up to Fleur but it had to fit the profile of his primetime current affairs show. He would have preferred to brief Fleur on her own; agents in general, and the lanky and waspish April Grosse in particular, were a constant irritation in the life of the Director of News and Current Affairs.

Despite this, Walter was in his most genial mood, satisfied that he had at last achieved his aim of getting his top reporter back to work. It only remained to educate April Grosse as to the realities of

BBC budgets, but he had no wish to do that with Fleur present. He preferred to maintain a personal relationship with his 'talent' that did not involve anything so crass as discussions of money.

Grosse by name, gross by nature, Walter thought. 'Of course, April, and we will. I thought perhaps you and I could crunch some figures tomorrow.' He smiled benignly at Fleur. 'We are renowned for our generosity to our favourite daughters.'

April grunted sarcastically. 'You're tight as a duck's arse, Walter' she said.

Walter gestured his injured innocence and turned back to Fleur, who had been listening to the sparring between these two old adversaries with quiet amusement. 'What do you want, princess? Anything you need – within reason.'

Fleur felt slightly embarrassed. She owed this man so much and over the past year her only regret had been the feeling that she had let him down. 'That's very sweet of you. I'll leave the details to you and April,' she said. 'Just give me a top crew, equipment that actually works, not that rubbish we had in Libya, and whatever's necessary to get me there and back in one piece.'

April harrumphed in annoyance in the background. The close relationship that had developed over the years between these two made her negotiating job that much harder. In her view it was unprofessional to treat television executives, even those who seemed as well intentioned as Walter Bloom, as anything other than the mean and unprincipled bastards they were.

'Only the best for you, my dear. Can we shake hands on your return to the fold, then?'

'Subject to contract,' April cut in sharply.

'As always,' Walter agreed without looking at her. How did such a harridan come to have such a girlie name as April? He stood up and came round his desk to give Fleur a hug. 'Welcome back, princess. Don't worry; we'll wrap you in cotton wool while you're over there. When this one's a success perhaps Joe will let you out to play with us again.'

Fleur wagged an admonitory finger at him. 'If you got to know Joe better you'd like him. You should think about using him.'

'My dear, at this moment I would be prepared to nominate him for a knighthood.'

'It's still subject to contract,' April repeated, offering a rock-hard handshake. 'What time tomorrow?'

Walter sighed theatrically. 'Civilised hour, say ten? Oh, and by the way Fleur, I gather there's some snail mail for you in the newsroom. You might want to pick it up as you go.'

If he had known what the outcome of that casual suggestion was to be, he would have bitten his tongue off.

8

Joe, in the way that lovers sometimes do, sensed her impending arrival well before she had reached the apartment and he was standing at the open door to welcome her when she stepped out of the lift.

Fleur was short, the top of her head barely coming up to his shoulders but, for all her small size, she conformed in every way to the golden mean, every part of her in proportion. She was remarkably beautiful, even as she was now, bundled up against the early spring cold, clasping a couple of rumpled envelopes in one hand. It was that photogenic face, combined with her determination, drive and talent that had made her the international success she was.

Fleur shed her outer clothing and they walked through to the sitting room where she dropped the envelopes on the coffee table.

'That your contract?' Joe asked.

'I left April to twist poor Walter's arm. This is fan mail, I'm told.'

'How about that. Out of the limelight for a year and still she gets fan mail. What a star.'

'Probably 'Demented of Deptford.'

'More likely 'Devoted of Dartmouth.'

They flopped onto the sofa beside each other. 'What have you been doing while I've been meeting and greeting?' Fleur asked.

'Homework mainly. Internet searches. Oh and I'm meeting the executive producer on Monday.'

'That's quick, hope they don't want you to start too soon.'

'They'll have to wait till we're both ready. What about you?'

'April and Walter are meeting tomorrow. They'll fight and argue as they always do. Probably have an agreement in a couple of days.

I'd guess a contract start on Monday. Then at least a week's prep before I go. Say a couple of weeks before I leave. I'd better update my research on Afghanistan. How did yours go by the way?'

'Okay. I've downloaded a lot of material on UNFPA and Two+One and there's a huge amount of information on overpopulation, a lot of it academic stuff. Some of the figures are quite worrying. The prediction is for a 50% rise in the world population in the next forty years. Could top out over ten billion and 99% of that growth will be in the developing world.'

'Problems all round,' Fleur muttered absentmindedly, cutting the envelopes open with her finger.

Joe nodded grimly. 'Came across a website…' He shook his head in disbelief. 'Just amazing, these guys are somewhere to the right of Genghis Khan, real xenophobic rednecks. One anonymous hero suggested solving the problem by 'nuking the bastards'. No particular bastards identified. Man, there are some real crazies out there.'

'Aren't there just,' Fleur agreed.

'Which is worrying because it makes the Two+One project seem like a true humanitarian approach.'

'Why would that be worrying?'

'Two+One is essentially a project initiated by a US multinational pharmaceuticals company, only taken on board later by the UN, and there's just something about the US playing at being Gaia's police force that doesn't sit too well with me.'

'At least the UN and US are trying to tackle the problem,' Fleur commented. 'And as a minimum it will mean some women in the third world won't spend their lives burdened by more children than they can cope with or feed.'

'If that's the true and only agenda.'

'You think it might not be?'

'I don't know, honey. I've agreed to take the job so I sure as hell hope it's kosher but my beloved country does not have a blameless record in foreign relations. Usually, no matter who's in power, what the industrial and military power block wants, it gets, so what's in it for the rich and powerful?'

Fleur grinned. 'Spoken like a true Democrat of the old school.'

'That's me,' Joe admitted. 'Be that as it may, they're always concerned with the bottom line and altruism is a net cost unless you can tweak it to your advantage. Aw hell, let's take the rest of the day off, have a glass of wine and relax. Go to bed?' he added hopefully.

'I don't think we should risk adding to the world population right at this moment,' Fleur said, straight-faced. 'You can make us tea. I'm going to read the mail.'

And a single icon hidden amongst what seemed like an innocent fan letter seeking her autograph changed both their lives forever.

9

Wenna was deep in thought as she returned home, unable to get the meeting with Charles Lovatt out of her mind.

The old red brick terraced house was four stories high, situated in a side street just down the hill from Hampstead underground station. In its heyday it had been the London home of an upper-middle-class family of the Victorian sub-elite, complete with a modest provision for servants, but it had long since been divided into separate apartments as London swelled its numbers and Hampstead became a desirable location much favoured by the creative fraternity.

Wenna's late father had bought it for his treasured daughter when she had first joined MI5, and she lived alone in the former servants' rooms on the top floor. The other flats were rented out through an agent; Wenna was a reluctant landlady and her contact with the tenants was restricted to a nod and a brief thin smile on the few occasions when they passed on the stairs. There was no elevator and the common areas were austere, with a musty smell that spoke of age and infrequent cleaning.

The house was dull and dark inside and out, unremarkable in any respect and this suited Wenna very well – the last thing she wanted was to draw attention to herself. It was not simply the necessity for discretion because of her work; it was equally that it suited her withdrawn personality. She used minimal makeup and dressed in a modest, corporate style; usually white shirts buttoned to the neck and a dark suit or a jacket with skirts to mid-calf, which fitted both the Security Services' 'in house' look and her personal inclination. Her eyes were clear grey and her naturally fair hair was swept back at the sides in typical Sloane Ranger style, revealing a face with fine bones and near-flawless skin.

Wenna had long since convinced herself that she was plain, although she had a neat, feminine figure and there had been plenty of approaches from men over the years. These had all been politely turned away. The fact was that she was simply not interested; she had never met a man who had raised in her the slightest flicker of personal interest, let alone sexual desire.

On the rare occasions female colleagues had talked of their male or female lovers, Wenna found herself excluded by incomprehension, she simply did not know what it felt like to want another person in that way. The only man she had ever truly loved had been her father, who had doted upon his only daughter. She missed him dreadfully and now the only family she had was her mother, and they had long since developed a relationship that was distantly dutiful.

Although she was almost always alone outside of the office, Wenna never stopped to consider that she might be lonely; there were always the absorbing intricacies of her work, the endless sequence of puzzles, the intellectual stimulation of testing herself against the minds of the enemy and, within the Service, of keeping up with the convoluted thinking of men like Charles Lovatt. Charles, who, with his high intelligence and occasional moments of whimsy, sometimes reminded her of her father.

As she mounted the stairs to her flat, her mind flicked from the house to her father then to her mother. Her monthly duty call was overdue, she must not forget. But as soon as the thought had come it was gone, replaced once more by thoughts of Fleur Nichols, as had been the case all day. Was it possible, even remotely possible, that she had gone over? Is that what Charles had hinted at? Well, stranger things had happened but somehow Wenna could not bring herself to believe Fleur was an agent for anyone but the media she served.

Wenna let herself into the uninviting interior of her flat, pulled back the heavy curtains to let in the last of the daylight, turned on the heating, poured herself a large gin and tonic and flopped into her comfortable old armchair. She thought about selecting a frozen meal but that was as far as it got, her mind was back on the Nichols file.

She was really quite annoyed at herself for not remembering sooner that Fleur's father was dead; it was a seemingly minor detail, an aside way back on the first page or so of her bio but even so, she should have picked it up the minute Fleur called Bloom 'Daddy'. So she was Bloom's 'princess'. That girl certainly had the inside running at the Beeb.

Wenna sipped her drink and brooded on the matter. She still considered she had been right to suggest reviewing the file. Equally, Charles was within his rights to insist it remain active if he saw potential and thought he could get continued authorisation. And he did not have to explain his reasons to her.

So why was she, who had wanted the file closed, now being so obsessive about it? She turned that question over in her mind and could come up with no better explanation than that, fired by the meeting with Charles, her instincts, somewhat dulled of late, had belatedly kicked in. She was pleased now that Charles had not been prepared to abandon the intercept. If both of them were instinctively interested in Fleur Nichols, albeit perhaps for different reasons, then maybe she had been wrong. It was unlike her, but perhaps for once she had shot from the hip. She needed to think the way that Charles would think.

The least that could be said was that Fleur Nichols was indeed a very interesting woman. The war against terrorism had long since become as much as anything a war of ideas, fought out in the media as often as in the streets. In a very real sense then, now that she had resumed work, Fleur Nichols was in the thick of that war. From the point of view of the Security Services, the Western media were not always allies. The question was then not so much whose side she was on as how she was viewed by the enemy. If Charles was fishing, then perhaps Fleur was the bait.

Satisfied she had worried all the meat she could from this particular bone, Wenna determinedly put all thought of work aside, reached for the palm-sized Ctab she kept at home and tapped a single digit.

'Cavendish House.' There was a lot of excited deep-throated barking in the background. 'Get down, dammit,' the voice said commandingly.

'Hullo, Mummy,' Wenna said, 'it's only me.'

10

Auriol called the university and told her supervisor she was sick. She felt quite justified because she was indeed sick, sick at heart, sick with worry about Simone. Just how ill was she? Surely even the most conservative GP would not send someone to a specialist without good reason. And she did not know what to think about Simone's cold and distant attitude of late, her anger and the harsh words that numbed Auriol's mind and left her emotionally distraught. If Simone were truly ill she only had to say, Auriol would have dropped everything to look after her.

So Auriol ate nothing; wandered tearfully from room to room, desperately trying to determine what to do. What was she to think? Last night, in bed, Simone had brushed aside all her anxious enquiries about her health; excluding Auriol from her life in a way she never had previously. Suppose the headaches were simply an excuse? Was the harsh truth that Simone was getting tired of her, that she no longer loved her? Had she let herself go, was she no longer attractive? Was it all her fault? Had Simone found another lover? Please God no! Would she come home that day and tell her that their marriage was over? And which would be worse, Simone's illness or her rejection? If she is ill I can nurse her back to health, Auriol thought desperately, but if she no longer loves me, if she's found someone else, then I've lost everything.

By the time they met Auriol had given up all hope of a relationship; was no longer even looking. There had been no one since those guilt-laden teenage fumblings at her girls' school; the school that was aware of such goings on but blithely assumed they were just teenage crushes, temporary hormonal aberrations that the girls would grow out of. Well she never had, it was not in her nature. Then, when all hope seemed lost, out of nowhere had come Simone.

When they met she was sure she had blushed and stammered and hung around her like the naïve teenager she had once been. Simone later assured her it had not seemed like that, and reminded her that she had been the one to make the first move, taken the risk. At first Auriol thought she had misheard but no: 'Will you have dinner with me?' Simone had asked and with those words Auriol's life had changed, as she then thought, forever.

Now she did not know what to think. All she knew was that if she lost Simone her world would end.

She went upstairs to the bathroom; washed and dried her tear-streaked face, then went and lay down on the bed they shared. She forced herself to think positively. Simone was a little unwell, that was all. She had been overworking. She would come home having seen the specialist and it would be some minor problem. No other woman. That was unthinkable nonsense; she was worrying herself sick about nothing. Simone would hug her and kiss her and laugh at her for being so silly.

She would need pampering for a while until those headaches went away, that was all. That was what her life was all about, caring for Simone, attending to anything and everything that she might want or need. She would spend the day tidying the house and making herself look attractive and preparing a perfect meal. Then, when Simone came home she would take her in her arms and all would be well, all would be the way it was. Perfect. Absolutely perfect.

Even so it was a while before the tears finally stopped and the pain in her chest subsided.

11

Fleur had said nothing to Joe the previous afternoon when she had first spotted the encryption in the fan letter. The letter itself was handwritten, brief, and almost certainly composed by someone for whom English was not a first language.

'Deer Fler Nikols,' it said in spidery ballpoint, 'I am wantin to be on the tele one day and I think your very famus. Could you give me a Autograf. Plaese find paper.' It was signed 'Alex'. Enclosed was a blank sheet of cheap writing paper in the top right hand corner of which was the crude childish drawing of an ice cream cone. The address for reply was in Southwark.

Eighteen months before, in the dining room of an upmarket Doha hotel, a man with a swarthy complexion, neatly trimmed beard and an Italian suit, had drawn a similar icon on his palm with a very expensive ballpoint pen. ‘Very bad,’ he said, and he had smiled, a thing he seldom did. ‘Degenerate Western food. If you see this, then it is me.’ The man had been the Head of Communications for Al Qaeda East. Amongst other far more important things they had talked about an old British film called, ‘Ice Cold in Alex’.

As far as Fleur knew he was still alive.

There was absolutely no doubt that the letter was journalistic gold dust, an invitation to make contact with a top terrorist, one with whom she had already established a relationship of trust. The problem was, apart from an address that experience told her would be false, there was no way to acknowledge her interest, let alone set up a meeting. The postmark was undecipherable and the letter was undated so there was no way of telling how long it had been sitting in the BBC post room but intuitively she felt it was recent. Was it a teaser, warning her to prepare for another more explicit contact? Or was there something in the letter she had missed?

She had taken Joe and the problem to bed with her, electing to say nothing to him about the letter for the time being; his reaction would be predictable and she needed time to think. Now, with a second cup of morning coffee in front of her and Joe safely at work on the Hub researching his documentary, Fleur went back to the letter and read it again. Nothing. Yet somewhere there had to be a telephone number, an email or a suggested meeting place. There had to be, or what was the point? Unless it was indeed a teaser and there would be another letter, a letter with a contact point. As realisation struck, Fleur jumped up and ran into the kitchen.

‘What is it, hon?’ Joe called.

‘Nothing, just remembered something,’ Fleur mumbled as she rummaged amongst the rubbish in the kitchen bin.

‘Oh, okay,’ Joe replied absent-mindedly.

She emerged triumphant with the other letter, the one she had barely read before discarding it, as you did with things like that. She straightened it out on the kitchen table.

It read, ‘Fleur Nichols you are a grade one hot bitch and I would like to pull down your knickers and fuck you stupid. I have a VERY big cock would you like some?’ It was signed ‘BIG Johnny Mills’ and there was a Roamer number.

Stuff like this happened, usually written by a pimply faced adolescent; it was part of the downside of fame. Of course yesterday she had only read the first line before she crumpled it up and aimed it at the garbage. If she had read the whole letter then something might have clicked in her mind. John Mills was the star of the 1958 movie 'Ice Cold in Alex'. They had expected Fleur to be bright enough to put this little puzzle together. She had her contact number.

'Joe, I'm going out for a minute,' she called as she shrugged on her coat.

'What? Where?' Joe called back.

'Won't be long, just a phone call.'

Joe appeared in the hall before she could reach the door. 'What's going on?' he asked, puzzled.

'Darling, this is business, I have to make a call quickly.'

'Well what's wrong with your Ctab or …' Joe indicated the Hub.

'No, not from here.'

'Why not?'

Fleur sighed. Joe was going to be persistent. 'It's a contact and I don't want the call to be reverse-traced back to me, just in case, okay? I won't be long.'

'Is this about…?'

'No it isn't,' Fleur said quickly. 'Something else. I'll tell you about it later.' She kissed him lightly on the lips. 'It's business, Joe, sometimes this sort of thing happens.' There was a slight edge to her voice.

'I'll come with you...'

'No! Just trust me, Joe, I'll be fine. See you later.'

And she was gone, leaving Joe worried and uncertain.

12

Dilip Khan's examination room at the venerable St Thomas' Hospital in Lambeth was one he shared with two other consultants and was therefore without personal adornment. There was an examination couch with a curtain screen against one wall, a simple imitation wooden desk with an old fashioned upright chair, writing pads and a cracked pen holder and a cupboard in the corner with one door partly open revealing boxes of tissues and a packet of latex gloves. In front of the desk was another elderly chair with a faded cushioned seat and worn padded armrests. Beside the desk was an old, faded-looking communal Comset screen on a metal trolley with wheels. It was an office from another age. Not so much as a single family photograph or grandchild's work of art offered relief from the clinical austerity of the room.

Khan was perhaps sixty, dressed impeccably in a dark blue suit and conservative tie. His smooth brown face, which he thought was composed, was in fact creased with worry and he was unaware that he was playing nervously with his steel-rimmed glasses. He was feeling exceptionally uncomfortable at having to face this particular patient since she was in a sense a colleague, one who, because of her qualifications, was more able than most to visualise the harsh reality of his diagnosis. A naturally kindly man, his expertise and many years of experience had never helped him come to terms with the brutal necessity of relaying bad news. And the news he had just delivered to Simone Gofre was as bad as it got.

She was sitting rigidly upright in the chair facing him across the desk, her hands held loosely in her lap. Her eyes were fixed on his face but he sensed that she was looking straight through him. A muscle was flickering on her cheek and her nostrils were flared wide.

The silence had become acutely embarrassing. 'Of course I can arrange for another oncologist to see you. Would you like a second opinion, Simone?' he asked.

Simone stirred and focussed on him. It was a shock, yes, worse than she had allowed herself to believe, but she knew enough about the human body and had had time to consider the possible outcomes so the diagnosis was not a total surprise.

'I think I can recognise the inevitable when I'm faced with it,' she said, her voice tightly controlled. 'It's inoperable because of its extent and the fact it's in the spine?'

Khan nodded. 'And has progressed to the lungs and lymph nodes. Ultimately it will affect the brain, as I am sure you will realise.'

'Yes. So, not a happy prognosis.'

'I wish it were otherwise.'

'I'm going to be boringly predictable and ask how long I have.'

The surgeon spread his hands. 'I will not prevaricate. Perhaps eight weeks. But most probably less.'

'But not more.'

'It is not impossible. However, in my judgement it is unlikely.'

'It seems so sudden, and I've had relatively few symptoms so far,' Simone said, almost to herself.

'That is the only fortunate aspect of the diagnosis. It can happen that way.'

'I have work to finish.'

'I understand,' Khan said sincerely. 'But realistically you may have to prepare for someone else to take over. Of course we can help progressively with the pain'

'Until we reach morphine, which is the end of the line.'

'At that stage there is always residential palliative care.'

'I won't need that.' It was said definitely, as if she had consciously made a decision that would preclude that requirement. But she had not; it was a purely instinctive reaction.

'You have support at home?'

Simone thought of Auriol. She would not take this well. Not at all well. 'Yes I have,' she replied.

'If there is anything at all I can do…'

'The big question is, how much longer will I be able to continue work?'

'To be frank, you should probably stop now, make the most of your time.'

'Given that's not an option?'

'Well…' In some ways Dilip Khan found emotional histrionics easier to deal with than this cold, analytical reaction. 'Very difficult to say but perhaps, if we can control the pain effectively and if the Unit will allow you to continue whilst under medication, say three weeks, maximum. Do you wish me to talk to the Director and the Unit GP?'

'Only if you can support my continuing to work.'

'Simone, it's obviously important to you, so I will support it but only for, shall we say, four weeks at the absolute maximum and under daily medical supervision.'

Simone agreed. She knew that without the consultant's support she would face an uphill battle persuading the Director to allow her to continue at the Unit and she had formulated no plans beyond working for as long as she could.

At that moment, despite the devastating news, Simone Gofre was still sane.

13

Fleur glanced at her watch. It was a few minutes after noon. The taxi driver double-parked outside the cybershop in Shoreditch High Street while she paid him. She slipped between the closely parked cars onto the teeming pavement; it seemed that for many the cost of parking and vehicle entry to the extended central city area was no deterrent. London was its usual hive of frenetic activity, which for some observers was a sign of vitality and contemporary pace and for others a panicked rush towards eventual societal implosion. For Fleur, as for most others who lived here, it was no more than the normal hurried, variegated background to her life; the city's disadvantages, dangers and irritations were noted, but only in passing.

The shop, with its rows of privacy booths that lined the walls and formed a central island, was a somewhat grubby, uninviting, blandly functional place with something of the atmosphere of an old-time betting shop. It smelt faintly of human sweat and spent bio-diesel. At least it was less well patronised than the more upmarket establishments and Fleur selected a booth as far away from other users as she could manage.

She swiped her credit card and the Hub lit up with a smorgasbord of advertisements. Fleur entered the system, disabled the video link, and then called the number. It rang several times before it was answered.

'Yeah?' The voice was young; the speaker had an uneducated London accent blended with something more exotic. In a city as cosmopolitan as this, that would raise no eyebrows.

'Alex wants to talk to me,' Fleur said.

There was a moment's silence, then the speaker said cautiously, 'My name's not Alex.'

'And it's not Big Johnny Mills, either,' Fleur said brusquely, 'so let's not waste each other's time. We'll meet up and have an ice cream, okay?'

Another silence. Fleur knew she was dealing with small fry here and was pretty sure a conversation was going on at the other end, courtesy of the mute button.

Then: 'Thanks, yeah okay. So we meet at...'

'No. I decide. That's the deal.' It was they who were seeking a meeting after all and experience had taught her that she needed to demonstrate up front that she was no pushover. She told him the location and gave him an hour to get there. 'You will recognise me of course.' She was certain of that.

'I'm George,' the young man said. And it must have sounded unconvincing even to him.

Fleur smiled to herself. They had little or no sense of humour but at least, unlike the Western Secret Services that were their sworn enemies, they did not expect you to believe their cover.

'Don't be late,' she said and cut the connection.

The shop was beginning to fill up and she was feeling hungry. The adrenaline surge of chasing down a story had that effect. She checked her watch and, out of habit, wiped her hands with anti-bacterial gel. If she hurried, there was just time to pick up a hot beef sandwich at Marksteins.

14

A longstanding failure to maintain the track meant that, for most of the journey, the train was forced to proceed at a modest pace but to Simone it seemed that the journey was taking no time at all, that she was being rushed pell-mell into a future over which she had no control. For a person used to a structured and ordered life, that was hard to accept. She found it difficult to focus her thoughts; her mind was flickering wildly from one unrelated thing to another.

Above her head a flashing light on the brightly coloured electronic route map of the line showed exactly how far they had travelled towards their destination. She stared out of the grimy carriage window at the blur of buildings flashing by. They were out of the urban sprawl of greater London but between the city and

Oxford there was barely an acre of railside land that was not developed to some extent. Its cities seriously overpopulated and becoming more engorged every day, Britain was fat with people and its gross human excess was oozing out across the landscape. The cost of this self-indulgence was being paid by the shrinking countryside, paid in pollution and escalating environmental degradation. Yes, Simone thought, we humans are the most dangerous kind of virus, the kind that blindly, mindlessly reproduces until it kills its host and brings about its own extinction. Not unlike the virus that was forcing cell division and transformation in her own body, leading to the cancer that was killing her.

The irony of her own position did not escape her. She was a lifelong high achiever, one of the elite band of scientists working on virus replication, those who could adapt existing viruses and create new ones, work that was dedicated to saving human life and, not coincidentally she had to admit, to the creation of substantial profit. Amongst other things she had been lead researcher on a series of vaccines for the control of the ever-evolving avian flu. How many people had that saved? Impossible to say but in total, probably as many as were alive two thousand years ago. You could re-populate the world with the people she had been instrumental in saving. Science was not always blind to the impact of its findings but it had its own unstoppable momentum.

Simone's thoughts flicked from the problems of the world to problems closer to home. How was she to break the news to Auriol? That dear woman she had bullied and patronised and dominated and loved and cared for and been faithful to for years; the lover who doted on her and had built her whole life around their relationship. She knew she had behaved badly in recent weeks, since the headaches and body pain had started and brought with it the first indications that something serious was afflicting her. She may not have been a medical doctor but she knew more than enough about human anatomy to understand the implications and her anxiety and stress levels had risen exponentially as she waited for the results. And she had taken it out on Auriol. She had to make that right somehow.

Dear Auriol. How was she going to cope on her own? What could be done to lessen the impact; how best to repay some of that devotion in the few weeks she had left? At that moment Simone had no idea. It was way too difficult to deal with but she knew Auriol would be waiting anxiously for her at home. She would have to think of something. Perhaps she could delay the truth; a white lie would buy her some time to work through the problem.

Her thoughts jumped again. How was she going to put her case to Colin Burcastle? The Operational Director of Genphree Biotics was as fiercely protective of his own interests as he was of the future of Genphree itself. Within the organisation, the work done in the PC4 laboratory where Simone worked provided the basis for a fair percentage of the vast downstream profit the company generated internationally. For that reason, and the bio-security of the unit, he would be reluctant to take a chance on her.

Burcastle was a busy, rotund little man, more a politician than a scientist and a bit of a white rabbit. Beneath a façade of absolute confidence and competence, he was prone to sudden panics and quick decisions followed later by equally hasty emendations. He did not like situations that he would describe as 'messy'. Colin Burcastle had to be placated because there was no way Simone intended to spend her last weeks vegetating at home waiting, counting down the days until death, laden with its instruments of pain, came to take her when it would.

She would have to reassure Colin from the outset, present herself as composed and confident, very much aware of the potential problems but in control of them and with the best interests of the unit and the company always at heart. All she had to do was pull herself together, plan the meeting in advance, control not only what she said but also the tone of her voice and the way she said it, address him with confidence, permit no hint of weakness.

'Good afternoon, Colin,' she said out loud, practising the moment. The scholarly looking young man sitting opposite her peered up from his eBook, then away in embarrassment as he realised she was not talking him but to someone in a private world of her own. Simone did not even register his discomfort.

The train slowed down gradually as it approached Oxford. Simone steadfastly ignored the pain in her back. She had prescriptions in her handbag and she would get them made up, take a painkiller before the meeting. I have so much to offer the world she thought, there are not many individuals who can genuinely make a difference but I can, even my last few weeks are important.

The human ego fights to the last, ignoring surrounding decay, believing itself immortal.

15

Fleur paid off the taxi in a side street and walked through to Hampstead Heath, entering the gently undulating park with its well-used walkways and stands of mature trees via one of the car parks. It was a fine spring day with scudding clouds and patches of clear blue sky, but the wind was chill and most of the walkers exercising their dogs or children and the joggers wired for sound were moving at a brisk pace. It was not a day for sitting still for long to admire the view across one of London's few green lungs and the occasional seats were sparsely occupied.

A young man was sitting hunched up in his padded jacket on the one that Fleur had nominated. He was looking up and down the path in front of the seat, careful not to make eye contact with the occasional passer-by. She looked around for the other one that she was sure would be somewhere within sight. Any experienced reporter used to the rules of clandestine assignments soon acquired a degree of tradecraft more usually associated with the Security Services.

She thought she spotted him behind a distant tree whose budding leaves did not yet offer much by way of cover. Whoever it was would have declared the area clear of watchers and Fleur was not unhappy about that. She would have gained nothing from this contact if the other side thought they or she were under surveillance. She was well aware that being a terrorist associate in London in these days was a hazardous business: MI5 had upped their game in recent times, concentrating on identification, infiltration and intercepts.

Fleur approached the seat from the rear, across the grass. 'Afternoon, George,' she said, leaning over beside him.

He actually flinched with surprise, moving away from her. 'Make this quick,' she said, 'because nobody is going to believe you and I are a couple.' Fleur walked round and sat beside him.

He was even younger than she had supposed from hearing him on the phone, perhaps not more that eighteen, his light brown face still pimpled with youth. His moustache was thin and straggled over his upper lip. 'Er, okay...' he said nervously. It was hard not to feel sorry for him, he was probably aware that he was only here because he was expendable.

'Relax,' Fleur advised him. 'The sooner you deliver the message, the sooner you'll be on your way.'

'Would you like to meet a very important person to discuss a matter of world signa– significance?' he blurted out, obviously having learned the words by rote.

'I'm a journalist,' Fleur said. 'What sort of dumb question is that?'

'That a yes, then?'

Fleur sighed. She had been expecting to meet someone a bit further up the food chain than this. 'Is this serious, George? Because right now you need to convince me you are for real or I walk away.'

'It's for real, yes,' he said anxiously.

'So who is the meeting with and what is it about?'

'I don't know.'

And of course he wouldn't know. The Georges of this world would never know. They were never party to information of any value; they were cut-outs, stalking horses; bearers of seemingly innocuous messages with built-in deniability.

'Then I suggest you go back to whoever sent you and get your pitch right. I don't make a move until I know who I'm dealing with and why. So here is what we do. I will be in the tearoom of the Grosvenor Hotel tomorrow morning at eleven, having coffee. This time send someone who knows a hell of a lot more than you do. And they'd better not be wearing a t-shirt and jeans. I'll wait for exactly thirty minutes, then leave. Understood?'

The boy was clearly taken aback. Although divorced from it, he came from a culture where women did not speak to any male in that way. 'Grovener?' he said stiffly, 'How'd you spell that?'

Fleur stood up, ready to leave. 'Ask the ice cream man,' she said 'he'll know.'

16

As soon as she walked into the Director's office it was evident he had already received the news. Burcastle came round from his desk and grasped her hand in both of his, anguish written all over his rotund face. Had she not known him better, she could have believed he was in deep distress over her condition.

'My dearest Simone, I am so desperately sorry,' he said, oozing sympathy. 'Anything I can do, anything at all, you only have to say. A chair, please take a chair.' He tried to usher her towards a seat but Simone waved him aside. This was not going to be easy and it was time to take control.

'Thank you, Colin, but I'm not a cripple. Although there is something you can do.'

Burcastle spread his hands. 'Whatever is possible.'

'I understand the severity of my illness and all the implications that will have but I want to continue work until I decide it is time for me to leave.'

'Ah…'

'You have a problem with that?'

He gestured vaguely towards his Hub. 'In your highly specialised position and particularly in view of your current project, personal health is a tricky area. I was thinking you might want a day or two to tidy up matters here, then...'

Simone felt a flood of bitter, illogical anger rising inside her as she watched him return to his desk. It was bad enough having to deal with a death sentence without having to pander to this pompous little shit. Did he seriously think she would endanger her life's work and her post-mortem academic reputation for the sake of a few extra days at the coalface? She controlled herself with difficulty, aware that her body language was screaming abuse at him.

'Do you really want someone else to take over when I'm about to finish engineering the human-to-human transmission of AF/G5? Have someone else come in at this late stage, someone who's not up to speed with the work and the protocols? You'll need to headhunt someone very special and the security clearances alone will take longer than I need to complete the work. Do I have to remind you that time is money so far as the Board is concerned?

'Of course not...' Burcastle said unhappily.

'I think you'll find Mr Khan will support me on this.'

'Ah, he may. He said something in his report. But of course he does not know what you are really working on, does he? So the risk, Simone, the risk for you and for us all, still remains. How could it be justified, hmm?'

The bloody man wanted to cover his arse, that was all, Simone thought savagely. He didn't want her to drop dead in the lab; anywhere else was fine but not in his lab, that was way too 'messy'. Stay calm, she warned herself, or you will lose.

'I know that Mr Khan has already supported my staying on for at least four weeks. I think we can both rely on his expertise; the prognosis of my mental and physical capacity is his area after all. In a sense he's the one who is taking the professional risk, if indeed there is any. There is a positive here; the extra time will enable HR to advertise internationally for someone to replace me. Then that person can take over and put our new little beast through the hoops. It would tidy things up nicely, don't you think?'

Burcastle was looking above her head, deep in thought. Simone held her breath, willing him to agree. She had played the only card she had and if it won her the trick she might be able to extend her stay.

'Perhaps if you were to accept additional daily evaluations by our own doctor as well as your GP and Mr Khan, then possibly I could agree for a very short while. On a day by day basis of course.'

Simone stepped forward and offered her hand. Burcastle half stood and shook it somewhat reluctantly. 'Perfectly acceptable. Trust me Colin, I will know when the time comes to go.'

After she had left the room, Burcastle waited until the sound of her footsteps had receded into the distance, then he called security. 'Tell Annie Morris I want to speak to her,' he said. Annie could be relied upon to keep a close watch on things down on the floor and if anything did go wrong, the more people who were in the loop and shared the risk, the better.

17

Fleur arrived home to an unusually cool reception. Joe was working on the Hub and did not come to the door to greet her. 'Hi, darling' she called out as she shucked off her outer clothing and went to him, throwing her arms round him from behind and nuzzling his neck.

'Hi, nice to have you back in one piece,' Joe said calmly as he switched off the Hub.

'You're grumpy with me,' Fleur accused, releasing him.

'Of course I am.'

'I know. I'm sorry I was short with you before I left but I had to pick up this meeting and I didn't want to get into an argument about it before I left. I wanted my head to be clear.'

'Okay. So I was right to be worried. Whatever it was, you knew I wouldn't agree. But you went anyway.'

'It was work, Joe.'

'Sure, and dangerous, right?'

'No. Not at all. It was a meeting to set up a meeting, that's all.'

Joe took her hand and led her to the sofa. 'We never had a pact that said no secrets. We've never had to. Maybe now we do,' he said.

Fleur took his hand in hers and kissed it. 'No secrets, I promise.'

Joe relented, smiling reluctantly. 'So why not tell me what the hell's going on.'

'Okay.' She moved away to sit opposite him. 'The fan mail. There were only two letters and they weren't really fan mail.'

Joe made a face. 'I'm not going to like this, am I,' he said.

'It was a message from an old contact. One of the letters had an icon identifying the sender and the other had a contact number. It took me a while to work it out, my brain must have gone rusty in the last year.'

'So who is this guy?'

Fleur shook her head. 'It was a way of authenticating the contact. He won't be here in person. If your countrymen ever caught up with him they probably wouldn't bother with a trial.'

'What are we talking about, Al Qaeda?'

'Not exactly. Maybe the Osama Martyrs or Al Qaeda East, names come and go. The struggle has been reborn in recent years and for a long time now there's what you might call a franchised organisational structure in place'

'Great! I just knew I wasn't going to like this.'

‘I’m not in danger, Joe, they need me. As we said before, they’re fighting a media war and I’m useful to them.’

‘Tell that to the families of all the journalists who’ve died over the years.’

‘This is London, not a war zone.’

‘Want me to list the bombings?’

‘Okay. I mean they don’t target journalists especially, certainly not here. When someone gets killed they tend to be collateral.’

‘And this is supposed to make me feel good? Anyway I thought they were fighting their media war on the net.’

‘They are but on the net they tend to be preaching to the converted and mostly in Arabic at that. Don’t underestimate the power of TV. They don’t, they use it when it suits them.’

‘When it suits them.’

‘Seriously, Joe, if this is for real it could be a world exclusive.’

‘Sure. They don’t want anyone else around when...’

‘You’re not listening! They’re offering to set up a meeting with one of their top operatives and they reckon they have a big story to tell.’

‘Of course they do. Fleur, they’re looking to use you.’

‘There’s nothing new in that and remember it works both ways.’

Joe looked away from her. ‘I don’t like it,’ he said.

‘Look at it like this. If it comes off I may not have to go to Afghanistan.’

Joe said nothing.

‘This has to be a safer option,’ Fleur pressed. ‘I can take it one step at a time and I dictate the schedule. If my instincts tell me it’s not kosher, I’ll pull out.’

‘You’ve already agreed, haven’t you?’ Joe said, looking back at her.

‘I set up a meeting. It won’t be the final one, just one more along the way. Eleven tomorrow morning at the Grosvenor, what could be safer than that?’

‘Not going could be safer than that but if it’s this or Afghanistan I don’t figure there’s much of a choice.’

Fleur went over and hugged him. ‘You can trust me, Joe. I’m good at this and I’m very careful. Now I’m going to have a shower, then we’ll go out somewhere to eat.’

She stood up and headed for the door, her movements brisk and businesslike. Joe was suddenly visited with a premonition of unwelcome change. In the year they had been together Fleur had never seemed quite this animated and he could count on the fingers of one hand the number of times she had wanted to go out anywhere; she had been content to stay with him, secure in their private haven.

'Fleur...'

She stopped by the door.

'I'm worried,' he said.

'Joe, you could worry for America.'

'I'm worried about your safety but I'm also worried that once we're both back at work it will change things between us.'

Fleur smiled at him but he suspected her mind was partly elsewhere. 'Nothing will change,' she said. 'Not now, not ever. You're my soul mate.' She blew him a kiss and was gone.

18

Simone stopped her car in her usual place in the driveway. She switched off the engine and sat for a moment trying to compose her mind. She knew Auriol would have heard her arrive and would be waiting for her in the house, armed with questions, emotionally dangerous. In normal times she dealt with Auriol's high maintenance devotion with calm acceptance. But these were far from normal times.

Despite what she had thought earlier, she decided that prevarication would not serve; there was no way Auriol could be gently prepared for this news and ultimately her reaction would be the same. Her distress was one more burden that had to be borne.

As she got out of the car and locked it with the remote access card, the next-door cat, a cute little black and white, was stalking across the lawn with a dead chaffinch hanging loose in its mouth, bloody beak gaping open. It stopped for a moment and stared at her as if daring her to condemn the killing, then walked on ignoring her. Simone remembered that somewhere she had read that in the wild, prey animals felt no pain as death was upon them, that they were in a Zen-like state, mercifully unafraid and unfeeling. Well, she thought grimly as she walked to the front door, that mercy certainly didn't apply to humans.

As she expected, Auriol was at the door to greet her. She was dressed as for an evening out, made up and looking at her best, apart from black rings under her eyes that no amount of makeup could hide. They kissed and hugged and before Simone could say anything Auriol spun away, drawing her by the hand into the dining area and showing off the table dressed with a candelabra and the best china.

'I thought we'd celebrate,' she said. 'Whatever the news, we'll celebrate dealing with it together.'

Simone's heart sank. She had expected to find Auriol tearful, distraught and in despair. This pretence of emotional control and pragmatism was far worse, far more difficult to deal with.

'Wonderful darling,' she said, 'how very sweet of you.'

'It's fish,' she said 'I know it's expensive but you like it so I thought, yes, why not?'

Auriol put on her apron and fluttered around the kitchen attending to the meal, making meaningless small talk, the effort of staying calm and not asking questions evident in her brittle chatter, the abruptness of her movements and the tension that lined her face. Simone sat in the comfortable kitchen chair and watched her, uncertain what to do for the best. At least for the moment her pain had lessened, the new pills seemed to control it much better. She would wait, let Auriol, no, let them both have the pleasure of this meal together before she said anything. Let them both pretend for a little longer.

Afterwards they pottered around between the kitchen and the dining room together, tidying up and feeding the dishwasher in simple domestic companionship as they had done so many times before. That done they retired with their coffee to the sitting room and their individual chairs opposite each other in front of an aromatic apple-wood fire in the old open Victorian fireplace. It was wasteful and would probably soon be illegal but it was also comforting. Auriol sat bolt upright on the edge of her chair, her whole body stiff with questions, staring at Simone with an anguished half smile on her face. It was time, Simone knew.

'My darling, the news is not good,' she said.

‘Yes.’ The single whispered word was squeezed out from between severely compressed lips.

‘I want you to understand; there’s no doubt or argument about this. No matter what we may wish, we cannot pretend things are different.’

Auriol was gripping her hands together on her lap now, staring fixedly at Simone, wide-eyed, leaning towards her, mouth slightly open as if about to beg for mercy. But in this human world there was no mercy to give.

Slowly, carefully and as gently as she could Simone explained what was wrong with her and what the prognosis was. ‘We have about two months,’ she concluded, ‘a little more if we’re lucky but we can’t be sure of that.’

For a moment Auriol was quite still. Then she sank slowly back into her chair, the life going out of her eyes. Her body, which had been sustained by determined hope, seemed to collapse in on itself.

‘We just have to face up to things and deal with it as best we can,’ Simone said.

Auriol had thought she would prefer Simone to be ill rather than leave her for another woman but no, anything was better than this. ‘It’s not true,’ she said in a lifeless voice.

‘It is true.’

‘There has to be a way...’

‘No. It would be stupid to pretend.’

Auriol sat up suddenly. ‘I heard about this doctor in South America. There was a program, a documentary about him…’

‘We saw it together, Auriol. The man’s a fraud. We mustn’t delude ourselves. At this stage of the disease there’s no cure’

Auriol was shaking her head vigorously. ‘But you’re a doctor, Sim. You work with things like this…’ There was sheer panic in her voice.

‘Different discipline, my love. A doctorate, even two, does not a medical doctor make. This doctor cannot heal herself. Believe me, if I could, I would.’

‘But it’s so bloody unfair...’

‘I’m pretty damn pissed off about it myself,’ Simone said, hardly believing she could manage irony at a time like this.

Auriol was on her feet now, fists clenched at her sides. 'There's no bloody fucking God,' she screamed.

'There never was,' Simone said quietly. The sacrilegious expletives were not Auriol. Somehow she had to calm her down or she would literally have a fit.

'We could have been together forever. We could have had babies. I still can, Sim, or we could've adopted. God knows there's enough hetero women in the world who breed kids they don't want and can't keep!'

'You must stay calm, Auriol. We have to talk about this sensibly.'

'It isn't sensible. It doesn't make any sense at all. Your vaccines keep these bloody women alive and they live forever breeding more and more kids and you die. Don't tell me to be sensible!' She was shivering in shock and fury.

Simone got up and went to her, holding her close. 'I need you to let the anger go, darling,' she said. 'We have to be strong and make the most of the time we have.'

'I hate them,' Auriol said bitterly, 'I hate all the women you've saved. I'd kill every one of them myself if it saved you.'

And she means it, Simone thought. At this moment she would kill for me. She loves me that much. Then, for the first time since learning of her death sentence, Simone's control broke. She burst into uncontrollable sobbing and then it was Auriol who was holding her, soothing her and smoothing her hair as if she were a child.

19

Charles Lovatt had come down to Wenna's desk first thing to sit alongside her as they reviewed the latest audio button. Wenna said nothing while they listened, waiting for the least hint of 'I told you so', but Charles simply asked to hear it again.

'It seems we may have struck lucky,' he said, as if they had had no previous discussion about the Fleur Nichols intercept.

Wenna was not one to leave things hanging in the air. 'I was wrong,' she said. 'I owe you a bottle of Dom Perignon.'

Charles smiled non-committedly. 'Clever girl, Fleur, choosing a location like that.'

‘Yes, I thought so. Makes our job a little easier too.’

‘Coincidental, I trust. Who are we sending?’

‘Jilly and Samantha.’

‘Yes, they should blend in nicely.’

‘Be interesting to see who picks up the meeting for their side,’ Wenna commented.

‘I doubt it will be anyone of real consequence at this stage. If indeed they do have a big story to tell they’ll take extreme precautions,’ Charles replied.

‘Given this is the second meeting, they’d have to declare themselves to her soon I’d have thought, Fleur is too astute to be manipulated,’ Wenna commented.

‘I agree. We probably won’t get audio of the meeting but fortunately Joe Kendry is getting edgy about the whole thing so she’s bound to talk to him afterwards,’ Charles said thoughtfully, ‘With any luck she’ll give us a complete re-run.’

‘I’ve said we want everything from the intercept as of 10am this morning. I didn’t want to risk the software not being tripped.’

‘Excellent. Now the level of our interest has increased we should have a word with Archives, get them to go in-depth on Fleur… And Joe Kendry.’

‘In theory it should all be in her file but I’ll double check anyway,’ Wenna said.

Charles looked at his watch. ‘Interesting times,’ he commented, ‘perhaps we should meet for lunch in my office at one; I’ll have something sent up. By then we may have things to talk about. What do you say?’

‘Yes, certainly,’ Wenna agreed. ‘I don’t suppose you have any idea what the big story might be?’

‘Absolutely none,’ Charles replied. And this time Wenna believed him.

Charles stood up to leave. Apparently as an afterthought he flicked the anonymous sticker she had left on her Hub. ‘Nice to have an admirer with a poetic bent,’ he said as he walked away.

20

The tearoom in The Grosvenor was less a room than a sumptuously equipped and appointed alcove off the ornate main entrance hall of the hotel, serviced from a manager's station near the alcove entrance.

Fleur deliberately arrived ten minutes early and asked for a table with a view of the entrance as she was expecting a friend. She ordered black coffee for two to be served later. With the waitress's attention turned elsewhere, Fleur settled herself with her back to the wood-panelled wall and had a surreptitious look around. The tea room was moderately busy; perhaps half full with a fairly predictable mid-morning clientele of upper management business escapees making sotto voce big talk, and mature Sloanes sharing gossip and comparing husbands.

So far as Fleur could tell there was no one taking the slightest interest in her and there was no one who looked even slightly out of place. She relaxed without even being aware that she had been tense. Her concern had not been for herself but for the possibility that her contact would abort the meeting if he thought either one of them was under surveillance.

He arrived at exactly 11am, walking confidently up to the manager and looking around the alcove. His Middle Eastern complexion betrayed his origins but he had adopted a very European look. He was of medium height, elegantly dressed in a pinstriped suit, white shirt and sober tie, clean-shaven, and looked to be in his late twenties. He carried a slim document case under one arm. A commodity broker perhaps, or currency dealer or corporate solicitor.

He came across to her and held out his hand. 'A pleasure to meet you,' he said, taking the seat opposite her. His middle-class English accent was almost impeccable.

'And useful for both of us I hope,' Fleur replied, taking his hand and smiling warmly at him for the benefit of any onlookers.

There would be no exchange of names or any need for such pleasantries. He was clutching his document case and looking round the room, ostensibly for the waitress, who was already on her way to their table. Fleur realised that despite his appearance of calm and control he was very nervous, which was hardly surprising. He was personally vulnerable and he had, of course, no reason to trust her beyond any assurances his superiors had seen fit to give him, if any.

It would also have been difficult for him or an accomplice to scan the room before the meeting.

The uniformed waitress arrived and served them coffee from a faux Georgian coffee pot and minute almond biscuits on a silver tray. Fleur thanked her and said nothing until she was out of hearing and they had both sipped their coffee.

'Someone wishes to meet me,' she said.

'And you have agreed.'

'Yes. Provisionally.'

'You understand there is a high level of risk for us in this.'

'Perhaps for me as well.'

'We are placing a great deal of trust in you.' He was looking at her earnestly over his cup, holding it with both hands as if to stop it shaking, and speaking not much above a whisper.

'Why are you wasting my time stating the obvious?' Fleur asked, her tight smile barely taking the edge off her words.

He hesitated before answering. 'Because I have to ask you to repay that trust.'

'How?' Fleur asked bluntly.

'By asking you to travel to where he is for the meeting.'

'He wants to meet on his own turf, is that it?'

He replaced his cup carefully in its saucer and spoke without making eye contact. 'No. Somewhere neutral, somewhere where the risk for both sides is minimal.'

'Like?'

'The location is New Zealand.'

Fleur said nothing for a moment, absorbing this information. It seemed extreme to travel half way round the world for a meeting that might take an hour or two at the most. However, it made sense in that New Zealand was a politically non-aligned country well known for being stable and independent, almost boringly so. It was probably as safe a meeting place as could be found for both of them and depending on where he was, the journey might not be as long for him as it was for her.

The cost of a return ticket and accommodation would completely clean out her bank account and probably Joe's as well. The BBC might spring for the fare in return for an exclusive but she could not approach Walter before the big meeting, she was sure that would be seen as a breach of trust.

'That's a hell of a trip,' she said, 'is the location negotiable?'

He gave a slight shake of the head. 'I'm sorry.'

'Well, I don't know...'

He seemed to divine the problem. 'If you agree to go we will arrange the itinerary and pay all your costs,' he said.

Well, that solved that problem. It also gave a clear indication of the importance they placed on this meeting; they were not people who spent a dollar if they did not have to.

'Who am I meeting?' she asked.

His lips tightened. 'Names are not important at this stage,' he said.

'They are to me,' Fleur responded, 'I may have to put off another assignment to pick up this meeting so it had better be worth my while.'

'I am not told everything,' he said, 'it is not necessary. But I was warned you would ask that question and as a sign of good faith I can say that you will be very privileged to meet this person and that he gives instructions to the man who likes ice cream. Is this enough to convince you?'

It was. While the latest evolution of Al Qaeda was heavily de-centralised these days, there was still a small shadowy group who oversaw major international action and provided what they would call spiritual leadership and guidance. The Hydra still had a central motivating brain. And anybody who could give orders to the Head of Communications was someone Fleur was more than happy to meet, especially if they were picking up the bill. There was something else however.

'After the meeting, will you expect to put any restrictions on how or where I publish the story?'

'No restrictions at all,' he replied confidently.

He knows more than he's letting on, Fleur thought. He must be high up in the UK franchise or he would never have been trusted with the answer to that question.

'I make the decision to publish or not,' she said 'I won't accept any pressure if I suspect I am being lied to or used to spread disinformation.'

A faint patina of sweat had appeared across his brow but his voice remained level and calm. Fleur sensed that he was worried about giving away more than he should before she had finally agreed.

'I am sure that has been taken into account,' he replied.

'I hope it has,' Fleur said, 'because that's the way it's going to be.'

He was fingering the zip of his document case nervously. 'You will go, then?'

'Yes. When do I leave?'

His relief was palpable. He opened the document case and took out a sealed manilla envelope, sliding it across the table to her. 'All the necessary information is in here. You understand that now we have made this arrangement, time is our enemy.'

Fleur understood. Being high up on the CIA's kill list, which her proposed contact most certainly was, would naturally tend to make you careful about your travel plans and who knew of them.

'So, when?' she asked.

'Tomorrow,' he said. 'And one last thing. We ask that you make no arrangements to pre-sell the story before the meeting and that you explain to your partner or family that you will be out of communication until you return.'

Joe was going to love that, Fleur thought. And it was going to be hard on her not to speak to him for the better part of a week but she at least understood the necessity for that level of security. She nodded acceptance.

He stood up, smiled briefly at her and walked away, leaving her to pay the bill.

21

Simone arrived at work late, a fact particularly noted by Fat Annie, who was still inflated by the level of trust Dr Burcastle had placed in her. Pretending ignorance, she greeted the scientist with her usual bonhomie.

'Mornin', Doctor Gofre.'

'Good morning, Annie.'

They went through the security ritual and Simone passed through the double airlocks with the negative pressure seals and into the laboratory.

''Ave a good day,' Annie said to her departing back.

The mix of American phraseology and London accent jarred with Simone. She recognised the injustice of it but felt like grabbing poor Annie and knocking some linguistic sensibility into her. Control. She had to control these irrational impulses, they were emotionally destabilising which was the last thing she needed after a long, hard night trying to placate Auriol.

For her part, Annie felt genuinely sad for Simone. She might be a bit of a strange one but you wouldn't wish what she had on your worst enemy. She did look worn out, poor thing and no wonder. You'd wonder why she came in to work at all in her state; she'd be better off at home resting up. Annie considered the boss was quite right to tip her off, Simone might be a doctor but she wasn't a proper one and she'd be no better than anyone else at looking after herself or the best interests of the Unit. Well, at least whilst she was here Annie would keep an eye out for her. She made a note of Simone's late arrival in the security pad. Then she added 'and she looked very tired.'

In the laboratory Simone made her way first to her desk, acknowledging a couple of colleagues with a brief smile on the way. It was what she always did and she knew it was important to preserve her rituals or word would get back to Burcastle. She sat at her desk and booted up the Hub, calling up the page with the last sequence she had been working on.

All this will continue whether I am here or not, she thought. No matter what I've achieved someone else will sit here facing the same sort of problems I have spent years trying to solve. It would be that way because so little could be achieved in one short life, even one that went full term; viruses could mutate faster than they could be identified and combated, and when it came to bacteria, well, some could replicate themselves a million times in seven hours. It was a race and not one that humankind was winning. She glanced around the lab that had been a second home to her since her late twenties. All around her, secured in their small deep-frozen containers in shielded cubicles behind shatterproof glass, were minute instruments of death, samples of the most potent, most deadly viruses that had ever existed. Forget atomic weapons, she thought, the real enemy to human existence was right here, too minute to be seen with the naked eye.

There were also some equally toxic mutations that man had created, even some she had created herself in the pursuit of knowledge, for the greater good of mankind, to save life, lengthen and improve it. Or such was the received wisdom that enabled her to pursue her career. Potentially vicious and lethal as they were, those at least she could control, unlike the rapidly multiplying cancerous cells that were ravaging her body. And that was the appalling irony of it all.

As her active sequence came up on the screen she felt eyes boring into her back. She did not turn round; she did not want their sympathy. She felt a flush of anger. He'd told them of course, they all knew. The bastard couldn't keep his mouth shut if his life depended on it, she thought bitterly.

22

Joe was surprised to discover that ConSept Productions actually had a London office, even if it was only a serviced facility in a modern block in a side road on the Fulham side of Putney Bridge. The immaculate young receptionist welcomed him with a professional smile and called Rose Petchek on the intercom.

She came out to meet him and offered a casual hand heavy with costume rings. The jewellery was a match for the rumpled ethnic-look dress that covered wide hips and a broad bosom and the mass of light brown hair that stood out around her head like a corona. Rose had a round owlish face, was heavily made up and she wore flat shoes that did nothing for fat ankles. She looked slow and unattractive, which put Joe instantly on alert. Knowing the business as he did, he was well aware that anyone who could afford to go through life sending out such negative messages had to be there on merit. She was one to watch.

'Hi, Joe,' she said. 'Good to meet you. Come on through.'

Joe acknowledged her greeting and followed her through to her modest office. She took her seat behind a thin-topped wooden desk covered with scripts, timing sheets, schedules, reference books, hard copy files and a thin Hub screen at one end. Against one wall was a whiteboard covered in dates and times under project headings and directors' names. Joe's name was not among them.

'Strange we haven't met before,' Rose said, indicating a visitor's chair to one side. It sounded rather like an accusation.

'Maybe a loss to both of us,' Joe replied. It would be very easy to dislike Rose Petchek he decided.

'Could be. Okay, down to business. We don't have a title for this project yet so for now we'll just call it Two+One. Your agent would've told you we're working with the UN on this one, right?'

'Yeah, he did. So who's doing what?'

'I'm producer, EP and project co-ordinator. The client will get final cut, that's the deal.'

'It usually is.'

'You are contracted as writer, line producer, director and presenter. You'll need a sound-cameraman who can sub as a travelling PA. Any ideas?'

'I'll take Phil Rogers if I can get him. I've worked with him before and he's based here in London. He's also got all his own gear.'

'Right. Put his agent in touch with me and we'll sort out the contract. We don't have a Hollywood budget, mind.'

'I'd gotten that impression,' Joe said pointedly.

Rose missed or ignored the sarcasm. 'You've seen the brief, we really need to deal to the critics out there, and you should bone up on what they're saying, then highlight the benefits of Two+One for the world as a whole, not just portray it as another worthy UN scheme. This is a sales and marketing situation, understood?'

'It's pretty obvious where the client would want the emphasis put. If Two+One is really as successful as we're told, that shouldn't be an issue.'

'Good. So we're looking at a running time of forty-seven minutes, straightforward documentary style, simple structure, voice-over rather than presenter to camera, no smart-arsed director's shots, lots of grateful women and cute kids, this is about the story and the product, okay?

Joe was rapidly heating up. 'Look, Rose,' he said, 'I know we're not making a movie; not likely with a crew of one, is it? You don't need to tell me how to do my job.'

Rose looked at him thoughtfully. 'My, was I doing that?' she said, straight-faced. 'There was me thinking I was doing mine. Ah well, talking of your job, we'll do post production here in London; I've arranged to lease a facility and an editor and we'll expect you to flash footage through to us pretty much as you shoot so we can get a rough idea of how it's going.'

'I'll try to rough cut it before I do that.'

'Right. I've arranged for a local contact to be available to you, details later. I'll leave the shooting schedule to you to work out on the spot but we've already lined up subjects for you to interview in Pakistan and contacts with the WHO and UNFRA clinics. I'll send all this through to your Ctab. All you have to do is tell them when you're coming.' She took an A4-sized envelope from a drawer and handed it over. 'All in there, including credit details for two airline e-tickets for three days' time.'

'Okay Rose, but I want you to understand, if this thing is to have any impact at all, we'll have to shoot some footage outside of offices and obvious set-ups. I need linkages and location background and cutaways and visual differentiation, maybe some vox pop stuff. I need product to work with in the edit suite.'

Rose seemed hesitant. 'Look, Joe, I don't want to cramp your creative style but I also don't want you wandering about Asia shooting a travelogue. Just use your common sense, right?'

'Of course.' It was the first time in the whole meeting that Joe felt he had won a point, however small.

'We need to get on to this, Joe, so I've made an appointment for you for eleven tomorrow at Genphree Biotics; they're near Oxford, where the university is. There's an interesting woman there, she came up with the original vaccine for H5N1 and created the Two+One virus. Thought you'd want to do a recce, talk to her, if at all possible, maybe take a Palmcam with you and get some pick-ups of the lab if you can't get your cameraman organised in time. Hope you don't mind.'

Joe opened his mouth to say what he really thought then rapidly closed it again. Arguing with a control freak like Rose Petchek would be singularly unproductive and in truth, the lab where the Two+One virus was created would have been his first port of call anyway. He felt obliged to make a point however.

'Okay, Rose, but now I'm on board I'd rather organise my own itinerary.'

'As of now you're on your own, Joe. I'm here as a backup if you need me,' Rose said, smiling at him for the first time. 'Keep me up to date. Treat me like I was your PA.'

Joe pocketed the envelope and felt obliged to return the smile; well aware he was being manipulated. 'There's just the small matter of money. Cash expenses and per diems,' he said.

Rose named a figure. 'It'll be in your bank account this afternoon,' she promised.

The amount was more than Joe had expected. Between that and his fee it was well worth putting up with Rose Petchek; from now on he could assume control of the project and he had every intention of taking Rose up on her offer to use her as a PA. When it came to making this sort of client-funded documentary the director may not be an auteur but at least while he was out on location Joe would be his own man.

For an hour Joe had not thought of Fleur at all. It was something of a record for the last year. Once he was out of the meeting and heading back to Putney Bridge underground station, she flooded back into his mind. For no logical reason a frisson of fear ran through him.

23

Jilly and Samantha were debriefed by Wenna and Charles in his office. The four of them had reviewed the footage the two women had shot at The Grosvenor Hotel, which Wenna had already watched live on a SysLink. Jilly still wore the brooch that housed the film button.

'The audio couldn't pick up a word they said,' Samantha offered. 'He seemed to be whispering and her replies were just a mumble.'

'We were two tables away and sideways on to them which wasn't ideal but we could hardly move around to get a better angle, that's the problem with latte reporting,' Jilly added, 'and that rather blanks the idea of using our tame lip-reader.'

'At least we know who she met,' Wenna commented.

'Which of them was driving the meeting?' Charles asked.

Samantha and Jilly exchanged looks. 'Him at the beginning, yah?' Samantha suggested, looking at Jilly for confirmation. 'Then she seemed to take over until he handed over the envelope.'

'Which looks quite thin, couldn't have held much,' Wenna commented.

'Absolutely.'

'And there were no spectators?' Charles asked.

'If there were, they were jolly good is all I can say.' Jilly sounded slightly put out at the suggestion that they may have missed something.

Charles raised his eyebrows at Wenna and she nodded. He beamed at his two surveillance experts. 'Sam, Jilly, thanks to you both. A super job as usual.'

When they were alone Charles leant back in his office chair and steepled his fingers. 'So, Mohammed Asami.'

'Indeed,' Wenna replied. 'Whom we have always assumed was a fringe player.'

'It bothers me that we know so little about him.'

'It seems he's actually a trusted middle man, perhaps a banker.'

'Paying our Fleur you think?'

'The envelope was rather thin. They wouldn't risk an e-transfer so it could have been high-denomination notes I suppose,' Wenna said dubiously.

'What was it then, a briefing document perhaps?'

'Perhaps,' Wenna said, although she was aware that Charles was speaking rhetorically.

'Do we think that at any point she might come to us with what she has?' Charles mused.

'Unlikely, I'd have thought. We'd hear about it on the news first.'

'Then we can't trust her, can we?'

'No,' Wenna said bluntly. 'She has a way of contacting these people that we haven't picked up on. Without the E-spy in her apartment we would have been none the wiser. She knows exactly what she's doing and she's playing the game.'

‘Which doesn’t necessarily mean she’s gone over.’

‘No, but it does mean she’s not likely to co-operate if we approach her, she has her own agenda.’

‘Sadly true. In that case what would you recommend?’

‘I think we should lock onto her Ctab, clean out her hard drive again, and put a team on her twenty-four seven.’

Charles looked thoughtful. ‘She is of course an honest and upright citizen with a high public profile and an impeccable security status. From what you’ve told me there is nothing in archives or on the net about her or this Joe Kendry to give us a moment’s concern.’

‘You disagree, then?’

‘No, I agree entirely. I am simply making the point that we must proceed with great caution, Wenna. Only the best will do. Deniability is the order of the day if at all possible. I do not wish to have to make awkward explanations to the Director General or the Joint Intelligence Council.’

‘Understood. It’ll take twenty-four hours to put the team together and that concerns me a little. Meeting on consecutive days is pretty unusual. It suggests things are moving fast.’

‘I will add my weight to your request for allocation,’ Charles promised.

‘And I don’t think we should forget about Joe Kendry. I want to include him if possible,’ Wenna said.

‘Very well, but not at the expense of leaving her free at any time.’

‘No, of course not.’

‘We may at some point, perhaps quite soon, have to consider who we bring into the loop.’

‘The Cousins you mean?’

‘Perhaps. Not formally though. I prefer to use the unofficial network first.’

‘I seem to remember you telling me once that there was no such thing,’ Wenna said with seeming innocence.

Charles smiled ruefully. ‘Perhaps I did. Nonetheless, the unofficial route tends to reduce everyone’s accountability at least in the short term. It so happens that an old sparring partner of mine is in the country preparing the way for a brief and hopefully uneventful visit from his President in a few weeks’ time.’

‘I’d lost sight of that. You think there might be a connection?’

‘We have no reason to suppose so but it’s a ball we need to keep our eye on.’

‘If the President was a target in any way at all that would certainly come under the definition of a big story, but why would the opposition want to involve a journalist before the event, whatever that event was? It hardly makes any sense.’

‘The key to this,’ Charles said deliberately, ‘is to find out what is in that envelope.’

‘In view of her profile even I wouldn’t suggest we try a physical search of her apartment. At least, not yet.’

‘No. But whatever is in it, I want to know before she goes public. If necessary we can slap a suppression order on her and whoever she’s selling it to.’

‘I’d better get moving,’ Wenna said, ‘the sooner we put this team together, the better.’ She stood up to leave.

‘When you’ve done that,’ Charles said, ‘I think we should go and talk to ‘Daddy’, don’t you?’

24

Covent Garden had once been a thriving fruit and vegetable market, its narrow Victorian streets and buildings cluttered with lorries and vans loading and unloading, and porters pushing long wooden carts overloaded with sacks and boxes and trays of produce from all over the country and around the world. The chaos was supervised with a lenient hand by police officers from the historic Bow Street Police Station, who saw their job as facilitators and seldom had to intervene, apart from extricating lost motorists or evening-dressed attendees at The Royal Opera House who had become trapped in the milling throngs of workers and market traffic.

Here, all-night revellers took advantage of the fact that the pubs opened in the early hours of the morning to ease the thirst of the muscular porters who passed their lucrative employment down through the family line. It had been a world of its own with its own rules, rituals and traditions and continued through the generations until the market finally moved to a new location in South London. Then, in a few short years the whole area became gentrified and partly pedestrianised and a vital and vibrant community became an increasingly distant memory. Although a lot cleaner now, the congestion of people and traffic was hardly any less.

Joe and Fleur met for lunch at a bustling Italian restaurant in a side street close to the Opera House, considering themselves fortunate to secure a pavement table. Such was the noise and bustle that there was little chance of their conversation being overheard. After Fleur had told him her news Joe maintained a distant silence until they had eaten and their plates had been cleared away.

'New Zealand,' Joe said flatly.

'That's good, isn't it?'

'Is it?'

You're determined to be grumpy, aren't you.'

'Reckon I'm entitled to be.'

'It's the nearest thing on the planet to a safe haven,' Fleur protested. 'Five million people and forty million sheep. Politically neutral, clean, green and nuclear free. What could be better?'

'Somewhere a hell of a lot nearer home,' Joe said tetchily.

'Can you think of anywhere nearer home that would be safer?'

Joe was silent for a moment as the waiter approached to top up their glasses of water and Fleur tucked the envelope away in her handbag.

'I don't like the fact they're paying your expenses,' Joe said, changing the subject. 'It means they're calling the shots.'

'Do you have any idea what the airfare to New Zealand is these days?' Fleur asked rhetorically, 'More than we could afford that's for sure. They have a story they want to get out and they're prepared to cover the cost. And I've made it quite clear I don't take orders and I won't be used.'

'I just feel uneasy about the whole damn thing. I mean, why you?'

'Oh, thank you for that ringing endorsement of my journalistic ability and status in the industry!' Fleur said tartly.

Joe grimaced, accepting his error. 'Okay, big mistake, really dumb, sorry.'

'They want the credibility my name can give their story and they want my contacts with the only Western broadcaster that has any standing at all in the Muslim world.'

'Point taken, sweetheart. I wasn't putting you down; I am just so damn worried. Especially since they want you to stay out of contact. What's that all about?'

'From their point of view it's Security 101. They trust me but only so far. Communications can be monitored. It's their weak point and they know it.'

'But you'll take your Ctab…'

'Too damn right. But I won't use it and I won't mike up or take any wearables. I'll play by the rules.'

'So we won't be able to talk to each other for… how long, a week?'

'Probably, but time will fly. I could pick up this meeting and be back in time to go to Afghanistan.'

'Don't wind me up, babe, I'm stressed enough already.'

'I'm serious. We've already had this argument. Afghanistan is definite money, this meeting may or may not be.'

'Then is it truly worth it?'

'It's the chance of a world exclusive, end of. As to money, you can bet on me making it pay somehow. I just don't know how much yet. Now, can we change the subject? How did you get on with Rose?'

Joe sighed. He knew pressing Fleur any further would be a waste of time. What he was seeing now was not his lover but the seasoned professional, and he had better get used to it. He dragged his mind back to his meeting with the unlovely Rose Petchek.

'She's a bully and a control freak but I can live with that,' he said.

'Is she pretty?'

Joe laughed for the first time for days. 'She's as ugly as sin and what's more she flaunts it.'

'Good. When does she want you to start?'

'Yesterday. And, since you'll be gone tomorrow, that suits me very well.' Joe found a grin from somewhere. 'I think we should go home and make the most of our last day.'

'Afterwards.'

'After what?'

'After I've called Walter.'

'Great. We have to ask his permission now?'

Fleur kicked him under the table. 'I need to tell him I'm taking a short break before Afghanistan. If I don't, he'll only worry what I'm up to.'

'Him and me both.'

'Think positive, Joe. We're damn lucky. We've got each other and the chance to make good money doing what we enjoy. Let's face it, darling, we've got a lifestyle to die for.'

Before Joe could reply the waiter brought the bill.

25

Charles had suggested they meet in Kensington Gardens and take in the spring air, wanting to make the whole thing sound relatively unimportant, but Walter Bloom had declined. His bulk testified to the fact that he was not a great one for physical exercise and it was said of him that being more than five minutes away from his newsroom gave him panic attacks. He was absolutely convinced that without him the whole structure of the BBC news service would collapse, a view not universally shared by his staff.

Walter was also aware that Charles Lovatt seldom if ever made social calls. Whatever he wanted it was business and Walter much preferred to conduct business on his home territory, so he invited him for afternoon tea.

When Charles had introduced Wenna they sat around a small table in a corner of his office and Walter poured. 'Very finest Ceylon warehouse floor sweepings,' he announced. 'Best we can do on my budget.'

'Walter, every time I meet you, you complain about your budget,' Charles said, mock-seriously. 'What do they do with all the taxes I pay?'

'Waste them on the Security Services. Now, what can I do for you?'

'Just a bit of background on one of your favourite employees.'

'You know I can't do that. Privacy Act.'

'Of course.'

'Any point in asking why?'

'I'd rather you didn't.'

'What I do for the sake of my country. Who, then?'

'Fleur Nichols.'

There was a silence, and then Walter said; 'Now, first of all she isn't an employee, she's an independent contractor, secondly I have a Director General who is almost as paranoid about privacy issues as I am and thirdly why would you want information on the best foreign correspondent in the Western world when you could search her on your Hub in the comfort of your own very expensive office?'

'A little additional background, perhaps,' Wenna suggested.

'From your personal and professional perspective,' Charles added. 'You can rely on our discretion; we make a practice of listening, not talking. Oh, and I'm sure the DG would approve if you thought it appropriate to inform him of our request.'

Walter pointed a chubby finger straight at Charles's heart. 'Try to bully me Charlie boy and you'll get the square root of bugger all.'

Charles waved the very idea away. 'Wouldn't dream of such a thing, Walter. We are here as supplicants after all. In your hands entirely.'

Walter harrumphed at them. 'Right,' he said 'so long as you understand I'm scratching your back and I expect reciprocation.'

Charles smiled amiably. 'Whatever is possible, Walter.'

'Okay, she's thirty-two, born in Britain, mother American, father British, they divorced when she was eleven, both now deceased. She was taken to America by her mother and finished her education there. After high school she trained as an actress, which is why she's so good in front of the camera. When her mother died in a car crash she returned to the UK to be with her father and lived with him until he died four years ago. He was a professor of Arabic Studies at Cambridge, took her under his scholastic wing, taught her all he knew I'd say. She's bilingual, very bright, has won a stack of awards and has a nose for a story almost as good as mine. That the sort of thing you want?'

'And more recently?' Charles asked.

'She took a year off.'

'That would be after she met Joe Kendry.'

'Right,' Walter said sourly.

'What do you think of him?' Wenna asked.

'I try not to. He was born with 'loser' tattooed on his forehead. God knows what she sees in him.'

‘Is he her weak link, then, do you think?’ Charles asked.

‘No doubt about it. She’s worth ten of him but she’s obsessed with the little turd. You can’t say a word against him.’

Charles looked thoughtful. ‘Walter, would you say that Fleur is sound?’

‘Absolutely. One hundred percent. That girl is kosher, I’d stake my mother’s life on it.’

‘And Kendry?’ Wenna asked.

Walter’s chair protested as he moved his considerable bulk to a more comfortable position while he tried to phrase a dispassionate response. He failed. ‘Limited ability,’ he said finally, ‘thinks he’s God’s gift to humankind and he’s got my top talent dancing on his dick – pardon me Wenna but he pisses me off – also, he’s American. This man you want me to trust?’

Charles smiled wryly and changed the subject. ‘So Fleur has done no work for you for the last twelve months, then,’ he asked.

‘Nor for anybody else so far as I know. I’ve only just managed to get her back in harness.’

‘Doing what?’ Wenna put in.

Walter looked uncertain. ‘Are you talking to anyone else about this?’ he asked, ‘because you’re asking for commercially sensitive information here.’

‘Only you, my word on it,’ Charles assured him.

‘Right. Well, she’s just agreed to go to Afghanistan for us.’

‘General background or something specific?’

‘Something specific. Is that why you’re here? Is it to do with Afghanistan?’

‘At this stage we can’t rule out anything.’

‘Look Charles,’ Walter said anxiously, ‘is there something I should be worried about? Are you telling me she shouldn’t go in?’

‘I don’t know,’ Charles replied honestly.

‘Come on Charles, this cuts both ways. There has to be some give and take. I won’t stand for Fleur being hung out to dry.’

‘We would never knowingly put her in danger,’ Wenna said. ‘So what is her assignment?’

There was a silence whilst Walter Bloom gave attention to his tea, clasping the cup in both hands and staring into it as if by so doing he could divine what his reply should be. He was under no obligation to answer but on the other hand having Charles under a moral obligation had its attractions. One of which was the possibility of finding out what he was up to. Walter smelt a story. A big one, and he was seldom wrong. After a moment he looked up, a decision made.

'We had an approach from the Afghan rebels, Muslim freedom fighters, Taleban, whatever you want to call them,' he said, 'they swear their people have been targeted by the Americans with some sort of virus and they're dying faster than they can bury them.'

'You believe that?' Wenna asked.

'Look, I'm not a fan of the American military but biological weapons, mass murder? I don't think so. It may be just a bid to get some anti-American propaganda across. However, these people don't usually bullshit us, there may be something going on out there. So, I'm sending Fleur to find out. Or I was, now I'm not so sure.'

'How did they make contact?' Wenna asked.

'Disposable Ctab,' Walter replied. 'Usual thing.'

'So how can you be sure the call was authentic?'

'We record all incoming material and they gave the news desk the code.'

'What code?'

'They've been in touch on and off over the years so we've established a two-way code system. Common journalistic practice. Saves time and angst for both sides.'

'So she didn't know the Taleban had made contact until you told her.'

'That's right.'

'When did you brief her?'

'Day before yesterday. Mid-morning.'

'Is there any chance,' Charles asked, 'that Fleur might have contacted them on her own, after that?'

Walter Bloom thought that one over. 'She might be able to but it wouldn't be like her,' he replied. 'We've worked together a lot over the years and I think she trusts me. If there'd been any out of office contact I'm pretty sure she'd tell me.'

'But you couldn't be certain,' Wenna said.

'Obviously not but I don't believe it.'

'When will she be leaving for Afghanistan?' Charles asked.

'Not until the week after next now,' Walter replied.

'Now?' Wenna enquired. 'You mean because of this conversation?'

'No. She called and left a message not long before you arrived. She's taking a week's break before she goes.'

'So, she's just had a year off work and now she wants a holiday?' Charles mused.

'That's what I thought. I was going to make a gentle enquiry along those lines myself but wherever she is and whatever she's doing she's not returning her agent's calls or mine.'

'Do you have any idea where she might have gone?'

Walter's heavy sigh and helpless shrug were a plea for understanding of the problems that beset a well-intentioned would-be employer fighting a losing battle against the power of lust.

'She's probably shacked up at home with lover boy, oblivious to the world. Who knows?'

Wenna exchanged a look with Charles. If that was true there was a good chance they would find out what Fleur was up to even if Walter Bloom didn't.

Walter spotted the look and leant towards them, testing the strength of his chair in the process. He pinned them with a glare that had frozen many a junior editor. 'Look after that girl,' he said, 'don't put her in danger or this little conversation won't stay private for long.'

'Your loyalty to Fleur is very commendable,' Charles said with a nod of acceptance.

'And another thing,' Walter added, 'I smell a story, and if you don't want my people ferreting about and getting under your feet, you'd better keep me in the loop.'

Charles smiled. 'Always assuming there is a loop to keep you in,' he said as he and Wenna got up to leave. 'Wonderful tea, Walter, my compliments to the canteen ladies. Thank you so much. Let us know if you manage to get in touch with Fleur. Oh, and of course silence is golden. Especially so far as Fleur is concerned.'

As they closed the door Walter called up the audio copy on his personal Hub, transferred it to a flash drive, then deleted it from the Hub. These days it paid to be careful, especially around people you actually trusted.

26

They had hurried home, switched off the Hub and, secure from interruptions, gone straight to bed. Now, with evening approaching, they were lying awake, side-by-side, holding hands across the covers, sated and drowsy with pleasure. But although rested and relaxed in body, neither was relaxed in mind.

Fleur was thinking ahead to the interview that might be the most important she had ever conducted. As always when dealing with people of power and influence it was important to set the tone at the outset or, as experience told her, they would ride roughshod over the interviewer, pursuing their agenda hard, controlling the questions and thus their own responses, ensuring their point of view was dominant.

She had no idea what sort of man she would be meeting but she was quite sure he would be intellectually able and very media savvy; he would be a man to be treated with respect and caution. He would certainly not be in awe of her but equally she must be sure she did not permit him to intimidate her; if she fell into the trap of accepting a subservient role that for cultural reasons he might expect, she might miss the chance of a lifetime. And anyway she had no intention of ending up as an unquestioning apologist for his ideas.

Even at the risk of him aborting the meeting she was determined that would not happen. Joe was right, there was the risk that, despite the warning she had given them, there was no great story to reveal and she was there simply to be used to disseminate propaganda. But she did not believe that, it offended her instincts that it should be so. She felt the beginning of a headache: best to do what she usually did and rely on experience and instinct at the time. She relaxed and tried to empty her mind.

Beside her Joe was breathing quietly and staring at the ceiling, trying to consider probabilities logically and not let worry take over and distort his judgment. He was finding it hard. All his concerns were for Fleur; he was utterly confident he could manage his own assignment and handle Rose Petchek. It was obvious Rose had organised the project in such a way as to give him little opportunity to explore the subject matter as he should and normally would, to probe for dramatic elements, look for story twists, identify the money shots and pick the telling interview. If she had her way she would surround him with minders and leave him no area to apply his craft and he was determined that would not happen. Once he and Phil were on the road he would find ways around any constraints that were put on them. None of that caused him any anxiety.

As always, it was Fleur. He was still not convinced by her arguments; it simply was not a safe world out there and she was so small and vulnerable, despite her experience and tenacious spirit.

The sense of unease he had felt since they started talking about both returning to work was back in full force. But was it based on any real evidence of risk or was he simply being selfish and controlling? If Fleur were ever to work again then nothing she was ever likely to do would be without danger, that was the simple truth of it. Still she had half agreed that they could do a risk-free project together when they both returned and that was worth looking forward to. For now, he wanted reassurance from her. He rolled over onto his side so he could see her profile.

'I want you to promise me,' he said, 'you take care, not risks, okay?'

'The same goes for you,' Fleur replied emphatically.

'Every move you make, think it through first. The slightest sign of danger and you pull out.'

Fleur turned to face him. 'You're more at risk than I am, I'll be worried all the time.'

'You'll be too busy. Anyway, the dreaded Rose has done her best to wrap me up in cotton wool.'

'I'm beginning to like her. The one thing you're not to do is wander off into the countryside on your own, understood?'

'It's okay, Phil will hold my hand. Problem is, there's no-one to look after you.'

'Joe, I've already explained, they need me, I'm safer on my own than if I had a complete SAS unit with me, they'll see to that.'

'You don't have any idea where to go or what to do when you get off the plane,' he protested.

'It will all be arranged,' Fleur reassured him. 'These people are old hands at covert meetings. There will be a message or someone there to give me instructions.'

‘I just wish I could at least talk to you.’

‘I know but it isn’t possible. I will call you as soon as I can after the meeting, I promise.’

‘Hold you to that. And… Hey, I’ve just had a brilliant idea.’ He sat up suddenly. ‘Since you’re leaving at some ungodly hour why don’t we go to the airport now, book into a hotel for the night and be on the spot for the morning?’

‘What about your meeting?’

‘I can pick up Phil in Hounslow and still get to Oxford in time.’

‘Well, that’s great. I’d better start packing.’ She slid out of bed, suddenly enthused. She grinned across to him. ‘You’ve got ten minutes to get dressed’ she said, ‘I’m a fast pack and you’re not going anywhere naked.’

27

They left the underground at Westminster and walked across Parliament Square, past the front of the Houses of Parliament and into Victoria Tower Gardens where Charles found a seat not occupied by vagrants, flicked off a couple of pigeon feathers and sat himself down. He had insisted that the labyrinthine corridors of the BBC Centre were claustrophobic and he felt in need of fresh air. Despite the brightly cool spring day, Wenna was not convinced he would find any in central London and would much have preferred heading straight back to the tiered concrete bunker that housed their office.

Charles was clearly in contemplative mood. ‘I sometimes think,’ he said, ‘that the day of the gentleman may be over. If true, that would be very sad, would it not?’

Wenna glanced at him sideways, trying to divine where this was leading, but he was staring straight ahead at the stone wall that blocked their view of the river.

‘My father used to say that we needed fewer gentlemen and more gentle men,’ she replied.

‘An interesting observation but nonetheless I think that in general he might have agreed with me.’

‘Quite possibly.’

‘There are so many drawbacks to being a gentleman these days. Or for that matter being a lady. The polite rules of society, the ones that used to enable us all to rub along with each other without too much friction, do not seem to hold anymore.’

‘Well, we’ve pretty much given up commonly understood and accepted social rules,’ Wenna agreed, ‘and, for the good of the many, replaced them with legislation.’

‘I made a mistake,’ Charles said abruptly.

Wenna was taken aback. ‘About what?’ she asked.

‘I should have had E-spy fitted in her bedroom,’ he said. ‘But I was too much of a gentleman… And I should have included video.’

Wenna considered that. ‘I’m rather glad you didn’t,’ she said truthfully.

‘Thank you,’ Charles said, still not looking at her. ‘However, it was a mistake, one that you should learn from, and it may have lost us valuable information.’

‘The surveillance team will be in place first thing in the morning,’ Wenna reassured him.

‘I saw you checking your Ctab,’ Charles said, ‘anything?’

‘Nothing. The E-spy picked them up returning, later they went out again. Since then nothing.’

‘Dinner on the town, do we think?’ Charles mused, flicking a well-shod foot at a scruffy pigeon, the boldest of a gang that was loitering with intent to beg. ‘A celebration perhaps, or a farewell?’

‘At least we know they haven’t flown the coop. I put a port watch on them first thing this morning, just in case. It’s very tempting to send in a team while we know they’re out,’ Wenna hinted.

‘Dangerously tempting, Wenna, and I might buy it if we knew where they were and how long we had.’

‘I’d quite like to get back to the office,’ Wenna said, ‘I want to put a watch on both their bank accounts.’

Charles nodded and they stood up to resume their walk along the Embankment.

‘So is Walter Bloom right when he says Fleur hasn’t made her own contacts with the enemy on the Afghanistan assignment? What do you think? Do we back his opinion?’

Wenna considered the question as they walked briskly along Millbank. A lot hinged on the answer. 'Yes,' she said eventually. 'I think he's right.'

'Why?'

'Partly instinct and partly because he knows her better than we do.'

'We are agreed then. For us, Afghanistan is a red herring,' Charles said.

'Coincidence, I suspect. This other thing came up after she had agreed to do the BBC job. That's why she's delayed Afghanistan for a week. She thinks it will take that long to finish whatever else she has going with Asami.'

'A week is a long time to arrange a meeting, however complex or important,' Charles commented.

'She may not know when and where the meeting is yet. She may be covering herself by allowing a week,' Wenna suggested.

'She may. Tell me, why are you still interested in Joe Kendry?'

'Because he's with her and he'll know everything that's going on. It may be coincidence he was offered an overseas contract at exactly the same time as Fleur meets up with the enemy. Maybe. I just don't like coincidences. Plus, as you suggested, he may be her weak spot, our way in to her if you like, and if we think that maybe the other side thinks so too.'

'At least we know what he's doing, courtesy of their Hub,' Charles commented.

'To be honest I can't suggest a realistic connection between a UN documentary on the Two+One project and whatever Fleur is up to but I wouldn't be prepared to rule it out,' Wenna commented.

A chill wind had got up and was whipping her hair into strands. 'If you've had enough fresh air,' Wenna said pointedly, 'we could take a taxi.'

'No need,' Charles said, stepping up the pace, 'nearly there now.'

Charles may have been a gentleman, Wenna thought, but there were times when he could be densely insensitive to the needs of a lady whose shoes were not designed for power walking.

28

Simone arrived home a little later than usual and the sun was low in the sky, throwing a chill dappled light from the trees in the front garden onto the solid Victorian façade of the house. It was oddly reassuring to see such evidence of seeming permanence. The house looked so firmly rooted in the ground it stood on, sitting blunt and foursquare to the world, defying time and weather as it had for the better part of two hundred years, and it could easily, she thought, last that long again. But not forever. Nothing is forever. One day even this haven of ours will crumble to dust, the natural state of the universe being one of irreversible degradation. It was not a depressing thought, simply, she accepted, the way things were.

She had had an unexpectedly good day, the pain had been in partial remission, no more than a dull background irritation and she had put aside all thoughts of her certain future, immersing herself in her work. Now, however, as she parked her car as usual beside the old wooden shed, she was feeling tired, ready for a meal and a peaceful evening at home.

Simone let herself in the front door. There was no Auriol to greet her. She called out but got no reply. She walked through to the kitchen, which was empty and showed no signs of a meal having been prepared. Nor was Auriol in the sitting room, which was cold, with the fire unlaid. With a sinking feeling in her breast, Simone headed up the stairs.

Auriol was lying on her side on their unmade bed, still dressed in her nightclothes and dressing gown, as she had been when Simone left that morning. She was ashen-faced, her hair in disarray, her eyes red and bloated with tears, and she was clasping Simone's pyjama top to her face like a comfort blanket. She stared at Simone as if she was a ghost, her mouth hanging slightly open and her hands shaking with involuntary convulsive movements. It seemed likely she had been there in this state all day.

Simone felt a sudden anger. If either of them was going to collapse in a heap it should be her, not Auriol. This was nothing more than self-indulgence. Simone was hungry and tired and in no mood to pander to Auriol's defeatist emotional collapse. It was time her lover shaped up and faced the inevitable as she had, there were things they still had to organise and do. Yet she knew that shouting at her would only make things worse. Somehow she had to shake

Auriol out of her despair and persuade her to focus on what had to be done.

Controlling her annoyance she sat on the side of the bed and took Auriol's hand in hers as a friend or family doctor might. 'This is not good enough, Auriol,' she said firmly.

Auriol's body shuddered as she looked at Simone with wide, pleading eyes. She tried to speak but gave up on the effort, clutching the pyjama top to her as if in fear that Simone might wrest it from her.

'You're letting me down. Don't you think things are bad enough without you putting me through all this as well? Don't you?'

Auriol's head was nodding but whether in distress or agreement it was difficult to say.

'Pull yourself together, Auriol or I will walk out of this room and leave you to it. Now, are we going to talk about this or not?'

'I… can't,' Auriol, managed at last.

'Yes you can, you just did.'

'When you left this morning… It was like you were leaving forever.'

'Auriol,' Simone said brutally, 'I am going to die. That is a fact. There's no way round it. I'm sick and I'm going to get worse. This is a progressive illness. We have a few weeks together and then you'll be on your own. We may not like it, I certainly don't, but it will happen and we need to accept that and organise things for your future.'

Auriol struggled up into a sitting position. 'I don't have a future,' she said bleakly, 'not a future worth living.'

'I won't hear that nonsense,' Simone said briskly. 'You had a future before you met me and you'll have a future when I've gone.'

Auriol shook her head in mute denial.

'Yes. I've made out my will leaving my share of this house and all my assets to you. This place will be too big for you when I'm gone so I suggest you sell it and move back into the Oxford flat.'

'I don't want to talk about things like that.'

'We have to.'

'No. It makes it seem like… Like it's real.'

Simone threw her hands up in a despairing gesture. 'Heaven help me! Get this into your head, Auriol,' she insisted, 'we're both going to die. If we'd lived to be ninety, one of us would still have died before the other, one of us would have been left alone. It's only a matter of timing. We begin the process of dying the day we're born and when we go is just a matter of luck and the mix of our genes. You know that as well as I do, so why are you living in denial, pretending that somehow everything is going to be all right? I've got bad news for you. There are no fairies at the bottom of the garden, there never were. Face up to it, Auriol.'

Auriol had a stubborn look on her tear-ravaged face. 'Six years, Sim, six short years. It's not long enough. Nowhere near enough.'

'Well, that's all we got,' Simone said grimly, 'so the best thing we can do now is shape up and make the most of the time we have.'

There was a sudden spark of hope in Auriol's eyes. 'We could go on holiday, somewhere warm. Maybe a better climate would…'

'No!' Simone exploded. 'You're doing it again. Let me make this clear. I am going to continue working until I'm forced to stop. I need to keep myself occupied. The last thing I want is to be sitting at home or on a beach somewhere with nothing to do but dwell on my aches and pains and wait to die. I'm not that kind of person. Surely you know me better than that.'

Auriol seemed to shrink back into herself, her eyes never leaving Simone's face. Simone stared back at her, willing her to understand.

'I went to church, said twelve Hail Marys,' Auriol said in desperation.

'If I thought Hail Marys would cure cancer I'd say them myself,' Simone responded bitterly. 'Didn't that boy-fiddling priest of yours cause you enough distress when we were first together? Telling you that loving me was a sin, that my job was the work of Satan? How many nights did I have to love you off to sleep before you got over that?'

Simone stopped and took Auriol by the shoulders, forcing her to make eye contact as a sudden thought occurred to her. 'You haven't been talking to him again, have you?'

Auriol said nothing but looked away guiltily.

'Oh great, that's all I need! What did he say, that my cancer is God visiting his wrath on me? Bet it was some crap like that. That's why you're in this state, isn't it? That evil bastard! I wish there was a hell because he'd be the first one to rot in it for sure. Come here, babe.'

Simone pulled Auriol to her and held her tight. 'We have to look after each other, sweetheart, do you understand?'

Auriol nodded into her chest as Simone stroked her dishevelled hair.

'And no more religious mumbo jumbo, okay? I don't want him upsetting you anymore with his fundamentalist bullshit.'

Auriol pulled away, the better to see Simone's face. 'But what am I to do then?' she pleaded.

Simone kissed her. 'I've got a busy day tomorrow. On top of a day's work, there's some film director Burcastle wants to lay out the red carpet for. So what you will do is have a shower, get dressed, then get that lazy arse of yours downstairs and get me something to eat, I'm starving,' she said, smiling.

After a moment Auriol smiled weakly in return and, driven by the strength of Simone's will, got up to do as she was told.

29

'Just remember,' Fleur said, 'forget about us for a few days and concentrate on your work and looking after yourself.'

Joe blew her a kiss. 'Not much point in promising that, is there?'

They were dressing rapidly, having elected to miss the mediocre delights of the hotel breakfast in favour of an extra half hour in bed. Joe was looking morose and faintly ridiculous in flapping shirttail and brown socks.

'You're being pathetic. This is work time, sweetheart, and once you get started you won't have time to think about anything else. And please put your pants on, it's time to go,' Fleur said briskly, patting his behind as she passed.

'You couldn't wait to get them off last night,' he said, pulling them on.

'Concentrate. And cheer up. It won't be long, I'll almost certainly be back before you are.'

'At least we can talk before then. You can call me as soon as your meeting is over.'

‘I will… I might have to give him some escape time though,’ she added as an afterthought. ‘Now, where’s the room card? Okay, got it.’

They hugged each other hard but Fleur turned her face away when he tried to kiss her.

‘I haven’t got time to get made up again,’ she protested, grabbing her handbag, suitcase and carry-on bag and heading for the door.

It was a hasty, scrambled goodbye, one to be regretted later.

***

Fleur arrived at the airport seven hours before she was due to check in. It was not an error. Knowing that Joe would string things out and probably use it as an excuse to put off his meeting at Oxford, she had told him a small white lie, let loose a casual hint about the flight time and he had not thought to question her about it. She did not consider it a hardship to spend so long at an airport; she was one of those rare people who, despite years of worldwide travel, actually enjoyed the experience.

Heathrow, the busiest airport in the world, a multi-storied super-city full of retail delights, offered endless opportunities for closet shopaholics and avid people-watchers like her. Even now, with international flights at a cost premium, the place was alive with people of all shapes, sizes, colours and origins, a colourful bedlam of a place, the recycled air spiced with a cacophony of languages from around the world.

It would take a week to explore every offering of this busy, glitzy metropolis and she, who had scarcely spent an hour alone in the last year, revelled in the opportunity to indulge herself, to do as she pleased, eat junk food free of guilt, to wander at will, accountable to no-one. In what seemed no time at all, her Ctab alarm buzzed her, recalling her to duty.

She passed through the security checks, presented her health certificate, found herself a seat in the departure lounge and composed her thoughts. She felt a familiar thrill of excitement about the uncertainties of what was to come. This was going to be the biggest story of her life, of that she felt certain.

She felt a touch of guilt about being excited at leaving Joe and at deceiving him. She put the guilt aside; she was not taking pleasure in being away from him, she was a journalist for God's sake and entitled to take satisfaction from what she did well and, she told herself, it was a small thing to hint at an earlier flight time, not at all important and done for his own good. Still, it bothered her.

She extracted her Ctab from her handbag. She did not want to call him direct in case he was driving, so she left a short message for him on her home Hub, something to cheer him when he returned that night to an empty apartment. She just hoped it would not occur to him to time-check the message but knowing him it was the kind of small detail that would pass him by. Then the flight was called, she presented her pass and boarded the aircraft.

***

Half way round the world the man she was to meet boarded a plane not long after she had, having been subject to health and security checks every bit as stringent. In his case, however, he had a number of passports and a variety of names to choose from.

30

Phil was waiting in the doorway, on the lookout for him when Joe parked the hire car outside the unassuming terraced house in a Hounslow side street. He was older than Joe by a decade and shorter by a head, with a wiry body and an infectious grin that spread across his heavily freckled face as he spotted Joe and ambled out to meet him.

'You locked it, mate?' he asked, indicating the car. 'You better had or the pond life round here'll have it away in two secs.'

Joe grinned and flicked the remote at the car, which responded with a barrage of flashing lights. 'They can't be that fast even in Hounslow,' he protested.

'It's the quick and the dead, mate, I tell yer. Come in and say hello to the missus.'

'We haven't got long, Phil, the traffic is bound to be a pain in the butt.'

'Just a quick cuppa. She's shot the kids off to school early and got herself made up special.' Brooking no argument, Phil took his arm and escorted him into the house. 'Here he is, the American ambassador come to see you,' he called out as they walked down the entrance hall and entered the modest but spick and span kitchen.

Alma Rogers was a year or two younger than her husband, considerably shorter than him but of similar build. Her naturally dark blonde hair was cut short and curled tight in the retro fashion of the moment, framing a narrow, pretty face that was slightly over-made-up.

'Alma,' Joe said, holding out his arms for a hug.

'You should've taken him into the lounge, Phil, what you thinking of?' she complained, pink-faced and flustered when Joe released her.

'Don't talk wet,' Phil said fondly. 'He's practically one of the family. Where's that tea? We haven't got all day.'

'You had breakfast, Joe?' Alma asked as she poured.

'Couldn't eat another thing,' Joe assured her, deliberately avoiding an outright lie. He knew full well that if he admitted to so much as a twinge of hunger, in no time at all he would be sat down in front of a huge cholesterol-laden English breakfast with no hope of getting away for another hour.

'Oh, okay then,' Alma said, sounding a little disappointed, as she carefully placed her best china teacups in front of them. 'Earl Grey, you do like that, don't you?' she asked uncertainly, 'You had it last time but I never know with you, you might just have bin pretendin', to be polite, like.'

'Alma, I've been accused of many things in my life but never of an excess of politeness,' Joe responded, before emptying his cup in one go. 'That was great.'

'You must've bin parched,' Phil said, trying to catch up.

'A top up,' Alma said, teapot in hand.

'Really, no,' Joe said hastily. 'We have to be on our way.'

'What time'll you be back then, one-ish? Time for your dinner?'

'Not exactly sure, Alma,' Joe said.

'I'll have it ready for one and if you're a bit late I'll just keep it in the oven, alright?'

'Well, I don't like to trouble you...' Joe replied, aware that he had already implicitly agreed.

'Don't be daft. What trouble? Tell him Phil…'

'Better had, Joe, if you don't, I'll get it in the neck.'

'Well, we can't have that,' Joe replied, smiling his thanks.

'Right, that's that then,' Alma said, satisfied, as the men got up to leave. 'Just be careful what you're up to, you two. There's lots of idiots on the roads these days.'

Phil gave her a peck on the cheek. 'There always was luv, and like I always say, it's only the good die young and that lets both of us out, right Joe?'

'I'll bring him back in one piece,' Joe said, giving Alma another fond hug.

'Promise?'

'Absolutely. Cross my heart and hope to die.'

'Don't say that,' Alma protested, 'it gives me the creeps.'

***

On the way to Oxford Joe briefed Phil more fully on the project. Phil sat quietly in the passenger seat, nursing his almost-new lightweight steady-shot Procam; buffing up the lenses as he took in what Joe was saying.

'So what you want to give them is a doco that looks like a movie, right?' he asked eventually.

'Hole in one, Phil,' Joe replied as they eased to yet another halt, the A4 traffic clogged up again for no obvious reason.

'Don't reckon I'm going to get on with this Rose Petchek bird, Joe. She sounds like one of them bossy know-it-all tarts, a right pain in the arras.'

'She is, but with any luck we'll only need her to pay the bills.'

'She can do joined up writing then?'

'She's not dumb, just not as bright as she thinks she is.'

'Mmmm,' Phil grunted, unconvinced.

An hour later they were free of the worst of the traffic and driving down minor roads that snaked through orderly farmland. As they got close to their destination Joe stopped the car to check his directions.

‘I want to get some pick-ups outside this place before we go in,’ Joe said, ‘set the scene, okay?’

‘Who’d ever believe what’s hidden behind these leafy lanes sort of stuff, right?’ Phil said, reaching onto the rear seat to check his equipment bag and tripod.

‘That’s it,’ Joe said as they set off again.

‘What if it’s not in a leafy lane?’

‘We’ll cheat it. There’s bound to be a leafy lane around here somewhere, we’re in the middle of the good old English countryside for God’s sake.’

Next time they stopped it was because they had found the perfect leafy lane, dappled prettily in the mid-morning sunshine, and it was not until they had got the shot Joe wanted and driven on that they discovered, halfway down the same lane, the tree and shrub-obscured entrance to the Genphree Biotics Laboratory complex. They overran and reversed clear of the entrance so that Phil could get a shot of the turn into the entranceway with its guardhouse, security camera array and double metal gates.

As they returned to the gate they were both amused to see that a uniformed guard, alerted by their behaviour, was out in the road filming them with a Palmcam.

‘Smile for the camera, Phil,’ Joe said

‘Everybody wants to make bleeding movies these days,’ Phil grunted.

After an examination of their identity cards and a phone call to confirm their appointment, the camera-happy young guard was deputed to accompany them to the main building.

The grounds comprised several acres of immaculate lawns, mature trees and shrubbery and dotted here and there were ponds decorated with water lilies and appropriately aged statuary. Set amidst this pastoral splendour was the original dwelling, a brick-fronted, slate-roofed Georgian manor. This grand old house had been retained as little more than a façade, having been subjected to many recent blandly ugly, flat-roofed extensions, plus a bleakly inappropriate secure-fenced car park to one side.

They pulled up outside the front entrance where an expensively dressed, corpulent man in his early fifties was posed like an eager politician, waiting to greet them. The guard handed Joe a swipe card and indicated the car park.

'I'll park the car for you sir,' he said, 'the card will get you out of the car park, hand it back at the guardhouse as you leave, please.'

Colin Burcastle stepped forward to greet his guests. 'Sorry about all this security fuss,' he said, 'necessary these days I'm afraid. I'm Colin Burcastle, Director of the Unit.'

'Joe Kendry,' Joe said, 'and this is Phil Rogers, he's a magician with a camera. He'll make you and this place look like a million dollars.'

Phil gave Joe a hard stare and mouthed 'bullshit' when Burcastle was not looking. Praise embarrassed him.

'Delighted to meet you both,' Burcastle enthused, unaware of the byplay, 'always pleased to meet one of our American friends. We'll have morning tea in my office, then I've arranged for you to be taken on a personally conducted tour by Dr Gofre.'

'She being the creator of the Two+One virus, I'm told,' Joe said.

'Quite so, an exceptionally brilliant woman. I knew you'd want to speak to her.'

'That's great but I'd like to get some exterior shots of the building before that,' Joe said, 'maybe one of you entering the front door here, as if you were just arriving for work?'

'Oh, of course, I didn't realise, yes...' Burcastle said, suddenly flushed but evidently inordinately pleased.

It always works, Joe thought as Phil set up for the shot. Make them the star and they'll eat out of your hand.

That chore completed, they were led into Burcastle's office, in one of the tall-ceilinged ground floor rooms of the old building where he personally served them tea on a rather pretentious silver tray.

Note to all Americans thinking of living in England, Joe thought; the cliché is for real, so prepare your bladder to receive vast quantities of tea or face social and professional ostracism.

Burcastle needed no encouragement to tell them on camera about the unit and what it did, he was obviously immensely proud of his domain and what he believed it had achieved.

‘Our motto translates as ‘For the future of Man’. In the most gender-inclusive sense of course,’ he added hastily as he finished his peroration.

Joe cut to the chase. ‘So, from what you’ve said, your job here is to create new vaccines and antidotes, so the Two+One virus was a first, I mean the first time you had actually created a new virus?’ he asked.

It was an obvious and innocent enough question but Burcastle hesitated before answering. ‘Not exactly,’ he said, and then, to stave off further questions, ‘there have been others but this is the only one to achieve public acclaim, shall we say.’

Joe was intrigued and very tempted to pursue the question but sensed from Burcastle’s body language that it would be counterproductive. It was time to get him back on side. He looked across to Phil and got a nod, the interview was safely in the can.

‘Okay, that was great, Colin. Ready for the grand tour when you are. And of course we’d like to interview Doctor Gofre afterwards if that’s okay?’

‘Of course, would you care to use this office?’

‘That would be perfect.’

Burcastle went to the door. ‘Jane, ask Doctor Gofre if she would be kind enough to join us, would you? She will be waiting in reception, I think,’ he said, with his back to them.

Phil raised an eyebrow at Burcastle’s deferential tone and Joe straight-lined with his index finger, indicating for Phil to record at will during the interview.

Burcastle returned to them, a concerned look on his face. ‘There is just one thing,’ he said, ‘Doctor Gofre has been quite ill of late. I must ask you to limit your tour and your questions so as not to tire her.’

An alarm bell went off in Joe’s head. Questions piled up in his mind that he could not possibly ask at the moment. He was not here to investigate or interrogate, he reminded himself, but to put together a client-friendly documentary, and in a sense Burcastle represented the client.

‘I’m really sorry to hear that,’ Joe replied sincerely, refusing to look at Phil, who he knew would have picked up on the same vibes he had. ‘I’ll try not to keep her too long.’

It was barely a minute before Simone Gofre walked straight into the room without knocking. She nodded briefly to Burcastle, and then addressed herself to Joe and Phil before she could be introduced.

'Hello,' she said, 'I'm Simone Gofre, which of you is Mr Kendry?'

Joe was somewhat taken aback by the abruptness of this approach. He had had no preconceived ideas about what a scientist might be like as a person, beyond a naïve assumption that scholarship would somehow necessarily equate to social graces. Well, Simone was living proof that he was wrong about that. She was evidently not a people person and, he suspected, would struggle to tolerate those who were not her intellectual equals, which might explain her dismissive attitude to Burcastle.

In dress and appearance she looked more like a high-ranking business executive than a scientist. She was tall and slim with short dark hair turning grey at the temples and seemed to be at least ten years his senior. Her eyes were alert but looked dull and sunken in a pale face and there were deep worry lines on her brow. She looked tired and, from her stiff body language, under stress. Joe wondered what was wrong with her; whatever it was it seemed to have hit her hard. He stepped forward and offered his hand. Hers was cool and thin-fingered but she had a firm grip. She was wearing a wedding ring on the third finger of her left hand.

'I'm Joe Kendry,' he said, 'and this is my cameraman, Phil Rogers.'

Simone nodded briefly to them both. 'I gather you want a tour of the facility, will you film as we go?'

'Yes, here and there, but the idea is mainly to get a feel of the place. Then we would like to do a piece to camera with you...'

'Meaning?' Simone interrupted.

'Sorry. An interview on camera about your work with the Two+One virus. Colin has kindly offered us the use of this office.'

'Has he.'

'You get to sit in my chair for a change,' Burcastle said with an edgy laugh.

The man is nervous of her, Joe thought. Simone was giving Burcastle a steely look but he was not meeting her gaze. He might be the boss, Joe mused to himself, but there was no doubt who was the stronger personality.

'You are welcome to it, Colin,' she said to the Director, her tone non-committal. Then, focussing on Joe, 'We'd better be getting along.'

Burcastle saw them to the door. 'I'll see you back here in what, half an hour or so?'

Simone seemed prepared to ignore him so Joe replied, 'That should be long enough for us. What do you think, Doctor Gofre?'

'Ample, I should hope, I have work to do. This way.' As they were walking she said, 'I suppose you don't want to see the admin offices, dispatch, staff canteen and that sort of stuff so we'll just go round the lab loop.' It was not really a question, more a matter of informing them of her decision.

Joe was intrigued by her. It was clear Simone had an agenda that did not include spending any more time on them than she had to. She probably was busy, Joe thought, but her lack of empathy, her abruptness and indifference and body tension spoke of some other driving force. One thing was for sure, the promise of on-screen stardom that had seduced Burcastle was certainly not going to work with her; she obviously had no interest in self-promotion. If the interview with her was to secure anything other than monosyllabic responses he had to find a way to engage her interest in talking about herself and her work.

She led them down the corridor and through a side door out of the old part of the building and into the new, an area that was partitioned off into discrete sections linked only by the windowless corridor they were in. In the distance the rubber-floored corridor looped round the rear of the old building, the whole lit by fluorescent lights. She stopped them by a security desk manned by an earnest-looking young man with rounded shoulders and heavy glasses. Simone ignored him and picked up some papers from his desk, handing them to Joe.

'I put this lot together earlier, it'll save a lot of explanations. Map of the facility, PR brochure, my CV, company structure, that sort of guff. There's also a vid with lots of pretty pictures of viruses. Virology 101. No Latin or words of more than four syllables.'

'Thanks,' Joe responded quickly, covering Phil's derisive snort.

A second security guard joined them from a door behind the desk. She was short and rotund with a significant chest and ample hips and looked in danger of bursting out of her uniform at several points.

'Annie,' Simone said, 'these are the people the Director told you about. Short tour of the labs, alright?'

'Course, Doctor Gofre,' Annie said, issuing the two men with clip-on visitors passes. 'They have AE to non-PC areas?'

'Yes, my authority, but no PC authorisation of course.'

'Can you translate, please,' Joe asked with a smile. "This is a foreign language to us.' He thought he detected a slight sigh before Simone answered.

'We have twelve different laboratories, each with a different level of physical containment. No unauthorised entry is permitted to any of the PC labs. This one,' she pointed to the room behind them, visible through plate glass windows, 'is the lowest containment level. From here on, as we progress down the corridor, the PC level goes up. Most are PC3. The last one, where I work, is PC4.'

'So we can't enter any of the labs without special permission?' Joe asked, the disappointment showing in his voice. 'Not even this one?'

'Not likely. Security, see.' Fat Annie answered.

'Nobody mentioned this. How do we get permission?' Joe asked.

'A double first and ten years' practical experience in a secure virology lab would be a good start,' Simone responded blandly.

That's the nearest to humour she's come this far, Joe thought grimly. Day one and this project was already doomed to visual mediocrity. He turned to Phil, who was looking increasingly long-faced.

'Okay, Phil, we have to live with the rules. Just one down the length of the corridor, then pan every second lab as we pass, that should be enough.' As Phil set up for the shot he turned to Simone. 'This place must be more secure than Fort Knox,' he commented.

'It probably is,' she agreed. 'We're monitored by half a dozen government departments, plus the World Health Organisation and the National Institute for Biological Standards and Control and they all take their job very seriously indeed. As they should.'

Phil gave him the nod and they began their progress down the corridor with Fat Annie trailing along behind. Simone saw Joe looking back at her in surprise.

'No visitor is allowed outside the reception area without a security escort, even if you are with a senior member of staff. Security here runs on facts and observation, not on trust,' she said.

'Why?' Joe asked. 'I mean, why that level of security?'

'It's directly related to the risk. Our library stock is high risk.'

'What are we talking about, library stock?'

'You name it, Mr Kendry, and we probably have it. Rabies, Yellow fever, HIV, Polio, Ebola, Swine Flu, SARS, Bubonic Plague, Polio, Hepatitis A, H5N1 through 9, Avian Flu and quite a few that just have Genphree numbers.'

'Why? I mean, why only numbers?'

'Because amongst other things we create both new and genetically altered viruses. That's part of my job. They're sequentially numbered.'

'How the heck do you keep these things safe in there?'

'Mostly they're in deep freeze, minus eighty degrees keeps them quiet.'

'Let's hope the power never goes off.'

'Multiple emergency generators. A 9.0 earthquake directly below us might be a problem.'

'Then?'

'Select your pandemic. Humans lose, but it might save the planet,' she said laconically.

They turned the corner of the corridor and from here on the labs were all sealed off from corridor access and offered only blank walls and double door entry. Phil dutifully took pot shots of them and kept the audio running.

'Okay, dumb question of the month,' Joe said, 'but just for the record, why do we need to store such highly dangerous organisms, let alone create new ones?'

There was that slight sigh again. 'Because, Mr Kendry, we need to know the enemy, be ahead of the game, be ready for when they mutate and evolve, which they do all the time. Viruses are present wherever there are cells to infect. They are the most common biological entities on earth. We need to observe them in action. This is war and most of the time they are winning. Usually the best we can hope for is an honourable draw. Bacteria and viruses own the world, not us. Humans have evolved alongside them, with them and despite them; they are in us and all around us; they and we were destined to do battle from day one in the primaeval ooze. This facility and others like it all over the world are the biological equivalent of Military Intelligence.'

At last, a quote I can use, Joe thought. 'How high is the risk factor in the Travel Warning Zones these days?' he asked casually as they continued.

'Depends where you are. Stay out of the slums and away from poultry and poor people, sanitise your hands and you're fine. Avian Flu needs five transitions before it can transfer human to human and it can't do that. Not yet, anyway.'

'But it will?

'Bet the bank on it.'

'My office,' Simone said, indicating the blank wall with the single door and the security station outside. 'End of the line, I'm afraid.'

'This is where you created the Two+One virus?'

'Amongst other things, yes.'

'Any chance of opening the door so's I can get a shot of the inside?' Phil asked hopefully.

Fat Annie stepped forward, bristling. 'Sorry, mate, no can do,' she said definitely.

'There's nothing to see anyway,' Simone added, 'through that door are just the inner security, reception and decontamination areas. The lab is beyond that, through a double air lock with negative pressure. And anyway, even if you were allowed in, bacteria, and especially virons, are so minute there's nothing to see, so unless you think static high-powered microscopes and thick plate glass would make riveting viewing, you'd be wasting your time.'

'Virons?" Joe asked.

'They're the tiny particles responsible for viral infection. Think something a hundred times smaller than a human cell and for the most part, as deadly as a bullet in the brain.'

For once Joe was glad Fleur was not with him. 'Know what, I guess I'm glad I can't get the shot I want,' Joe said. 'Shall we go do your interview now?'

When they had returned to Burcastle's office the Director was evicted from his desk and settled for a chair in the corner and Simone took over his usual seat as Phil set up the camera and Joe found himself another chair safely out of shot.

'Do I look at you or the camera?' Simone asked, for the first time showing some interest.

'Ignore the camera and relax. Imagine you are at home in your sitting room and I've dropped by for a cup of tea,' Joe replied.

He registered the momentary shadow that flickered across Simone's features. He had touched a nerve there but had no idea why.

'What exactly do you want to know?' Simone asked. 'You should understand that some of my work is completely embargoed and much of the rest is commercially sensitive.'

In the corner Burcastle was nodding emphatically.

'Understood,' Joe replied, 'we're only concerned with the development of the Two+One virus and getting some insights from the person responsible for creating it.'

Simone nodded briefly. 'That seems alright,' she said. 'If you go off track I'll tell you.'

I'm sure you will, Joe thought. He counted Phil down and turned his attention to Simone.

'Doctor Gofre, as I understand it there are two quite different aspects to your work. On the one hand you save human life by creating vaccines and antidotes and on the other you created the Two+One virus, which prevents life. Do you see any contradictions in those two features of your work?

'None at all. The fact that we work on ways to improve the health and well-being of existing humans in no way denies the fact that there are simply too many of us and we need to drastically reduce the human population of this planet. We have reached plague proportions.'

'I take it then that you support the UN project both personally and professionally.'

'Of course. I just wish the take-up was greater.'

'Why do you think it isn't?'

Simone answered without hesitation. 'Mainly because of the opposition of the major religions. They all seem to agree that their Gods intend us to reproduce at exponential rates. I suppose the idea is to provide a ready supply of followers or new martyrs to the cause. I don't always agree with Karl Marx but religion is undeniably the opiate of the masses; a prime example of incoherent belief surviving despite undeniable scientific knowledge that completely refutes it. It seems to be an inherent weakness in our species and it may yet doom us all.'

In the corner Burcastle cleared his throat, evidently becoming concerned that the interview was veering into areas of controversy. Simone and Joe ignored him but Joe changed tack anyway.

'I imagine you would also be aware of the criticism aimed at the project by some who say that we should allow nature to take its course; that the population will stabilise naturally over time?'

'If nature takes its course, millions in the Third World will die from war, starvation, and preventable illnesses. Those that survive will have a short and brutal life, a deprived, bare and pointless existence full of disillusion and bitter resentment, without any hope of a rewarding, fulfilling, contributing life. In the meantime, by sheer weight of numbers, we will have damaged this planet beyond repair,' Simone replied vehemently.

I'm on a roll, Joe thought, at last she's talking from the heart about matters she passionately believes in.

'Even so, there will always be those who don't accept your view,' Joe offered.

'Naturally.'

'Why do you think that is, if the project is so obviously valuable?'

'Because numbers equal power in most cases: economic, political, social, military or religious power. The very basis of the democracy we enjoy comes down to numbers for and against. We are a number and power-driven species, Mr Kendry, haven't you noticed?'

Burcastle was moving uncomfortably in his seat. The others in the room continued to ignore him.

'Is the Two+One virus safe?' Joe asked.

‘What the hell do you mean?’ Simone demanded, fixing him with a stony glare. ‘You think we would ever have allowed anything out of this establishment that wasn’t?’

‘I’m acting as devil’s advocate,’ Joe said quickly, ‘we’re setting out to ask the questions and provide the answers before anyone else does.’

‘Someone has said it’s not safe? Who?’

‘It came up during my internet research.’

‘Search the internet long enough and you’ll find convinced flat-earthers,’ Simone said dismissively.

‘There is chat amongst some in the online scientific community about the possibility that Two+One could interact with another virus…’

‘Online scientific community? That’s an oxymoron, Mr Kendry. Only those who can’t secure reputable publication end up quoted on the internet.’

Burcastle moved uncomfortably in his chair. This lady really does not take prisoners, Joe thought.

‘That’s a no, then?’ he asked.

‘That’s a no. The virus has been genetically neutered. It can no more breed than a castrated male. You want a more scientific explanation?’

‘I think our audience will be happy with that graphic explanation,’ Joe replied blandly. ‘One last thing, the population stats show that Western women are having fewer babies, below replacement in fact.’

‘True.’

Burcastle interrupted from the corner. ‘Just a moment, Mr Kendry, are you suggesting the Two+One project is unnecessary? Exactly what spin are you attempting to put on this?’

‘No spin, Mr Burcastle. As I explained before, I’m attempting to deal with any criticisms of the Two+One project up front, so that we can refute them. There have been allegations that the project is racially motivated...’

‘What garbage!’ Simone exploded.

‘The world population increase is all happening in the Third World,’ Joe persisted, ‘amongst black, brown, poor, ill-educated and deprived people.’

‘Precisely,’ Simone said, ‘which is why Two+One is aimed at those people, because they are the ones in need.’

‘The suggestion is that the productive nations of the west will be swamped by a tidal wave of the indigent poor if nothing is done, hence the Two+One project,’ Joe said.

‘That is a political argument,’ Burcastle put in anxiously, ‘nothing to do with us, we are scientists.’

Simone gave him a withering look and he subsided. ‘Two points,’ she said, addressing Joe. ‘Firstly the Two+One project has the complete support of the UN and you could hardly call that body racist, and secondly, the major causes of overpopulation in the Third World are, in equal measure, religious dogma, poor education, female subjugation and poverty. Those are the problems; scientists simply try to provide a small part of the answer.’

‘Gentlemen, I think...’ Burcastle began.

Before he could finish Simone stood up. ‘What I think is that you have quite enough to make up your story, Mr Kendry. I have work to do that is considerably more important than answering any more of your questions. Excuse me.’

And she was gone, leaving a slightly flustered Burcastle to escort his visitors to the car park.

‘I hope that was all satisfactory,’ he said hopefully as they shook hands at the car.

‘Mr Burcastle, thank you for your co-operation. I found the whole experience very enlightening,’ Joe responded.

***

After a long silence in the car on the way back, Phil said, ‘You’re a top bloke but you can lie like a demon.’

‘Only when strictly necessary,’ Joe replied.

‘‘Very enlightening’! What a load of bollocks,’ Phil said, grinning.

‘You never know, we may need to come back,’ Joe said. ‘Never burn your bridges.’

‘S’pose not. He was a bit of a prat but she was a right madam. Fancy being married to that!’

‘Mmm, I wonder what’s wrong with her.’

'Case of terminal bloody arrogance if you ask me,' Phil responded.

'Did you have a good look at her? That woman is ill and it isn't just a head cold.'

'Maybe she caught one of her own bugs.'

'Not likely. With all those security protocols in place that should be pretty well impossible and if it were true they'd never have let us anywhere near her.'

'Which would be fine for my money,' Phil retorted. 'She's so far up herself she can't see daylight.'

'An interesting woman, nonetheless,' Joe said thoughtfully.

'Makes me realise how lucky I am with Alma, she's a princess compared to that one. Like your Fleur.'

With a guilty shock Joe realised that he had been so immersed in work that he hadn't thought about Fleur for over three hours. Which was exactly what she had predicted and he had denied.

31

Charles Lovatt had the hideously expensive turbot; his companion ordered the only marginally less expensive eye fillet, suitably rare. They were in the wood-panelled and leather-seated Condor Club in Pall Mall, a venue they had visited together before and both found congenial. As London dining clubs went it was relatively new, being hardly more than a hundred years old and as such it lacked the cachet of age that the landed elite and the nouveau riche alike seemed to find so seductive. It tended to draw its membership and clientele from the city's legal and financial fraternity and was not favoured by politicians from either side of the political divide, which suited them both admirably.

'So, Donald, congratulations are in order I gather,' Charles said when they had put aside their plates and ordered coffee, 'your own fief to rule over.' By an unspoken tradition established over the years their paths had crossed, they did not discuss business on empty stomachs when out of their respective offices.

'Not sure about that, Charlie. Some would say it was a poisoned chalice,' Donald Costello replied.

He was a head taller than Charles Lovatt and a year or two older. His hair was thinning and he was slightly stooped, his well-cut suit tending to hang on his lanky frame. His brown eyes were noticeably sunken beneath fierce bushy eyebrows and there were prominent veins across his high, patrician cheekbones. Costello was nearing the end of a long and successful military and Security Services career and had recently been appointed head of a secretive Counter-Terrorist Intelligence Unit reputedly reporting direct to the White House. He was not finding that appointment an easy ride.

'But you're the capo de capos,' Charles said. 'Direct access to the boss and when you say jump the other agencies all ask how high.'

'It's not quite like that. I've got the Director of National Intelligence between me and him and eighteen other security agencies all busy protecting their own backyards. The CIA is supposed to be concentrating on field ops but they're still wasting resources, trying to get their analysis function back from the military. If the enemy knew how fragmented we are they'd praise Allah ten times a day instead of just five.'

'I can sympathise. You don't have a monopoly on inter-service territorial disputes and if you have the DNI, we have the Commons Intelligence Committee.'

'Accountability eh, Charlie, the bane of the Security Services.'

'Would a half decent brandy cheer you up?'

'Sure would but I'm going to say no, I'm due back in the Embassy in half an hour, meeting with one of your Foreign Office guys.'

'Good luck,' Charles said wryly.

'Thanks a million. Look, we'll have to have an office meeting with you and Six real soon. The Big Chief will be packing his bags before long and I'd like to know if there's anything going to keep me awake nights.'

'Not from my end, but there is a small favour I'd like to ask you.'

'Okay?'

'I'd like to know if a chap called Joseph Allan Kendry is one of yours and if not what you know about him and his girlfriend, Fleur Nichols.'

'He a US citizen?'

'Yes.'

'I'll get one of my guys to chase it up.'

'I'd like it to be done by someone very close to you, Donald. And no electronic trail would be good.'

'Uh-huh,' Costello said, looking interested.

Charles handed him a slip of paper, opening it out to show the two names and a list of personal details. 'They're living together. This is all we have on the pair of them.'

Costello took the paper and looked at the names. 'Is this woman who I think she is, the anti-American journo, works for your BBC?'

'Yes. She's half American I'm told.'

'You can have her. I can tell you right now that bitch isn't one of ours.'

'But you'd have a file on her. Anything you'd feel able to pass on about either of them would be appreciated.'

'Sure.' Costello tucked the paper away in his inside pocket, finished his coffee and put down the cup, waiting for Charles to say something more but when he remained silent he added, 'What priority?'

'I know how busy you must be...'

'But yesterday would be good?'

'Exactly.'

Costello stood up, looming over the table. 'Always happy to help out friends of the Good Guys,' he said. 'Uncle Sam's turn to buy lunch next I think.'

'Much appreciated.'

Costello hesitated. 'We're going to be singing 'Hail to the Chief' here real soon and Presidential visits give me severe migraines.' He patted the pocket where he had put the paper. 'Should I be buying painkillers?'

'No connection that I know of yet.'

Costello considered that for a moment. 'Charlie, when the time comes, you will share, won't you?' he said, offering a tight, humourless smile.

'You have my word,' Charles replied.

'I'll be in touch,' Costello said and, touching Charles briefly on the shoulder as if in confirmation, he set off across the dining room, weaving his long form between the tables, heading for the service counter. He did not look back.

Charles Lovatt sat for a while, pretending interest in the remains of his coffee, wondering about the decision he had made to approach the Cousins. He knew perfectly well that Donald Costello would never be satisfied until he knew exactly why Charles wanted that information.

Inviting Costello to the party was rather like inviting a stoat into a rabbit hole. If you were the rabbit you rather hoped, contrary to all historic evidence, that this particular stoat was vegetarian.

32

Wenna watched Alexander Jones as he scooted his office chair across to her Hub desk and sat down beside her. He was both the most talented and the most irritatingly self-confident of her agents and certainly, if the other women in the section were to be believed, far and away the most attractive. Wenna could not see it, despite his immaculate dress sense, brilliant hazel eyes, boyish face, perfect skin and casually barbered fair hair that flopped forward over his forehead. She thought he was too obvious, almost a caricature of the self-obsessed pretty-boy hetero male and she had no idea if this was calculated or not. She also suspected him of being the anonymous poet.

What she was sure of, and it was his saving grace so far as she was concerned, was that behind that carefully maintained, slightly effete façade was a sharp and devious mind. For that reason she had selected him as her understudy on the Fleur Nichols file and given him four hours to bring himself up to date, reckoning that if he was half as good as he thought he was, he should manage that with ease.

'What have you got for me, Alex?' she asked.

'Not a great deal I'm afraid. Finance first?'

'By all means. Anything of interest?'

'She's paid nothing in for the past ten months, been living on what she saved from her last BBC assignment by the looks of it. No outstanding debts though and credit cards are just in the black.'

'How has she been spending her money?'

'Mortgage, rates, insurance, clothes shops, chemists, supermarket, the occasional meal out, nothing unusual.'

'And that's up to date?'

‘As of this morning. Our friend Joe Kendry, however, is in funds to the tune of thirty-seven thou, deposited two days ago.’

‘The payee being?’

‘The transfer was made against the account of ConSept Productions. Presumably his fee for this documentary he’s making,’ Alex replied. ‘I assume we’re not especially interested in the company?’

‘Not particularly,’ Wenna replied, ‘but I do propose to keep one eye on Joe. Nothing from the shadow team or the intercepts I suppose?

‘Seems neither of them has been at the flat for the last twenty-four hours,’ Alex replied. ‘All we have are some emails for Joe from a Rose Petchek, making contacts and arrangements for him to film in the Far East.’

‘Where?’

‘Pakistan.’

Wenna looked thoughtful.

‘Which could account for them not being at home last night,’ Alex suggested. He grinned impishly at her. ‘Final night of fiery passion before he takes off for the Orient.’

‘Check his credit card; see where they spent the night. I mean, why bother to go somewhere else when they have a perfectly good bed at home?’

Alex sighed theatrically. ‘Ah, Ms Cavendish, where’s your sense of romance?’

Wenna ignored the question. ‘I want to know where they are, Alex, and what they’re doing. I want the red spot on them. I don’t like it when our targets disappear off the radar.’

‘Well it seems likely they were together until this morning, then we know from the chatter that he has a meeting at a biological research lab near Oxford.’ Alex looked at his watch. ‘He should be there now. Oh yes, and there was a message from her to him on their home landline.’

‘Saying?’

‘I love you,’ Alex said, smiling innocently.

‘Nothing else?’

‘Nothing else.’

‘Very odd,’ Wenna commented.

‘Ah, but it’s the sort of thing lovers do when they are parted by circumstance, isn’t it? It eases the pain,’ Alex replied blandly.

‘You think she expects to be away from him for some time?’ Wenna asked.

‘Possibly, but not necessarily. When you’re in love, five minutes can be an eternity.’

Wenna looked at him sharply but he was straight-faced. She shook her head; it made no sense to her. ‘We need to know what was in that envelope,’ she said. ‘It’s a reasonable assumption that when she met Mohammed Asami she found out who she was going to meet and where. It was a map of the next move.’

‘I doubt if it will do much good but I could ask George,’ Alex offered diffidently.

Wenna stared at him.

‘I’ve been running the little toad for a couple of months but he’s come up with nothing so far, he’s still somewhat nervous.’

‘And it didn’t occur to you to tell me about this?’ Wenna asked grimly.

‘No time,’ Alex responded cheerfully. ‘It wasn’t until I briefed myself on the file first thing today that I discovered he’d met Fleur Nichols. It was probably the first job he’d been given.’

‘I expect you to be a bit more on the ball than that, Alex. And I also expect to be kept in the loop.’

‘That’s a bit hard. Mea culpa and all that but he’s a newbie. Okay, he’s been a naughty boy, keeping that little snippet to himself. He’s not playing the game properly and I will speak severely to him. Can I suggest something?’

‘Yes?’

‘If we think she’s arranging a higher level meet, perhaps we should take off the shadows and rely on the intercepts, upgrade them if necessary.’

‘You think they might be watching her?’

‘It wouldn’t surprise me. And if they are, we might spook them.’

‘I’ll think about it,’ Wenna said slowly. ‘In the meantime, I want you to monitor the port watch on both of them, and have a trawl for any interesting incoming arrivals in the last week. Then go back through the whole file and all the chatter. I have a nasty feeling we’ve missed something.’

‘If you’ve had the file I doubt anything has been missed,’ Alex said sweetly.

‘What?’ Wenna said, only half listening.

‘Just flattering my beautiful boss,’ Alex said, straight-faced.

‘Well don’t bother,’ Wenna said abstractedly. ‘Just get on with it.’

33

Joe arrived home late afternoon, having finally extricated himself from Alma’s culinary clutches, feeling bloated, rather tired and suddenly lonely. Over the last year he had lost the habit of being content with his own company and, back in her familiar apartment, he was acutely aware of Fleur’s absence. The silence was loud in his ears, jarring his senses, and the fragrant scent of her was everywhere.

He poured himself a stiff drink. They were going to be out of contact for at least a week and apart for probably two, better get used to it. He pulled the curtains open and stared morosely out at the river. It was barely four o’clock but already a dull grey mist was rolling in from the direction of the Thames estuary, creating a gloom to match his mood. When he had last pulled those curtains she had still been here.

He closed his eyes and tried to picture her face. He found that oddly difficult to achieve; the best he could manage was a vague, almost ghostly impression of the whole person, which appeared not in front of his closed eyes but somewhere at the back of his mind where memories rested. It was disquieting not to be able to recall the detail of her; he had spent so long gazing at that face in the last year, he had felt sure he would be able to recall it at will. They had never taken photographs of each other; no physical record existed for either of them to call upon in the absence of the other. Now that it was too late, it seemed like a glaring omission.

Joe looked at his watch. She would be, what, almost halfway there by now. At least on board the aircraft she was reasonably safe, such was the level of security these days. It had been many years since there had been any successful attempt at hijacking or bombing a commercial flight.

Just as well then that he didn't know she was still at the airport.

He switched on the Hub. He had successfully exorcised all thoughts of Fleur, at least for a while earlier in the day, by immersing himself in work. Maybe it would work now. The message icon flashed on the screen. Rose Petchek no doubt, anxious for feedback on the meeting at Genphree Biotics. He sighed, already composing the email in his mind.

He opened the message.

'I love you,' it said.

34

Wenna had been in meetings for most of the day, absorbed with section administration, budget allocations and other housekeeping matters but Fleur Nichols was never far from her mind. The instinct that had served Wenna so well in her career to date told her that the game was getting away from them. While she was prepared to concede the likelihood that Fleur was innocent of any wrongdoing, except probably withholding information, it was certain that the enemy she was dealing with were at the very least about to pull off a major propaganda coup. And if that coup had any connection with the upcoming visit of the American President, now public knowledge, then the Security Services would all end up with a serious amount of egg on their faces. And included on the list of potential scapegoats was Wenna Cavendish.

Alex Jones had been conspicuous by his absence for most of the day. Wenna was reluctant to show her unease by calling him and demanding an update and by the time he finally appeared in the early evening she was in a thoroughly bad mood. He drew up his chair beside hers and seemed undeterred by her frosty demeanour.

'George apologises profusely and pleads fear of consequences for not coming forward earlier,' Alex said.

'And that's all you have?' Wenna demanded.

'I believe him; he actually doesn't know anything useful. He simply secured Fleur's agreement to a meeting and passed the message on.'

'To whom?'

'Our friend Asami.'

'Where, of course, the trail goes cold.'

'The last address we have for Asami turned out to be a boarding house in Peckham where he stayed for a week over a month ago. God knows where he is now. George has never met him, only contacted him on a disposable Ctab, as you'd expect, a very professional cut-out.'

'I am not in the mood to hear praise of the enemy's tradecraft thank you,' Wenna said tartly.

Alex permitted himself a wry smile. 'No praise intended. Next item on the agenda, Joe is back at the apartment, alone.'

'You're sure he's alone?'

'The shadows say he went in by himself and there's been nothing on the audio.'

'Where is she, Alex?

'A rhetorical question I imagine. One other thing. They stayed last night at an airport hotel half a mile from Heathrow.'

'What! Why the hell didn't you tell me straight away?'

'Because it can't be relevant. We have a port watch on her and she hasn't gone anywhere.'

'False passport...' Wenna thought aloud.

'Must have been a thin one if it was in the envelope Asami handed over and I don't think the BBC goes in for forgery,' Alex commented.

'What then? Think, man, think!'

'Of course she could have hopped the channel and taken off from anywhere in Europe. We haven't gone EU-wide at the moment.'

'We should, then,' Wenna said.

'Can I use your Hub? Mine is acting up at the moment,' Alex asked.

Wenna was suddenly still, staring at him fixedly.

'What?' Alex asked, uncomfortable with the intense scrutiny.

Wenna slapped her hand down on her desk hard, glaring at him.

'What exactly have I done?' Alex asked, and when no reply was immediately forthcoming, 'or not done?'

Wenna ignored him and manually punched a number into the Hub board. After a bare couple of rings a distinctive voice said; 'Bloom.'

'Walter, this is Wenna Cavendish.'

'Uh huh. Don't tell me. You've got an exclusive for me'

Wenna ignored the irony. 'Just a question at the moment,' she said.

'Why am I not in the least surprised. Go ahead.'

'You told us Fleur had been an actress at one point.'

'Yes, so?'

'What name did she use?'

'Fleur Nichols.'

'She used her own name?' It was hard for Wenna to keep the disappointment out of her voice.

'No, that was her stage name, not that she ever did much professional acting. When she started in journalism she kept it. She thought it had a better ring to it than Janice Firth.'

Wenna turned to Alex but he had already booted up the second Hub screen. 'So her birth name is Janice Firth...'

'What did I just say?' Walter asked testily.

'One last question. What's the name in her passport?'

'Firth, for God's sake. Janice Firth!' Walter roared. 'Any more questions? Because I'm not on your payroll and in case you've forgotten I have a newsroom to run.'

'Walter, thank you. We're in your debt.' Wenna said, peering across at the screen Alex was using.

'You most certainly are and I'm not likely to forget it,' Walter assured her, ringing off.

Wenna cleared the line and looked at Alex. He nodded and cleared his screen. 'Done,' he said. 'Now we just wait.'

'We've lost her,' Wenna said grimly. 'Wherever she's gone she's out of our jurisdiction.'

Alex was well aware this was no time for levity. 'But wherever she is, we're likely to have friends,' he said placatingly. 'It's an electronically small world these days.'

'Don't look for the upside, Alex,' Wenna said, bleakly. 'There isn't one.'

35

Fleur was uncharacteristically edgy and it had nothing to do with the flight. She had been allocated an economy window seat in an otherwise empty row of three, on a flight that was barely three-quarters full. The flight attendants were working their way towards her, serving dinner and light conversation, making slow progress down the aisle.

She was thinking of Joe; wondering where he was and what he was doing. She looked at her watch, still on London time. It was six thirty. By now Joe would be safely home. She slipped off her shoes and settled more comfortably in her seat. She didn't think she should eat, not right now. If she wanted to end this trip the same dress size as she started, after a day grazing at the airport, any further overindulgence was definitely contra-indicated.

Her mind was working at full speed, ranging wide over one thing and another.

Somewhere in the world a man who was personally responsible for ordering and organising hundreds, if not thousands, of deaths over the years was flying to meet her and she had no real idea what to expect of that meeting. But it was not that consideration that was making her uneasy, it was something else she could not identify; some deep-rooted instinct for danger was shadowing her thoughts.

Often, she had noted, the most obvious dangers, such as those presented by her upcoming meeting, were less fearful than those unseen. Unseen, unseeable dangers like those confronting Joe in the contaminated zones of Asia. It occurred to her that before Joe had entered her life she would have faced this assignment without fear or doubt. In the last year however she had become seduced by the illusion of safety. She and Joe had built an enclosed, self-sufficient world in the haven of her apartment and, just as the reality of flight required defiance of the laws of gravity, so the opposite had applied to them, they had succumbed happily to the gravitational pull of their love and that had altered the time and space around them. A year had flown by, weakening their ability to cope with risk, and they had not noticed the passing.

The trolley had arrived by her row. Whatever was on offer, the smell was enticing. Fleur declined with a smile and a gesture. At least when it came to calories she could be strong.

36

Simone knew instinctively that she would not last out her allotted month at the laboratory. Well before then, despite the regime of pain control and no matter how fierce her determination, she would be too weak to continue work even if her brain was unaffected, which seemed unlikely.

Burcastle was watching her like a hawk and so was Jen, the company GP. Simone sensed that her condition was worsening more rapidly than had been expected, that soon she would be on injections. Fortunately, what she needed to do could be done within the next fourteen days. In her mind, that was also the length of time she gave herself before her mental and physical capabilities collapsed irretrievably.

She was driving home in the early evening. Burcastle had sought, to use his words, to 'release her early' that day in view of her stressful morning with the filmmakers. In truth Simone would not have been sorry to leave early, these days she tired rapidly and it had crossed her mind that one day soon she would have to give up driving. But she had declined. She did not want anyone at the laboratory to think she could no longer sustain a full day's work. In fact she had stayed on later than usual, just to make the point.

She drove slowly and carefully through a light early evening mist, oblivious to the irritation and abusive hand signals of other road users, thinking about what remained to be clarified and organised for Auriol's benefit. There was a lot of bureaucracy involved in dying. Auriol was still in great distress, unwilling to accept the reality and inevitability of what was to come. The problem now was how best to organise her future care in the short time Simone had remaining. If Auriol continued to be completely irrational about it, refused to think about the future let alone plan for it, what was best to do?

It was not Auriol's fault, it was simply the way she was, and she was unlikely to change her whole nature in the space of a few weeks. It did not occur to Simone that Auriol, as a mature woman, should be allowed to be in charge of her own destiny; it had never been that way between them. From the day they met it had been Simone, with Auriol's contented acquiescence, who had taken control of their lives. It was understood, and taken to be natural, that

Auriol would love with unquestioning adoration and that Simone would love with pragmatic dedication.

They had struck a balance in the relationship that an outsider might have considered one-sided but which, to them, was both normal and rewarding. Simone had assumed responsibility for them both and it did not now occur to her that, just because her circumstances had changed, she should abdicate that responsibility. Whatever she did, it would be in Auriol's best interests and however hard the decision; she would make it for both of them.

Simone knew that however she resolved the problem of Auriol's future, it would have to be soon, before she became too ill to think rationally herself. That would happen towards the end, she knew; Mr Khan had warned her of that. But exactly how soon would it happen and how rapid would the onset be once it began? Would she be able to recognise what was happening and react in time or would it be like switching off a light, one minute alert and in possession of her faculties, the next a mumbling idiot, lacking all decision-making capability? She had no idea and suspected that even the doctors would not be able to give her a definitive answer. Best then to prepare everything well in advance, to do all that had to be done now and not procrastinate, to protect Auriol in the short term.

In the fields on the outskirts of the village, lights on in the gathering gloom, the bulldozers, earthmovers and diggers were still at work, crawling determinedly across the land like articulated insects, ripping up the sod as they had been threatening to do since the local council had granted planning permission for yet another vast housing estate.

The sight filled her with instant, irrational anger. Irrational because she had known for months what was to come and had long grudgingly accepted the inevitability of it. All over southern England new towns were being mooted, planned or under construction as the population mindlessly expanded to fit the available land. What fired her anger now was the sudden harsh reality of it.

Where this morning there had been pristine grazing land divided by hedges and the occasional tree, there was now a scene of desolation; the trees dying on their side, the hedges grubbed up and piled in huge heaps ready for the bonfire of the inanity.

Will they ever stop, she thought sadly. Will there ever come a time when the politicians realise that continued growth is a policy for human disaster, that an economy based on endless expansion is not sustainable? No, probably not, she thought as she drove on, leaving the devastation behind, what would be the electoral chances of a political party that advocated policies as obvious as a population cap, lateral economic growth and an altered standard of living to fit a sustainable future? Bleak is the word that came to mind. Greed will always win out against common sense. There will be no changes except those dictated by disaster and by then it may be too late.

As she entered her drive and parked in her usual spot she was pleased to see that there were lights on in the downstairs rooms. At least Auriol was up and about and, it was to be hoped, in a more rational state of mind. Simone sat for a moment in the car, composing herself. She was due for another of the heavy-duty analgesics that had kept the pain at bay, reducing it to a dull background ache and making life bearable. What are my chances of staying on at work once I'm on morphine injections, she wondered. But she knew the answer to that and put the thought aside as soon as it arrived, easing herself out of the driver's seat and locking the hybrid with a brisk flourish of the remote. It was time to be positive.

In the house Auriol greeted her as she always did, with a hug and a kiss. She had dinner cooking and to Simone's great relief, seemed in control of herself.

'So, how is my film star?' Auriol asked with a brittle smile, the import of which Simone totally missed. 'Did the director think you were wonderful?'

'The whole thing was a crass and idiotic waste of time. I got rid of him as soon as I could,' Simone replied.

'I hope you weren't rude, Sim. You can be a little short sometimes. What was he like?'

'Oh, a self-important urban liberal with delusions of intelligence and an irritating American accent, none of which is forgivable.'

'But it was all about you, about your work and how important it is, wasn't it?' Auriol asked as she busied herself laying the table.

'Maybe,' Simone said grudgingly, 'but I've got more important things to get on with while I still can.'

She saw Auriol's shoulders hunch up and knew she had once again touched a sensitive nerve. She was suddenly annoyed with her, annoyed that she had to be permanently careful of what she said for fear of precipitating an emotional outburst. The pain in her side had come on again and seemed to be working its way up towards her shoulder.

'I'm going to have a shower before dinner,' she said abruptly, aware that despite her irritation, she had ducked the issue and not admitted that she had to take her medication. That was another taboo subject. This has to stop, she told herself as she went upstairs. It really does have to stop.

Left alone, Auriol blanked her mind and concentrated fiercely on the preparation of the meal. Everything was fine; everything was going to be just wonderful. Pray for a miracle the priest had said and that was what she had done, determinedly and repeatedly that afternoon. Not even the annoying HR woman from the University insisting on knowing when she would return to work had deterred her. And above all she must not let Simone know how devastated she was or Sim would become angry with her and she really could not bear the thought of that. Love, she had convinced herself, the kind of absolute love she felt, could cure anything. She held that comforting thought with her until Simone returned, when she busied herself serving the meal.

Simone had had time to restore her determination and after they had eaten she returned to the battle to impose reality on Auriol. They were side by side on the sofa, in front of the open wood fire in the sitting room and Auriol had been determinedly talking non-stop in a voice shrill with cloaked anxiety about the minutiae of her day, blocking any attempt by Simone to move the conversation on to more serious matters. Finally Simone lost her temper.

'Auriol, shut up!' she demanded, and then, softening at the sight of Auriol's crumpled face, she added, 'Please be quiet, dear and listen,' in a gentler tone.

Auriol sat rigidly still, staring into the fire, knowing that whatever Simone wanted to say, it was nothing she wanted to hear.

'We need to talk about funeral arrangements,' Simone said. 'I want to be cremated. I'll make all the arrangements ahead of time so you won't have to concern yourself with that, understood?

Auriol nodded dumbly. Simone took Auriol's face in her hand and turned it towards her. 'And I want my ashes to be scattered on Dodman Head in Cornwall, will you do that for me?'

Auriol nodded, her eyes blank and uncomprehending. Simone shook her head slightly as if to wake her up. 'You know why it has to be there?'

'It's where we went for our honeymoon,' Auriol replied in a monotone as Simone released her.

'Exactly. And one last thing. I've stipulated in my will that my reference books are to go to Lady Hall Students' Library. Apart from that I've left everything else to you. You shouldn't have any financial worries.'

'Thank you,' Auriol said, barely audible, like a child who had been given an unwanted gift but felt obliged to make a polite response for the sake of form.

Simone summoned all her resources and delivered her final instruction, which she thought of as her final gift. She took Auriol's hand and curled it up in hers.

'And I want you to find another partner eventually. I don't want you to be alone,' she said calmly.

Auriol did not reply. She was listening but not hearing. She had retreated into the private world she had created to protect herself and Simone. In this world there was no loss, no pain, no death, only eternal, blissful togetherness.

37

'Auckland, New Zealand, via Singapore: the flight left an hour ago.'

Wenna and Alex were in the Director's office confessing, as Wenna saw it, to serious sins of omission. It was dark outside; the thick, shatterproof windows overlooking the river, capable of withstanding anything but extreme firepower, were barred with cream blinds that matched the institutional colour of the walls and the room was lit by the raw glare of overhead neon eco lights. It could easily have passed muster as an interrogation room and Wenna was tense in expectation of the grilling to come. Alex had literally taken a back seat and had been unusually subdued since bringing Wenna the information. Like her, he was expecting a roasting. Charles Lovatt, however, seemed unmoved by the news.

'Do we think Auckland is the intended final destination?' Charles asked mildly.

'She presented an Auckland return ticket. Singapore is simply a refuelling stop.' Wenna replied tightly.

'So, I trust we have we asked our good friends in Singapore to ensure she stays on the flight or to keep her under observation, just in case Auckland is an expensive blind and she intends to jump ship there.'

Wenna indicated Alex with a gesture. 'We've already done that and also contacted the night desk at Wellington SIS to arrange for the plane to be met when it lands in Auckland.'

'Good. And what did you tell our New Zealand colleagues?'

'We said she was a priority IT contact, watch, report, do not touch, and asked for a twenty-four seven shadow team at distance. Since it was a request to allocate substantial resources I took the liberty of using your code, so they will want confirmation of at least partial funding or their accountants will have a fit. I just hope the SIS have enough quality personnel to do the job.'

Charles made a note and spoke without looking up. 'I was there at a Commonwealth Heads of Security Services meeting last year. They're only about a hundred and fifty strong including the tea ladies but as to their ability, I think they're probably rather more than useful.'

He looked at his watch and did a rapid mental calculation. 'Fortunately we have about twenty hours in hand.'

'It could be worse,' Alex pointed out hopefully. 'We'll get top co-operation from the Kiwis.'

'Thank you, Alex,' Wenna said, 'but we all know we've been playing catch-up right from the start. The fact is we've been out-manoeuvred and I should never have allowed that to happen.'

Charles had been scribbling notes on a desk pad. 'If it helps, I suspect that if I had been fed the same information in the same sequence, I would have made the same decisions,' he said. Seeing her disbelief he added: 'Don't forget I was also at the meeting with Walter Bloom but I didn't pick up on the possibility that Fleur might have a passport in another name. You did. Also, even if we had known where she was going earlier, we could have done nothing more than we've done now. As of this moment we have lost nothing.'

Wenna felt unable to appreciate Charles's attempt to absolve her of blame. She was convinced that her failure to cover all the bases was what had cost them the target: the bird had literally flown. She was volcanically angry with herself, the more so because there seemed little hope of redeeming her mistake. They were now in the hands of a small foreign service who, willing as they might be, she still suspected lacked the expertise to conduct the kind of delicate surveillance this case required. Charles had personally instigated the enquiry and had trusted her to watch over it. If she were the Director she would not have been so forgiving of this botch-up.

'Thank you,' she said distantly.

'So, if the flight left this evening, I wonder where she was all day,' Charles said, 'since you tell me she and Joe Kendry booked out of the hotel quite early this morning and he went off to Oxford.'

'The simple answer is, we don't know,' Wenna responded, 'and what's worse, we have no way of finding out unless she shows up on the Heathrow security scans.'

'Sometimes we look for the complex answer where a simple one will do,' Alex put in. 'She may just have gone for some retail therapy.'

Wenna glared at him and he made a wry face. Charles was smiling behind his hand. 'We must live with what we cannot know,' he said, 'and turn our minds to Joe Kendry for a moment. He's back at the apartment I gather.'

'Yes, but booked on a flight to Pakistan tomorrow morning,' Alex answered, 'with his cameraman, a guy called Philip Rogers.'

'So Fleur and Joe will end up in the same quarter of the globe within a day of each other, which as you pointed out before, may or may not be a coincidence,' Charles commented.

'We could ask our friends in Pakistan to keep an eye on Kendry,' Wenna suggested.

'I think we should,' Charles replied. 'Although I strongly suspect they will do that as a matter of course. Western media plus camera, red flags and all that.' He smiled amiably at them. 'This is all becoming rather interesting, don't you think?'

‘I think there’s too much we don’t know,’ Wenna replied, ‘which means we can’t possibly make any informed decisions.’

‘You have a wonderfully exact mind, Wenna,’ Charles said, smiling benignly at her, ‘it’s unfortunate we operate in such an inexact business. However, that is half the fun of it. Now, let us turn our minds to the next move. What might that be, do you think, Alex?’

Alex Jones looked unhappy at being singled out for attention; he had been more than willing to concede the lead position to Wenna at this meeting.

‘Well,’ he said uncertainly, ‘on the face of it we’re the spider at the centre of what will hopefully be an information web so, like the spider, we sit and wait I suppose.’

There was a moment of silence. Wenna at least had the advantage of knowing what Charles was up to, having been on the receiving end of his abstruse teaching methods often enough in the past. Alex, however, was considerably discomforted, sensing that for some reason he couldn’t fathom, he had given the wrong answer. Finally Charles nodded as if accepting Alex’s assessment. Alex relaxed but Wenna knew better.

‘A nice analogy in many ways,’ Charles said, ‘although I would prefer that in our case we should be more of an active hunter. With that in mind let us consider our options. Would you give us your assessment please, Wenna?’

‘Our options are pretty limited,’ Wenna said cautiously, well aware that Charles clearly had something in mind. ‘As far as we know Joe Kendry’s activities are legitimate and have nothing to do with Fleur Nichols. They’re both honest, upright citizens in good standing and so far they’ve committed no actionable offences in law. Fleur has arranged a meeting with the opposition but we don’t know who that might be, except that it’s a reasonable presumption that it’s someone of high standing in the Al Qaeda family, possibly AQE. It may take place in Auckland. For a freelance foreign correspondent that’s a legitimate activity and it’s taking place outside our jurisdiction. The meeting must be of considerable importance to the opposition because they’re allocating considerable resources and putting one of their top operatives at risk.’

Wenna waited but got no response.

'They almost certainly have in mind a propaganda coup of considerable proportions but what, we have no idea,' she continued. 'We would want to establish who Fleur is meeting and what the purpose of that meeting is. As things stand, the best way of achieving that is by letting the meeting take place, relying on observation to identify who it is she meets and debriefing her on her return. That scenario requires her co-operation, which we have no reason to suppose she won't provide, but it may be after the enemy have succeeded in their propaganda aims and from our point of view, that's too late. We may be able to prevent publication, but only, of course, in this country. In short, I agree with Alex. We sit in our web and hope we may be able to counter-attack later.'

Charles sat back in his chair and steepled his fingers, settling in to what Wenna recognised from past experience as lecture mode. It was his way of mentally proofreading decisions he had already made.

'You know,' Charles said, 'we have become used to the idea that the latest version of Al Qaeda is not a structured organisation, rather a kind of extreme religious and cultural meme, but I am beginning to wonder if we have not been slightly misled in that. It has become clear in the last few days, if it wasn't before, that AQEast, for example, still has senior organisational figures who have authority and access to funds from what we might call head office, and it seems Fleur Nichols is about to meet one of them. It seems they may be looking for a different and non-Arab outlet for whatever information they wish to be disseminated. Whatever they're up to, they want worldwide, non-partisan coverage and they want Fleur to be the carrier, presumably because of her contacts with the BBC. This has been in the wind for a while, hence my original interest in her. Whatever this meeting is about, it is of vital importance to them and therefore, to us. We simply have to know what they are up to before they go public. All of which provides ample justification for a proactive approach despite the fact that our options are limited; do you agree?'

Wenna found herself nodding in unison with Alex, her mind whirring, but trying to double-guess Charles was time ill spent at the best of times.

'Good, let us hope the Director General agrees,' Charles continued with a dry smile. 'My view is that if the opposition is prepared to spend money and take risks then we must do the same. Alex, I want you to take over this file from Wenna as of now. You will report directly to me.'

The bottom dropped out of Wenna's world. She knew she deserved to lose the lead role in this operation but the harsh reality of it was hard to bear. Charles turned his attention to her. 'Wenna, I want you to go home and get a good night's sleep...'

Wenna nodded dumbly. This, she thought, was the way careers were made and destroyed; there would be no sacking, the Service was more civilised than that. In a few months there would be a quiet sideways appointment followed by years of frustration in an administrative backwater and an early pension. It was tough but it was the way things were.

'Tomorrow you will pack your bags and leave for New Zealand. I want somebody over there that I can totally rely on,' Charles said.

38

'There's a story in there, Phil, I can feel it in my water.'

They were thirty-seven thousand feet above Saudi Arabia and Joe had been deep in thought for most of the time since they left Heathrow.

'What?' Phil asked, emerging from a detailed perusal of the in-flight magazine.

'The lab. There's something about that place that's not quite kosher.'

'You playing Shylock Holmes again?'

'Journalistic instinct. And it's Sherlock.'

'No it ain't. You want your pound of flesh out of that lab and you don't reckon you've had it so far.'

'Maybe, but think about it. Who ever knew there was a place just outside Oxford, heck, that close to London, storing enough viruses to wipe out the population of the world. I mean, just one of them on the loose would do the job.'

'Don't wanna think about it, thanks.'

'And she's making more of them. Like there aren't enough of them already. And you can bet she didn't tell us everything. So if we know that much, what don't we know?

'Plenty,' Phil suggested, well aware that nothing he said was actually registering with Joe.

'And what do you think is wrong with our Doctor Simone Gofre?' Joe continued. 'That is not a well woman.'

'We'll probably never find out. All I know is she's an Olympic class ball-breaker.'

'I sniff an impact doco, Phil, the sort of thing that sets off a government enquiry. I mean, what exactly are they up to in there? I'm going to talk to Fleur when we get back. If she fronts it we'll have a sale to the BBC pretty much in the bag. You be able to shoot it for us?'

'Course, but these people are international, them and their mates've got enough money to buy Africa. I can't see us getting in that place again to do an exposé without someone hefty on our side, and we're certainly not going to get into those containment areas, are we?'

'Nil desperandum. I'll think of something. We've got Dr Gofre on video admitting she manufactures new viruses. We bullshit that Director with the weak handshake. Give him the chance to tell his side of the story, that sort of thing. Relax, Phil, we'll find a way to get in there, right inside, even if we have to use a robot.'

'Get real, Joe, what're you talkin' about? You have contacts in the army?'

'Okay, so we send in Simone Gofre with a Palmcam. The more amateur it looks the better, gives it a feel of reality, brings it nearer to home.'

'She'll blank you, I'd bet on it.'

'She's got an ego the size of Texas. By the time I've finished with her she'll be grabbing the camera out of my hand and running for the lab doors.'

'Well, I suppose,' Phil conceded. As Alma often said, the man could charm the birds out of the trees. 'Reckon we could pre-sell it?' he asked.

'I might be a bit cheeky and put together a demo from what we've already got, just add a piece to camera.'

‘We can do that. We’ve got plenty in the can. Just so long as our friend Rose Petchek doesn’t get wind of it, she’s likely to go apeshit and start throwing writs around.’

Joe isn’t listening. ‘The Danger Within,’ he said.

‘What?’

‘The title. Fleur will just love it.’

And for the first time for several hours his thoughts returned to Fleur and the pain of her absence struck home like a king hit to the solar plexus. I will stop this, he promised himself yet again, I must or I’ll never get this job done.

‘Bastard, innit?’ Phil commented sagely, ‘when you can’t even have a decent textual relationship with the missus.’

He was grinning at Joe, but his attempt at humour went unacknowledged. Joe was back in a world of his own.

39

Fleur was aware that she was about thirteen or fourteen years of age. She was sitting in the shade of a grandmother tree that spread its branches out over the water of the river-fed pond where the family bred their fish and snared wildfowl in season. There were thin reed beds in the pond edges where the small fry lived and the skeleton of a dead tree out towards the centre that the larger fish used as a haven from the eagle-eyed herons.

Fleur’s job was heron scarer but the day was warm and she was drowsy and at peace, in tune with the world around her, her slingshot and collection of pebbles unused in her pocket. Her woollen shift seemed a burden to wear but a bigger burden to remove, so she had lifted it up above her knees to cool her legs. A GodsEye, the sunlight glinting from its tiny lens, flew in and hovered above the pond, watching her. She smiled and waved at it and it dipped slightly before moving on. It provided a special sense of security to know that the Gods were watching over the world.

She was brought suddenly alert by an eruption in the water further along the bank. She could not imagine what it might be; certainly it was too big to be a fish and swimming was forbidden in the pond. She got stealthily to her feet and moved with a hunter’s care between the trees to investigate.

The girl that emerged naked from the water seemed to be a year or two older than her, and taller, with shoulder-length fair hair that the water had darkened and plastered close to her head. She was obviously a late one because she had no breasts and her legs still had the bony look of the young. She was also deformed, with a strange growth dangling out between her legs above her first silky woman's hair, but her face was beautiful and the water droplets sparkling in the sunshine made it look as if she were covered in a thousand tiny flames. She seemed vaguely familiar yet she was also a stranger.

Fleur stepped out from her concealment to confront the intruder. Whoever she was she had no right to be swimming in the family pond.

'Who are you?' she demanded.

The girl, startled at Fleur's sudden appearance, backed away, covering her deformities with her cupped hands. Her mouth opened and closed but she said nothing.

'Well? This is my family pond, you shouldn't be swimming here.'

The girl looked turned away and spoke over her shoulder. 'I didn't know. It was hot and I didn't know where I was...' Her voice was unusually deep and it broke now and then into attractive highs and lows. She looked embarrassed and confused.

'Who are you?' Fleur asked in a slightly more conciliatory tone. At least the intruder wasn't being hostile.

The girl shook her head. 'I don't know.'

'Don't be stupid, everyone knows who they are. What's your name?'

'I don't think I have one.'

She's like Nesta, this one, a bit slow, Fleur thought. You have to tell them what to do. 'Better get your clothes on,' she said.

It was time to return to the family and show off her find. Maybe she would be allowed to keep the stranger if she had no family of her own. She might be slow but she didn't seem completely incapable so they could probably find something for her to do. Unless she was a runaway, that would be a problem. More likely her family had turned her out because of her defect. She'd heard there were families like that.

The girl looked around helplessly, hands still cupped between her legs. 'I don't have any clothes,' she replied eventually.

Fleur dug in the pocket of her shift and handed over her spare slingshot. Realising that would barely cover the deformity, she emptied her bag of stones and offered both to the girl. 'Tie this round you,' she said.

The girl turned away and after a few moments of inept fumbling had covered herself. Fleur felt sorry for her; if she looked like that she would be embarrassed too and want to cover up. The girl stood irresolute, waiting for Fleur to tell her what to do.

'Better come with me and meet the others,' Fleur said, 'but remember, I found you and you belong to me.'

The girl nodded. 'What's your name?' she asked. She could obviously talk well enough.

'Flower,' Fleur replied as she led the girl away, 'and since you don't have a name I'm going to give you one. I'm going to call you Jo.'

But the girl felt insubstantial when she took her arm and her voice had become lighter and more confident.

'...like the fish or the beef, madam?'

Fleur struggled into wakefulness. All she could remember was that she had been with Joe, the rest was irretrievably lost. She fretted that it might have been important, a premonition of some sort, an augury. The flight attendant was serving the row immediately in front of her. It gave her time to compose her mind. No matter how hard she worked to keep thoughts of Joe from intruding into her work time, it seemed that she would never be able to keep him out of her dreams.

40

Charles Lovatt and Donald Costello retired to a private interview room after the meeting of the Joint Intelligence Committee at the Foreign Office, called to finalise security details for the imminent Presidential visit. As such meetings went it was fairly typical, with the usual inter-departmental rivalries and territorial disputes evident to all the players but hidden to the official records beneath a thin veneer of voluble co-operation. In fact there were no decisions to be made, Costello and Lovatt and their teams had done all the organisational work long since, but there were protocols to be satisfied for such high-level visits and the legitimate interests of the other security agencies had to be respected, like it or not. Despite maintaining a politically civilised façade in the meeting, Charles most certainly did not like it, a fact not lost on Donald.

'Cheer up, Charlie,' he said as they closed the door with a sigh of relief and took facing armchairs, 'I get the same at home. They all want their speaking rights but they sure as hell don't want to take any responsibility if they can avoid it.'

Charles nodded reluctant agreement. 'If I had a glass in my hand I'd offer a toast to a dull and uneventful visit.'

'And if I had one I'd sure as hell drink to that,' Donald replied with a wry grin. 'This place wired by the way?'

'Normally only used by the locals so, probably not. I was wondering if you have any news on Fleur Nichols or Joe Kendry?'

Costello shrugged. 'They're clean,' he said reluctantly. 'He's a documentary maker with a strong left wing bent, like most of them, known for making earnest and boring but meticulously researched public service documentaries. He's not the brightest star in the US sky; bit of an Okie if you know what I mean. You're welcome to keep him and so far as we're concerned she's a Brit anyway.'

'I have to ask you, Don, do you own either of them?'

Costello laughed. 'Hell no, not interested.'

'None of your people had a file on them?'

'Not until you put their name in the frame.'

'One more thing. Do you have anything running in New Zealand at the moment?'

Costello eased himself back in his chair and considered the question. 'You're beginning to interest me now, Charles,' he said.

'Anything?' Charles persisted.

'Fact is, historically we haven't always got on too well with those folks down there,' he said, his eyes fixed on Charles's face. 'They've had this dumb anti-nuclear policy going for decades so we don't really talk the same language. You know that.'

'But you have interests there, Operation Deep Freeze operates out of Christchurch airport, for example.'

'Oh yeah, sure. They service our boys on the Antarctic ice shelf.'

'And a listening post at Waihopai Valley, also in the South Island.'

'Well, yeah...'

'And what do they get in return?

Costello shrugged. 'We keep lines of communication open and throw them some chicken feed now and then. They're members of Five Eyes of course.'

'Okay, but none of your agencies have any operations down there at the moment?'

'No.'

'And if they had, you'd know.'

'Likely. Very likely. Now, it's time to share, Charlie, why the interest in little old New Zealand?

'Because that's where Fleur Nichols is headed and we think she has set up a face-to-face with the enemy.'

Costello was suddenly alert. 'Who, exactly?'

'No idea, but we think they're paying for her trip, so it has to be someone on the list.'

'So... you're running her then?'

'On a very long leash. I have Wenna Cavendish riding shotgun. Just one thing, Don, this is for information only, not action.'

Costello made a small gesture of acceptance. 'What about the boyfriend?' he asked.

'Joe Kendry has taken a job for the UN, making a documentary in Pakistan.'

'Interesting.'

'No obvious connection as yet but we're keeping a close eye on him.'

'Anything I can help with?'

'Not at the moment but I wouldn't hesitate to ask.'

'Please do. This is your show, understood, but I'd really like for you to brief me properly. I'd like to know what your end game is. Can you do that?'

Charles hesitated only briefly. Denying that entirely reasonable request from his country's major anti-terrorist ally was not an option. 'Of course,' he replied.

But he was not at ease in his mind.

***

When he returned to his office in Thames House it was early evening. Charles felt slightly distrait, his mind running through options and coming up with no ready answers. They were in a holding pattern. He booted up his Hub and talked it through the security gates to the Level OpZ files, the ones that were inaccessible to any below his standing and deniable to all but the most rigorous investigation. The Hub asked for an ident and reference.

'Donald Costello,' Charles said. 'US five A.'

After a moment the file appeared. He spent the next half hour reading and re-reading it but found nothing that he did not already know or suspect.

He logged out and blanked the screen, then called Alex Jones to ask for an update. In recent years technology had transformed intelligence work, he mused as he waited for Alex, but in the end, success or failure still depended on people. You had to know them and you had to trust them. But in this business trust was also high risk and Charles Lovatt was instinctively risk-averse.

41

Fleur reset her watch to New Zealand time as the aircraft approached Auckland airport. Having slept surprisingly well during the flight she felt quite bright and alert and as the moment of first contact loomed closer, she felt a flush of adrenaline-enhanced excitement. She knew that she would have to have all her wits about her from the moment the aircraft touched down. To steady her nerves she settled in for a professional worry session. The worst possible scenario was that one of the British or American counter-terrorist organisations had become aware of the upcoming meeting. She could see no way in which that could have happened but she knew it was not impossible and if they had, then she would be followed from the moment she passed through customs.

Fleur had no concerns about the fact that what she would normally consider to be the enemy was dictating her every move. Much as she wanted this exclusive, they wanted her and her contacts even more. The greatest fear she had was that, experienced professionals that they were, if she was followed then they would most certainly spot the watchers and call off the meet. This was almost certainly a one-off opportunity and if it was aborted the trust they had placed in her as a politically unaligned commentator, one they could do business with, would be compromised, probably beyond repair. There was, however, nothing she could do except trust herself to spot and avoid any watchers before any contact was made.

There was a change in the monotonous drumming of the engines and the seat belt signs came on as they ran into a patch of still air turbulence; they were losing height as they approached landfall but from the window she could only see blue sky above a carpet of thick cloud. She looked at her watch; they were due to land in fifteen minutes. She lost the focus of her earlier train of thought; wondered where Joe was, how he was and what he was doing. This is the last time, she promised herself, the very last time I let him take risks. The aircraft tipped easily on one wing, straightened up and dipped into the cloud layer.

***

Auckland, a sprawling city built across a narrow neck of land that separates the Tasman Sea from the Hauraki Gulf, enjoys a climate typical of a maritime city set on a southern hemisphere isthmus; namely it is capable, as the locals are happy to confirm, of delivering four seasons in one day.

This day, at the end of a hot Indian summer, the entire city sweated beneath a layer of fog that had come in with first light and hung around on and off throughout the morning like an unwanted guest, every now and then promising to depart and leave clear blue skies, only to renege on its undertaking and return to do its humid worst.

The airport had been closed to international flights at various times during the morning, then briefly re-opened as windows of opportunity occurred. In these circumstances the decision to re-route Fleur's flight was taken late, too late to save Callum West the tiresome, traffic-clogged journey from the Security Intelligence Service Northern Region office in Wellesley Street, to the airport.

When he arrived and checked in at the airport security office, it at first seemed that flight 207 bringing Fleur Nichols would land on time then, with ten minutes to go before the scheduled arrival time, the flight was suddenly re-routed to Wellington. By the time news of this decision had reached the Security Office the aircraft was already a third of the way to its new destination.

Callum West muttered a few choice epithets under his breath and commandeered a staff Hub to contact the SIS Head Office at Defence House in Wellington and forwarded the case instructions and the photograph of Fleur. Having been handed the file, he was in no way happy at having to rely on others to keep track of the suspect but he assumed that she would re-book and return to Auckland on the first available flight. Head Office had perhaps a quarter of an hour to meet the plane, which should just about be enough, so he decided to sit it out at the airport and await events.

42

Wellington, the southernmost city in New Zealand's North Island, has long been the home of the nation's parliament. It has been said, usually by Aucklanders, that Wellington was chosen as the country's capital and its legislative and political centre simply to punish politicians for their temerity in being politicians and to instil in them a proper sense of their limited worth. Certainly, if weather was the criterion by which a nation's capital was to be determined, Wellington would have struggled to make a case for itself. Not for nothing is the city notorious for its wind, which gathers itself out in the Southern Ocean and is funnelled between the two landmasses of the North and South islands through Cook Strait. Storms brew up with remarkable speed, churning up the turbulent waters of the Strait and forcing the hardy inter-island ferries to scurry for cover in the inner harbour or across the water in the sheltered fiords of the Marlborough Sounds.

At such times Wellington airport, exposed to the sea at both ends of its main runway, is no place to try and land an aircraft of any size, let alone an international flight, and as the weather had steadily deteriorated during the one hour flight from Auckland, the decision to on-fly to Christchurch was an easy one for aviation authorities to take. It did, however, create further problems for the SIS, which was unused to playing pass the parcel with inbound 'subjects of interest'. In such circumstances, bureaucratic delays were inevitable.

The disruption to the flight plans did not concern Fleur at all. Since she had been headed for Christchurch anyway it simply saved her time and the minor inconvenience of a domestic flight. It meant that she would arrive an hour or so early but provided her reception committee had monitored the international flight details, and she was sure they would not have left that to chance, then all would be well.

The weather improved to offer a beautiful clear day and the new flight path followed the coast of the South Island, passing between the sea and the spectacular Kaikoura Ranges, which still held a fleck of last winter's snow here and there. According to the in-flight magazine, there were whales to be seen in the bay off the coast of Kaikoura township, but not on this day and not from this height, even though they were already descending towards the flat Canterbury Plains and the airport on the outskirts of Christchurch city.

Back in Auckland, Callum West heard the news about the further re-routing of Fleur's flight with some trepidation. There were only a handful of officers stationed in the Southern Region office in Christchurch and he knew none of them personally. When his frustration became too much to bear he rang the Southern office anyway, only to be told that they were waiting confirmation from Wellington and had had to bring in someone from leave to cover the unexpected arrival. As he blanked the call and dialled up Wellington HQ, Callum had the distinct feeling that this was not going to be his day.

43

Simone Gofre woke suddenly, tense and alert, adrenaline pumping, a fight or flight response to the nightmare that had ridden her emotions hard. She was laying on her back, only partly covered by the bedclothes, her eyes wide and staring. Gradually, as she returned to reality, she relaxed and pulled up the covers in a reflex action, protecting herself from the night. Whatever the nightmare was, it had fled from the grey light of early morning filtering through the curtains, never to be recalled.

Beside her Auriol was snoring peacefully, her body turned away and her legs tucked up in a comfortable foetal position. What Simone might have seen of her face was hidden by stray strands of hair that moved slightly as she breathed. It's the only time my poor darling has any peace these days, Simone thought, these few brief night hours.

They had bickered and argued last night and it had ended up once again with Simone shouting Auriol down because she was implacably opposed to accepting reality. Then Simone had felt guilty. Shouting at Auriol was like beating an importunate but obdurate puppy. Afterwards the guilt had made her feel even angrier. The fact that she was right and Auriol completely wrong made no difference, Auriol seemed incapable of understanding what now had to be done.

It was vital that Auriol returned to work. She must not lose that job; she would need it to keep herself occupied, to prevent herself from falling into the kind of deep despair that Simone knew she was capable of. Left alone in this empty house she would simply waste her life in bitter regrets.

Despite this self-justification, in her heart Simone knew that this particular argument had been largely her fault. She had not in fact had a bad day at all, the pain had been under reasonable control and she had wrung some major concessions out of Colin Burcastle and the unit doctor, when she had really thought that this time they would block her determination to continue working as long as she could.

It had been a pre-emptive strike. Simone had known that any day now she would have to begin morphine injections to control the pain and that would involve taking syringes into her PC4 containment unit, something she suspected would give Burcastle an apoplectic fit. In that she had been absolutely right.

'My dear girl,' he said, 'the rules are explicit...'

Simone had let him get away with the 'dear girl', something she would never normally have done. 'Of course they are and for good reason,' she had responded. 'But they were never meant to cover these circumstances. For once in your life, Colin, bend a rule.'

He had not given in easily or quickly. The whole scenario had forced him way outside his comfort zone. ‘I really don’t think I…’

‘Consider the alternatives.’ Simone had suggested. ‘No doubt you’ve already begun the recruitment process; for all I know you may already have someone lined up to take over from me…’

‘Oh we’re not jumping the gun, I can assure you…’ he said hastily.

‘It wouldn’t be jumping the gun Colin; it would simply be good business. But think of this: let me finish and I can leave you with a completed virus ready to work on and you’ll be absolutely on schedule. No delays to explain.’

‘Yes, true, but… Well, I’m very sympathetic to your wishes but I’m not entirely my own boss you know, I have to be sure I can justify any decision I make…’

‘Precisely my point, you have an international board to account to and they have millions invested in my work, work they will be very keen to see completed on time.’

Colin Burcastle was by now looking extremely uncomfortable. Simply having Simone Gofre in the same room as him for any length of time had that effect on him, let alone when she was in such a demanding mood. He felt himself to be in a no-win position and that did nothing at all for his stress levels.

Just by looking at him Simone knew she had him at a tipping point and pressed her advantage. ‘Pharmaceutical behemoths are not known for extreme generosity to junior executives who make promises they can’t deliver on. It won’t be my future that is on the line here, I don’t have a future to be worried about, but you do.’

‘Since you are being so pragmatic about your own future, Simone,’ he said ‘there is the matter of the medical…’

Simone cut him off. ‘You know perfectly well I’m under constant medical supervision, Colin, and I’ve also arranged for an update on my psychological profile to be on your desk in the morning. Let me repeat what I told you the last time we had this sort of discussion: there is very little risk in my continuing to work long enough to finish this project and what little risk there is falls on other people’s shoulders, not yours. Plus, in the hugely unlikely event that anything went wrong I am the perfect fall-guy, I won’t be around long enough to contradict anything you say.’

Beneath the level of his desk Burcastle was rapidly dry-washing his hands, caught in the agony of indecision. Simone could even feel some sympathy for him. She understood that he just wanted her and her relentless demands to go away. Like many middle managers he was less competent than those he had to manage and lived in permanent fear of discovery; under those circumstances every decision was stressful and decisions that carried such a high potential for risk, a nightmare. Not that she was prepared to let him off the hook until she had what she wanted.

'I don't need it in writing, Colin, your word is good enough.'

'When?' Burcastle asked eventually. 'When would you want, I mean to start…'

'Injecting? Not yet, I'm just preparing the ground for what I know is inevitable. Maybe in a couple of days. I'll know when the time comes, believe me.'

'And your work is on schedule?'

'It is, and so long as I remain alive and relatively pain-free I'll be finished in about a week.'

'A week…'

'Possibly less. I intend to work this weekend and next if necessary, just to make sure.'

'Then you'll be…'

'Yes, finished and gone.'

He had caved in then, still obviously reluctant and beset by the pain of difficult decision-making, the root cause of which would never be eased by a simple injection.

'Very well, then,' he had said. 'You will be missed, Simone,'

You won't miss me, Simone had thought, you'll be glad to see the back of me, like every man I've ever known. Even my father.

Simone eased herself up in the bed and sat up supported by her pillows. She took one of the tablets laid ready on the bedside table and swallowed it down with a mouthful of water from a tooth glass Auriol had put there for her. Auriol snuffled and turned over onto her back, still fast asleep.

Replaying the meeting with Burcastle in her head had given her a real sense of satisfaction. Right up until the moment she had that remembrance of her father; that beautiful man she had loved devotedly and who had, in return, offered no more than gentle, patronising acceptance of her presence in his life. What she would have given for some of his abundant, vivid intellectual sunlight to have been shed on her instead of being wasted on his academic contemporaries whose intellects were so patently inferior to his.

It was not even as if she had to compete with siblings for his attention, she was an only child: a distantly tolerated, occasionally petted, but always lonely child, lost from an early age in a bewildering adult campus world of flawed, self-indulgent intellectualism; an enclosed world where status and advancement depended on playing the publication game, not on talent or ability. The frequent and sometimes embarrassingly effusive public demonstrations of affection and fellowship within this elite clan seldom felt genuine to her budding feminine intuition.

Alienation from that world was acceptable, even desirable, but alienation from her father was not. When her distress became intolerable, she had exploded in anger; taken out every book and file she could find in his study, piled them in a heap on the lawn and set fire to them. As a scream for attention it could hardly have been louder or more blatantly obvious. Yet the only result had been incarceration in a boarding school, it being thought, as her beloved father had explained to her, that the caring discipline would teach her a more balanced and enduring set of values than he had been able to. She was branded, it seemed to her, as his only failure.

She never knew what went wrong in his life when she was no longer there to observe his moods and contend for his attention but when she was fourteen he left her forever, without a word of goodbye, without, so far as she knew, so much as a thought for her. It was not an heroic death; he drank half a bottle of whisky then locked himself in his car and poisoned himself with carbon monoxide. There was no note, no indication of motive. She was granted an exeunt for the funeral and distinguished herself by a furiously petulant tirade aimed at her astonished mother for her incompetent care.

However, it had not been her mother's function, it seemed, to care for him; he batted for both sides, she explained, and that function of care had been usurped long since by his boyfriend of many years, who was now nowhere in evidence.

Simone had forgiven her father everything except his selfish decision to leave her without a word. What bitter irony, she thought, that now her own body had decided to suicide without consulting her.

Beside her, Auriol kicked out beneath the covers, fighting some dream foe of her own, and Simone was brought sharply back to the problem of her future. It would be out of the question for Auriol to take care of her once she became too ill to care for herself, she would collapse in a heap at the sight of Simone in the last stages of her illness. Besides, she had ample morphine available and if she were sparing with its use, she and not the cancer would decide her last day. And on that day she would be alone. Come what may, she would spare Auriol that final pain.

The problem now was that Auriol would never take any steps to secure her own future. Whatever needed doing, Simone would have to do it. It was a harsh truth but there was only one way in which Simone could ensure Auriol was set up in a new life whilst she was still around to monitor it, and that was to insist they separate. And they had to part while Simone was still competent enough to enforce the decision.

There was no easy way; no matter how it was put it would seem like abandonment. No matter what Simone said, Auriol, being Auriol, would feel that she was unwanted, no longer loved or needed. Knowing that, telling her would be an impossibly hard thing to do, but tell her she must, and somehow fortify her to see this thing through.

Not yet though. They still had time, a few last precious days. Simone leant over and kissed Auriol gently on the forehead, a butterfly touch.

44

The pilot brought the aircraft in for a whisper-perfect, copybook landing at Christchurch airport despite a bumpy approach. Enjoying a sense of temporary community, Fleur joined in when, prompted by relief as much as admiration, the passengers broke out into a spontaneous round of applause.

Compared to Heathrow, the terminal, although ultra-modern, was modest in size and the security checks here seemed self-indulgently casual by comparison. There was no evidence of any watchers and the only security activity was a sniffer dog and her handler patrolling the baggage carousel for the scent of drugs or possibly, Fleur supposed, for explosives. She collected her flight-hardened suitcase, loaded it onto a trolley and headed for Customs.

There were no armed men to be seen in the inner concourse and at Customs, whilst her British passport provided no special privileges, she was passed through with a smile and no comment except 'enjoy your stay', which was more courtesy than she had met with in much of her international travel. She headed for the green exit, very aware that the steady eyes of the strategically placed Customs officers were on her as she passed. Above the exit portal was a colourful sign that read: 'Haere Mai. Welcome to Paradise.'

Then she was out into the main concourse, facing a glass barrier that funnelled people left or right, behind which waited a gathering of friends and relatives and limousine drivers. Watchers could have been anywhere in that throng but there were no standouts that she could spot.

She scrutinised the placards held up by the waiting drivers without seeming to be too interested. Amongst them she noted a young man of Middle Eastern appearance wearing a grey suit, neat white shirt and tie and holding a cardboard placard headlined 'Southern Range Tours'. Beneath, handwritten in capital letters, was 'Mrs Gelato'.

Fleur smiled at the choice of pseudonym as she manoeuvred her trolley through an excited and voluble family group of substantially built Pacific Islanders who were exchanging enthusiastic hugs and greetings with arriving relatives, and approached the young man. He saw her coming and obviously recognised her. So, they had sent him photo ID, Fleur thought.

'I'm Mrs Gelato,' she said, straight-faced.

He was looking at her intently, as if to eliminate any lingering doubts as to her identity. 'Yes, you are,' he said finally.

'Well, are you my driver?' Fleur asked when he made no move.

'No. I'm waiting for someone else,' he said. But at the same time he removed an envelope from behind the placard and shoved it into

Fleur's hand. Before Fleur could react he had slipped away in the crowd and was gone. Whatever arrangements had been made for her, being chauffeur-driven was obviously not included.

Fleur abandoned her trolley at the collection point near the exit from the concourse and, grateful that experience had taught her how to travel light, hauled herself and her luggage into the female toilets. Secluded in a cubicle she opened the envelope. It contained a brochure for the Waimanu River Resort, an international Lodge in North Canterbury, a set of car keys with a tag giving a vehicle registration number, a hand-drawn map showing the location of the car in the multi-storey car park, a car park ticket, a ten dollar note and a map of North Canterbury with the route to Waimanu Lodge marked from the airport.

Very efficient, Fleur thought. But then she would have expected nothing else. Obviously even in remote and secular New Zealand, the revitalised Al Qaeda had a well-organised body of sympathisers. It did strike her as faintly patronising that they obviously thought she might have been so poorly organised that she would arrive half way round the world without being able to provide herself with at least enough of the local currency to pay a car park fee.

The biggest problem she faced was persuading the recalcitrant automatic ticket dispenser to accept her money and issue an exit ticket. Having cleared that hurdle she found the car without difficulty and checked it over. It was a nondescript saloon a few years old, showing current warrant of fitness and registration stickers and the fuel tank was full, with a red plastic five-litre spare can in the boot. They were leaving her no cause for complaint; being stopped by the local constabulary for minor traffic law breaches or running out of fuel miles from anywhere was definitely not an option on this trip.

Much of the central city had been completely rebuilt in recent years following a succession of earthquakes and the roads were pristine, almost manicured compared to much of London, and traffic was mercifully light. Driving, not historically Fleur's favourite occupation, was almost a pleasure. Once clear of the city environs Fleur picked up Route 73 heading towards the towns of Darfield and Sheffield. She was feeling tired and jet-lagged and considered stopping overnight in a pub or motel but decided against it, the probability being that the facilities available at what sounded like a fairly up-market Lodge would be worth the wait. At least the roads were remarkably free of traffic, the weather continued to be kind and the early evening countryside with its backdrop of the Southern Ranges was stunningly beautiful, even to the eyes of a confirmed city girl.

***

Fleur had been clear of the airport for fifteen minutes by the time Katy Tan, irritated at having to cancel a hair appointment and return to work, arrived to learn that Fleur's flight had long since been cleared and 'Ms. Janice Firth' had already passed through immigration and customs.

It seemed that Southern Region was going to carry the can for this one even though it was hardly their fault. She dutifully checked the return flights to Wellington and Auckland, the regional and international flight bookings, then the airport rental car agents, the accommodation bureau and the information centre, but there was no record of Fleur Nichols or Janice Firth. She had vanished and all Katy would be able to report with any certainty was that she was somewhere in the South Island but where or with whom or in what vehicle, if any, they had no idea.

Katy checked her watch. It would be about six in the morning in London and the one certainty was that the person on the other end of this news would not be starting their day well. She was just glad that she would not be the one telling them. If this case was anything like as important as it sounded, then something very unpleasant was about to hit the fan.

She put in a call to Callum West in Auckland.

***

Fleur turned onto Route 77 to Coalgate and soon after encountered her first road kill. The bloody remains of an adult opossum were splayed across her path and above her a kahu, a harrier hawk, disturbed from its prey, was circling slowly, wings full spread and flight feathers extended, waiting for her to have the decency to go away and leave it to its meal. Fleur steered round the carcass; she was not overly superstitious but she certainly did not want the animal's blood marking out her vehicle, it would have felt too much like offering a digitus impudicus to fate. Behind her the kahu settled on the carcass again, sinking razor-sharp claws into the exposed flesh and ripping out entrails with a viciously curved beak. This was his paradise, not hers.

After two and a half hours' driving, Fleur was in the foothills of the Southern Alps, following a clearly signed tourist scenic route, heading towards the upper reaches of the broad and braided Rakaia River. A prominent sign guided her to a turn-off and the access road to Waimanu Lodge. She felt a sudden tightening of her stomach muscles, a familiar nervous reaction. Wish me luck, Joe, she thought. Wish me luck, darling.

45

Joe spotted Phil taking the capsules as they were progressively losing height, preparing to land at Quaid-e-Azam Airport. 'What's that, Phil?' he asked.

'Nothing much.'

'Come on, Phil, what?'

'Aw, just blood pressure that's all.'

'Since when?'

Phil shrugged. 'Last year or so. Like I said, it's nothing.'

Joe made a face. 'Heart problems aren't nothing, Phil, have you got it under control?'

'Course I have. That's what the pills're for.' He grinned at Joe and gave his thigh a friendly punch. 'Thank the Lord for the drug companies, eh? What'd we do without 'em?'

'Die early in some cases I suppose,' Joe replied, 'but even so I have problems with the ethics some of the multi-nationals apply, or don't apply.'

'Joe, my old mate, I sometimes think there ain't nothing in the world you wouldn't find a problem with if you was in the mind. What's got into you this time?

Joe shook his head. 'Don't know,' he said.

‘Missing that Fleur again, right? I told the missus what you’d be like. I went, he’ll be a pain in the arras until we start work, you’ll see, and she goes, quite right too. Fat lot of use she was, God bless her.’

‘Yeah, okay, I miss Fleur but it’s not just that. I just feel something’s not right. Call it intuition.’

‘What for, us or her?’

‘No idea.’

‘Right then, best thing is, forget all about it ’till it happens, that’s what I say. Now, stop moaning and tighten your seat belt.’

Joe forced a grin. ‘You’re such a mother sometimes,’ he said.

The aircraft made disturbingly loud mechanical noises as the undercarriage and flaps were lowered and it lined itself up on the landing strip by the Jinnah Terminal.

‘Know what the pilots call these jets?’ Phil offered. ‘Flying bricks, mate. Know why? Because they can’t glide, when the engines cut out they drop like a brick, so they have to fly them onto the ground to stop from crashing.’

‘Well thank you for that input, Phil, but I think it’s rather more information than I really need right at this moment,’ Joe said wryly.

The aircraft touched down, bounced heavily and then settled into a fast-braking dash down the runway with the engines screaming in back thrust.

‘See what I mean?’ Phil said smugly as the jet slowed to taxi speed and turned towards the modern white-fronted terminal. ‘If there’s a God and he meant us to fly he’d’ve given us wings, I tell you.’

Joe hushed him with a gesture. ‘That could be construed as taking God’s name in vain, it’s bad karma and in this country it would go down like a lead balloon.’

Phil sighed. ‘Remember the good old Church of England? You could say what you liked about them and nobody gave a rat’s arse.’

‘The C of E does still exist, Phil,’ Joe pointed out. ‘Anyway, I didn’t know you had any fears about flying.’

‘I don’t. Just making small talk like, trying to cheer you up.’

The co-pilot broke into their conversation, praising Allah and welcoming them to Karachi, City of Lights, sometime capital of the Islamic Republic of Pakistan, and probably the most populous city in the world where, he told them, the time was 10am and the outside temperature was a mild 34 degrees. He wished them a good day, thanked them for flying with his airline and ordered them to stay in their seats until the seatbelt signs were turned off, an instruction that a good proportion of the passengers immediately proceeded to ignore, joining in a general scramble for the overhead lockers. Phil and Joe, like the patient and experienced travellers they were, sat tight.

On the tail end of the disembarking passengers, they had an easy run through to customs. The terminal, as modern and efficient as any in the world, was thick with a dense and colourful throng of people, reflecting the diverse ethnic mix of the city, their background chatter a blend of Urdu, Punjabi, Sindhi, Kashmiri, Seraiki, Pashtan and Bengali, with now and then a smattering of half a dozen other Indo-Asian languages. It was pleasantly warm and the air held a faint blend of scents that went unnoticed to the majority but were new and exotic to the visitors.

The concourse was patrolled by stone-faced and heavily armed soldiers who obviously viewed the Westerners with particular suspicion but did nothing to impede their progress through to Customs. Here their passports and bags were subject to a thorough search whilst in the background they were being closely observed by a burly man in an ill-fitting suit with an interesting bulge beneath his left armpit who might as well have been holding a placard advertising 'low-level Security Services'. He and the Customs officer exchanged a none-too-subtle look and then, somewhat to their surprise, having not even been asked the purpose of their visit, Joe and Phil were allowed to pass.

They had barely taken two steps towards the exit when the security officer stepped up to them. 'You will come with me,' he said blandly, indicating a door behind him.

Phil opened his mouth to speak but Joe got in first. 'Of course,' he said.

The office they entered had all the featureless, impersonal and Spartan hallmarks of an interrogation room. Behind a simple, spindly-legged desk sat a tall, sparely built man of about Joe's age. He stood as they entered and came round the desk to offer his hand and a thin smile.

'Hello, welcome to Pakistan, Mr Kendry,' he said in barely accented English. 'My name is Syed Siddiqi and I have been appointed to be your consultant during your stay.'

'That's very kind,' Joe said, 'but we're on contract to the United Nations and I have no doubt they'll provide any consultancy we need. In fact we're being met by Bill Mathews, who heads up the mission here. He's probably wondering where we are at this moment.'

'We offered to meet you on his behalf. He is expecting to lunch with you at your hotel.'

Joe shook his head. 'I don't understand. Who do you work for?' he asked, as if he didn't already have a pretty good idea.

'My office has responsibility for the security of important visitors to our country,' Siddiqi replied. 'Mr Mathews and the other UN staff are very happy to work closely with us when necessary.'

Supposing they had any options, Joe thought. It seemed worth one last try. 'I hardly consider myself an important visitor,' he said, 'and we're experienced travellers, well able to look after ourselves.'

Siddiqi gave a slight shake of his head. 'I'm afraid we must insist,' he said. 'Like many countries in the world we have dissidents in our midst who frequently resort to violence.'

'My research suggested that things had been pretty calm of late.'

'I will be straight forward, Mr Kendry. We decided to provide you with extra protection because of the reason for your visit. There is considerable political and religious opposition to the operation of the Two+One scheme in this country and there have been attacks on some of the clinics recently.'

'Recently? That's news to me.'

'After consultation it was decided not to publicise these events.'

'Why?'

Siddiqi's face tightened. 'The international press have their own agenda which always seems to include making more of these things than the events merit. We do not wish to give, what is the word, yes, succour, to our enemies, Mr Kendry, any more than we wish to attract the kind of negative publicity that we certainly would attract if anything happened to you during your stay.'

And that, Joe thought, if not the truth, is at least part of it. It was obvious that if he hoped to achieve anything at all while he was here it would be wise to be seen to be compliant, at least for the moment. 'I understand, Mr Siddiqi. Thank you for explaining things to me and we'll be happy to take your advice.'

Behind him Joe heard Phil give a faint snort of amusement that he rapidly covered with a cough. Siddiqi stood up, looking somewhat more relaxed.

'Then, if you would be kind enough to hand over your passports, I will happily escort you to your hotel. Your baggage will be delivered to your room.'

They were led out of the terminal building beneath the shade of the pedestrian overhang and ushered into a black limousine with darkened windows that took off smoothly into the crush of traffic. The ride downtown afforded them little opportunity to gain an impression of the real city as the route they took passed mainly up-market shopping complexes and office blocks, the architecture of which was mostly either modern international, with just a hint of Muslim creative influence, or renovated colonial. They could have been in any of a number of cities in the world. The hotel too was truly international in design and function, only the occasional artwork and the ethnicity of the staff marking it out.

Siddiqi supervised them booking in, handed over their passports to the reservations clerk and accompanied them to their adjoining rooms. He handed over a card. 'Please do not leave the hotel for any reason without telling me. Your lunch appointment with Mr Mathews is in the dining room here at twelve thirty and we have booked office suite 3A for three this afternoon.'

'Er, what for?' Joe was genuinely puzzled.

'For your first interview. We have arranged for a number of women who took part in the Two+One scheme to be here at various times over the next two days. You will understand that in parts of our society there is a certain social stigma attached to what they have done and we have to protect them as well as you.'

Before Joe could reply the security officer from the airport appeared, herding in front of him two porters carrying their luggage, which they placed in the rooms. 'You may see Waseem now and then during your stay,' Siddiqi continued, indicating his bulky, cold-eyed assistant. 'I hope you will find that reassuring. Of course the hotel has additional security. Now I will leave you to rest before lunch, do call me if I can be of any further help.'

'One thing,' Joe said.

'Yes.'

'Can I call you Syed?'

***

'Can I call you Syed!' Phil mimicked sardonically when they had been left alone.

'Sometimes, Phil, you're a bear of little brain. Do you seriously want him permanently on our case?'

Joe flopped down on his bed while Phil lounged in an easy chair. 'I reckon he'll be on our case no matter what. Him and that thug Waseem,' Phil complained.

Joe sighed. 'Phil, has it occurred to you that this room might be bugged?'

'No.'

'I thought not. Let's hope we're not that important. For the moment let's assume not.'

'Okay, in future I'll keep my big gob shut. What I'd like to know is how come they know so much about us and what we're here for, I mean who's dobbed us in?'

Joe started to unpack. 'Probably our lunch date,' he suggested.

'Why would the UN want us in bloody handcuffs? It's their doco for Christ's sake.'

'Bill Mathews has to live and work here. Co-operating with the authorities, keeping them up to date with what the UN is doing in their country, who's coming and going and why, would make a lot of sense to him. He may even not have an option, especially if there really is a violent reaction here against the Two+One project.'

'Yeah, well, we could ask him.'

'I intend to. Let's hope it is him because the possible alternatives are less attractive.'

'Like what?'

'Like Rose Petchek setting us up to fail.'

'Why would she?'

‘I don’t know, and that’s what bothers me, I hate not knowing. In London she was saying she’d arranged UN contacts here for us, including clinic visits, no mention of a permanent security attachment. And not a word about recent attacks on UN clinics. So what are we dealing with, are there warring factions inside the UN? If so, whose side is she on and what’s their agenda?’’

‘And if it’s not the unlovely Rose playing secret squirrel?’

‘Well, you can bet your bottom dollar the British Secret Services are all over the airports like a rash. Maybe they monitor all flights to this part of the world and tip off their counterparts here.’

‘Oh, great.’

‘Whatever it is, let’s hope the explanation is simple and innocent because no matter what the risk I intend we should make the film we came here to make.’

‘Fat chance with the local spooks looking over our shoulder all the time.’

‘Let’s be charitable for a minute. The Security Services may have genuine concerns for our safety. The fact that this is a Muslim country doesn’t mean it isn’t vulnerable to Islamic extremists. In all the years of Islamic extremism, most of the dead have been fellow Muslims. The Shias and Sunnis have never seen eye to eye, and whoever comes out on top, if you’re not singing from their song sheet you’re an apostate, a bigger sinner than the people of the Great Satan, America.’

Phil threw his hands in the air. ‘You’d make a good schoolteacher, you. What I reckon is they’re mad, the lot of ‘em. Bloody psychotics.’

‘They’re no more psychotic than the Catholic Inquisition were in their day. Those priests tortured maybe a million people. They burnt them alive because they thought they were possessed by devils. Muslim extremists have a long way to go to match that score.’

‘C’mon Joe, you making a case for them?’

‘No. I just don’t think they are psychotic in the usual sense of the word. They’re fanatics, drunk on religion and the euphoria of common conviction. They believe they have genuine grievances.’

Phil yawned. ‘Whatever, either way they’re still bloody dangerous. And I don’t see what it has to do with the spot we’re in right now.’

‘It might explain why we’re in this spot at all.’

Phil yawned. Philosophy was not his strong point and when Joe started lecturing, he soon got bored. ‘Question is, how do we get out of it?’ he asked.

‘I’ll find a way.’

‘How?’

Joe swung his legs off the bed and made for the en suite. ‘Why waste time seeking answers when we should be exploring the questions,’ he said.

The reply left Phil none the wiser. ‘That a wossname, a quotation, is it?’ he asked.

‘No, it’s an evasion,’ Joe’s disembodied voice replied from the bathroom.

***

Bill Mathews, despite a workaday name, turned out to be an American bureaucrat of the old school: a tall man in his early fifties with a full head of perfectly greying hair and square-jawed, film star looks. He was dressed in an expensively cut light-coloured casual suit and formal tie that in earlier times would have passed muster amongst the British Raj. He had the relaxed, socially confident manner of the Ivy League elite and there was about him an understated but evident presumption of superiority that Joe found inherently distasteful.

Putting aside his personal prejudices, Joe found an actor’s smile and managed some expat small talk whilst they ordered and were served. The hotel was obviously busy and the dining room almost full, the background hum of conversation in many different languages an ample cover for their own discussion. There was no sign of Syed Siddiqi but Waseem had been sitting in an alcove in the foyer when they entered, reading a newspaper, trying and failing dismally to be inconspicuous.

After what he considered to be the minimum period that politeness decreed, Joe turned the discussion to matters of the moment. ‘I have to say, Bill,’ he began, ‘things have not quite worked out the way I expected.’

‘That so?’ Mathews could do a very refined version of bland.

‘I was promised open access to people and places in order to make this film in the way it needs to be made to fulfil the contract. I certainly wasn’t told there had been attacks on the UN clinics. As it is, Siddiqi has effectively taken over our schedule and is organising where we go, who we see and under what circumstances. We’re virtually limited to this hotel. It’s very frustrating to be restricted in this way.’

‘I’m sure it is, I can understand it would cramp your artistic instincts but there are risks to be considered and it is a case of when in Rome, I’m afraid.’

‘Given that we’re both working for the UN, can’t you bring your influence to bear?’

Mathews spread perfectly manicured hands in a gesture of hopelessness. ‘If only I could. The fact is we are all here on sufferance, valued friends for the most part, but still strangers in a strange land.’

‘Prisoners more like,’ Phil put in.

Mathews looked at him with faint surprise, as if seeing him for the first time, then returned his attention to Joe. ‘Syed Siddiqi is an important man and a useful one. The UN has many different interests here and he opens doors for us when he can. He is also privy to information that neither you nor I have and if he thinks, for your own safety, he should restrict your movements whilst you are here then I suggest it would be wise to comply. Of course, anything I can do to assist, I will with great pleasure.’

‘Suppose that left me in a position where I couldn’t make the film, couldn’t fulfil the UN contract?’

‘That would be regrettable but it would be entirely your decision. There is a great deal at stake here, Joe, in particular the future of the Two+One project in this country. It is too important to be prejudiced for the sake of a single publicity event and I am sure that is the view our masters would take. Syed and I have agreed to do our best to enable you to make a film, although perhaps not quite the one you had in mind, and we will. I can probably even access some filmed material from the Pakistan Television Corporation that might offer some local colour. However, we do expect your co-operation. Can I assume we will have that?’

After a beat Joe said, ‘You can assume I will do my very best.’

‘Excellent. I believe your first interview is in half an hour and I have a meeting, so…’ he stood up and offered a brief handshake. ‘I will leave you to your work.’

Joe and Phil watched in a mutually disgusted silence as Mathews walked away without looking back. Phil broke the silence. ‘Fat lot of use he was,’ he commented. ‘Makes you wonder exactly who he’s working for.’

‘Doesn’t it just,’ Joe replied. ‘And I wonder how much of this Rose Petchek knew before she sent us. She wanted me on a tight leash right from the start. Somehow we’ve got to find a way to get out on the streets without a minder, but that’s a problem for later. Right now we have a beauty parade to attend.’

46

By the time she turned into the long tree-lined drive that led to Waimanu Lodge, Fleur was feeling the deadening effects of jet lag. The drive passed a series of linked and landscaped man-made lakes large enough to enjoy their own small islands. Around the lakes were scattered stand-alone mini-mansions and a small block of low-level apartments. Further on was an immaculately groomed eighteen-hole golf course that ran down to a broad, fast running river and ahead of her was the main Lodge, the size of an average five-star hotel.

This was an international retreat for the seriously rich; the last place you would expect to meet up with a terrorist. Which, she supposed was the point. The opulence of the surroundings also served to emphasise how important this meeting must be; she permitted herself a wry smile, the bill for this little get-together would have made a serious dent in the AQE entertainment budget.

An immaculately dressed porter came to take her luggage and escort her to reception where a young woman who looked as if she had just stepped out of the pages of ‘Hotel Vogue’, took her passport and booked her in. By the special magic of faceless service reserved for the very finest establishments, her luggage and car disappeared.

Here it seemed she was to be known by the name in her passport, Ms Janice Firth and, curious as she was, she was wise enough not to ask questions about the booking that had been made for her. She did ask if there were any messages for her but there were none. She was shown to her room, which was elegantly decorated and furnished and the size of a small apartment. It smelt fragrant and cool. The picture window overlooked one of the lakes and had a glimpse of the river in the distance and beyond that a backdrop of mountains. Her baggage was already placed on the baggage stand by the double-fronted wardrobe.

It was early evening and there seemed little likelihood that contact would be made until the next day. She ordered room service and unpacked. At any other time, in any other circumstances, she would have called Joe but talking to her beloved was something she dared not do.

Despite his absence, that night she slept well.

47

Charles Lovatt did not take kindly to early mornings, they tended to make him irritable. This was a fact of which Alex Jones was very well aware and he had not been looking forward to this first meeting of the day.

'And how exactly did they manage to lose her,' Charles asked coldly.

'It seems the flight was diverted twice at the last minute due to weather and they just missed her. She landed at Christchurch and is now somewhere in the South Island. Obviously that was always her destination.'

'There's barely a million people there, surely to hell they can track her down.'

'Let us hope so, sir.'

'Nothing from Wenna yet?'

'Still in the air I imagine.'

'Give her the good news as soon as you can. Anything else?'

'Just that Joe Kendry has started a kind of diary, reporting back to the Hub in her apartment.'

'Saying what, exactly?'

'It seems he's not too pleased with the reception he's getting in Pakistan.'

'Why not?'

'Our friend Siddiqi has him on a short rope and Joe is not amused. He wants to go walkabout in Karachi armed with a camera and a host of good intentions.'

'Well, no doubt Syed will keep him out of trouble. Decent of Kendry to keep us up to date. I don't really see him as a player but we should still download what he sends, you never know.'

'He may try to give Syed the slip of course.'

'Not sure he has the cojones for jumping bail but I suppose it's possible. Not our concern unless he does skip and meets someone interesting. If that happens you can be reasonably sure Syed will know about it.'

'But can we be reasonably sure he will share?'

Charles covered a yawn with the back of his hand. 'Nothing is absolutely certain. For all we know Syed may decide to let him run just to see what happens. Anyway, Joe Kendry is far from our biggest problem… We have an appointment to keep.'

48

The woman seemed to be in her late thirties, thin and gaunt looking, her clothes hanging on her worn body, her weathered peasant face framed by a dull-coloured headscarf. She seemed bewildered and lost in the modest-sized but well-appointed conference room. With her was an equally worried-looking young man in his early twenties with a pencil thin moustache and a wasp waist, wearing an impeccable white shirt and dark slacks that hung on his hips. They were sitting side by side on conference chairs that were backed against a blue wall screen. Behind a desk on the opposite side of the room was Syed Siddiqi. He stood in a single, sinuous movement as Joe and Phil entered, his eyes fixed on Joe's face.

'Your lunch went well?' he enquired.

'Thank you, yes,' Joe replied, indicating for Phil to begin setting up.

'You found your conversation with Mr Mathews instructive I hope.'

'I certainly did.'

'Good. All the women you interview wish to be anonymous. I'm sure you understand. More women have been arranged for tomorrow morning. You must say how many you wish to interview. The boy with her is your interpreter, since I will not be able to be with you all the time after today. You may call him Jamal.' He made an imperious gesture and Jamal shot to his feet and came to stand respectfully in front of Joe. 'Please begin whenever you wish,' Syed advised as he returned to his observation post behind the desk.

Phil was checking his light meter and muttering under his breath. Joe gave him a hard sidelong look as he shook hands with Jamal, who seemed a little flustered at such formality. 'I'm Joe,' he said to the young man. 'Good to meet you. Tell me, will all the women speak the same language or will we have problems later?'

Jamal flashed a quick look at Siddiqi before answering. 'No problems. Most speak Gujarati, understand some English but also I speak others if we need.' His English was accurate but several degrees of competence below that of Siddiqi.

'Okay, that's fine.' He turned to Phil. 'Ready for a take, Phil?'

'Ready as I'm going to be,' Phil grumbled.

'No countdown. Start on MCU. In the unlikely event we get a moment I'll leave the CU's to you.' He turned back to the interpreter. 'Right, Jamal, ask the lady to tell us something about herself.'

There was a brief conversation between them, then the woman composed herself and began a measured response. She was looking up at the ceiling, then down to the floor and frowning in concentration, now and then hesitating for a moment before continuing. When she finished Jamal began the translation, stopping now and then to check his accuracy with her.

'I am twenty-seven years old. I am a married woman but my husband is not with me. I have six children, four have lived; one of them is a girl who has been kept. My parents came from Kathiawar in 1948 after the partition and the formation of the Islamic Republic of Pakistan by the beloved Muhammad Ali Jinnah, may Allah reward him. We are poor. My family heard of the people who were offering money for women like me so they sent me to the clinic. Now we have been paid the money and my family is pleased. That is why I am here.' Jamal looked apologetically at Joe. 'That is what she says,' he concluded.

'Thank you, Jamal, and thank the lady for me,' Joe said blandly. He exchanged a look with Phil, who flicked off the camera and stood back to see what Joe would do now.

Joe walked over to Siddiqi, his face serious with concern. 'I have a problem,' he said.

Siddiqi looked enquiring. 'The woman is not suitable?'

'The woman has learned her speech well, she has obviously been rehearsed, but that's no use to me. In fact I only filmed this meeting to prove to you that no-one watching it will ever believe what she's saying, even though it's undoubtedly true. They will think it's a set-up, you know what I mean by a set-up?' Siddiqi nodded abruptly, as if this was a ludicrous question. Joe continued, 'they will think she's an actress playing a part and, to be truthful, not a very good actress.'

Siddiqi shrugged 'She is just a poor woman, she has done her best for you.'

'I know, and I thank her and you for arranging this meeting but I need to make this film in a different way.'

'What do you propose?'

'We need more freedom. We can't make the entire film in this hotel. We need to visit these women in their own homes, meet their family, shoot footage of their neighbourhood, see how they live so we can show visually why they made the decision to join the Two+One project and see how they have benefited from it. We need to visit the clinics and talk to the doctors; we need what we film to be seen to be real. I am sure the World Health Organisation and the United Nations would be very grateful to you if you could help me make a film that is more interesting and professional.'

There was a silence. Siddiqi was very still.

'Of course we would be very happy for you or Jamal or Waseem to be with us while we film, perhaps just at a discreet distance. That would help us enormously,' Joe continued.

Siddiqi shook his head. 'You ask a lot, Mr Kendry. I have explained the risks to you.'

'We will sign a disclaimer,' Joe pleaded, 'any risk will then be on our heads.'

'You may take the risk but I would take the blame,' Siddiqi said. He paused. 'Even so, I will think about it. But I promise nothing.'

'Thank you, Syed, I am very grateful.'

'Yeah, me too,' Phil said.

Joe hoped that, despite his language skills, Siddiqi was not quite so familiar with the concept of sarcasm.

49

Charles and Alex met Donald Costello in a small wood-panelled coffee bar on the first floor of an elegant listed building a short walk from the American Embassy in Grosvenor Square. Charles introduced Alex and ordered for them, leading the way to a table in a corner. It was obvious from the outset that Costello had picked up on Charles's discomposure.

'Well, Charlie, do we wait for the coffee or do you tell me straight out?'

'It's not good news but I have no reason to suppose it will have any impact on your interests,' Charles began.

'I have many interests,' Costello responded, 'and most everything that happens in the world impacts on one or another of them. I assume it has something to do with our journalist friend.'

Charles nodded. 'She's gone missing somewhere in the South Island of New Zealand.'

Costello was stone-faced. 'When?' he asked.

'We had a message from the boys in Wellington in the early hours this morning.'

'So the Kiwis fucked up.'

'They blame the weather; fog in Auckland, storm in Wellington, so the flight was re-directed twice at the last minute and eventually landed at Christchurch. It's obvious that was her final destination anyway because she hasn't re-booked.'

'So how much confidence do we have that these guys will ever track her down?'

The coffee arrived and was ignored. 'They're usually pretty reliable,' Charles said when the barista had departed, 'but I've sent Wenna over there to keep an eye on things.'

Costello looked away, deep in thought. Then he said: 'Anything I can do?'

'Not at the moment. I'm sure Wenna will have them on their toes. I'll keep you in the loop,' Charles replied.

Costello drank his coffee in one go and replaced the cup with an appreciative nod. 'Columbian I suspect, one of their more innocent exports.' He stood up, ready to leave. 'Chances like this don't happen very often, do they, Charlie?' he said, leaning forward over the table. 'We really wouldn't want to miss this opportunity to offer whoever she's meeting our hospitality.'

'Even if we miss out on him we'll still be able to debrief her when she gets back,' Charles responded. Even to him that sounded like a very poor substitute.

'Sure we've got her but we want him, don't we, Charlie. Look, I have to get back and babysit a President. Thanks for sharing. I'll be in touch.'

Costello left a thoughtful silence behind him. 'Considering this has nothing to do with the Presidential visit so far as we know, Mr Costello seems very interested,' Alex commented.

'And that,' Charles replied, 'is something we should be very aware of.'

'You think he might take a closer interest than we would want?'

'The thought that a high-ranking enemy might slip through our fingers will exercise him considerably, you can be sure of that.'

'How exactly do we handle that situation?' Alex asked.

'With extreme care.' Charles paused. 'Alex, there's a little something I want you to do for me. You do keep in touch with old friends, don't you?'

50

Wenna arrived at Auckland airport and was met by a grim-faced Callum West, who saw her through the formalities and escorted her to the privacy of the airport security office where he faced up to the embarrassing task of telling her they had lost Fleur Nichols.

'No excuses really,' he concluded, 'Southern missed her by about ten minutes.'

Wenna was tired and jet-lagged and this was the last news she wanted to hear. 'Does London know?' she asked.

'Yes, we contacted them straight away.'

'This makes things very difficult, we can't get the police involved,' Wenna pointed out.

'I appreciate that. I did wonder if there is anything else you could tell us that might help locate her.'

'Not really. We had her monitored but the other side made all the travel and contact arrangements and their tradecraft is pretty good.'

'Okay. We have a team working on it in Christchurch so perhaps we should base ourselves there.'

'Certainly. What approach are they taking?'

'Well, she must have the use of a car because public transport in the South Island is virtually non-existent and unless this is a fast turnaround meeting she'll have to stay somewhere, so we're working our way through taxis, car rentals and accommodation lists. I'm sure you have a good relationship with your banks, so if she uses a credit card we'll know.'

'But if she's being driven by someone else, using cash and is booked in under a false name, what then?'

Callum was a personable and successful young man, used to the interested attention of women, and a degree of respect from his colleagues. He had liked the look of Wenna Cavendish when he first saw her; she had seemed like his idea of a typical English rose and while he was well aware that some criticism of his office was due, he felt she could have been a little more collegial and understanding. A little personal warmth would not have gone amiss either.

'Then we caucus and try another tack.'

'We may not have time. There's no way this man will want to remain in one place for a minute longer than he has to.'

'If you have ideas, please share them,' Callum said coolly.

'Have you had any interesting arrivals in New Zealand lately?'

'We're not a major destination for international terrorists,' Callum replied blandly. 'We're more often the target of illegal immigrants who travel on false passports then destroy them on arrival and claim to be refugees. However, it wouldn't be too difficult to infiltrate this country. New Zealand passports command a high price but if you can afford it they can be bought on the international market. They're either genuine but issued in a false name, genuine but stolen and altered, or good enough fakes to pass. So the answer is, if we knew our man's name and he travelled on his own passport, no problem, but since we don't and he probably has a choice of passports then we'd be wasting our time pursuing that avenue.'

Wenna was looking at him closely, as if doubting what he was saying. But then she nodded acceptance, fished out her Ctab and switched it on. Predictably the screen offered a brief message from Alex confirming he knew they had lost Fleur and telling her that the Cousins were not impressed, warning her to keep one eye open for friendly but unwanted and possibly over-eager co-operation. He also told her that Joe Kendry was in Pakistan and sending a diary of his activities back to his Hub in Fleur's apartment but so far there was nothing to suggest a connection with Fleur's meeting. He told her they had arranged a night owl so she could call any time of the day or night, and wished her good luck. And I'm going to need it, she thought.

Callum West watched her as she pocketed her Ctab, her face clouded with thought. 'Anything that helps us?' he asked.

'Er… Sorry. Nothing,' she replied.

I do hope she's not going to play this too close to that distracting chest of hers, Callum thought, we're supposed to be in this together. But what he said was: 'Then I'll book us flights to Christchurch.'

51

In Karachi, after their abortive first attempt at an interview, Joe and Phil retired to Joe's hotel room to consider their next move. By unspoken agreement they were silent until the door was firmly closed behind them, then Phil, who had struggled throughout to keep his opinions to himself, could contain himself no longer.

'He won't do it Joe. We're not welcome here and he certainly don't want us running about the place on our own. He'll just stuff us around until we run out of budget.'

Joe, sprawled in a chair, nodded slowly. 'Could be.'

'We're talking to the wrong people, we need to get in on the ground floor, like.'

'Meaning what, exactly?'

'It's like this. Even if your mate Syed lets us out of this prison, he'll have us watched like a hawk. These women aren't goin' to talk to us proper with him or his goons about, are they?'

'No way.'

'So I reckon it's time for me to pull a sneaky one.'

'Like?'

'What happens is, later on, I do a Harry Creepers down the back stairs and chat up the night porter, pretend I want a bit of nightlife without my business partner knowing. I've got half a bottle of Johnny Walker in me bin, bet that does the trick.'

'Phil, if there are any risks to be taken on this job, I'm the one who takes them, not you.'

'Wouldn't work, Joe. I'm a peasant, you're not, I'd fit in downstairs, they'd talk to me, tell me what we want to know. You'd stick out like a whore's tits. I take the Palmcam, have a butcher's round the neighbourhood, see what I can find out and come back in the way I went out. Dead easy.'

'I didn't know you spoke Gujarati,' Joe said pointedly.

'Most everyone in this hotel speaks some English. I'd get by.'

'If Syed found out, we'd be on the next plane. It wouldn't be the first time a hotel porter was on the payroll of the Security Services.'

'Worst case, you plead shock, horror, surely not and all that stuff and send me home. You stay on and shoot it yourself. Way things are looking you hardly need me anyway.'

'I don't know.'

'You're the boss, Joe, but I'm going anyway because we're both only as good as the last job we did and if we come back from this with our tails between our legs it's my arse on the line as well as yours.'

'This makes me very uncomfortable,' Joe said slowly.

'You've had the willies ever since we got here and I think you're right. There's a story out there and we're being kept away from it. Why, that's what I want to know, and so do you. And we're never going to find out sat on our fat arses in our hotel rooms, are we?'

'You can be so eloquent at times, Phil.'

'That's a yes then.'

52

Fleur took breakfast in her room and then had a leisurely shower. Given the business at hand she deliberately applied conservative makeup and as she did so, mulled over what to wear. Something discreet without being an obvious concession to Islamic dress codes she thought, but in fact her options were relatively few, given that she was travelling light. In the end, after consulting the weather out of her window, she settled for a lightweight trouser suit and high-necked white blouse, business-like but cool, and low-heeled shoes. After further consideration she abandoned the idea of taking her handbag; he might view that with suspicion and she wanted him at his most relaxed. She did however decide she would take her Ctab. Even switched off it would be a comfort to have it with her; there was a picture of Joe on the screen.

Then there was nothing to do but wait. Restless, she wandered about the room and, spurred by idleness, toyed with the temptation of her Ctab. She had left it switched off according to the agreement she'd made in London and because she was certain that contact would be made direct at the hotel. Would they know her number? They seemed to know a lot else, including the name on her passport, so why not that? What harm would it do to switch it on, just in case? She hesitated, very well aware that succumbing to the temptation would be unprofessional and knowing what was behind it.

It was Joe. The thought that, despite their agreement, he might have called and left a message. If he had, at least she would know he was safe. It would clear her mind for the meeting to come.

She took the Ctab and walked over to the window. It was a beautiful day with just a few puffball clouds decorating a clear blue sky. A light breeze was playing with the flags on the golf course and the drooping willows along the riverbank. In the distance, beyond the river, the irregular humps of the folded mountains sat stolid and unmoving, as if impervious to the tide of time. The colours were distinctive, a melody of grey, brown and greens overseen by the rich blue of the sky.

Already there were a couple of golfers testing the course and a ride-on mower was bumbling about between the trees in the landscaped slopes leading down from the golf course to the river.

Tranquil, Fleur thought, that's the word to describe it. Maybe one day, if they were ever wealthy enough, she could come here with Joe.

She switched her Ctab on and off again immediately as the room Hub rang.

'Yes?' she said, deliberately holding her voice steady.

'I thought we would meet at the third hole,' the man said in carefully enunciated English with a strong hint of a Middle Eastern accent. The voice was deep, resonant and confident, that of a man used to public speaking.

'Of course,' Fleur replied.

'You will know me,' he said. 'I will be not playing golf.'

The phone went dead. Well now, Fleur thought, a terrorist with a sense of humour.

53

Joe found the waiting intolerable. Two and a half hours had passed since Phil had left, warning him, unaware that he was quoting, that he 'may be some time'. The most appalling thought was that if anything had gone wrong and Phil was in trouble, he simply wouldn't know until Syed came to confront him and order him out of the country. If anything serious had happened to Phil he'd never be able to face Alma or Fleur again. He should never have let him go, the blame was entirely his. He had the executive authority and had failed to employ it; now, he was increasingly sure, there would be a price to pay.

Time moved with painful slowness, ticking on towards the third hour since Phil had set out. Panic was setting in. Suppose Phil was lying in a Karachi gutter, bleeding his life away. At what point should he bite the bullet and inform Syed that Phil was missing? He took out the card that Siddiqi had given him and placed it beside the room Hub set. He didn't even know if Phil had his Ctab with him, he hadn't thought to ask.

Then, when his nerves were almost at breaking point, the bedroom door eased open and Phil edged in, turning his back to close it quietly behind him.

'Where the hell have you been?' Joe demanded furiously.

Phil grinned at him. 'Knock it off,' he said, 'you'll wake the neighbours.'

'I've been going mad here.'

'Relax, me old mate, have I got news for you,'

Joe held up his hands and took a deep breath, forcing himself to relax. 'Okay, start from the beginning and give me chapter and verse,' he ordered.

Phil dropped into a chair and put his camera down beside him, grinning from ear to ear. 'Okay, it's like I told you, we peasants understand each other. We may not speak the same language but we speak the same language, know what I mean? Farooq and me,' he held up his hand with the first two fingers entwined, 'like that mate. Anytime we want out of here, we're in business.'

'Farooq being the night porter?'

'Right.'

'So we can only get out when he's on duty.'

'I wouldn't have chanced it with the day boys, they're much more likely to be in Syed's pocket. Besides, half a bottle of JW only goes so far. What's the matter, you think I should've scored us the freedom of the city or something?'

Joe held up a placatory hand. 'Sorry, Phil, you've done brilliantly. So you palled up with Farooq, then what?'

'Well, we had a bit of a Pidgin English gossip, him and me, and I reckon I know why our mate Syed doesn't want us let loose. No wonder the locals've turned against the Two+One project. There's this rumour going about that it's killing people.'

'What! That's ridiculous!'

'Seems there's been a lot of unexplained deaths in the last few months, specially men, and Two+One's getting the blame. Farooq reckoned it's got to the point some men won't sleep with women who were in the scheme in case they get infected.'

'Has this got to the authorities yet, are they doing anything?'

'That's what Farooq was grizzling about. He reckons it got to the media but was closed down pretty quick, the official line is that it's extremist propaganda, they blame the deaths on natural causes,' Phil replied.

Joe looked thoughtful. 'Which could be the case, especially if you include avian or swine flu as natural causes; this is a TW zone after all. You should never underestimate the power of rumour though. I wonder why Bill Mathews said nothing about this, he must be aware of it. And probably Rose Petchak knows as well. '

'I reckon we was supposed to come here, shoot what we were told, take what we were given and be sent home none the wiser. Then they'd use our film to combat the rumour when it got out.'

'You may be right, Phil. But it isn't going to be like that.'

'Hang on. There's more. I got into one of the clinics.'

Joe stared at him. 'You got into a Two+One clinic in the middle of the night? How come?'

'Simple. Asked Farooq where the nearest one was, just dropped it into the conversation casual like, then wandered down to have a look. It was a bit of a trot but I kept me hood up and head down. The clinics are open twenty-four seven, most of them anyway. Seems a lot of the women don't want to come in during the day. You know what, soon as you get away from the hotel district this place smells a whole lot different I can tell you. Bloody whiffy. Anyway, I got some good background stuff plus, get this, an establishing shot of the clinic inside and out.'

'You're a genius, Phil. Didn't anyone in the clinic ask you who you were?'

'Yeah. Met this young Aussie doctor, nice bloke. Told him we was a documentary unit working for the UN and I was researching background. Thought I'd better level with him 'cause we might want to go back.'

'Damn right we will. Did he know about the rumours?'

'Not half. The place was empty when I was there and he reckoned trade's down a whole heap since the rumours started. He blames the Mullahs, they was always dead against it.'

'Didn't he ask why you were doing research in the middle of the night?'

'It was only half eleven for God's sake and I reckon he was glad of someone to talk to.'

'What did he think about the deaths, natural causes?'

'His opinion, the authorities got a big problem. He reckons the death count is up all right but it's more likely a new strain of virus. And it's being sat on at top level because Roflu isn't working and there's no new vaccine. Just his opinion, mind.'

'Phil, whether he's right or wrong, we've got to get this doctor on film.'

'Funny, thought you'd say that. Didn't want to flash the camera about too much at the time in case it stopped him talking.'

'Good. But we have to play this carefully, let Syed think we're playing along with him. I'll send what we've got back to my Hub, just in case we're stopped and our camera's confiscated.'

'What about Rose Petchek?'

Joe smiled grimly. 'Oh, I don't think we need trouble her with bad news just yet, do you, Phil?'

Phil yawned widely. 'I wouldn't trouble her with a ten-foot barge pole, mate,' he said. 'I'm off. Past my bedtime.'

54

Auriol was asleep in the armchair in front of the fire in the sitting room, exhausted by her chronic stress. Her chin had dropped onto her chest; her arms were hanging loose beside the chair and her legs had fallen apart, tightening her skirt across her thighs. She was, Simone observed, relaxed to the point of inelegance.

The question was, should she wake her and suggest they go to bed or leave her in peace for a little longer and take a chance on her being able to get to sleep again later. It was a simple enough problem and one that in normal times Simone would have resolved with an instant decision; now it seemed impossibly difficult. She felt a wash of regret for a decisiveness that she seemed to have lost; she had always been a natural problem solver, which had been an essential part of her life's work. Work that was now rapidly approaching its premature end.

And what had it been worth, this life of scholarship and unrelenting work, what value could she put on it after all those years of endeavour? No high value that was for sure. Her mind jumped from one loosely connected thought to another. She had been, barely still was, at the forefront of the worldwide race to control our minute toxic enemies, but as she had told Joe Kendry, it was a race that might never be won.

Why should she, with her damaged body and increasingly failing senses, waste what was left of her life combating an enemy that had no ethics, no concept of conservation and which would continue to mutate and prey on human life to the point of mutual extinction. That may well be, she considered, what the future held.

From the pragmatic, non-ethical, scientific standpoint there was a simple Malthusian response; reduce the availability of potential hosts.

Her mind wandered on, pursuing the line of thought. It had worked in an involuntary way in medieval times with the Black Death and many other epidemics that historically had kept human numbers in check: the viruses had had an explosive effect, then faded away to relative obscurity. Now we had vaccines, new era antibiotics, phages, so any such reduction would have to be deliberate policy. Politically and ethically inconceivable of course, but could we afford ethics when the enemy accepted none? Perhaps the existence of ethics in human society could be its greatest and ultimately fatal weakness. Yet what was the point of a human society without ethical standards, it would tear itself apart. Which is what it was doing anyway, ethics or no, by breeding beyond the support capacity of the planet.

So had that annoying little documentary maker been right? Had she made the problem worse by saving lives, was her work doing nothing more than helping to overpopulate the planet? Well, if that was true, there was nothing she could do about it, she didn't own her work, the company did. They and they alone dictated the use it was put to and they were driven by a profit motive that paid only lip service to ethics and gave no consideration to a macro, holistic view of human existence. But in a sane world should not she, the mother of her creations, have some say over the ultimate use her work was put to? And if she did, what would she say?

Simone's mind slowed to a halt and left her back in the reality of her living room with Auriol sprawled in the chair opposite her. She wondered if she had been making any sense, or if her previously incisive and coherent intellect was already beginning to fail. That she was still capable of criticising her own thinking at least gave her hope.

Immersed in her thoughts, she had for a short while been able to ignore the increasing pain and distant nausea. The chair creaked as she shifted to a more comfortable position and the noise disturbed Auriol, who came to slowly, covering a yawn with her hand.

'I was dreaming about you,' she said.

Simone found a smile for her. 'Happy dreams I hope,' she said.

'Yes. Have you been asleep?'

'No.'

'What have you been thinking about?'

'Nothing much. Just the nature and purpose of human existence, the future of humankind, you know.'

Auriol stretched and straightened herself in her chair. 'Oh, that's good then,' she said drowsily. 'Have you taken your pills?'

55

Fleur made her way unhurriedly through the Lodge foyer and out into the grounds, heading for the golf course. As she walked, she mentally composed herself, knowing she would have to be intellectually alert for the confrontation to come. The paved and edged path she was taking led through an area landscaped with young trees and shrubs and emerged to skirt the open edge of the course, winding along a ridge that gave a spectacular view of the river basin below.

In the distance to her right was the golf clubhouse and pro shop and ahead the third tee, evidently chosen as the location for the meeting because the path led conveniently right by it. The course was thinly populated and a golf cart had just left the third hole carrying away its cargo of brightly dressed players. Then she saw him. He was standing on the path with his back to the course, facing towards the river, watching the lawn mower wend its way between the trees and out of sight.

As she drew closer she was faintly surprised by his appearance. He was light-skinned; she thought ethnically Arab; short but heavily built and perhaps sixty years of age. He was clean-shaven, expensively dressed and immaculately presented and, had she not known better, Fleur would have taken him for a wealthy international businessman. Which, in one aspect of his life, perhaps he was. For now she was sure this beardless, Western façade had been selected for the purposes of this meeting and to match whatever passport he was using. He turned to greet her as she approached him, his look guarded but not unwelcoming. He did not offer his hand.

'Good morning,' he said evenly, 'I am Salah al-Rashidi.'

He did not have to say anymore, she knew exactly who he was, and the reason for the extreme caution surrounding this meeting became instantly clear. He was widely thought to be the latest Head of Operations for AQE and she had seen photographs of him furnished to the press by the CIA, taken from old video footage, but he had looked nothing like this; it seemed to her that the Arab dress and Islamic beard had been his disguise and this was the real man. It crossed her mind that it was a deliberate sign of good intentions that he had given the name by which he was internationally known and internationally hunted, whether or not it was genuine.

'And I'm sure you know who I am,' Fleur said calmly. Now the moment had come, any remnant nerves had fled and she was coldly professional.

'I do,' he replied. 'So. I think we have the preliminaries over with. I have information for you of the highest importance and I wish you to make it known to the world through the BBC. I know you can do that.'

'Perhaps I can but, forgive me for being sceptical, why me and why the BBC? You've used your own media outlets successfully in the past.' She knew the answer of course but she wanted to put the first question.

High above them a hawk circled, riding a thermal, head jutted forward, watchful and ever predatory, wings adjusting now and then to the occasional cross current. Fleur looked up uneasily, sensing eyes on her. There's nothing for you here, she thought. She didn't register the tiny dragonfly hovering over the tee behind them, its underside mottled blue and white, a perfect camouflage against the backdrop of the sky.

'When you hear what I have to tell you,' al-Rashidi said, 'you will understand. If the information is seen to come from those sources, no-one in the West will believe it, and it is important they do.'

'And why me?' Fleur asked.

There was a nervous flicker in al-Rashidi's left cheek and he made occasional involuntary movements, changing the position of his feet, twisting his torso slightly, and looking quickly left and right as he spoke before returning his attention to her face.

'You were recommended because you have shown in the past that you understand, have some sympathy for, the problems of the Muslim world,' he said, 'and because you have an open mind. Also you have the necessary media contacts to ensure this story is told.'

'Some people have accused me in the past of being a sympathiser. I warn you, it's not true, I'm Western neutral.'

'Even so, all that matters to me is that you will listen without prejudice and you can get the story into the international media through a credible source like the BBC.'

'Suppose I had refused this meeting?

'Then the BBC would have sent you to Afghanistan. We would have met there. That was a backup arrangement but it was much more dangerous for both of us. Too many informants, too many drones.'

So far so good, he was being remarkably forthright and was sparing her the extremist rhetoric he had commonly used in the past, quite rightly understanding that that would only serve to alienate her. 'They and I will need to be absolutely convinced before I do anything,' she said.

'I will convince you. To begin, why do you think I have taken the risk of coming here if not to reassure you? We were well aware that you would not listen otherwise.'

'Very well, but from my point of view this might still be a disinformation exercise,' Fleur pointed out.

'You must judge,' al-Rashidi said, apparently unconcerned. 'You must trust me or not when you have heard everything.'

An electric golf cart pulled up behind them and disgorged four enthusiastic Asian players who entered into an animated discussion before lining up their first shot.

'Shall we walk?' he suggested.

***

On the far bank of the river a wide-bodied four-wheel drive was parked on the edge of the gravel foreshore between two old man willows. A fly fishing rod was leaning against one of the trees and a chilly-bin sat beside a pup tent, suggesting an overnight stay.

The driver, dressed in unremarkable neutral colours that blended into the background, was seated under one of the willows, back to its trunk, seeming to scour the water with a dull-coated monocular. The monocular had a number of functions including a massive zoom and a communications app that, courtesy of the dragonfly, was presently showing a perfect overhead shot of the third tee and the meeting taking place there. The driver zoomed in on the couple standing beside the golf course, then went to a close-up of the man and sent the video image by SatLink to the National Reconnaissance Office, half a world away. There the full facial hair evident on all other images of him held on file was removed by computerised reconstruction and a further comparison made. There was a delay before it came back identified positive.

When al-Rashidi was joined by the woman the same process was repeated but she came back negative wanted, but on file. The file downloaded and identified her. She was a journalist, possible sympathiser. Well, that figured, the operative thought. What the hell, they had identified and located Salah al-Rashidi, which was all that mattered. The equipment had audio capacity but at this range it could only pick up a muted mumble.

Then al-Rashidi and the woman moved off the ridge, slightly down slope and into the trees and, even from above, were temporarily out of sight.

***

'I think it's time you told me your story,' Fleur suggested.

He was leaning against a tree, facing back up the slope, from which position he could keep an eye on the path they had just left and the golfers behind. 'Suppose,' he said, 'I told you that I have evidence that the CIA has mounted a murderous campaign against the Muslim world?'

'The CIA?'

'Americans, who else but CIA?'

'This murderous campaign, are you talking about what they call the War on Terror?'

'No. This is something new.'

'My first reaction is I haven't come halfway round the world to listen to propaganda.'

Al-Rashidi's face tightened in anger. 'This is real, and I will prove it. We had a source inside the American Security Services, may Allah grant him peace...'

'He's dead?'

'A martyr, yes. They caught him and killed him.'

'In general, the Americans tend to put traitors and spies on trial, not kill them out of hand,' Fleur said.

'They killed him. Fake auto accident,' al-Rashidi said emphatically.

Fleur shook her head uncertainly but she was well aware that in the world this man inhabited there was little that was impossible. 'Presumably he told you something before he died,' she prompted.

'He was an IT expert, a specialist in computerised anti-surveillance. They employed him to clean rooms where very secret meetings were held. He did this but put in equipment of his own. That is how he had a record of the meeting where this satanic plot was discussed.'

'And what is this plot exactly?'

'You know of the Two+One project?'

Fleur stiffened. 'I do.'

'It was the Americans who sold the idea to the United Nations, they wanted to reduce the world Muslim population by sterilising our women.'

'Or to reduce poverty and deprivation in the Third World, depending on your viewpoint,' Fleur put in.

Al-Rashidi ignored her interruption. 'But our people are wise to that foul plot and very few have taken their blood money, so the Devils came up with another scheme. They have had a genetically altered virus created. It is contained within a substance that is almost the same as the birth control linctus. They have mixed up the two so no one can tell the difference. Now those few women who take Two+One will contaminate any man who lies with them and eventually the men die.'

Fleur's mind was whirling. 'Just a minute, doesn't it kill the women?'

'Eventually it will, I'm sure, but now it is mostly the men who are dying.'

'So you're saying that this virus is somehow active against the Y chromosome?'

'Maybe. Maybe not. Women have died also. Maybe it just takes longer to kill women. I am not a scientist. We need to obtain a sample and test it.'

'Why haven't you done that?'

'We have samples but no facilities for sophisticated tests or autopsies. You can do that and add it to your proof.'

'And how did the CIA manage to create their own virus and contaminate the drug without anyone noticing?'

'Exactly, we do not yet know, but it is possible the laboratory they use is in England.'

'This is crazy,' Fleur said, 'you're talking about an international conspiracy to commit genocide. They'd never get away with it.'

'They have. It is already started.'

'If large numbers of people were dying then we'd know about it, it would be all over the international media.'

'They are not stupid. They know that, so the apostate authorities say it is a new sort of bird flu and they keep it quiet to stop any panic. Meantime, people die.'

'But all you have to do is tell your people not to take the birth control and this alleged plot will fail.'

Salah sighed. 'Do you know how many millions of Muslims there are in the world? How many languages they speak? How few have access to radio or television, let alone computers? I tell you, maybe twenty-five percent. We cannot reach them all in time. Many are desperately poor and will take the risk for the sake of the money, they believe the American lies. We need this to be stopped at once.'

'If this virus exists, it certainly does need to be stopped but I have to tell you, I'm having trouble believing a word of this.'

***

In the pup tent across the river the sniper assembled her rifle of choice. It was a Barrett M107 .50 calibre with a range of nearly two kilometres. It was fitted with a state of the art silencer and a scope sight with a laser tracker.

Her movements were quick and efficient; this opportunity might not occur again and she had a reputation, honed in Afghanistan and Iraq and Somalia, of which she was quietly proud.

Now and then she glanced at the monocular to confirm the target had not moved and, as she worked, she repeated a Buddhist mantra to calm her nerves, relax her muscles and slow her breathing.

With the rifle assembled she placed it in a fishing rod cover for the few steps to the willow tree. She climbed quickly and athletically, securing herself a well-camouflaged position that also provided a good view of the Lodge grounds.

She looked through the monocular but the dragonfly showed that the target was still behind the tree where he had taken up position a few minutes earlier, so she put the monocular aside and used the rifle scope, continuing her breathing exercises whilst zeroing in the weapon. She knew she would only get one shot but then, that was all she ever needed.

***

'You must realise how crazy the whole thing sounds to me,' Fleur said. 'I'm sure you believe every word you say, and I'm no fan of the CIA, but for me to go public with something so bizarre, well, I'd have to have proof that stacked up one hundred percent.'

Al-Rashidi reached into his trouser pocket and handed over a ladies watch. 'This will not tell the time; in here is a cache button. On it there is a visual record of the meeting where the plot was discussed,' he said. 'There are faces on it that can be identified. There is also an interview with me, a record of everything I have told you with numbers of dead and interviews with some of those who have suffered.'

Fleur turned the watch over in her hand, then strapped it on her wrist, thinking hard. 'If your man is dead, how did you come by the information?' she asked.

'He was able to deliver it before they found out about him. He sent it to us by disposable Ctab, then he destroyed it, but he was too late, they suspected him and they killed him.'

'Perhaps, but a hell of a lot of people get killed in the US every year in auto accidents. Can you prove they murdered him?'

'No. But it is a convenience for them, is it not?'

Fleur let out a long breath. If there was even a shred of truth in this it was the story of the century but maybe that's all it was, a story. 'Let's look at what we've got,' she said slowly. 'An informant who is dead, a record of a meeting which, given the state of computer technology today could easily be faked, and staged interviews with some of your own people. It won't stand up. Sorry.'

The tic on al-Rashidi's cheek had become worse and his voice had become harsher. 'You haven't seen the evidence on the button.'

'You've told me what's on it and it's not enough.'

'You are a freelance journalist yes, you investigate things. Investigate this, take a sample of the linctus and have it analysed, go to these countries and talk to people, isn't that how you do your work?'

'To get the BBC to fund an investigation of that size I'd have to have a lot more evidence beforehand and if you funded it, well, it would seem like propaganda.'

Al-Rashidi's whole body stiffened. He forced himself upright, away from the tree and focussed his gaze on her. 'What do you want, what would it take to convince you?'

'Get a sample of the linctus analysed then come back to me. I'm sure you can arrange that if you had to. Money buys anything. If it's been altered, then I'll go to the BBC for funding.'

Al-Rashidi shook his head. 'We do that, and then there will be something else. They will say we altered it. They will find scientists to disagree, you know what will happen. Time will pass and nothing will be done.' He looked away, his face grim. 'So, it seems I will join the great band of martyrs.'

'What does that mean?' Fleur asked, at a complete loss.

'I will give myself up into your custody. At the offices of the BBC. You can interview me, show the button cache, then hand me over to the British authorities.'

Fleur stared at him in utter astonishment. 'Are you serious?' she demanded.

'I am. I can be replaced. And what is my life worth when my people all over the Muslim world are dying of this foul disease every day?'

A sudden coldness struck at Fleur's heart. Just looking at him she could tell this man was deadly serious. The fact that he was prepared to sacrifice himself was not evidence of the truth of what he was saying but regardless, he was offering the scoop of a lifetime, for her and for the British Security Services.

But what did any of that matter, because if there was any truth at all in what he said, then Joe was at great risk. She simply could not take that chance.

'You have gone pale,' Salah said, a certain satisfaction in his voice. 'Do you believe me now?'

Fleur took out her Ctab and showed it to him. 'Do you have a family?' she asked.

Al-Rashidi shook his head. 'That is not relevant.'

'My man, my partner, is in Pakistan right now,' she said, 'he's making a documentary on the Two+One project for the United Nations. I'm sure he can get us a sample of the linctus. If he confirms what you say about the unusual number of deaths, then I'll accept your offer to give yourself up and you have my word it will be a truly explosive story. You'll get all the exposure you want.'

Al-Rashidi hesitated. 'He knows you are here?'

'He knows I'm in New Zealand, not who I'm meeting or why. And I won't tell him.' There was a small white lie hidden in there, but a necessary one.

Al-Rashidi gave a grim smile. 'A trusting man, then, to ask no questions.'

'Yes, he trusts me, and so should you.'

He looked at his watch and mentally calculated the time difference. 'Very well then. If you can wake him up.'

Fleur, heart thumping with fear, walked clear of the trees, back up towards to path, unconsciously wanting to put distance between the two of them. She had lied about her reasons for the call; securing an exclusive face-to-face interview with Salah al-Rashidi in the hallowed halls of the BBC was incentive enough to co-operate with him, the truth or otherwise of his extraordinary allegations would come out later. For now she simply had to get Joe out of Pakistan.

Al-Rashidi followed her up the slope, a few paces behind her, as if he were reluctant to let her out of earshot. Fleur reached the path, quickly checked there were no golfers nearby and turned away from him, cupping her face with her free hand as she flicked on her Ctab and auto-dialled Joe's number.

Al-Rashidi stopped and waited, focussed totally on the woman in whom he had just placed such trust.

***

On her miniature screen on the monocular the sniper watched with cool satisfaction as the woman emerged from the shelter of the trees and walked up towards the path, followed by the target. The shot would be angled upwards against a background of clear sky above the path. She put down the monocular and eased the butt of the rifle back into her shoulder, switched off the laser beam for fear he would notice the tell-tale red spot before she had him locked in her sights and double checked the range and wind deflection. It never paid to hurry these preparations.

The woman had stopped on the path and, unless either of them moved, was in the line of fire behind the target. Perhaps she would get lucky; if not, well, that was the fortune of war. Al-Rashidi was walking slowly up the slope towards the woman, presenting a clear opportunity for a body shot. But the sniper was a perfectionist and she waited. He stopped, seeming to be listening to the woman. The sniper breathed out and held her breath, ensuring the rifle remained motionless in her hands. She switched on the laser tracker, noted its position on the nape of Salah's neck, moved it up a fraction, and then gently squeezed the trigger.

The large calibre, high-velocity bullet struck Salah al-Rashidi squarely on the back of his head with enough force to stop a rhinoceros, smashing through his skull and exiting through his forehead above his left eye socket. The bullet passed on in a fraction of a second to splatter Fleur's suit with Rashidi's blood and tissue and strike her left temporal lobe, dropping them both to the ground like abandoned rag dolls. Unimpeded, the projectile finally buried itself a second or two later in a barren mountainside over a kilometre away. The only sound had been the faint whine of the projectile's passage and the insignificant thump of the two bodies falling to the ground. There was no one close enough to hear.

Beyond the river the sniper left the tree that had concealed her within seconds of taking the shot. She had no need to check to see if Al-Rashidi was dead, a professional knows instinctively when they have done their work well. He was number 127 in her tally. She strode quickly to the pup tent, recalled the dragonfly, stripped the rifle and bundled it up in a sports bag, dismantled the tent and fly rod and stacked the lot in the back of the four-wheel drive. In less than two minutes she had left the scene and was on her way back to Christchurch.

56

'Where is Wenna?' was Charles Lovatt's first question when Alex Jones entered his office.

'She's in the SIS office in Christchurch, giving them a good grilling I imagine.'

'They bloody well deserve it.' Charles said grimly. 'What else?'

'Well, I'm rather puzzled by the latest episode of Joe Kendry's diary.'

'What's he up to now?'

'It seems that despite being under virtual house arrest, he's ended up investigating an allegation that people are dying in Pakistan because of a contamination of the UN's Two+One viral contraceptive.'

'Just a minute, that sounds very much like the story the BBC were going to send Fleur Nichols to Afghanistan to report on,' Charles put in.

'Yes, it does. And I get the impression Joe thinks he's on the trail of some nefarious right wing CIA plot. Which of course would please him enormously.'

'So, she was going to Afghanistan, he's next door in Pakistan and both would have ended up covering the same story. Do we think this is coincidence?' Charles asked thoughtfully.

'Seems unlikely.'

Charles brooded for a moment. 'If there is a connection, then Joe and Fleur don't know about it or we'd have picked that up on the intercept.'

'Unless they're both a lot cleverer than we gave them credit for.' Alex did not sound convinced by his own suggestion.

'In which case they are both players in the great game, which seems unlikely. Coincidence is actually beginning to look like an option.'

'Except...'

'Precisely. Except that neither of us believe in fairies. The question is, what connection, if any, might there be between the contamination stories in Afghanistan and Pakistan and Fleur's sudden flight to meet the enemy in New Zealand?'

'Probably unknowable at the present time.'

'Unfortunately true. For the moment it seems to be a case of wait and see. I think we both smell ratty here.'

'Indeed.'

'Better let Wenna in on this guessing game.'

'Will do.'

'And put one of your people on nights pro tem.'

'Already done.'

Charles declined to commend Alex's diligence. 'Anything else? That little job I asked you to do for me, for example?''

Alex looked slightly embarrassed. 'I was puzzled to know why you thought I still had those sorts of contacts.'

Charles grinned mirthlessly. 'It's a question of who watches the watchers. One day you may be a star of this little organisation of ours. We have to be very sure about you, don't we, Alex?'

There was a constriction in Alex's throat. 'And since I'm here and we're having this conversation, I'm guessing you are, sir,' he managed.

'Tell me Alex, was there ever a time when you seriously thought of going over to the Cousins? Maybe keeping a foot in each camp?'

'Never. Not for moment.'

'They never approached you?'

'Yes, they did. Which of course you know because I reported the fact over a year ago.'

'Yes, quite, I'd forgotten.'

Like hell you had, Alex thought. 'You were right of course, the American branch of the Cambridge network is alive and well,' he said.

'And what do these old chums have to say?'

'More than I expected. They don't really seem to like the guy.'

'Can't say I'm surprised; he can sometimes rub people up the wrong way. So?'

'The consensus of opinion, or perhaps I should say biased gossip, is that he's clever but a loose cannon. Presently running his own show and managing to get up everyone's noses. His loyalty is undeniable but he is, and I quote, 'very Pentecostal about the enemy', which can lead him to extreme attitudes and perhaps flawed decisions. He's driven by personal hatreds in a very fundamentalist, Old Testament way. One guy actually described him as being afflicted by paranoid-messianic delusions. I thought that was a bit harsh but he has a tendency to make his fellow practitioners nervous. Even so, he's good at his job and as of now is very much in the President's good books. The man is absolutely untouchable.'

Charles had steepled his fingers as he listened, watching Alex closely. 'So, there is a faction that would like to see him gone, which does not surprise me. However, I'm surprised they were so open with you about one of their own, and such a senior one at that,' he mused.

'I hinted that I was possibly available. They didn't want him to get in first.'

'Ah, that would explain it.'

'When we met him, I thought he came across as a reasonable bloke, actually,' Alex commented.

'Yes, on his day Don Costello can be very personable. As you knew anyway because he was the one who tapped your shoulder a year ago, wasn't he? He may be all the things his colleagues said about him but he also has a sharp eye for available talent.'

It was said amiably but Alex couldn't escape the conviction that he was being interrogated. 'Well he made a mistake that time because I was not and am not available,' he said, a little more forcibly that he had intended.

Charles smiled benignly. 'I'm very pleased to hear it, Alex,' he said.

57

Despite the pleasantly warm ambient temperature, the atmosphere in the austere SIS office in central Christchurch could fairly have been described as chilly. Callum West was very aware that he was being kept in the dark and he did not appreciate that one little bit. Whatever it was Wenna Cavendish was keeping to herself obviously had some relevance to the Fleur Nichols enquiry. On that basis alone he felt that he should have been kept in the loop but evidently Wenna did not see things that way. It smacked of a lack of trust and he was unused to being excluded from enquiries; normally his experience and expertise were valued. Not, it seemed, by this haughty import from the old colonial power.

He was also feeling for his junior colleague Katy Tan, who had been on the end of a pretty stern interrogation from Wenna that had elicited nothing new of value and left Katy doubting her own abilities. Thanks for that, Callum thought grimly.

For her part, Wenna was far too worried about her missing target to spare time to consider whether she was making a good impression on the locals or not. She had taken the risk of calling Fleur's Ctab in the hope of tracing the call but, not surprisingly, it was switched off. She knew all too well that Fleur's meeting was probably happening at this very moment and that it was likely to be of short duration. Any hope of monitoring that meeting was probably already lost and despite Charles's reassurance, she still felt that she was to blame for that.

The message from Alex Jones on her Ctab had given her further cause for concern. For the life of her she couldn't see what the connection was between the BBC story in Afghanistan and Joe Kendry's suspicions of what was happening in Pakistan. Still less could she see how those two matters could be connected to Fleur's presence in New Zealand, but like Charles and Alex, she was instinctively sure that a connection existed.

She put aside that problem for the moment and returned to her immediate concern, Fleur Nichols's whereabouts. The locals, having lost her, seemed to have done everything they could to try and put things right but their efforts had so far all come to a dead end. She became aware that Callum and Katy were looking at her with what seemed remarkably like hostility. She was sure she must be wrong, there could be no possible reason for that. Probably they were just as concerned as she was, and looking to her to take the initiative.

'We have to take a chance,' she said. 'Call in the police.'

'And tell them what?' Callum asked.

'She is a person of interest. Locate and inform us. Priority one.'

'Priority one isn't a term we use and anyway it won't impress them if they don't know what it's about,' Callum said, 'we're more likely to get a reaction if we said she was a suspect wanted in another jurisdiction.'

'We can't say that, she isn't a suspect.'

'What exactly is she then?'

'A witness. A vital witness.'

Callum shrugged. 'We can try that. You do understand the problem though, don't you? Supposing they find her, they have no authority to detain her even long enough to check her identity.'

'I understand that perfectly well,' Wenna said tersely.

'And of course the same very much applies to you,' Callum said, stone-faced. 'Your writ doesn't run here. And, forgive me for stating the obvious, but we're on your side.'

Wenna was aware she was being put in her place for not sharing all she knew with him and was instantly resentful. Wasn't this arrogant young nobody aware of how serious this case was? She stopped herself. No, of course he wasn't, how could he be? She took a breath and made an effort to redress matters.

'I'm sorry if I've been a bit short with you, Callum. I'd like to share more but believe me, it would not be appropriate and it wouldn't help us find her. I just think we have no option now but to try the police, whether they can help or not.'

'We'll have to download a photograph,' Callum said, only partly mollified.

'Yes, let's do that. We don't have much to lose now.'

58

Simone arrived home after nightfall. She parked in her usual spot, switched off the lights and went to get out of the car. As she did so she noticed for the first time two empty bulk size plastic sugar bags on the floor in front of the passenger seat and a bottle of wine and a supermarket checkout receipt on the seat itself. She stopped half in and half out of the car, staring at what must have been her purchases.

The problem was that Auriol normally did their shopping and she did it online. Simone had no recollection of visiting the supermarket herself in recent days and yet it looked as if she must have done. And what was the explanation for the sugar? If she had bought that much sugar what had happened to it? Simple memory loss can happen to anyone at any time but it seemed she had had a complete mental blackout, yet had continued to function. And for how long had she been like that?

Before she had time to consider the matter any further Auriol came rushing out of the house in a state of great distress.

'Sim! Where have you been? I've been worried sick!'

Simone was at a loss for words but knew she had to placate Auriol somehow. 'Calm down, I'm here now and I'm fine.'

'But where have you been? You called me from work two hours ago and told me you were just leaving. I phoned the police and everything...'

Simone sighed. 'Well you'd better go and un-phone them, hadn't you,' she said, forcing a smile.

Auriol pointed accusingly at Simone's feet. 'And why have you got mud on your shoes?'

Simone had no idea. 'They've been water blasting the old building at work,' she lied quickly.

Auriol was not to be put off. 'But where have you been for the last two hours?' she insisted.

Simone found herself becoming irritated with this continued questioning. She grabbed the bottle of wine and flourished it in front of her. 'Calm down, Auriol. I've been shopping.'

'For two hours?'

Simone stood up and closed the car door. 'Seems like it.' She locked it with the remote.

Auriol looked completely disbelieving. 'You never shop. You hate it. And anyway we've got wine in the cupboard.'

Simone took her by the arm and led her towards the house. 'It was a sudden impulse, a whim, that's all,' she said with simulated confidence. 'Come on, let's go inside and have a glass, it's getting cold out here.'

Auriol allowed herself to be led but was not giving up. 'And what do you mean, seems like it? You've obviously been somewhere and bought wine, don't you remember?'

Simone sighed. There were times when Auriol could be annoyingly tenacious. 'What is this?' she asked, 'an interrogation?'

Auriol stopped and turned to face her. 'Yes,' she said with rare determination, 'that's exactly what it is, and it won't stop until I find out where you've been for the last two hours and why you've had your Ctab switched off.'

Simone shivered. 'Let's do this inside,' she said, encouraging Auriol forward. What am I going to say, she wondered, what the hell can I tell her when I don't have any answers myself?

'You will tell me, Sim,' Auriol said doggedly, 'and if you can't remember I'll call your office and see if they know anything.'

Simone felt a sudden jolt of panic. They were at their front door; Auriol's hand was on the latch. She removed Auriol's hand, pressed it to her lips and kissed it. 'Whatever you do, sweetheart, please don't do that until I've had time to think,' she said. It was as near as she had ever come in her life to begging for anything.

59

There was a time when virtually all Japanese tourists travelling overseas did so in large, well-organised parties with strict itineraries and officious tour guides. Those days had long gone, particularly at the upper end of the market. The tendency now was FITs, free independent travellers, who arranged their own schedules and travelled singly or in small groups with similar backgrounds and interests.

The two golfers who approached the third tee on the Waimanu Lodge course in their electric cart were brothers-in-law, both senior managers in the advertising business in Kyoto, enjoying a dream holiday bought by half a lifetime of unrelenting, pressurised endeavour.

When they saw the bodies they were initially stupefied. Even to people like them, who had no personal experience of violent death, it was obvious that this was what was confronting them. The man was a few metres down the slope from the path, face down, arms and legs at unlikely angles, a large section of the back of his skull missing and a stomach-churning pool of blood around his upper body which the blowflies had already found. The woman was closer to the path, on her back, her head lying in a smaller pool of blood, an open wound along the side of her head just above her ear, her mouth partly agape and blood trickling and clotting down the side of her face. Both bodies had the utter stillness of death. There was no sign of anyone else in the immediate area, or of a weapon.

Taka Yamazaki was first to react. Many years of watching viewer-generated news items and interaction with the Japanese media had taught him all he needed to know about citizen journalism. He abandoned his golf clubs and took out his Ctab while Kenji Morita, unwilling to face the reality of what they had chanced upon, turned away, summoned up his English and called the Lodge office.

Taka was not an expert cameraman but he knew enough to include a pan of the area to take in the golf course, the clubhouse, the Lodge in the distance and the river valley setting and to add a brief commentary on their location. Of course a lingering close-up of the bodies was mandatory to capture the full horror of these brutal deaths in this sylvan setting. There was no doubt this footage would play around the world and it would be a Japanese exclusive, one for which his contacts in the media would be very grateful.

From the direction of the Lodge there was the sound of engines hurriedly fired up. Near at hand there was a still silence but for gentle birdsong. As they waited, Taka forwarded his recording to his good friend Satoshi Nakamura in Tokyo. Satoshi had contacts at NTV's Nippon News Network and they, with associated websites, wireless web services and top selling newspaper Yomiuri Shimbun, would know exactly how to handle its exploitation.

Then common humanity reasserted itself. The voyeurism that is regularly excused by the socially ingrained but rarely defensible concept of 'the public's right to know' no longer sustained him. He bent double and vomited violently against the side of the golf cart.

60

'I am pleased to tell you I can assist you as you requested, or nearly so,' Siddiqi told Joe when they were seated and the waiter had brought them iced fruit juice.

Joe had arranged the meeting in the congenial atmosphere of the lounge of the hotel. He trusted Phil in every way that truly mattered in a friendship but not when it came to keeping his opinions to himself in delicate circumstances, so Joe had decided to meet Syed Siddiqi on his own.

The delicate circumstance in this case was Joe's intent to create a believable deception to convince Syed, who undoubtedly spent a good part of his life being lied to and was therefore likely to be adept at identifying a deceiver, that Joe, although annoyed, was at least compliant. Joe was by no means an accomplished liar, even less so a willing one, but it was not too difficult an acting role, he only had to put out of his mind any thought of his other clandestine options and be himself.

No matter what proposal Siddiqi came up with, Joe fully intended to make as many late night forays as he could and get to the bottom of the rumours that Phil had picked up. However, if Siddiqi were offering a compromise there would be no harm in appearing to accept wholeheartedly. At the least it would save him from the lie direct, he could simply use the lie oblique, the lie of omission; there was no moral obligation whatsoever, as he saw it, to admit any part of his real plans to Syed's scrutiny.

'What do you have in mind?' Joe asked.

'I have spoken with Mr Mathews and we are agreed that you can be permitted to film at a UN clinic so long as the location is not revealed on the film.'

Joe considered that for a moment, then nodded. 'And I get to select the women I want to talk to?'

Siddiqi shook his head slowly. 'That would create problems for us. We will arrange the women but will permit you to interview them in the clinic.'

'On my own?'

‘We cannot remove all security but we will be discreet. And I have arranged for what I believe you call ‘local colour’ videos to be sent to you here from our television broadcaster. They were described to me as being of international broadcast quality, so I am sure you will find them suitable.’

Joe sighed heavily. ‘Don’t think I’m not grateful,’ he said reluctantly ‘but it’s not exactly what I had in mind. The idea was that I shot all the material I needed myself. I suppose I can cut some of it in during editing.’

‘It is the best I can offer,’ Syed said flatly. ‘Do you say yes or no?’

Joe spread his hands in a theatrical gesture of unenthusiastic acceptance. ‘I am in your hands,’ he said with what seeming grace he could muster, ‘whatever you can arrange I will accept.’

Siddiqi sipped his drink and returned his glass to the table between them, watching Joe closely. ‘You are happy with our arrangements then?’ he asked.

Joe leant forward and placed both his hands flat down on the table in the universal gesture of utter frankness. ‘No,’ he said. ‘I’m not happy, not happy at all. I like to get my own way. I like to shoot a film the way I want to shoot it and I want everybody to jump when I say jump but… I’m not stupid. I know that this time I’m not going to get what I want, so I accept the inevitable and I’ll make the best of a bad job. And if that sounds ungracious then I apologise but at least you’ve heard the truth.’

Siddiqi visibly relaxed. ‘We should never apologise for telling the truth,’ he said.

Later, when Joe returned to his suite, he found Phil waiting impatiently for him. ‘Well?’ Phil asked, ‘how’d it go?’

Joe maintained a sober look. ‘Reasonably well, tomorrow we get to have a supervised tour of a clinic and we meet some carefully selected ladies.’

‘Right, so he’s come round a bit but did he buy your bullshit?’

Joe smiled smugly. ‘I just wish Fleur had been there; she’d have loved it. It was an Oscar-winning performance and he bought it hook line and sinker.’

Phil made a face. ‘Impressed with your modesty, was he?’ he asked.

61

Detective Inspector Robert Purau arrived at Waimanu Lodge to find that he had been preceded by the forensic and scene of crime teams and that he was one casualty short. Sergeant Wayne Pedder explained the absence of the second body.

'She was still alive. Just. So I called up the rescue chopper, she's on her way to Christchurch hospital. I arranged for a woman officer to keep an eye on her there.'

'What're her chances, any idea?'

'The medics reckoned fifty-fifty.'

Purau looked around at the roped-off crime scene and the white-coated figures working there. 'What's it look like?' he asked. 'Domestic, love triangle, murder-suicide, what?'

'It's likely to be a bit more complicated than that, sir,' Pedder replied. 'There's no weapon and nobody heard a shot. Looks like a professional hit.'

'Drugs?'

'Not on either of them or in their rooms. But he's got three passports in different names.'

'So who do we think they are?'

Pedder consulted his Ctab. 'The name he booked in under at the Lodge is Mohammed Kamal and one of the passports is in that name... It was stamped at Manila and Auckland.'

'Country of origin?' Purau interrupted.

'Egypt. The other passports are from Saudi Arabia and Pakistan.'

'And her?'

'Booked in as Janice Firth and that's what it says on her flight documents but her English credit cards are in the name of Fleur Nichols. She's also got journalistic accreditation in that name and a BBC security pass.'

'How long have they been here?'

'They both arrived last night but not together.'

'Separate rooms?'

'Yes.'

'Searched them?'

‘Had a quick look. He was travelling light. Apart from the passports he’s got a change of clothing, a return ticket Auckland to Manilla, domestic return Christchurch to Auckland, a copy of the Koran, an Asian credit card in the name of the second passport, rental car keys and paperwork from Christchurch, and an unused disposable Ctab; some Kiwi dollars and Malaysian currency.’

‘Did she have a Ctab?’

‘Seems she was about to make a call when she was hit. Prior to that it hadn’t been used for two days or more.’

Robert Purau had been a rep rugby player in his time; he was a man with a commanding physical presence and a deceptively quick mind, son of an Irish mother and a Ngai Tahu father. In a career spanning thirty years he had dealt with more than his fair share of murder enquiries and he had acquired an instinct about the ones that were going to cause him trouble. He had become progressively more depressed as the slightly-built Pedder answered his questions. There were calls to be made, to HQ, Interpol, immigration, customs and the SIS. He was not optimistic about this case; a professional hit, a dead Arab, a seriously injured British journalist and probable spook involvement was not likely to add up to a successful outcome for local cops.

‘Call HQ for me, Wayne, tell them I want the Armed Offenders Squad guarding that woman. And forensics to go through both their bedrooms in the Lodge. And get some of the local boys across that river, it’s too late of course but that’s probably where the shot came from.’

‘Right, sir. And I’ve got a Japanese interpreter on the way. The two guys who found the bodies don’t speak much English.’

Purau groaned. ‘Do you have any good news?’

Pedder looked non-committal. ‘The woman is still alive so far as we know so that’s a positive, oh, and one of the Japanese guys took a video of the scene,’ he offered.

‘Why don’t I think this is good news?’ Purau said grimly. ‘Okay, you’re in charge here, I’m going to the hospital.’

His Ctab rang. ‘John Fortune here, Bob.’ Purau sighed. The bloody press already. ‘How are you feeling, this fine day?’ Fortune asked.

Robert Purau knew this was going to be a long day. 'Oh, fluffy ducks, bro, fluffy ducks,' he said sarcastically.

62

The young woman in the four-wheel drive passed through the outskirts of Christchurch City heading towards the International Airport. She drove carefully, partly because she was still unused to driving on the left-hand side of the road but mainly to ensure she did not attract any undue attention.

She followed Memorial Drive to the roundabout giving onto the airport complex and turned right past the International Antarctic Centre. Once past the tourist attraction she slowed down as she approached her destination. The sign at the guarded entrance said: 'Gate Three. US Antarctic Program. Air National Guard Detachment 13. Flight Operations. Restricted Area. Authorised Personnel Only.'

Turning in, she stopped at the guardroom and handed over an innocent-looking swipe card. It galvanised the security officer into action and she was ushered in off the street and into the safety of the US base. According to her instructions the vehicle she had used was power-washed, the interior stripped and cleaned, the odometer altered and, immaculate and sterile, it was parked in a secure garage ready, after an appropriate lapse of time and some re-griming, for return to the up-market hire company that owned it.

The young woman was treated with hushed respect and accorded de facto officer status, since none knew her actual unit or rank but all knew what the instructions on the swipe card implied. She personally stripped, cleaned and boxed the Barrett, trusting that job to no one else. In little more than an hour she was aboard a USAF flight, bound for America. Neither she nor her equipment was listed on the manifest.

Whoever she was, she had never been in New Zealand.

63

Callum West flicked off his Ctab, his face telling the story. He saw no point in beating about the bush. 'That was Wellington;

they've had a call from Christchurch CIB. Fleur Nichols, or Janice Firth if you prefer, stayed last night at Waimanu, a high country Lodge a couple of hours north of here. She was found this morning on the Lodge golf course, she'd been shot.'

Wenna had been expecting bad news but this information stunned her. 'Is she alive?' she asked.

'Apparently. Not so the Arab gentleman she was meeting, he lost half his head to a sniper's bullet.'

'Have they named him?'

'Not to us. Fleur Nichols is in the Neurological Department at Christchurch Hospital under guard and the officer in charge of the case is on his way there now.'

Wenna thought of Charles Lovatt. She could just imagine his reaction to this. She wondered about calling him immediately but it was the middle of the night in London and she needed answers to at least some of the questions he was bound to ask. She felt drained and mentally battered but this was one time when she needed all her wits about her, there was no time for self-recrimination now.

'We'd better get going,' she said, 'see if we can retrieve anything from this mess.'

Like international hotels, hospitals tend to have an architectural sameness and this one, despite overlooking an extensive park in the centre of what the locals liked to call The Garden City, was no different; it was big, post-earthquake modern and constructed like a blocky institutional maze. Outside the main entrance there was a gaggle of reporters and news cameras, held at bay by security guards. Callum talked his way past the guards and seemed to know the layout, leading them straight to the Neurological Unit. There was no mistaking the room Fleur was in: outside the door were two heavily armed AOS officers and a substantially built, middle-aged man in a smart dark blue suit who was in close conversation with a staff nurse as they approached.

Callum introduced them and showed ID. Detective Inspector Purau nodded resignedly. 'Right, and you'll want answers and I can't give them.'

'Why not?' Wenna demanded sharply.

Purau turned slowly to fix her with a glare that would shatter glass. The nurse and the two AOS officers watched wide-eyed to see how this would play out. 'My name is Bob Purau,' he said slowly, with calculated politeness, 'and I'm in charge of an investigation into what may be a double murder. What that means, Miss Cavendish, is that, as things stand, I decide who gets to know what and when and how. And for a start I want some answers from you before you get anything from me, do we understand each other?'

Callum stepped in fast. He did not know Purau but he well knew the type; obdurate, smart, and as an investigator he'd be like a terrier after a rat. Pulling rank or otherwise pressurising this man would be totally counter-productive.

'Sorry, Bob,' he said, 'don't want to get off on the wrong foot. Anything we can tell you we will.' He turned to the nurse. 'Is there a room we can use?'

'There's the nurses' tea room, second door on left, that's all. And I'll tell you the same as I told the Inspector, Miss Nichols is in a coma and can't be seen by anyone, so don't waste staff time pestering us about her condition. You'll be told if there's any change.'

I could get a job as a UN peacemaker, Callum thought wryly to himself. What he said was, reading her name badge: 'We quite understand, Caitlin, we'll be quiet as church mice, promise we will.' And he grinned at her, the boyish grin working its usual magic.

'Don't try that on me,' the staff nurse said brusquely, but she walked off down the corridor with a slight smile and the hint of a sway to her hips.

Wenna, irritated by this time-wasting exchange, led the way to the nurses' tea room. She found the seemingly endemic informality in this country somewhat unsettling but was smart enough to realise that it was time for some social acclimatisation.

'I apologise, Bob,' she said when they had closed the door of the cubicle-sized room behind them. 'This hasn't gone well for us, so far. What do you want to know?'

Purau nodded acceptance of her apology. 'Okay, Wenna. I understand about 'need to know' but for a start who are they, why were they here and why are you interested in them?'

Wenna drew breath, trying to work out how much to say. 'Fleur Nichols is a well-known UK journalist. We became aware that she had been invited to meet someone we might be interested in, so we followed her. Unfortunately the plane she was on was diverted at the last moment and we lost track of her.'

'Who was she meeting?'

'We were hoping you could tell us that.'

Purau shook his head. 'Take your pick of three names on the passports he had. Three different countries of origin, no ID on him,' he handed over the passports. The names meant nothing to Wenna. 'The forensic people will have fingerprints and there'll be no shortage of DNA samples but the chances of him being on record here are nil,' Purau continued, 'and it'll be a long haul going through Interpol.'

'We may be able to get a photo ID,' Wenna suggested.

'Not likely, there's not much left of the front of his face. Whatever rifle they used took bullets that would drop an elephant. They weren't taking any chances, that's for sure, they wanted these two dead.'

'They were shot from some distance then?' Callum put in.

'Across the river'd be my bet. It was a targeted, professional hit,' Purau confirmed. 'I'm a hunter myself and I can tell you this, whoever it was, he sure as hell knows his stuff.'

'No trace of him I suppose,' Wenna said hopefully.

'Not a sniff. At first I thought it might be drugs, but it isn't, is it?'

'No' Wenna admitted. She hesitated for a minute as Purau watched her. Then, deciding they would probably want a lot more co-operation from him before this was over, said, 'The chances are he was an international terrorist.'

Purau sighed. 'Then we'd better hope our Fleur recovers and tells us all about it,' he said.

'Amen to that,' Wenna said, already thinking ahead to the difficult conversation she would have to have with Charles. An unpleasant thought flittered across her mind. Had Fleur been used as bait, and if so, just how much involvement had Charles had in setting the hook?

64

The video of the murder scene had arrived in Japan long before Bob Purau even arrived at the Lodge. It had been quickly passed on through a line of contacts to Nippon Television in Tokyo where it was assessed and accepted for transmission, shown on the early morning news, then released for international distribution.

It arrived on the BBC news desk at two in the morning local time and the night duty staff immediately recognised one of the bodies as being that of Fleur Nichols. The question of whether or not to wake the irascible Walter Bloom was academic, they were well aware that he would have considered not doing so to be next door to treason. The three of them tossed coins to see who should be the unlucky one to tell Walter his favourite journalist was dead. The loser added a generous nip of whisky to her coffee before making the call.

It took a moment or two for Walter to grasp the reality of what he was being told and when he did he vented his spleen on his unfortunate staffer. 'Listen, Brogan, you'd better be damn sure this is not some photoshopped scam or your arse is on the line. Double check the source with Japan, you done that?'

'There hasn't been time...' Brogan began.

'You bought the bloody rights didn't you, why didn't you ask them about it then? I want to know this is kosher, so get the back-story to the video; there must be someone there who speaks English. When you've done that, if it stands up I want the story prepped for when I arrive, I'll edit it myself, got that? And try and tie up world rights to any territories they haven't sold to.'

'On it now...'

'Then get the hell off this phone,' Walter demanded, 'I have a call to make. Then I'm coming in. No, wait, hang on, call Television New Zealand and the local cops there as well, see what you can find out.'

He cancelled the call, satisfied that his instructions would be followed to the letter. Beside him his wife, long used to night-time calls, stirred and came half awake.

'Not Simon is it?' she mumbled.

'No. Business. Go to sleep,' Walter replied distractedly.

He called up his work Hub and extracted Charles Lovatt's personal Ctab number. His call was diverted and answered by the night owl Alex Jones had employed. By this time Walter was in full flight.

'This is Walter Bloom, BBC news, I want to talk to Charles Lovatt.'

'I'm sorry, Mr Lovatt is not available at the moment, can I help or take a message?'

'No you bloody well can't. Get the bastard out of bed and do it now.'

'I'm sorry sir,' the night owl said carefully, not quite sure how to handle this. 'Maybe if I had some idea what this was about…'

'Tell the little shit he's got my best girl killed and I want him on the phone now and talking fast or his name gets plastered all over the next news bulletin.'

He abruptly cut off contact. The night owl blinked rapidly twice, then, still unsure, made the call.

65

Simone Gofre woke in the morning from a fitful sleep to an empty bed and with a clear recollection of exactly what had happened the previous evening before she arrived home. The knowledge of what she had done left her with a mixed reaction. On the one hand it was totally out of character and certainly illegal and on the other she felt no guilt whatsoever; it was a protest born of frustration. Increasingly these days individuals were being disenfranchised and ground down by a mind-numbing burden of bureaucracy and legislation. Democracy, she felt, was in need of an application of the principles of Occam's razor.

She could clearly remember calling Auriol and telling her she was on her way home. Then she had made the irrational decision to make a personal strike against the destruction of her countryside. She had driven to the hypermarket, bought the sugar and wine and headed home. On the way, within what had seemed at the time like a dream, she had stopped at the partly prepared subdivision, marched onto the site and poured sugar into the fuel tanks of those bulldozers and JCB's that the contractors had been unwise enough to leave with their fuel tanks unlocked. Then, still in a semi-dream state, she had driven home, arriving with no recollection of what she had done and no recall of it until this moment.

A jagged stab of pain interrupted her reverie and caused a sharp intake of breath as she moved slightly in the bed. She was probably overdue for an analgesic. She had taken two in the middle of the night but their effects were not lasting so long these days and they barely dulled the pain anymore.

The smell of a cooked breakfast was wafting up the stairs of the cottage. She was not feeling very hungry but whatever Auriol brought she would try to eat, the girl was worried enough about her as it was. The blackout that Simone had finally admitted to had panicked her even more than her being late home, if that was possible.

Simone edged herself up into a sitting position and contemplated a visit to the bathroom. She believed she had convinced Auriol that the blackout was a one-off event, probably unrelated to her condition, but she could not believe that herself. She heard Auriol coming up the stairs, no doubt armed with more of her pills and a breakfast tray. Despite the now continuous nagging pain in her chest she had to find a morning smile for her.

She felt a moment of panic. What if the blackout happened again, what if it happened when she was at work? Would she still be able to function as she had last night or would she gradually lose rational control of sections of her life?

Could she be sure she would continue to enjoy recall as she had this morning or would she gradually lose her memory?

66

In Fleur's brain there was no frame of reference for the nothingness that had come upon her so suddenly. In essence it was very simple: one moment she was, and the next she was not. It was as if she had been switched off: alive then dead.

She returned to consciousness with a mind-stunning headache and no concept of the passage of time. She did not open her eyes or move for some while, her pain-panicked mind lying numb and inert, incapable of rational thought. Awareness of her situation came slowly, one sense at a time. There came a moment when she knew she was lying on a bed, then that she was pleasantly warm and that there was a background humming noise which she could not identify. There was a smell, faintly antiseptic, faintly metallic. After perhaps three or four minutes, by an effort of will she forced her eyes open but what she saw through blurred vision made no immediate sense to her and she suffered an overwhelming sense of disorientation.

She was looking at a bland off-white ceiling and a green wall that completely surrounded her limited peripheral vision. She was unwilling to move her head for fear of ratcheting up the pain, so she lay where she was, trying to make sense of what little she knew.

One of the green walls broke apart with a swish and a young woman in nurse's uniform entered her fuzzy field of vision and looked down at her with a warm smile. She was sturdily built, with short black hair, brown eyes in an open brown face and a rose birthmark on her cheek. There were medals on the breast of her uniform and a nametag that read 'Sesimani'. Fleur stared at her, trying to bring her into better focus.

'Ah, you're back with us, you had us worried, girl,' the young woman said. She had a pleasant, light voice and spoke English with an unfamiliar accent.

She took Fleur's wrist and held it, consulting a watch hanging from her breast pocket as she did so. Her touch was warm and gentle. Nothing of what was going on made any sense to Fleur; it was as if her body belonged to her but her senses to someone else. The young woman laid her arm down on the sheet beside her, moved away to the end of the bed and picked up a clipboard on which she made a note.

'You'll be right now,' the nurse said.

Fleur finally found her voice but it was hoarse and harsh, alien sounding. 'Where am I?' she asked.

'You're in hospital, girl and you're going to be just fine.'

'Why am I here?'

The nurse hesitated a moment before answering. 'You had an accident, honey,' she said.

Fleur absorbed that for a moment. 'What happened to me?' she asked.

'You've got a nasty bump on the head but you'll be right.'

Fleur was sure that there were a lot of questions she should be asking but for the moment she could not think of them. 'My head hurts and I'm thirsty,' she said, slurring her words.

The nurse smiled at her. 'We can fix that,' she said, 'and we won't let anyone bother you till you're feeling a lot better.'

She turned to leave but Fleur made a croaking noise that stopped her. 'You want something?' Sesimani enquired.

'Who am I?' Fleur asked.

67

Simone made the decision as she stood under the shower. Auriol had brought her breakfast in bed and fussed around her when she couldn't eat it all. It would go on like this till the very end if Simone did nothing about it and there was no point in delaying any longer.

Auriol was never going to face the reality of the situation so Simone had to deal with the problem for her, and she had to do it now. She had to confront Auriol with the only possible solution before she lost her rational capacity and with it, her ability to enforce the decision that alone would secure a future for her lover when she was no longer here.

She dried herself and dressed slowly as she thought how best to broach the subject. She was aching all over and every muscle in her body felt stiff despite the warm shower and she found it difficult to concentrate her thoughts. In a way it did not matter how she put it, Auriol would react badly no matter what.

The deep-seated, nagging pain was still there despite the powerful medication she had taken, so she knew in her heart that today was also the day she would have to begin self-injection if she was to get through even a few hours' work. Work that, with any luck, she could finish in just two or three days, provided there were no further blackouts or, if there were, that they did not disable her to the point where she couldn't function. If that happened at work there would be no way she could avoid coming under the eagle eye of Fat Annie, who would have no hesitation in reporting even the most minor incident to the already panicked Colin Burcastle.

Auriol was in the kitchen, feeding the dishwasher with the breakfast tableware when Simone joined her. She looked up, scanning Simone's face for something more to worry about. Simone went up to her and hugged and kissed her.

'You know I love you, don't you?' she said.

Auriol blushed and smiled uncertainly. 'Of course I do Sim,' she said.

'And you know I'm going to die, quite soon,'

Auriol looked away from her, her mouth tightening in a grimace of denial. She shook her head emphatically but said nothing. Simone took her face in her hands and forced her to look at her.

'You're going to do what I tell you, my darling, and you're going to do it because you love me and I love you and it's the best for both of us. I don't want you here the day I die, understand?'

'No!' the word came out in a rush, a general denial of all Simone had said and anything she was likely to say that Auriol did not want to hear.

'Yes!' Simone responded firmly, stepping away from her. 'Today you'll begin to pack, tonight we'll have a last dinner together and tomorrow you'll leave for your sister's. You will stay there until the flat in Oxford is free and you'll go back to work as soon as you can. You won't return here.'

Auriol was staring mutely at her with that whipped puppy look that Simone had been dreading, the muscles in her face had gone loose and her arms hung lifeless from slumped shoulders. Somehow Simone managed to harden her heart.

'I want you at least half packed by the time I get back tonight,' she said, 'and there will be no arguments, no discussions about this, Auriol. We'll both behave in a civilised way. When my time comes I want to know that I've done everything I possibly could for you.'

Simone took Auriol's face in her hands again and kissed her on the lips. 'I'll see you tonight,' she said, and walked out of the room leaving Auriol standing still and inert, staring blankly after her.

***

Simone drove cautiously, trying to compose her mind for the day to come. In her shoulder bag was the syringe case and a phial of morphine. It would have to be declared to Fat Annie on arrival and from then on Simone knew she would be under even closer scrutiny than usual. Well, it wouldn't be for long and then she could at least walk away with the satisfaction of a body of work professionally completed.

She passed the development site with its idle machinery and puzzled hard-hatted workmen and a lone policeman leaning against his patrol car talking to a man in a suit. Observing the scene she felt a quiet satisfaction; she had at least slowed them down for a day or two. It was her small gift to a world that needed a million more such gifts and she felt completely justified in what she had done, regretting only that despite her high intelligence and superior education, she hadn't done more, earlier, to save humankind from its own follies.

She was vaguely aware that some would criticise her actions as childish and irrelevant but it was a distant, fey thought. She, who had been brought up to abide by a powerful code of ethics and stood by them all her life, felt no guilt. Ethics were a human construct not universal law.

68

Wenna and Callum were not allowed to see Fleur and were at first denied a meeting with her neurologist, a young American consultant on an exchange visit; something to do with privacy legislation. It took some furious calls to Wellington and high-level SIS intervention with the reluctant bureaucrats of the District Health Board before the surgeon was allowed to discuss the case with them. When he did it was in his office in the presence of a minder from Human Resources and what he had to say was not good news.

'She's conscious and the long-term prognosis is good but she's suffering from anterograde amnesia,' Mr Hu told them.

'Meaning what exactly?' Wenna asked.

'The bullet struck her left temporal lobe a glancing blow,' he touched the side of his head just above his ear to indicate where, 'and impacted on a region underneath the cortex called the hippocampus, causing the amnesia.'

'Is it likely to be permanent?' Callum asked.

'Probably not. I'll have a better idea once the trauma and sensory shock has passed, but nothing is certain because memory for both facts and events appear to rely on the integrity of the hippocampus, which in this case has been disturbed.'

'Could you explain to us in layman's language what this is going to mean for her; give us your professional opinion?' Wenna asked.

'Okay. There are different kinds of memory, including short and long-term, explicit and implicit. We use implicit memory sometimes when we perform on autopilot everyday things such as driving a car. You know sometimes you can drive many miles completely safely without being aware and suddenly you wake up to normal consciousness again. Perhaps you've experienced this yourself?'

'It happens to us all I suppose,' Wenna confirmed.

'So, for the time being the patient has lost both her implicit memory and her explicit memory,' Hu continued. 'This means she has no recollection of her past life or events and doesn't know who she is, even how old she is. She can't reconstruct the events prior to the shooting. At the moment she's living in the present and can only do simple things. Memory is a complex matter and not completely understood, so I'm afraid I can't give you a more accurate prognosis than I already have. Recovery, when it occurs, tends to be random and varies from patient to patient.'

'Is she in pain?' Callum asked.

'To a degree,' the consultant responded. 'There are no sensors for pain within the brain itself, but she's been sedated and given painkillers because she complained of a quite severe headache.' Callum and Wenna looked puzzled. 'It's probably referred pain, there would have been considerable trauma to the neck and upper spinal muscles.'

'When can we see her?' Wenna asked.

'Perhaps after rounds, say an hour.'

'And she remembers nothing of past events, not even her name and wouldn't recognise people she knew well?' Callum asked

'As I have already explained,' Mr Hu said with just a hint of impatience.

'How soon before she can travel?' Wenna asked.

'Where to?'

'Britain.'

‘Probably sooner than you might think. There should be no physical impairment once the wound has partially healed. I’ll let you know.’

Wenna’s Ctab dinged quietly and the neurologist took that as an excuse to end the meeting. Alex Jones said a brief hello and handed the call over to Charles Lovatt.

‘How come the media had the story before I did?’ Charles demanded.

‘I sent a brief on the secure line through Wellington and I thought I should confirm how Fleur was before I called you direct,’ Wenna replied.

‘Unfortunately your brief arrived after the media report,’ Charles said with a touch of acid in his voice. Then, a slight change of tone: ‘Are you telling me she’s still alive?’

‘Yes and she’ll recover we’re told… But...’

‘No need to be coy, Wenna. The whole world has got the story thanks to a couple of media savvy Japanese golfers and if anyone has hacked our Ctabs we’re in deep trouble anyway.’

‘Damn! Did they identify the dead man?’

‘No. Have you?’

‘Choice of three aliases and there’s not enough left of his face to get a likeness. It’ll be down to fingerprints and DNA,’ Wenna replied. ‘Whoever the sniper was they certainly knew their stuff and they used some fairly heavy artillery.’

‘Wonderful,’ Charles said gloomily. ‘Passport photos?’

‘If you believe them. He could have had cosmetic surgery. I’ll send them through to Alex for evaluation.’

‘What about Fleur’s Ctab?’

‘Nothing, it’s been cleaned. But she may have been about to make a call when she was hit.’

‘Right. How bad is she?’

‘She’s come out of a coma but is suffering from amnesia.’

‘Prognosis?’

‘The consultant can’t say but he expects eventual recovery. For now she doesn’t know who she is, let alone what happened.’

‘Stay close, Wenna.’

'She's been moved out of Intensive Care to a single room. I'm camped outside her door along with two AOS men, she's safe and no-one will have access except us.'

'Good. I had Walter Bloom on my back in the middle of the night threatening to make an 'MI5 implicated in death of journalist' exposé of the whole damn thing. We've got to get her back home as soon as possible, we need to know what she knows and fast.'

'Understood. At least we can tell Walter that Fleur will live, that should spike his guns.'

'I doubt it but it might buy us some breathing space,' Charles replied. 'And he's bound to send someone over there to interview her, which we most definitely do not want.'

'Don't worry; I'll keep her secure. The consultant hinted it might not be long before she can travel.'

'Better double up on the guard, there's every chance the enemy will blame Fleur for setting up the hit.'

'That had occurred to me.'

'Wenna…'

'Yes?'

'When she comes round, she'll need a friend. Make sure it's you.'

69

Joe Kendry was shaving the old fashioned way when his room Hub trilled at him. He wiped off his face, walked through to the bedroom, put it on speakerphone and answered. 'Yes?'

'Joe, this is Rose Petchek…'

He was instantly alert. She sounded amiable enough but any unexpected contact from Rose was both unwelcome and unlikely to improve his day.

'Hello, Rose, what can I do for you?' he asked guardedly.

Rose did not waste time with a preamble. 'The good news is that you'll be paid in full, plus a bonus for the inconvenience.'

'Rose, what the hell are you talking about?'

'The plug has been pulled on the doco, Joe. I want you both on the first available flight back to the UK. Meantime send me what material you have and then delete it, understood? No copies, the confidentiality clause still stands.'

Joe was dumbfounded. 'Rose, this is crazy,' he said finally.

'The client has pulled the project. We have to live with these things, Joe, you know what this business is like. You should be glad you're getting paid. It ain't always that way.'

Joe's mind was spinning. He had to be careful what he said. 'But I've just negotiated…'

'I don't care what you've negotiated, Joe,' Rose interrupted, 'get your ass out of there, you don't have any support or any protection anymore.'

'So you've told Syed Siddiqi and Bill Mathews.'

'You're unofficial as of now, got that? I suggest you start to pack.'

Joe was framing another question when the line went dead. He hitched up his robe and sat down suddenly on the bed, his mind buzzing, anger slowly building. The whole thing stank to high heaven. Something had triggered this, but what? It couldn't be anything to do with their plans for a late night foray, he was as sure as he could be that no one knew anything about that. It could only be that his insistence on visiting the clinics and interviewing the women in uncontrollable circumstances had touched a raw nerve.

If this was the case, no matter what the UN clinic doctor thought, it gave credence to the rumours about the unexplained deaths and their connection to the Two+One project. There was a cover-up going on and Rose Petchek was either in on it or had been leant on.

As Rose had said, they were on their own now, although Joe didn't doubt for a moment that they would continue to be under surveillance for as long as they were in the country. Well, if they were on their own, so be it, but for sure the bastards were not going to get away with it. He had one last card to play. He called Phil on his Hub.

'You want to come and talk to me?' he asked. 'Bring the gear.'

Phil, alerted by the tone of Joe's voice, was there in barely a minute.

'What's up, boss?' he asked.

Joe told him. Then he said: 'First of all we're going to send Rose that garbage we shot before, then we're going to do a piece to camera for ourselves: what we intend to do tonight, who we're going to see and why, the rumours, our suspicions of who's behind it, the lot. Then we send it all to my home Hub, just in case. Tonight we go out the back door and get every inch of footage we can. If we don't have a documentary we may have an exposé instead. You okay with that?'

'Too damn right I am,' Phil replied. 'But how'd we explain not going straight to the airport?

'We go talk to our large friend Waseem, I'm sure he'll be lurking around somewhere, and we ask him to take us to the best tourist shops in town. That'll buy us one more day. We want mementos of our visit to his beautiful country to take home for our wives, don't we?'

'Course we do, only natural.'

'Right, I'll get dressed, then it's show time,' Joe said without a trace of humour.

70

A great and pervasive darkness descended on Auriol once Simone had gone and she was left alone. Her worst fears had been realised. Simone had finally admitted that she had no more use for her. No matter what fine words she had used, no matter her protestations of love, that was what it came down to.

She abandoned the breakfast dishes and taking short, doll-like steps, walked stiff-legged to the armchair in the sitting room, placing herself in it carefully, as if she were in danger of breaking. She considered that she needed to think but thinking was not easy when her mind refused to function coherently. Did it matter? What was there to think about when all was said and done? Her beloved Sim had told her she was to leave and never come back, never see her again. She was to leave this house and the bed they had shared and be abandoned to the cold, loveless outside world where she would be as lost and alone as she had been before they met.

She stared into an unseen middle distance. Her world shrank, limited by the boundaries of her unfocussed vision. Simone had loved her, she knew that, but never in the way that she loved Simone. Simone had always had her work. It was her vocation, hugely important to her, filling the major part of her life; she talked about it with a sometimes ferocious enthusiasm. What passion she had left was given to Auriol and for most of the time that was enough. A share of her life force was all that Simone had to offer and Auriol accepted that with gratitude.

It was different for her. For Auriol, work was an annoying interruption to her real vocation of loving Simone. It went without saying that under no circumstances could Simone do any wrong and her least hint of a desire, her slightest wish, should be Auriol's command. Love for Simone filled her every waking moment, consumed her energy and her constant thoughts. It was a passionate, absorbing disease for which she had no wish to seek a cure. Loving Sim had, until recently, afforded her the greatest pleasure, the greatest happiness she had ever known.

And now it was over. There could be no doubt that Simone meant what she said. She was ill and, Auriol now accepted, she was about to die. She needed to be taken care of but she didn't want Auriol to do that for her. She would rather die alone than have by her side the one person who loved her more than anyone in the world. Auriol had heard the explanation Simone had given but it made no sense to her so, having no real sense of self-worth, she had assumed that somehow her rejection was her own fault.

A deep, hopeless despair consumed her. At the time when Simone needed her most, she had failed her, and with Simone gone from her life she couldn't conceive of how she could live. She could survive, no doubt, but not live.

After a while she got up and began to tidy the kitchen. Then she went upstairs, the black dog of depression at her heels, and made the bed before tidying the rest of the house. She swept and polished and cleaned with a determined, mindless thoroughness. She would not be there when Simone returned that evening, there would be no final dinner, that would be too much to bear, but she did not want Simone to come back to a dirty home.

When she had finished she left the house, locking the door behind her. She walked to her car, her mind in stasis, and drove away into a perfect spring morning.

71

When his secure line activated Charles Lovatt had a pretty good idea who it would be. 'Lovatt,' he said.

'Don here,' Costello said, 'I heard about the little problem down south, of course. Wanted to offer my condolences.'

'Thank you.'

'Always difficult when we lose someone.'

So he didn't know. 'Fleur Nichols is still alive,' Charles said.

There was a fractional silence. 'Well, that's good news, Charlie. Safely tucked up somewhere is she?'

'In hospital in Christchurch under heavy guard.'

'A public hospital…'

'Yes but I'm assured a platoon of marines couldn't get to her. Wouldn't want to run the risk of someone trying to finish the job.'

'Okay. So … Wenna's with her?'

'Yes.'

'Uh huh. Good girl, Wenna. Is Nichols talking?'

'She's just come out of a coma and she's suffering from amnesia, doesn't even know who she is.'

'But she will.'

'So I'm told.'

'Biggest fuck-up since Pearl Harbour.'

'You said it, Don.'

'Warned you about those useless bastards in New Zealand.'

'You did, Don.'

'Still, we can debrief her when she gets home. When're you bringing her back?'

'Soon as we can. Then she goes straight into protection. There's a lot I'm hoping she'll tell us but at the end of the day she's a witness, the innocent party in all this.'

'Is she, Charlie? Is she really?'

'She was under no obligation to tell us what she was planning. As far as I know she was just doing her job, following up what would have been a world exclusive. Unless you know something I don't.'

'Oh I doubt that, Charlie. I'm sure you've covered all the bases. Maybe I'm just not as trusting as you when it comes to journalists. They've been known to cosy up to the enemy before now, and this one is a well-known sympathiser, I'm sure I'm not telling you anything there.'

'No, but sympathy doesn't necessarily equate to complicity.'

'I just love the way you Brits play with words, Charlie. Now, anything Uncle Sam can do to help here?'

'Not at the moment but I think we should have a face-to-face quite soon.'

'Okay. Your place or mine?'

'Mine, I think. Tomorrow?'

'Sure. Not before ten though.'

'Eleven, then?'

'Look forward to it, Charlie.'

The line went dead. Charles called Alex Jones up to his office and played him back the recording of the conversation.

'What do you make of that, Alex?' he asked when it concluded.

Alex considered the question for a moment, then he said: 'He didn't ask who Fleur was meeting, who the dead man was.'

'Indeed he did not. Nor did he show any interest in who organised the assassination. However, I'm sure if we put those things to him he'd say it's our game, not his, and his concern was for the living and the possibility of extracting something positive from this mess,' Charles commented.

'Except that, until you told him otherwise, he thought Fleur was dead.'

'He did. So why did he not ask those questions, Alex?'

'If I were cynical I might say it was because he already knew the answers.'

'Perish the thought.'

'Absolutely. I notice you didn't mention anything about the diary Joe Kendry's so kindly keeping for us,' Alex observed.

'On balance I thought not. Would you have done?'

'No, but of course Joe has this conspiracy theory about the US and the Two+One project.'

'Well, that's Joe, isn't it.'

'We don't buy it then?'

Charles looked at him in apparent wonder. 'Don't you trust our Cousins, Alex?'

'I trust them to exactly the same degree you do sir,' Alex replied, straight-faced.

Charles sat back in his chair and stared hard at the ceiling as if seeking inspiration from on high. 'Whilst we're waiting for Fleur to recover, perhaps we should explore the world of Joe Kendry a little more closely.'

'Which part of his world, exactly?

'The part that got him sent so conveniently to Pakistan at exactly the time Fleur went off to meet the enemy. That part, Alex.'

72

When Fleur woke from a long period of sedation there was a rather severely pretty, fair-haired and conservatively dressed young woman sitting beside her bed, watching her intently. Fleur yawned widely and stared at her visitor, trying to make sense of the world she had woken to. She remembered being awake some time before in a small green room and speaking to a nurse with a foreign accent but that might have been a dream. Now she was in a larger room with dull cream walls and a window with full-length curtains. It was daylight but the curtains were drawn. Most of the equipment she had been attached to had been removed; there was just a drip in her arm feeding what looked like water from a transparent bag on a stand. Her temple was throbbing gently and she felt muzzy-headed.

'Hello, Fleur, how are you now?' the woman asked gently.

Fleur closed her eyes for a moment and opened them again but nothing had changed, she was still in the same monochrome cream room. It registered that she was in hospital. There had been a doctor, several doctors, and now she recalled, more than one nurse. Some of the things she had been told returned to her: she had been in an accident, they thought her name was Janice Firth or possibly Fleur Nichols, she was safe here. She had no idea why she needed to be told she was safe in a hospital. The woman was looking at her enquiringly.

'Who are you?' Fleur asked.

'My name is Wenna Cavendish,' the woman answered. She had a cultured, educated English accent. 'And I'm your friend.'

'Who am I? They said I had two names...'

'You are Fleur Nichols and you're a journalist.'

Fleur considered that. It did not seem very likely but the woman seemed honest enough and she obviously believed it, so perhaps it was true.

'Where do I live then?'

'In England, London.'

'So I'm in England?'

'No, New Zealand.'

'I don't understand… What am I doing here?' There was a hint of panic in her voice.

'You've had a nasty bang on the head, it will all come back to you eventually.'

'Why don't you just tell me?'

'I will. I'll tell you everything you want to know. I'm going to stay with you and take you back home as soon as you're well enough to leave hospital.'

Fleur felt reassured, instinctively wanting to trust this person, this friend of hers, even though she could not remember ever setting eyes on her until this moment.

The green walls swished apart and staff nurse Aroha swept in, oozing authority. 'That's enough talking for now.' She pointed a finger at Wenna. 'I'll tell you when you can come back.'

Wenna found herself complying. This was not her turf after all and she well understood that whilst you could perhaps negotiate with a doctor, you did not argue with a staff nurse.

Outside the room she found Callum West in conversation with Detective Inspector Robert Purau. Callum was handing a Ctab to Purau.

'It's Fleur's,' he said in explanation.

'Anything?' she asked, nodding to Purau.

'Clean as,' Callum replied.

'It seems to me,' Robert Purau said, 'that we may have a new problem on the horizon.'

'Have we?' Wenna asked.

'Yeah, we have. You're going to want to take her back to the UK, possibly before she recovers her memory, and I'm going to want her here as a material witness.'

'I'm sure we can get round that,' Wenna replied.

‘I’m sure we have to,’ Purau said pointedly.

‘She can give a statement to the Metropolitan Police once she’s recovered her memory and we’ve debriefed her,’ Wenna suggested. ‘And if there is ever a trial she can be subpoenaed to return here and give evidence.’

Purau nodded heavily. ‘As you say, if there is ever a trial. Have you had any feedback as to who might be responsible?’

‘At this stage we’re all guessing.’

‘Let me guess then. What we’ve got here is a highly trained and experienced sniper who knew exactly where his target was going to be. He was carrying heavy artillery; probably a purpose-built large calibre sniper rifle. He had access to backup and support here and I’d bet my dear old mother’s pension that he’s already left the country. Now, who do we think could manage all that and would want an Al Qaeda suspect dead? Do I hear anyone humming ‘Dixie’?’

‘Speculation might not be wise at this point,’ Callum warned.

‘There may well be political implications here,’ Wenna added.

Purau sighed. ‘I’m not really dumb, Wenna, I just look as if I am. Now let me tell you some Realpolitik here. This business is news headlines all over the world. I’ve got the Commissioner on my case and the Prime Minister is on his. The Opposition is having a field day; our MPs are angry as cut snakes at the thought of an assassination on our shores. Things like that don’t happen here; we just have ordinary, everyday hometown murders. Just to really make my day, outside this hospital is a big percentage of the international media. They’re hunting as a pack and they’re armed with dangerous questions and some of them are bright enough to do joined up writing. Trust me, they can add up two and two and make five as well as we can and what we don’t tell them they’ll make up. Sooner or later I’ve got to go out there and face them and when I do I want to be sure that what I say isn’t going to come back and bite me on the bum, so now would be a damn good time to let me in on all you know about this mess.’

Wenna considered what to say. She understood the detective’s problem all too well but that had to take second place to removing Fleur to a safe house in the UK as soon as possible. Throw him a bone, she thought.

‘I promise you I don’t have any more information at the moment,’ she said ‘but when I leave with Fleur, my office will be in continuous touch with the SIS and Callum can liaise with you. If Fleur can add anything to your investigation you can be sure you’ll know.’

‘I second that,’ Callum said.

Purau did not look convinced. ‘I want your boss to talk to my boss,’ he said to Wenna, ‘and both of them to talk to his boss,’ he added, pointing at Callum, ‘before the blame game starts.’

‘Not a problem,’ Callum reassured him.

Purau was not finished. ‘I know a dead enquiry when I’m faced with one,’ he said, ‘and this one was dead before I ever got to the scene. It’s not a case of who pulled the trigger, it’s who gave the orders and even if we knew the answer to that they’d never stand trial here or anywhere else. This was a kill mission from the outset, an institutional murder, and it’s like tax: if you’re rich and powerful, paying is a choice not a requirement.’

‘Nothing is impossible,’ Wenna ventured, knowing full well he was right.

Robert Purau pointed to the ceiling of the corridor they were standing in. ‘Oh look,’ he said, ‘porcine aviators.’ He handed Fleur’s Ctab back to Callum. ‘You might as well have that,’ he said, ‘I doubt it’ll be any use to me.’

And then they were looking at his broad back as he walked away down the corridor to face the press. The two armed AOS men stared straight ahead, faces unmoving, as if they had heard nothing.

‘The question is,’ Wenna said, ‘how are we going to get Fleur out of here past the media?’

After a moment one of the AOS men coughed slightly and held up a finger.

They both looked at him.

73

Joe and Phil left the hotel courtesy of Farook the night porter and made their way out into the back alleys of night-time Karachi. Here the streets were narrow and festooned above their heads with a complicated web of wires attached to posts that leant drunkenly this way and that, supporting a looming cat's cradle of power and telephone lines. Despite the late hour it was still warm and humid and the air was scented with the aromatic residue of the endeavours of several million people; the distinct and unique olfactory identity of the city.

Regardless of his bold assurance that he remembered the route, Phil made frequent reference to his Ctab on which he had scrawled out a rough map. They kept to the shadows and spoke only occasionally and in monosyllables, anxious not to draw attention to themselves. They were in a rundown area of mainly small, shuttered shops and dilapidated two-storey houses crammed close together, seeming to rely on each other for support. Notwithstanding the hour there was still some traffic and a few pedestrians about, whose business abroad was unreadable to the two Westerners. They avoided eye contact and kept up a busy pace.

The clinic was just another rundown shop, distinguishable from the others only in that it was open. There were lights on inside and the sign above the front door in, to them, indecipherable Urdu, was freshly painted. Phil led the way in and introduced Joe to the fresh-faced young man in the Surfers Paradise t-shirt who got up from the reception desk as they entered.

'Joe, this is Doctor Morgan.'

'Name's Steve, Joe.'

They shook hands briefly. 'Thanks for seeing us, Steve.'

'No worries. I'm not exactly overrun with customers as you can see.'

Joe looked around. 'On your own?' Joe asked.

'Yeah, I've got the night shift this week and I speak basic Gujarati so...' he shrugged, indicating there was no problem.

'You don't mind if we film this interview?'

'Go for it. There's no such thing as an Aussie that doesn't fancy himself in Hollywood.'

'I can't promise that exactly,' Joe said, as Phil busied himself setting up the camera, 'but it could well make the news back home.'

Steve grinned 'My mum'll be stoked,' he said amiably.

'But your employers might not be,' Joe felt obliged to point out.

'What're they going to do, sack me? Fine. There's always a job for doctors who'll work in the Third World.'

Joe looked across at Phil. 'Ready to go, Phil?'

Phil, ever the perfectionist, made a face. 'Lighting's dodgy but it should be all right. Give me the cue and we're away.'

'Right. Steve, if you just sit at the reception desk, we'll count down from five, pan round the room then come to you ready for my first question. You okay with that?'

Steve settled himself behind the desk and grinned acceptance. 'Loose as a whore's drawers, as my old man would say.'

Joe nodded to Phil. 'Five, four, three...' he mouthed a silent 'two, one' and as Phil panned the room to rest on the doctor, he said: 'We're in the back streets of Karachi, where Doctor Steve Morgan runs a clinic operating the Two+One project on behalf of the United Nations. First of all, Doctor Morgan, in your experience, how is the scheme working here?'

Steve spread his hands. 'As you can see, despite opening all the hours God sends, women aren't exactly rushing to take our money.'

'Why is that, do you think?'

'Because they're scared.'

'Scared of what exactly?'

'Religious persecution, street violence, scared of their men-folk and scared of dying.'

'Was it like this right from the beginning?'

Steve shook his head. 'Went off like a rocket at first. The men actually encouraged the women to take the cash. Some of them used it to buy Roflu vaccine for the family, which was fine by us. We're in a TW zone after all. Course, some of them just pissed it up against the wall.'

'Then what?'

'It all went a bit pear-shaped about three months ago. The Mullahs were always dead against it anyway and when people started dying the rumours began and that really slowed things down.'

'What were these rumours?'

'It got about that the linctus we supplied was contaminated and that's what was killing people, especially men. Bit of a panic set in, men wouldn't sleep with their wives if they'd taken the linctus for fear of being infected. Then supplies of Roflu ran low and the price went through the roof. It didn't seem to be working anyway. One way or another we found ourselves with no answers.'

'Is it true, are more people dying than usual, men in particular?'

'Seems like it, according to my GP friends.'

'Is it possible the linctus is contaminated?'

'That's what the extremists are saying but if I thought that, I wouldn't be here. What's more likely is we've got ourselves a Roflu-resistant virus in the population. I've heard rumours that the Brits are working on a vaccine for a new strain of the old H5N1 so you can bet it exists. I've been trying to persuade the powers that be to investigate but to be honest I don't think they want to hear what I'm saying. Behind the scenes it's become a blame game.'

'So who's blaming who?'

'The extremists blame the people for siding with the Great Satan and taking American money. Among themselves the people accuse the government of incompetence and corruption and the West of hoarding Roflu for their own use while good Muslims are left to die. The government are blaming the extremists for rumour mongering; they say the deaths are either natural causes or among people who haven't been vaccinated. And of course, on the streets everybody blames the Americans for everything, it's an international pastime, that.'

'And what do you think? Are the authorities, including the UN, turning a blind eye?'

'My opinion? Guilty as charged. Nobody wants to start a panic and they don't know what to do so they do nothing. Meantime they muzzle the press. Any day now they're going to have a full-blown epidemic on their hands. Does anybody care? Do they hell. The people who're dying are poor and brown, they breed like rabbits and there's a lot of them. They're not news and they don't have a voice in the corridors of power so I guess a few million of them will have to die before anything gets done.'

Joe nodded in agreement. 'Is it possible the Avian Flu virus has mutated,' he asked, 'or maybe been deliberately engineered or cross-bred with the Two+One virus, to create a new virus with a special effect on the Y chromosome?'

Wayne thought that one over for a moment. 'You'd need a virologist to answer that,' he said finally, 'but in the virus world it seems you can expect the unexpected.'

Joe thought back to his conversation with Simone Gofre. She had emphatically denied any such possibility but then, what were her allegiances? Was she to be trusted any more than anyone else?

They all turned to look as a short, stocky woman covered from head to foot in a black burqa entered the shop behind them. She hesitated just inside the door and Steve stood up behind the reception desk to welcome her. She shuffled a step or two nearer and her hands made sudden indistinct movements beneath her clothing.

Joe had just enough time to register the suspicion that perhaps this was not a woman, when the world exploded around him.

74

Charles Lovatt looked at his watch. 'We have about twenty minutes before he arrives,' he reminded Alex.

Alex Jones nodded briefly and went straight into his story. 'ConSept Productions have disappeared,' he said. 'The office is empty; the woman running it has been gone for at least two or three days. No forwarding address. It looked to me as though the cleaners had been in so I called on my Oxbridge buddies again. They were nowhere near as forthcoming this time but I got the distinct impression that ConSept was a Special Unit front. As in, fully-funded but completely deniable.'

'Ah. Of course. Which leaves Joe Kendry either as one of theirs or somewhat out on a limb. Have you had a look at his latest epistle?'

'Yes, I don't think he's one of theirs; his diary seems to refute that. He's too much of a conspiracy theorist.'

'Mmm. He does rather have it in for his own people. He seems convinced the CIA are hell-bent on genocide. A little extreme, I thought.'

'And yet...'

'Exactly. We have an allegation made to the BBC backing up what Joe's saying about Pakistan plus an assassination in New

Zealand of a top-level terrorist with Fleur involved. There's a pattern here but we're no nearer to unravelling it. Opinion, Alex?'

Alex considered the question. 'To some extent I'm with Joe on this one. My money would be on our Cousins' involvement but perhaps not in the way he suggests.'

'What then?'

Alex shook his head. 'Sir, I have no idea.'

The urgent warning chord on Charles's Hub interrupted them. 'Excuse me, Alex,' he said as he flicked on the monitor. 'Foreign Office Liaison thinks they have an emergency we should know about.'

There was silence as he read the screen message. Charles's face hardened. Finally he switched off the monitor and turned back to Alex. 'And they were right for once. Joe Kendry is dead. He was in a UN Two+One clinic in Karachi when it was hit by a suicide bomber.'

For a moment neither man said anything, absorbing the news. Alex spoke first. 'Question is, was he the target or just incredibly unlucky?'

'That will be for you to investigate,' Charles said grimly. He looked at his watch. 'Before you start on that we have a very interesting meeting coming up.'

***

When Don Costello entered Charles's office he was in sombre mood and greeted them both with a silent handshake before taking the seat Charles offered him.

'You heard about Joe Kendry?' Charles asked.

'We have an outreach embassy in Karachi; he was an American after all.'

'Not your favourite son, though,' Charles suggested.

Costello shrugged. 'I guess he just lucked out.'

'Wrong place, wrong time, you think?'

'Either that or the enemy mistook him for someone important. He was fishing in dangerous waters you know.'

'Making a documentary about a legitimate UN project?' Charles enquired mildly.

‘Which you don’t do late at night in downtown Karachi. What was he up to Charlie? I sure as hell don’t know and I’d like to make the point here that the enemy uses suicide bombers, our side doesn’t. Our methods, if we ever use them, tend to the more traditional.’

‘Which brings us to Fleur Nichols, Don. Is there anything you’d like to share with us now you’ve had time to look into that business?’

Costello looked unconvinced. ‘I don’t really think so,’ he said finally, leaving behind an element of doubt.

Charles smiled innocently. ‘Nothing personal, Don, but outside of this office you were the only person who knew Fleur Nichols was off to meet the enemy.’

‘Cliché time, Charlie. Appearances can be deceptive. In this case very much so.’

‘Can you offer an alternative scenario?’

Costello mulled that one over, then he said: ‘It wasn’t my game, okay? I don’t know anything about it. But let me take a guess here, let’s be creative. Suppose this guy was high up on our Shoot on Sight list. Suppose we had a unit on his case, waiting for him to pop up somewhere. Suppose he was followed from the Afghan border to New Zealand and the unit took him out. Nothing to do with Fleur Nichols at all. I’m not saying that’s what happened but it would explain it, right? I wouldn’t want you to think I’d breached your confidence, Charlie.’

Charles nodded as if in total acceptance. ‘And was Fleur also a target, added onto the list because she met him secretly and didn’t tell us?’ he asked.

‘I’d guess not. If she wasn’t on the list to begin with, then she wouldn’t be a target. She’d have been collateral. Unlucky, is all.’

‘Fleur and Joe, both unlucky.’ Charles said blandly.

‘You know it happens,’ Costello replied.

Charles gestured to Alex, who got up and moved the nearest of the triple monitors on Charles’s desk Hub so that Costello could see it. ‘Thought you should hear this, Don,’ Charles said. ‘We’ve had a low-level intercept in Joe and Fleur’s love nest for some while and he’s been sending back diaries to his Hub. Have a listen.’

Alex inserted an audio button, hit play and returned to his chair. Don Costello sat stone-faced as he listened to Joe’s suspicions of deliberate contamination of the Two+One linctus, the cover-up by US and UN interests and the allegation of mass genocide by the US Security Services.

'The little shit!' he exploded furiously when the recording ended. 'He's paranoid, a typical lefty conspiracy theorist who's bought into anti-US bullshit. We're better off without him.'

'You didn't know what he was delving into over there I suppose?'

'I sure as hell didn't.'

'Perhaps the enemy did you a favour, then.'

'You could say that.' He stared hard at Charles. 'So what now?'

Charles steepled his fingers as he considered his reply. 'My feeling is this should be kept from the press, at least for the time being. Unfortunately the idea that the US Security Services might want to reduce the recruitment potential of the enemy, under the guise of a humanitarian project to reduce over-population, is just plausible enough to gain a lot of traction in the media.'

'Charles, we've got enough battles to fight, you and I, without adding that one to the list,' Costello said forcibly. 'You know as well as I do the facts don't always stand in matters like this. The media would rather play his lies than our truth. We have to keep this under wraps. We need to send the cleaners into his apartment.'

'Not possible in this country I'm afraid. Listening in is one thing; destroying private correspondence is another. However, we may be able to stop its publication. I have another, possibly related problem. Walter Bloom, the BBC Head of News, is normally useful and co-operative but this time one of his own is involved, and a favourite one at that. I have to have a story for him that Fleur will back up.'

Costello registered the point with no more than a flickering cheek muscle. 'I would prefer all copies of that material were destroyed,' he said mildly. 'Any help we can give you to clear this mess up, we will. Can I offer our facilities to protect Fleur and help with her debrief. Who knows what she may have learnt?'

'Indeed,' Charles said blandly, 'but we think our facilities are adequate to care for Fleur.'

Costello spread his hands. 'What can I do to help, then?' he asked.

Charles smiled artlessly. 'You can tell me who's been crossed off your Shoot on Sight list,' he said.

75

Fleur was in a serene, sedated sleep in a darkened room when Wenna took the call from Charles. She left the comfort of the armchair in which she had been dozing to take the call in the corridor. Charles got straight to the point.

'Where are you, free to talk?' he asked.

'Hospital corridor and yes,' Wenna replied, already sensing trouble.

'Joe Kendry is dead, suicide bomber in Karachi.' He went on to tell her how it had happened, of Joe's diary report and his suspicions about lethally clandestine US involvement in the Two+One project. Then he said, 'That's not all. We had a word with the Cousins and it seems the dead man was Salah al-Rashidi.'

Wenna drew a breath. 'That would explain a lot. What about Fleur?'

'Collateral, they say. They may have trailed al-Rashidi from the Afghan border and she was simply unlucky.'

'Do we believe that?'

'I think we keep our powder dry, watch her like a hawk and beware of friendly fire.'

'And now it's going to look to the other side as if Fleur was a US agent and set up their Head of Operations for the hit. They're not going to be happy.'

'They aren't but it may take a few days for them to organise any reaction so the sooner you're both back here and in a safe house, the better. Meantime for God's sake don't tell her about Joe's death, I wouldn't trust her reaction.'

'At the moment she wouldn't understand what I was saying.'

'Good. And whatever you do, keep her and yourself away from the media.'

'That won't be easy,' Wenna replied, 'this whole country's buzzing like a nest of wasps over this intrusion from the real world. We've got TV cameras and journos from all over surrounding the hospital... But we'll find a way.'

‘When can you get her out of there, do you know?’

‘I’m hopeful for tomorrow.’

‘Good.’

‘She’s asleep at the moment but when she wakes in the morning she’s going to be full of questions. She’s lost her memory, not her mind,’ Wenna pointed out.

‘Tell her as much of the truth as you can. We want her on our side when it comes to the debrief, I don’t want her thinking we’ve lied to her. And I want you right alongside her if she recovers her memory.’

‘Let’s say when. And it could be any time according to the specialist, days or weeks or triggered by some event.’

‘Right, just make sure you’re joined at the hip. Let Alex have your flight number and we’ll arrange a reception committee. Bring her home safe, Wenna, I think al-Rashidi told her something before he died and we need to know what it was. I’m relying on you.’

‘I’ll do my...’ Wenna began but the line was dead. Charles was not given to extended goodbyes.

Wenna returned to Fleur’s room, her mind buzzing with what she had been told. What had started as a simple and secret fishing expedition had exploded into a horribly public worldwide media frenzy with the death of al-Rashidi and, if there was a fraction of truth in what Joe Kendry had alleged, looked to be heading for a political nightmare of the kind that the Secret Services most detest. No wonder Charles was unusually abrupt: he was going to have to make explanations to his political masters about this whole mess, and innocence and honest explanation would not necessarily stand him in good stead; MI5 was not universally esteemed in the corridors of Whitehall except, occasionally, as a repository for blame. And old rivals for funding and influence, MI6, would be delighted to wallow in the comforting mud bath of schadenfreude.

Fleur had not moved and was breathing easily, soundly asleep. Wenna stood looking down at her. With her petite body and elfin looks, her head bandaged across her brow line and below her chin, she looked frail and vulnerable, not at all like the hard-nosed journalist Wenna knew her to be. Wenna felt an unexpected wave of tenderness and moved to take the girl’s hand but stopped herself, not wanting to wake her.

She returned to her vigil in the armchair, her mind full of dread for the moment that she knew would eventually come, the moment when she would have to tell Fleur that Joe was dead.

76

Simone Gofre had finished the work she had set her heart on completing. Even had she been able, it was not for her to concern herself with further development, containment or future usage; that was for lesser brains. A new, artificially created Avian Flu virus had been born under her hands, one that had jumped the five evolutionary stages necessary to be capable of being transmitted human to human. It would take its place for now in the deep freeze cabinets that also housed phials of the most dangerous pathogens in the world, waiting for someone else to uncover its secrets, discover how to neutralise it and validate her work. It was done. She had finished.

Yet, when the moment came to report her final success and justify her insistence on continuing to work when under sentence of death, she found herself reluctant. The PC4 unit had been her second home and the source of her creative drive for half her working life; the thought of leaving it now was impossibly difficult to face, even though she knew she must. But not quite yet. The pressure was off, but no one knew that, so she could indulge herself by staying on for another day or so.

She was sitting at her Hub, apparently immersed in the mass of data on the monitor, but in fact in a daydream. Beside her on her work desk was the opaque plastic container that housed the two syringes she had worked so hard to be allowed to bring in. So far this day she had used just the one. Her mind was wandering, travelling back and forth over a life of high achievement, recalling the highs and lows of a twenty-five-year career that had immeasurably benefited humankind.

In the end though, it came back to this day and the harsh reality that her life was finished. She felt a vicious flood of anger. Ultimately, despite the degrees and awards and accolades, she had achieved nothing. A few people had lived who perhaps otherwise would not have, but who was to say that was a worthwhile achievement? She might have saved rapists and murderers for all she knew. And those she had saved simply added to the nine billion humans, and rising, that were destroying the planet with the sheer weight of their presence.

Humans had become the pre-eminent alpha predator and frequent wars, natural disasters and epidemics alone were no longer effective controls.

It had not always been so. Once the hunters had also been the hunted, prey for the great carnivores: Panthera leo, Ursus arctos, Carcharodon carcharias, Varanus komodoensis, Panthera tigris and their like. They, and a limited group of others, had the size, the ferocity and the voraciousness to prey on humans in the days when human numbers were much smaller. Now those great beasts had been driven to the point of extinction by a vast tribe of upright apes with large brains and insufficient intelligence to preserve themselves or the planet on which they are totally dependent.

But there was always another killer waiting in the wings, one ultimately even more effective than the great carnivores. Perhaps, having dominated the great beasts, humankind had, by providing a vast population of hosts, left itself vulnerable to the smallest predator of all.

The idea did not distress her, despite the fact that she had spent a working lifetime fighting the war against this particular foe. She recognised that her latest creation was a huge advance, an immensely valuable tool for science. Ultimately however, she sensed the battle would be lost.

Her thinking became confused; surely there was still hope. Those who followed her might not be as talented as her, but perhaps they would be good enough to keep the work going at least. She knew she had been special, perhaps unique in her abilities. She had been a scientific sniper, armed with a high-powered intellect, picking off the worst of the enemy one by one. Strip away all the intellectual, academic and scientific ostentation surrounding her creations and that's what she was: a highly educated, very experienced, professional virus killer. She felt a distant, clouded sense of relief.

She knew what she was and it sat well with her.

77

Despite a carefully moderated explanation from Charles, Walter Bloom was incandescent with rage. 'You promised, Lovatt, you promised to keep my girl safe.'

'She's alive, Walter, she's under guard and Wenna is holding her hand. She's as safe as can be.'

'No thanks to you.'

They were in Walter Bloom's office at the BBC since Charles could not put off the meeting and had no wish to let the irate Head of News loose in Thames House. It was vital that Walter did not go public prematurely with what he knew of the background to the story; that would add enormously to the political interrogation Charles was already coming under. He had not been offered tea.

'All thanks to me, actually, Walter. Remember Fleur deliberately ran from both of us, went off to consort with the enemy with not so much as a phone call to you or a tip-off to us.'

'They insisted, you can bet on that,' Walter responded, not in the least mollified. 'She was chasing a world exclusive and she'd have brought it back to me.'

'Possibly, but we were the ones who tracked her down and we're the ones who are keeping her safe, despite what some might see as her act of disloyalty.'

'Bollocks, Charles! Fleur hasn't got a disloyal bone in her body. She's an honest journalist and a bloody good one. Who's the dead man?'

The sudden change of tack set Charles aback only for a moment. He knew he had to throw this old newshound a bone. 'There are things I can tell you, but not for publication.'

'So?'

'This has not been confirmed but we believe it is Salah al-Rashidi. Head of Operations for AQE.'

Walter sat back in his chair and nodded acceptance. 'It had to be someone that high up. Who killed him, the CIA I suppose.'

'That's a dangerous presumption, Walter. It could have been an internal dispute. It wouldn't be the first time they'd assassinated one of their own.'

'I don't believe that anymore than you do. So who killed Joe Kendry?'

‘So far as we know Joe was collateral, the suicide bomber was after the clinic.’

‘Collateral. Like Fleur. Yes, of course,’ Walter said sarcastically.

‘We’ve come up with no connection between the two events.’

‘When’s she coming home?’

‘Next couple of days we think, and then she’s going straight to a safe house with medical facilities. I know you want to talk to her but so do we and we have priority. As soon as she’s recovered her memory and has been debriefed you can have your exclusive interview.’

‘I’ll have that, all right and remember, she’s a journalist and as soon as she’s got her memory back she’ll want to tell her story and you won’t be able to stop her.’

‘I can’t stop her telling her story but if I was forced to, I can stop publication.’

‘You threatening to section me?’

‘I need time, Walter. I have to know what al-Rashidi said to her before anyone else does, surely you see that. And I have to protect her; she may be a target from either side. I can do that, you can’t. You want her safe, don’t you?’

Walter crossed his arms and leant forward onto his desk, pinning Charles with a grim stare. ‘It’s like this, Charles. I run the premier news desk in the world. We don’t like buying in stories and regurgitating second-hand material. We break news, and sometimes, like now, we make it. Fleur is my girl and her meeting with al-Rashidi, the shooting and Joe’s death are my stories. If you gag me and someone else gets in first I promise you I will take it very personally and I’ll haunt you till the day you die.’

Charles spread his hands placatingly. ‘Let’s not follow that route, Walter. I promise, nobody gets any information ahead of you. I also promise to keep you informed of what’s going on and you will get first and exclusive access to Fleur as soon as possible. That’s almost going beyond my mandate.’

‘And for this I do what?’

‘Concentrate on the Kendry story and leave Fleur out of it. They kept their relationship pretty quiet; it’s unlikely anyone else will pick up on it. Live with what others are doing on the al-Rashidi shooting for now, play dumb, block any media enquiries about Fleur.'

'That's a big ask. Everyone in this business knows she belongs to us, they'll think we've lost the plot.'

'Then one day soon they'll have a nasty shock when you deliver the inside story, won't they? And you will, I promise you that.'

Walter sat back in his chair. 'Tell you what I'm going to do, Charles, I'm going to publish as much as I can, right up to the limit – you'd expect that, I hope. I'm going to authorise a documentary, which may very well link the two stories, and put my best team on it. But I won't screen that until I can add Fleur's story. Okay?'

Charles knew that was the best deal he was going to get without making an enemy for life. 'I'll take your word on that.'

'Never forget, Charles, I don't work for you, but for the time being and against my better judgement, I'll work with you. Now, you want tea?'

78

Wenna had slept little during the night and it seemed like the crack of dawn when the early-shift nurse came in to wake Fleur, see her washed and prepare her for breakfast and the consultant's rounds. Wenna was politely asked to leave and was offered the welcome opportunity to freshen up in the nurse's common room. By the time she returned, Callum West had the news she had been waiting for: Fleur had been cleared to travel and he had booked flights for her and Wenna later that morning on a domestic flight to Auckland, where they would be met and escorted to the International Terminal.

The day duty staff nurse handed over painkillers and a list of instructions for Fleur's welfare on the flight. She reported that the patient was alert, no longer sedated but still amnesiac and somewhat confused. She should see a doctor as soon as she returned home.

Wenna left a message for Charles and Alex with the night owl at Thames House to report their incoming flight number then turned her attention to Callum.

'Thanks for everything, Callum,' she said, 'sorry I have to leave you to deal with Bob Purau.'

‘No worries,’ Callum responded, ‘he’s an old pro. The real problems are back with you now. Glad you’re the one who has to give her the bad news.’ He looked at his watch. ‘Want to get her ready?’

Wenna entered Fleur’s room, somewhat depressed by Callum’s reminder, to find her sitting up on the side of her bed, perfectly made up, dressed in her travelling clothes and going through the contents of her handbag, her small suitcase open at her feet. Her head now had a smaller bandage worn like a bandeau and her short hair was sticking up above it in cute little tufts. Wenna found herself smiling. Fleur looked up as Wenna entered.

‘I suppose I do look strange,’ she said.

‘No. I’m just glad to see you looking so much better.’

‘I thought it might help me remember if I looked through my things but no luck. You were here last night, weren’t you?’

‘Yes, I slept in that chair.’

‘Why?’

‘Because that’s what friends do.’

Fleur pointed at her bandage. ‘So how did I get this?’

Wenna took a breath before answering. It was going to be like this; she would have to think carefully before answering every question, and there were going to be a lot of them, she was sure of that. ‘You got in the way of a bullet intended for someone else,’ she said.

‘Who?’

‘I was hoping you would remember that,’ Wenna equivocated.

‘I don’t. Was it someone I know?’

‘I think you just met them.’

‘Are they injured as well?’

‘It was a man and he’s dead.’

‘Who shot him?’

‘I don’t know.’

‘Do the police know?’

‘I don’t think so, no.’

‘But they think I might be in danger.’

‘Yes.’

‘So that’s why there’s policemen outside the door, to guard me.’

‘Yes.’

'So why am I in New Zealand?'

'You came here to meet the man who was shot.'

'Why?'

'Because you're a journalist and you came here to get a story from him.'

'What story?'

'Only you know the answer to that. Look, we have a plane to catch; can I answer some more questions later? Now I need you to get dressed.'

'I am dressed,' Fleur said, puzzled.

***

Half an hour later three nurses, one male and two female, walked out of the staff entrance at the rear of the hospital and headed towards the staff car park. They were one of a number of employees coming and going singly and in small groups. One of the female nurses wore a broad-brimmed sunhat and was arm in arm with the other. The TV journalists covering the rear exit gave them no more than a passing glance; it was shift change, they assumed.

The three got into an elderly, nondescript coupe with a sticker on its dusty rear window advertising the nursing trade union. It belonged to the wife of one of the AOF officers who had been guarding Fleur. With Callum at the wheel they drove at a steady speed across the side of Hagley Park heading for the airport. Three hours later Fleur and Wenna were on an international flight heading across the Tasman Sea bound for Singapore and eventually, Heathrow.

At about that time the waiting media saw the Armed Offenders Squad officers standing down and leaving the hospital and they knew they had been outwitted. Some of them broke for the airport, others, anxious to recover something from the debacle, rang contacts in London, warning them that Fleur Nichols was on her way. One, smarter and faster off the mark than the rest, did an internet search on Fleur, located her agent and left a six-figure offer on her Hub for an exclusive.

79

The only good news that Charles Lovatt had to take with him to the meeting was the fact that Fleur Nichols was on her way home. The Security Intelligence Co-ordinator reported directly to the Prime Minister and had taken the unusual step of asking for a personal meeting with him, a privilege more usually granted to the Director General. It was a privilege that Charles would happily have foregone at this moment.

'Charles, so good of you to come,' Sir James McCulloch said warmly. They were in his personal office, a wood-panelled Victorian relic into which the tousle-haired but immaculately dressed Whitehall mandarin fitted like a glove.

'A pleasure, sir, as always,' Charles lied.

'We live in interesting times,' McCulloch observed.

'The Chinese knew something when they offered that as a curse,' Charles commented.

McCulloch nodded agreement and got straight to the point. 'The media are in a feeding frenzy and the PM is not at all happy. There are some things we need to know. For example, how is it that Fleur Nichols, a known sympathiser who, I am reliably informed, was being monitored by you, is able to set up a meeting with a top AQE operative in friendly little New Zealand and MI5 know nothing about it? See the problem, Charles?'

'Indeed I do. The answer is that we did know about it but she slipped the net once she arrived in New Zealand. We were reliant on their SIS to track her once she arrived there but I don't blame them, last minute change of flights caught them out and we temporarily lost sight of her.'

'I have no interest in apportioning blame at this juncture, Charles, but it does not look good from any point of view. At least can you tell me what that meeting was about?'

'Fleur Nichols is being brought back here by one of my best people right at this moment. I hope to be able to answer that question when we've been able to debrief her.'

'Assuming she regains her memory.'

'We're pretty much assured she will. It's just a matter of time and managing her recovery.'

'And hoping she will co-operate.'

‘We can be fairly persuasive and I have no reason to believe that, despite being a journalist, she is not a loyal citizen.’

‘Let us hope so.’ McCulloch did not sound convinced. ‘Some members of the international press are questioning that fact, suggesting she might be an American agent.’

‘I don’t think so.’

‘The press are also blaming the Americans for the assassination. You agree with them on that at least?’

‘Officially they deny it.’

‘I’ll take that as a yes. The question that springs to mind is how come an MI5 operation somehow ends up as an opportunity for the Cousins to strike one off their hit list, mmm? Are we taking the special relationship that far these days?’

‘I can absolutely assure you that we did not co-operate in the assassination. They say they had followed al-Rashidi from the Afghan border and Fleur simply got in the way.’

‘And is that likely?’

‘It could be so.’

McCulloch leant forward on his inlaid desktop. ‘And how does the death of this American documentary maker fit into all this?

‘He’d been living with Fleur for a year and he was in the wrong place at the wrong time.’

‘As she was.’

‘Quite.’

McCulloch sighed heavily and eased back in his chair. ‘Does she know he’s no longer with us?’

‘Not yet. When she recovers her memory we’ll have to play things very carefully in that area.’

‘Indeed. It has come to my notice that the BBC are planning a documentary on this whole business; she is one of theirs after all. Media speculation we can dismiss for what it is but if the BBC goes to air with verifiable information not available to me, I should be quite put out, I think,’ McCulloch said mildly.

‘I will go out of my way to ensure that doesn’t happen,’ Charles replied.

‘Please do. I am aware of course that there may be things that, for operational reasons, you may see fit to keep even from me.

However, should that be the case, as you know, the Service will ultimately be held responsible for any unfortunate consequences.'

'As is only right and proper, sir,' Charles confirmed.

'You have nothing else you wish to tell me at the moment?'

'The situation is fluid but as of the moment, no.'

'Then let us hope for all our sakes that this fluid situation is not allowed to leak through our hands. What has happened already might be cause for adverse comment but if anything happened to Fleur Nichols from now on then I think it might be difficult to find believable explanations, don't you?'

'We have already made arrangements to keep her safe.'

'I'm sure you have. I trust they are effective.' He stood up and offered his hand. 'I won't keep you any longer.'

When he left the room, despite the fact that McCulloch had not once raised his voice beyond gentle enquiry, Charles felt that he had been subject to a harrowing interrogation. He had been left with absolutely no doubt as to the depths of the Service's failings to date and where, finally, the buck would stop.

Should he have told McCulloch about the Two+One allegations? Or would that have made him sound like a weak man desperate to shift the line of enquiry into new and, for him, safer areas?

There were too many questions and, until Wenna got safely back with Fleur, too few answers. He was on his own and, if it all went wrong now, he knew he would have few friends, even in the Security world.

80

Fleur, living in a present that began when she woke up in Christchurch Hospital, was aware that there was a lot she did not know, but she did at least know that at the moment she desperately needed someone she could rely on to fill in the gaps in her past. Wenna had been understandably preoccupied whilst they made their escape from the hospital and were shepherded by Callum West through the VIP corridors of Christchurch and Auckland airport terminals and onto the UK flight. Once aboard, they had been upgraded to Business Class and given paired places near a window. It had been arranged that the news channels on the monitors and audio on those two seats would be unobtainable so Fleur would have no access to unwanted input during the flight. Callum was not without some influence it seemed.

Now, relaxed in her seat, Wenna simply looked tired and drawn. From what little she had learned so far her new friend must have been under great stress in recent days. Even so, Fleur had too many questions to leave her in peace just yet.

'I want you to tell me all about me,' she said.

'I'll tell you what I can,' Wenna said guardedly. 'Where do you want to begin?'

'Where was I born, who were my parents, where did I live, where was I educated. That'll do for a start.'

Wenna smiled. Fleur had a straightforward, childlike quality about her which she found endearing. She was a woman it was easy to befriend. She answered as best she could, hoping the biographical files she was relying on were accurate. Fleur was not someone she ever wanted to lie to.

'So I'm half English, half American.'

'It seems so.'

'Where are my parents?'

'I'm sorry, Fleur, they're both dead.'

'So I'm an orphan. And a journalist.'

'A very well-known one. You've won awards and done a lot of television work for the BBC.'

'Did I come out to New Zealand to work for the BBC?'

'No. You came on your own.'

Fleur stopped for a moment to absorb that, then she said: 'How old am I?'

'I believe you're thirty-two.'

'Where do I live?'

'You have an apartment in Docklands, London.'

'Am I married?'

This was dangerous country. So far as she knew Fleur and Joe Kendry had not been engaged. Mindful of Charles's warning, a simple answer seemed best. 'No,' she said.

'I saw some people on the plane looking at me, am I famous or is it because of the bandage?'

'Both,' Wenna replied.

‘So I’m a famous English/American journalist with an apartment in London and I’m single. If I was beautiful I’d be quite a catch.’

‘You are beautiful,’ Wenna said without thinking, ‘very beautiful.’

Fleur looked at her but Wenna was hiding her embarrassment by evidencing great interest in the monitor screen on the back of the seat in front of her that was showing a movie with the sound muted.

‘Thank you,’ Fleur said simply. ‘So are you. Are you married?’

‘No. But I thought you wanted to know about yourself.’

‘I do. If I’m famous, do I have an agent?’

‘I’m sure you do, yes.’

‘Am I wealthy?’

Wenna hesitated. Having accessed Fleur and Joe’s bank accounts she had an excellent idea of their financial position but had no wish to reveal the fact. ‘I don’t know for sure but I imagine you’re able to pay your bills,’ she said, attempting a light-heartedness she wasn’t feeling.

‘I know some things,’ Fleur said. ‘When you mentioned London and England I didn’t remember them but I kind of knew about them. Same with New Zealand, it’s like I’ve heard of them but a long while ago. So I’ve got memory of background things like that but only when you mention them. It’s events, things and people that I can’t remember.’

‘Well that’s a good sign I should think.’ Wenna covered a yawn with her hand.

‘You’re tired aren’t you? Do you want to have a sleep while I think up some more questions?’

Wenna smiled. ‘I wouldn’t mind,’ she said truthfully.

‘That’s fine. You stretch out, I’ll make sure the bogeyman doesn’t get you,’ Fleur said, grinning.

This girl is incredible, Wenna thought. Gunned down only two days ago, still trying to recover from amnesia and she finds something to joke about. But if she knew what I’m keeping from her it would be a different story.

81

‘She’s on her way, Walter. Just thought I’d let you know.’

'Good. How is she?'

'Last report, coping remarkably well.'

'She got a doctor?'

'Doctor, psychologist and personal chef. It'll be red carpet treatment for Fleur I can assure you. And Walter, I have a request to make,'

Walter Bloom snorted. 'Now why am I not surprised. What is it this time?'

'You've given him a good run already. Keep Joe Kendry out of your news for a couple of days,' Charles suggested.

'That story's still hot, Charles. His remains have just been flown back to his people in the States and its headlining there, award-winning director terror victim and all that. No matter what I do he'll be on the other channels anyway.'

'I can explain excluding the other channels at the safe house but not the BBC, she's already been told she works for you.'

'Don't know...'

'It's for her sake, Walter. At the moment she doesn't know Joe ever existed. We need to break that to her slowly and carefully, don't you agree?'

'Mmm… I'll see what I can do, but the opposition is going to be giving it a lot of airtime – I hear they're rushing an hour-long doco to screen and you can bet they'll have an angle. Pressure's on me here, I want access to her, Charlie boy, and I'm not a patient man.'

'I understand but, well, we've had this conversation, Walter, you know how it has to be.'

Walter Bloom grunted reluctant agreement. 'Got some bad news for you, Charles. I took a call from April Grosse, Fleur's agent, been putting her off since the story broke. She's like a rattlesnake on steroids, seems to think it's all my fault. So I had to tell her...' Charles groaned. 'Relax, I told her Fleur went off on a hunt of her own, trouble is, she doesn't believe me and she's banging on doors trying to find out what's going on. Did I tell you she's married to the Labour member for East Hackney?'

'You didn't,' Charles said, 'and I'm sorry you have now. Can you try and keep her calm for a couple of days?

'Not my problem, Charles. She's worked out you spooks must have got her in protective custody so she's set her sights on Thames House. Expect a call.'

'Thank you for that, Walter.'

'Pleasure.'

'One last thing,' Charles said.

'Am I going to like this?'

'Probably not a great deal, but it is only a request.'

Walter sighed. 'Then the answer's no.'

'I've had a meeting with someone in the Cabinet Office. They're concerned at the prospect of your documentary on this case. They suspect you may have inside information best kept in-house. Any chance you could can the idea for the time being?'

'No.'

'Walter…'

'Charles, I am the most reasonable man in the world, a pussycat, a born gentleman, everybody's pushover. What I am not is a lackey for MI5 or the PM's office; so don't push your luck. I have no intention of letting the opposition walk all over me on this one. I know Fleur a hell of a lot better than you do and I can assure you when she's not loved-up she's tough as old boots. Once she's normal again she'll be back in front of the camera in a flash, Joe or no Joe, and the doco will be waiting for her. We look after our own and she's one of ours. You want her for what you can get out of her.'

Charles was rapidly becoming irritated at being lectured to. 'So do you, Walter,' he said tartly.

'Yeah, but we love her,' Walter Bloom said, and put down the phone.

82

Wenna woke to find Fleur gently shaking her arm. 'You've had three hours,' Fleur told her, 'and any minute now they going to bring us dinner or lunch or whatever it is.'

Coming too slowly, Wenna said: 'Thanks. How's your head now?'

'Feels a bit numb down that side but otherwise all right.'

Wenna ran her hands through her hair and adjusted her seat to the upright position. 'We'll have a doctor look at it as soon as we get there.'

'Where? Where are we going, to my apartment?'

'No. We thought it best we take you to a place where we can keep you safe until this thing blows over.'

'You think I'm still in danger?'

'It's not a risk we're prepared to take. Besides, the doctor advised rest and a peaceful environment to help you recover your memory.'

'Who is 'we'?'

'Let's say the Foreign Office.'

Fleur rounded on her. 'No, let's not. Let's tell the truth,' she demanded.

Wenna was brought up short. Somewhere along the way she had slipped out of her usual professional mode. She had let her guard down, looking on Fleur as a vulnerable, pliant victim when in fact she was still the old Fleur Nichols, just with a temporary memory loss: the grim determination and quick mind was still there. It was time to put things right if she was to keep Fleur on side.

'You're right. I'm still half asleep and old habits die hard.' She dropped her voice. 'I work for the Security Services and we're the ones who've arranged for your journey home.'

'Are you my armed guard, then?'

Wenna laughed quietly. 'No, we have people to do that if necessary, not me. I'm more like a cross between a tour guide and an agony aunt.'

Fleur gave her a stern look. 'I think you're more important than that.' She took Wenna's hand and grasped it tightly, her face relaxing. 'I don't want you ever to lie to me, Wenna. I know you're doing your job but you're my only link with my past and you're very important to me.'

Overcome by the plea in those immense brown eyes, Wenna squeezed her hand in response. 'Think of me as your sister,' she said, 'I'll do all I can to help you get your memory back, and when you have you won't need anyone to answer questions.'

Fleur smiled at her. 'Until then, be my guide and mentor,' she said. 'They won't send you back to your office when we get to England, will they?'

'No. I'll stay with you until this is all over,' Wenna promised, knowing that was one promise she would definitely be able to keep.

'Were you following me?' Fleur asked suddenly.

Wenna was taken aback. She looked away from Fleur to gather her thoughts. 'You have a disconcerting way of suddenly changing the subject,' she protested.

'So, were you? You must have been because I was shot and you were by my bedside when I woke up, so you must have been here before it happened.'

'Yes, I was following you.'

'So why didn't you stop whoever it was from shooting me?'

Wenna took a second to compose her mind. She was going to have to get used to these sudden changes of conversational direction from Fleur. 'You left London on a secret mission of your own to meet an informant in New Zealand, you travelled on a passport in your birth name, Janice Firth, not as Fleur Nichols, then officers there missed the flight you arrived on so we had no idea where you were or who you were meeting.'

Fleur digested that, then she said: 'Who was he? I asked you before but you didn't tell me.'

'Salah al-Rashidi.'

'Country of origin?'

'We're not sure. Possibly Saudi Arabia.'

'Why was he shot?'

'Because he was the Head of Operations for Al Qaeda East.'

'Who are they?'

Wenna smiled at the earnest little face confronting her. 'This is a long flight,' she said and, mimicking Fleur, 'I think I need some dinner or lunch or whatever it is they're bringing down the aisle at this moment.'

83

Simone Gofre arrived home in the early evening. She turned the car engine off and sat still for a moment, gathering the strength to meet Auriol for the last time, fully anticipating a dramatic scene of one kind or another. Her muscles felt stiff, the arm where she had injected herself earlier ached and she felt light-headed and slightly nauseous. She opened the car door and swung her legs out to rest on the ground, pausing again to compose herself. There was heavy cloud cover and a brisk breeze fluttered the leaves of the tree above her as she levered herself to her feet and walked stiffly towards the house, pointing the remote over her shoulder to lock the car behind her. The gardens had been let go in recent weeks, the lawns were badly in need of mowing and weeds infested the flowerbeds; neither of them had felt much like gardening lately.

The wind gusted, chilling Simone and moaning through the Hub aerials on the roof. She shivered as she unlocked the door, faintly surprised Auriol was not there to greet her but glad to be inside.

'Auriol, I'm here,' she called out.

There was no reply and her voice seemed to echo along the hall. She left her coat on the hallstand and walked through to the kitchen. It was clean, spotlessly clean, but empty. Although she knew that Auriol was not there, she walked slowly through the rooms on the ground floor, then methodically through the three bedrooms and the bathroom upstairs. The house was cold and silent, bereft of life. Simone returned downstairs, went into the kitchen and poured herself a large glass of brandy. It was medicinal, she told herself with grim humour. She took it into the sitting room and sat in her usual chair beside a cheerless fireplace.

After a while she got up again and went out into the garden. She opened the door to the old shed and looked inside and, as she had expected, it was empty. It was necessary to look, though, to make sure that Auriol really had gone. It would have been untidy not to. Simone returned to the house, put her coat back on and went to sit in the coldly unwelcoming sitting room. She sipped the brandy, feeling its warmth and thinking about Auriol. For once in her life the girl had taken decisive action. She had obviously decided that sitting through a last dinner making stilted small talk, for that's all there could possibly have been, was too much for her to bear. Simone felt the slightest twist of annoyance that there was not so much as a note. There should have been something, even if only another emotional outburst. Simply walking away in sullen silence was not like Auriol.

In a corner their Hub was blinking at her, telling her it was in sleep mode. Simone activated it and called up Auriol's Ctab. It rang repeatedly then went to her answer service. Well, complete separation was what she had wanted, what she had thought was best for them both. Simone returned to her chair and her brandy. It was over, love had gone from her world, only grey blankness was left and soon enough that too would be gone.

Later, she thought she ought to eat but the prospect of preparing a meal made her feel queasy. She poured herself another brandy and went upstairs to her bedroom. Sitting on her bed with her syringe case beside her she used her Ctab to call the local taxi company and order a cab for the morning. On the way home that evening she had twice found herself driving on the wrong side of the road, being blasted out of her trance-like state by the horns of oncoming motorists, without any idea of how it had happened. She no longer trusted herself behind the wheel.

She shrugged out of her outer clothing and wound a medical tourniquet onto her upper arm. She was beginning to become dehydrated and it was difficult to get a vein up to inject. She could have opted for morphine pills but that had seemed like a cop-out from a minor inconvenience and she was not one to ever avoid a confrontation with the tougher issues in life. I must drink more water, she thought, it would be ironic if I died of kidney failure before losing out to cancer. She sat for a moment shivering, the empty syringe in her hand.

It came to her then. She knew exactly how she could control her own end in a way that was both certain and appropriate.

84

The following morning, having been kept in a holding pattern for half an hour, the plane carrying Fleur and Wenna finally came in over the ponds at Staines Reservoirs for a faultless landing at Heathrow. As they were taxiing towards the terminal gate, still pinned by their seat belts, Fleur suddenly grabbed Wenna's arm.

'April Grosse,' she said. Wenna looked puzzled for a second. 'My agent. That's her name.'

'Yes, I believe so,' Wenna replied.

'And Daddy... Daddy, but...'

'Walter Bloom. He's the Head of News and Current Affairs at the BBC and your boss for a lot of the time. His nickname is Daddy.'

‘I have a nickname for the Head of News? I must be in favour.’

‘I suspect he regards you as his prime asset.’

‘So I’m a television journalist.’

‘I’m sure I told you that.’

‘You just said journalist. Foreign correspondent, yes?’

‘The best-known one in Britain by far.’

‘So what happened to me is probably big news.’

‘It is,’ Wenna confirmed.

Fleur was silent for a while. Then she said: ‘I want to call my agent.’

Wenna hesitated. From what little she knew about April Grosse the chances of her keeping quiet about Joe’s death were minuscule. Unless she could get to her first. ‘I’ll arrange that for you as soon as we’re settled into the safe house,’ she said.

They were taken off the plane first and ushered by Airport Police through customs and immigration to the VIP lounge where Alex Jones was waiting for them. They greeted each other briefly and Wenna took him aside.

‘She’s remembering things already. Call Walter Bloom and April Grosse and warn them to expect a call from her but tell them not to mention Joe’s death. Beg them if you have to.’

‘Should we let her make those calls yet?’ Alex wondered.

‘We can’t stop her, Alex. Trust me, she’s a very bright and determined lady and keeping her out of trouble isn’t going to be easy. How are things here?’

Alex brought her up to date with the pressures being piled on Charles Lovatt. ‘And outside we have a small army of media,’ he concluded, ‘they seem to have been tipped off you were on your way.’

Wenna gripped his arm. ‘I need to know before the debrief and before Fleur recovers any more of her memory. Has Charles said anything to suggest we had any involvement in setting al-Rashidi up?’

‘I think you can take it the answer is no. Charles was absolutely furious when he found out what had happened, he knew it would look as if we’d been in the Cousins’ pocket.’

‘You’re sure we’re not?’

‘I’d stake my career on it, and yours. If I had to plant a flag in the sand I’d say this was a Don Costello special.’

Ten minutes later a limousine with darkened windows left the VIP area in a hurry, snaking its way through the streets of the airport and out onto the main London road. Within seconds the media pack was on the chase, which continued into the city traffic where the most they managed was a few shots of the darkened windows and some blurred shapes inside. Finally they were left frustrated as the limo entered through the electronic gates of Thames House car park and disappeared.

Meanwhile an RAF helicopter took off from a secure area at Heathrow. It headed across the capital and up the east coast cutting inland to touch down at the old World War Two aerodrome at Martlesham Heath, much of which had long since been developed. A car with a driver who looked as if he had trouble fitting his bulk into his chauffeur’s uniform was waiting, and took Wenna and Fleur for the short drive to their final destination.

The sign above the gates as they passed through said: ‘Melton Hospital Rest Home.’ Once a repository for the mentally ill, it had long since been adapted as a hospice for mentally and physically damaged British servicemen, originally from the wars of attrition in The Falklands, Iraq and Afghanistan. It might have occurred to some to wonder why these unheralded derelicts of war, hidden away in the East Anglian countryside, needed high-tech security, with armed guards at the entrance and others discreetly patrolling the grounds.

At the rear of the main hospital building were a number of more modern chalets and it was in front of one of these that the car stopped.

‘We’re home,’ Wenna said, ‘I expect you’re pretty tired.’

‘Yes, but I’ve a lot of catching up to do and I need you to help me,’ Fleur said determinedly.

Wenna put an arm round her shoulders and ushered her through the door of the chalet as the chauffeur carried their cases in, hefting them as if they were weightless. ‘I will but before anything else you’re going to see our doctors, then you’re heading for bed.’

‘Plural? How many doctors do I need to look at a scratch on the head?’

85

There was not a mark on her. She was lying completely naked on her back on a stainless steel shelf that had been drawn out of a wall of deep freeze cabinets in the morgue. There was a numbered tag around her left wrist. The young police officer was standing just behind her, waiting.

'Yes,' Simone said, 'this is Auriol Preston.'

'Thank you. I'll leave you alone for a moment if you like,' the officer said and walked away to stand by the door without waiting for a reply.

Simone shivered slightly, partly because she had dressed quickly and too lightly in the dawn chill, partly an emotional reaction. She found it difficult to make a connection between the Auriol she had known and loved and the inanimate body before her, legs modestly together, arms neatly to the side, well-formed breasts that she had so often caressed now flattened and flaccid.

For the moment Simone felt nothing, emotionally completely distanced from what she was seeing. It was a cadaver, one that physically resembled her lover but it was not she. Auriol was elsewhere, or nowhere, but certainly not here, so it was not possible to feel bereavement. Not yet, not in this cold, sterile, alien environment.

But it should have been. Simone felt guilty that she did not instantly have what she assumed would be a more normal, visceral reaction. She stood frowning down at Auriol's face as if, by her disapproval, she could bring her woman back to life. Her hand moved slightly as instinctively she went to reach out for her but she stopped herself, feeling that to touch the body she had touched in living love would somehow be indelicate now. There could be no healing touch, so there would be no touch.

She took a step back, her eyes still fixed on Auriol's face, her mind in a confused whirl. There was a discreet, enquiring cough behind her. She turned away from the body and walked unsteadily to the door. An attendant entered to close the cabinet and Simone followed the officer into the mortuary office, where she was offered a seat. The officer composed herself behind the desk to complete the legal formalities.

'Are you her next of kin?' she asked.

'For what it's worth, yes,' Simone replied dully. She was overtaken by a sense of wild unreality; this was one of those appalling dreams she had been having lately. Cruel as real life often was, it surely should not inflict this bland, bureaucratic torture. The young PC was looking at her enquiringly, hands hovering over her Hub pad. She must have asked something and Simone had missed it.

'What?' she asked.

'Your name and address?'

Simone told her and as she was typing she asked: 'What did she do?'

The officer hesitated for a moment, then took a piece of paper from a folder and handed it over. 'I should check your ID first,' she said, 'but... She had this in her hand.'

The note was short. It was in Auriol's looped, girlish writing. It read: 'I decided to go before you. I'll wait for you there. God bless and keep you. All my love forever and beyond. Your Auriol. xxx'

The young constable was concentrating hard on the Hub in front of her, giving Simone time. After perhaps a minute during which no coherent thoughts of any kind entered Simone's mind she looked up and asked: 'Where did you find her?'

The officer cleared her throat and put on an official voice. 'She was in her car, parked near the lake in Rumerhedge Forest... Well, it's hardly a forest...'

'I know it,' Simone said. It was where they used to go when they first met. It was where they had exchanged their first clandestine kiss, where they had admitted their love, where they had finally decided to confront the world and to hell with what others thought. It was their special place. They had not been there for a long while.

'How?' Simone asked.

Young as she was, the PC intuitively understood what Simone was asking. 'The car doors were locked, the windows were closed and there was a plastic tube running from the exhaust to inside the vehicle. Some walkers found the car early this morning'

‘Carbon monoxide poisoning.’ Simone said blankly. ‘Exactly like my father. The death of choice for the people I love it seems. But she wouldn’t have known that.’

After a moment Simone added, ‘At least she didn’t suffer.’

Auriol would have wanted to spare me that, she thought, even at the moment of her greatest distress she was still thinking of me. And she had chosen somewhere symbolic of their love, not wanting to take her life at the house where Simone would have come home from work to find her body, protecting her interests to the last. It was a shaming thought.

‘Doctor Gofre...’ the PC said tentatively, ‘Could you give me any idea why...’

‘We were married. She killed herself because I took away from her the only thing that mattered to her. I might as well have killed her with my own hands.’

The officer swallowed hard, hating this part of her work. ‘What did you take from her?’

‘Myself. Believe it or not I was all she wanted in life.’

‘So, why did you...?’

Simone fixed her with a stare that bordered on the manic, cowering her into silence. ‘Because I am dying, because I wanted her to have a life after I’d gone, because I didn’t have the wit and intelligence to realise that forcing her to leave me was the worst thing I could possibly do, because I loved her enough to spare her from coming home and finding me dead. That enough for you?’

‘I’m sorry,’ the PC said with genuine compassion.

‘Don’t patronise me,’ Simone demanded. ‘It’s not sympathy I need, it’s my partner back and a cure for cancer and if someone with my intellect can’t deliver that I’m damn sure you can’t. You’d better get on or I’ll be dead before you finish.’

It’s the shock, the young PC thought. She’s temporarily deranged.

86

Fleur began her interrogation of Wenna as soon as they had finished the early breakfast that had been delivered to their chalet by a taciturn young woman, taller and bigger built than either of them, who looked as if she could eat both breakfasts, trays and all, and come back for more. Fleur sat Wenna down on the two-seater couch in the small living room and took her hands to make sure she stayed there.

'We need to do this logically,' she said. 'I want to know all you know about me and I want to know all you know about what led up to the shooting. And al-Rashidi. All you know about him as well.' Both were still in their nightclothes and Fleur looked even more diminutive than usual, the shaven strip down the side of her head with its plaster protection making her look like a damaged doll.

'Fleur, you're asking for what is almost certainly classified information,' Wenna protested.

Fleur shook both her hands, keeping hold of them. 'Wenna, I'm not stupid. You didn't fly half way round the world just to keep me safe. I'm not here just for protection. You want me to tell you everything I know as soon as I remember it. Okay, if that's the case start talking or there's no deal, whatever I remember stays with me. You said you wouldn't lie to me and that includes deliberately hiding things from me.'

Wenna hesitated, then released her hands and made an executive decision. She spent the next twenty minutes explaining how they had first come to know of Fleur's meeting with Salah, and a potted history of the War on Terror. Fleur sat listening, her brow furrowed with concentration. When Wenna finished Fleur was silent for a moment, then she got up and walked around the room, deep in thought.

'So, you bugged my apartment without a warrant, just on a hunch.'

Wenna shrugged. 'Face it, Fleur, it worked. Like you, sometimes we do what we have to and keep our fingers crossed. Blame me if you like but I'd do it again.' If Fleur intended to hang anyone out to dry for that it would be her, not Charles.

Fleur shook her head, she had already moved on. 'And although they're not admitting it, you think the American Security Services shot al-Rashidi and I simply got in the way of the bullet?'

'That's what I think but I have no evidence.'

'And now I'm at risk from AQE who assume I'm a US spy and lured al-Rashidi to his death.'

'It's logical.'

'You work closely with the Americans, don't you?

'Quite often, yes. We're obliged to.'

'So did you tell them I was going to New Zealand to meet al-Rashidi?'

'No, we didn't know ourselves; you played your cards pretty close to your chest. They say they didn't know who he was going to meet, they followed him from the Afghan/Pakistan border.'

'Pakistan, I know where that is. I know something about Pakistan.' She shrugged and gave up the struggle to remember. 'The Americans could have betrayed you of course,' she added.

'Nothing is impossible in your business or mine,' Wenna said, 'but we think not.'

'Who were you dealing with?' Fleur asked.

'That's a need to know situation,' Wenna protested.

'No lies, no evasions,' Fleur reminded her.

Still Wenna hesitated. Finally she said, 'We deal with different people but on this occasion it was Don Costello, who's a kind of high-ranking Presidential security adviser. At the moment he's here to cover a Presidential visit.'

'So he's CIA and his job is to protect the President?'

'I don't think he's CIA exactly. Same family though. And yes, part of his job is to protect the President.'

'And the US President is in this country now?'

'He leaves tomorrow.'

Fleur grabbed her hands again. 'And?'

'What?'

'What is it you're trying hard not to tell me?'

Wenna knew she had to change the subject fast or Fleur would be building a case against Don Costello that would eventually explode onto the media.

'You wanted to talk to your agent... And Walter Bloom at the BBC,' she reminded her.

Fleur shook her hands angrily. 'Later,' she said 'I know when you're avoiding things. Just tell me.'

'You had a boyfriend,' Wenna blurted out.

That stopped Fleur in her tracks. 'Had, past tense, as in he dumped me?'

Wenna bit her lip. Now the moment had come it was as difficult as she had always imagined it would be, perhaps more so because she knew Fleur as a person now, not just a subject of interest. 'I'm sorry, Fleur, truly I am. I didn't want to tell you until you'd recovered... He's dead.'

She could have added what she knew from Alex, that ConSept Productions, the company that had arranged for him to go to Pakistan, was almost certainly a US Security front operation and had since disappeared. That would only serve to inflame any conspiracy theories Fleur was harbouring.

Fleur did not react to the news of her lover's death. Clearly it had no immediate emotional impact but it certainly took her mind off Don Costello. 'Tell me about him. What was his name?' she asked.

'Joe. Joe Kendry. He was an American documentary film maker.'

Again, no reaction, just interest. 'When did he die, where?' Wenna told her and Fleur absorbed the information. 'Pakistan again,' she said, looking away from Wenna, 'and while I was in New Zealand. Was Costello involved? Is there any connection with what happened to me?'

God, she's quick, Wenna thought. 'Not that we've been able to discover,' she answered hastily. Then, to get away from Costello, 'Can you remember anything al-Rashidi said to you?'

Fleur's eyes lost focus for a moment. 'No, but I will,' she said determinedly. Then she added: 'He gave me a watch.'

Wenna's eyes widened. She looked at Fleur's arm. 'That one?' she asked.

'No, a smaller one.'

'Where is it?'

'I put it in my case.'

Wenna stood up suddenly. 'I think we'd better look for it right away.'

'Why would he give me a present?' Fleur asked herself aloud.

'Exactly,' Wenna agreed.

They headed for Fleur's bedroom where her case had been left on the floor beside the bed. Fleur stopped at the door. 'Wenna...'

'Yes?'

'Did I love him, I mean, truly love him?'

'Yes,' Wenna said with a catch in her throat, 'I believe you did.'

87

Yet again Charles Lovatt had been dragged out of bed by a call from Walter Bloom which necessitated an early appearance at his office and his mood was not equable. Once he had run the data button through his Hub a second time he was even less so. It had arrived by urgent courier and passed security only a few minutes before. Seeing who had sent it, he had known it was not going to be good news. Little as he might like it, the Director General was going to like it even less. Margaret Morton-Grace did not take prisoners when it came to bad press for her beloved organisation and there were certainly going to be questions asked when this went to air.

The video was shot in the usual unidentifiable setting against a white sheet backdrop and featured an armed ethnically-dressed cleric making no attempt to hide his identity. Charles recognised him, he had several aliases and under any one of them he was the most likely candidate to take over al-Rashidi's position. The production quality of the video was better than similar ones had been in past years but still not of normal broadcast quality. It was quite short and in the main a typical terrorist harangue about the evil empire America but towards the end it was chillingly specific. It denounced the brutal and unprovoked murder of innocent Arab businessman Salah al-Rashidi in New Zealand by agents of the Great Satan. It blamed the CIA, the US President and his British lackeys, and threatened retaliation against all those involved in the foul plot to kill their brother.

His direct line rang. 'Lovatt,' he said into the Hub speaker.

'Thought you'd be expecting me to call you,' Walter Bloom said, 'didn't want to disappoint you.'

'It's standard propaganda,' Charles protested, 'so I hope you'll ignore it.'

'Sorry, Charles, no chance of that. We probably weren't the only ones to get it and I warned you I wouldn't come second to anybody over this. Besides which, I'm sure it won't have escaped your notice that we've got the US President on our dirt at the moment and any threat to him is *news*, Charlie. All bets are off.'

'Don't you understand there's a threat to Fleur as well?'

‘It isn’t specific, and anyway, you’ve got her safely locked away, haven’t you?’

‘Not the point, Walter...’

‘This is the point, Charles: al-Rashidi is Fleur’s story and that makes it mine as well. I know the girl and there’s no way she’d want me to sit on this. What's more, what do I tell the Board? That I didn’t run this story because I wanted to do a favour for MI5? How d’you think that would go down? On top of all that I’ve got that appalling woman April Grosse trying to do a deal with the opposition behind my back, the bastards are offering mega-bucks for an exclusive with Fleur. Me? I’m relying on loyalty. So I don’t have any choice here, I’m going to cut them off at the pass and run as much as I can as soon as I can. Look at it this way, I’ve given you advanced warning, that’s the best I can do.’

Charles couldn’t see any way out of this impasse. He very much doubted that he would get away with trying to section the BBC on the grounds of National Security involving an assassination halfway across the world and the sort of generalised threat to the US President that had been made many times before. It was worth one more try though.

‘Non co-operation works both ways,’ he warned.

‘I’ll have to take a chance on that,’ Walter responded, ‘I don’t think AQE are stupid enough to blame Fleur for al-Rashidi’s death and you can’t hold her forever. The minute she gets her memory back she’ll be out of there and on the phone to me.’

Charles thought rapidly. What he knew and what he had no intention of sharing with Walter was that Alex was on his way back to the office from the safe house with the data button al-Rashidi had given to Fleur. It couldn’t be a copy of the one sent to the BBC so heaven alone knew what nasty surprises it might hold. It was time to rescue what he could from the situation.

‘I understand, Walter,’ he said. ‘And as a gesture of good intent I’ll talk to Wenna and get her to encourage Fleur to call you, even if she hasn’t recovered her memory. And she can call April Grosse as well, that might take some pressure off both of us, I’m still ducking her calls.’

There was a suspicious silence on the other end of the line. ‘I’ve got nothing to offer in return,’ Walter said.

‘Nothing required,’ Charles assured him. ‘I’m accepting the inevitable and storing up goodwill. Talk soon.’

He ended the call and asked the Hub to put him through to Wenna on a secure line. He didn’t share Walter Bloom’s confidence in the enemy’s rational assessment of Fleur’s involvement. He also needed to brief Wenna on his conversation with Walter Bloom and warn her to keep Fleur away from the news bulletin. It briefly crossed his mind that if Fleur saw the programme it might jolt her memory but he dismissed it, mindful of the psychiatrist’s advice to take one step at a time, that a brutal, confrontational approach might damage her emotionally for years to come.

***

Whilst waiting for Alex to arrive, Charles debated whether to call Don Costello. With the President in the country and not flying out until noon the next day he could hardly justify withholding the information he had received from the BBC, especially since it was about to be splashed all over the midday news. Costello would have seen and ignored the wild speculation in the tabloid press since the hit on al-Rashidi but worldwide TV coverage from a sober source like the BBC would be certain to enrage him, the more so if he got it second hand. The special relationship had its obligations and like it or not, Charles would have to act as messenger boy. But not, he thought, until he had seen the Al-Rashidi data button.

Alex arrived looking unusually dishevelled and worried after an early start and a hastily arranged return helicopter flight to Suffolk.

‘Have you seen it?’ Charles asked.

‘I’ll let you see for yourself.’ He handed over the button, looking grim.

Charles passed over the one from the BBC. ‘You look at this on the spare monitor whilst I see what has so obviously spoilt your morning.’

It was not long before Charles fully understood why Alex was looking so serious. The video was far more professionally produced than the BBC one. It opened with al-Rashidi, in full, formal Arab dress, sitting in an elegant wooden chair in what was evidently a corner of an equally elegant Middle Eastern drawing room. He seemed relaxed and spoke confidently and convincingly in near-perfect English.

'In the name of Allah, the merciful and compassionate,' he began, then outlined what he believed was a plot by the CIA, 'may Allah's curse be on them,' to subvert the hated UN Two+One project by contaminating the virus-based linctus they used. It was, he said, a satanic plot to reduce the worldwide Muslim population, particularly the males, by a deliberate act of genocide. It was a predatory, expansive and aggressive campaign against Islam. The US military were well-known cowards who panicked when faced with the harsh reality of war, more dangerous to their own allies than to any enemy they ever faced, and it was another way for them to wage the war without risking combat troops. A reduction in Muslim numbers would also find favour with their Zionist collaborators and the morally bankrupt religions of the Western world. He paused dramatically after he had finished the outline of his case, then prepared to deliver his coup-de-grace.

'In case there are those who will not believe without evidence, then I give that to you as well. It was obtained by one of our blessed martyrs, may Allah be pleased with him, who, like Hazifar Ben al-Yaman, exemplary in his obedience to Mohammed when sent to spy on the Kureish during the siege of Medina, worked within the very heart of the Great Conspiracy and gave his life to ensure the world knew what these evil beasts planned and put into operation. I offer it to you now.'

There was a slow fade and cut to a low-resolution, black and white video. It was shot from a single static camera that had been located at one end of an oblong conference room at about head height. There were five people in shot, two with their backs to the camera and three facing it. Of those three the most immediately identifiable was Don Costello, the other two were not known to Charles. They were sitting round a table that was noticeably clear of paper, recorders, Hubs or notepads. Despite the obviously clandestine nature of the recording, the faces of the three men facing camera were very clearly recognisable and the audio, whilst it hummed and buzzed here and there, was easy to follow.

What was recorded was a damning account of the plot exactly as al-Rashidi had outlined it. It seemed to be a meeting to confirm that the plan was operationally sound and that the early trials in rural Afghanistan were successful. Watching it, there could be no doubt as to who was responsible, what was to be done and the anticipated results. The men were grimly determined that this plan would tip the War on Terror totally in their favour and they showed no remorse at the prospect of the millions of dead that the plan entailed. The video cut off suddenly and went to black for a few contemplative moments until a slow fade-in returned the viewer to al-Rashidi in his elegant surroundings.

'So now you have seen the proof, so now you know,' he said 'peace be with you.'

And the video faded once more to black. The carefully constructed performance, and there could be no doubt that was what it was, was over.

'They're getting good at this sort of thing,' Charles said whilst his brain was spinning, trying to put together the implications of the two data buttons.

'I think we know what Costello will say,' Alex remarked.

'Oh yes. Question is, what do we believe?' Charles asked rhetorically.

'The BBC button looks as if it was intended to set the scene for the content in the second one,' Alex offered. 'It's part of the same intelligence continuum.'

'Which suggests they were pretty confident the al-Rashidi button would see the light of day,' Charles added. 'In which they may be right, since Fleur knows it exists and probably what it says. It will certainly get her journalistic juices flowing once she recovers her memory'

'Which could be quite soon judging from what Wenna was saying,' Alex commented.

'Who's seen this?' Charles asked, offering up the button.

'Just Wenna, she copied it onto her Ctab before I left, wanted to look through it herself.'

'Right. Enter it into archives. I need to be able to plead impossibility in case Don wants it to be conveniently lost.'

Alex nodded, then hesitated. 'They wouldn't really contemplate such a plan would they, not even as some kind of bizarre training exercise?'

Charles sighed heavily. 'The one thing I would be pretty sure of is that whatever this is, it isn't a training exercise. The men in that room all look far too long in the tooth to need training in any part of the craft. Even so, one way or another they've been compromised.'

'I'm just remembering,' Alex said, 'that this all ties in rather neatly with what Joe Kendry reported in his diary.'

'Plus the fact that, if your network information is correct, ConSept Productions was a Don Costello front,' Charles said, 'which suggests that he wanted Kendry in Pakistan for some reason. Kendry was a pawn.'

'And pawns tend to get sacrificed.' Alex commented.

'It could be something as simple as getting him out of the way so Fleur was free to go to New Zealand,' Charles mused. 'But that would suppose that they had Fleur in their sights before we did... Or that they had a mole in the AQE organisation here.'

'Either of which is possible,' Alex agreed.

'And either of which means we're playing second fiddle and I don't like that idea any more than Walter Bloom.'

'So .... Next move?' Alex enquired.

'I think we have Don here and indulge in a little sharing, don't you?'

88

Wenna called her office administrator and downloaded the numbers for Walter Bloom and April Grosse onto her Ctab. She was gambling that Alex was right when he had said they would both keep quiet about Joe's death if they were allowed to speak to her. Fleur was holding her own Ctab and watching what Wenna did.

'I know how to do this,' she said, thumbing the pad.

'I think you'll find your battery's low,' Wenna told her. 'Anyway, your Ctab is stripped.'

'What does that mean?'

'There's nothing on it, no stored contact numbers, no incoming or outgoing calls recorded, nothing, it's been stripped of all information.'

Fleur did not bother to enquire how Wenna knew. 'Why?' she asked.

'I imagine you did it before you left for New Zealand, just in case someone else gained access to it, someone you didn't want to know too much of your personal information.'

'So I didn't trust al-Rashidi, then.'

Wenna was calling Walter Bloom's number. 'I'd be surprised if you did,' she said, 'you're far too experienced for that.' She put her Ctab on speaker and handed it over to Fleur. 'Walter's on the line,' she told her.

Fleur took the call uncertainly. So far as she was concerned she was speaking to a stranger. 'Mr Bloom, this is Fleur Nichols,' she said.

'My dear princess,' Walter boomed, 'how lovely to hear your voice again.'

'I don't know what to say,' Fleur began, 'I haven't got all my memory back yet.'

'I understand,' Walter said reassuringly. And I'm not Mr Bloom to you, I'm Walter or Daddy, we've worked together for many years, Fleur.'

'Yes, Wenna told me.'

'How are you now, bad headaches I suppose?'

'Not really, no. Wenna is looking after me incredibly well.'

'I'm sure she is,' Walter said dryly.

'I'll come to see you as soon as I get my memory back, I know I'll have a story for you,' Fleur said.

'You certainly will, and about that, no matter what April Grosse says, talk to me before you talk to anyone else, promise?'

'Yes, I promise. I have to go now.'

'Okay, princess, talk to you soon.'

Wenna heaved a sigh of relief as she took the Ctab back and called up April's number. Walter at least was playing the game. She wasn't so sure about April Grosse but she was committed to calling her anyway to keep Fleur's confidence.

'Grosse.'

'April, this is Fleur Nichols.'

'Fleur, baby! Great to hear from you at last, I've been turning London upside down trying to find you. Your Ctab hasn't been on. Where are you?'

Fleur looked at Wenna, who shook her head. 'Sorry, don't know, and if I did I probably couldn't say but I'm safe and well.'

'Are those spook bastards looking after you?' April demanded.

'I don't think they are bastards and yes, I'm being treated like royalty.'

'Don't let them brainwash you, baby, you're not on their side, you're on your own. We have things to talk about, you and I.'

'I expect we do but not yet.'

'Have you talked to Walter Bloom?'

'Yes, just now.'

'You didn't agree to anything, did you?'

'I know I have a story and I promised to talk to him before anyone else.'

'Damn! Never mind what you told him, I've got a solid offer on the table that he'll never be able to match.'

'I'm told I've worked for him a lot, don't I owe him some loyalty?'

'You're freelance, Fleur. Your first loyalty is to yourself and your agent, that's the way the business is.'

Fleur sighed. 'At the moment I don't know what to believe but I will talk to you again when I get my memory back.'

'Keep in touch, babe, don't make any promises to anyone and keep your Ctab on, okay?'

'Okay. No doubt we'll talk soon.' Fleur cut the connection and handed the tablet back to Wenna. 'I thought talking to them might help me remember,' she said 'but nothing registered.'

'It will,' Wenna assured her.

She was much relieved that April Grosse's self-interest had overtaken all else in the conversation and that Fleur had kept it short and not begun to question either of them. 'Is there anything else you want to ask me?' Wenna added.

Fleur shook her head. 'I think I'll lie down for a while and try to make sense of what I know so far.' She wandered off to the far end of the chalet to the bedroom she shared with Wenna and closed the door behind her.

***

Once she was sure Wenna would not quickly follow her, Fleur plugged her Ctab into the electric socket to power it up and searched the net for April Grosse's number. She fended off her agent's insistent questions and secured her home Hub number. She got through and heard her own voice talking to her and without giving it any thought instinctively tapped in her access key. There were several audio and video messages that Joe had left over a period of several days. She sat on the edge of the bed and began to work through them.

The last one was his piece to camera shot in a Karachi hotel bedroom, setting out all his suspicions of a US-based conspiracy to subvert the Two+One project and the possible involvement of Genphree Biotics biologist Simone Gofre. It was Joe at his enthusiastic and committed best, making even these wildly unlikely allegations seem feasible.

Thirty seconds in, Fleur began to cry silently. Her body became rigid and the hand holding the Ctab shook with a palsied tremor. It was as if a screen in her mind had been drawn back, leaving her exposed to all the horrors of the events of her past that, until this moment, had been hidden from her. She heard small mewling sounds, unaware that they came from her. Her mind, full of unwanted knowledge, was yet for the moment blank.

Wenna came into the room in a rush, alerted as much by instinct as by the distant sounds of extreme distress. She took in the slumped figure sitting bowed on the edge of the bed with her Ctab clutched in her hand and knew instantly what had happened, if not how. She went to Fleur, sat beside her and put her arm around her shoulders. Fleur turned a red-eyed, mascara-streaked face to her, making no attempt to brush aside her tears. 'Where is he?' she asked in a voice clotted with pain.

'His body was flown directly back to his folks in the States,' Wenna said gently. Then she added: 'I suppose to the US embassy in Pakistan it seemed the logical thing to do.'

Fleur looked away making no reply. Wenna was at a loss as to what to say. She looked at the Ctab; the image was still locked on Joe's face in close up, the final shot of the clip filmed in the hotel bedroom. So somehow Fleur had accessed her own Hub and now knew all about Joe's conspiracy theories, which was not going to make life any easier for either of them. 'I tried to save you the shock of finding out this way,' Wenna said, 'for your sake we wanted you to recover slowly but I did explain that your boyfriend had been killed.'

'He wasn't my boyfriend,' Fleur said thickly. 'He was my soul mate. My forever man.'

There was nothing to say to that, so Wenna changed the subject. 'Do you remember everything now?' she asked quietly.

After a moment Fleur sat upright and dug in her handbag for a tissue. She wiped at her face, leaving it with black zebra marking. Wenna let her arm fall away. 'Yes, I remember everything now,' Fleur said, struggling hard to gain control of herself. 'I need to be alone. Nothing makes any sense at the moment.'

***

After she had left the room Wenna felt absolutely professionally and personally useless. There was nothing she could do to ease Fleur's hurt and this was no time to attempt a debrief. She had no personal experience on which to call to give her an insight into how Fleur was feeling but nonetheless felt worried and anxious for her. She wanted to tell Fleur all she knew at once in an attempt to get the revelations over and ease her distress. She felt oddly guilty, harbouring knowledge of the al-Rashidi recording with the devastating record of the covert meeting that was, in one sense, Fleur's property.

She called Charles and, discovering he was in a meeting with the Director General, spoke to Alex and told him about Fleur's traumatic recovery. They mulled over the problem and there was no escaping the fact that sooner or later Fleur would demand to see the al-Rashidi recording. Both felt that was an executive decision and therefore a problem they should lay at Charles's door.

There also seemed little point in protecting Fleur from the BBC news reports or the video that had been sent to them any longer; if they tried she might become suspicious of their motives. In a sense the more information they provided her with now the better, since it might keep her mind off the al-Rashidi recording for a little longer.

Wenna left Alex to bring Charles up to date and set her Ctab to record the BBC midday news.

An hour later Fleur re-joined Wenna. She had washed her face and wore no makeup. She looked more childlike, more vulnerable and, Wenna thought, more appealing than ever. Only her eyes, unnaturally bright and slightly sunken, suggested the fury that boiled beneath the calm surface.

'I am not recovered,' she said tightly, 'I will never recover, but you can talk to me now and I won't collapse in a heap.'

Wenna wanted to go to her and give her a hug but something in Fleur's body language precluded that possibility. Instead, she held up her Ctab and offered Fleur a chair. 'I have two items I think you should see. I want you to know everything that's going on.' She sat beside her and played back the BBC news item featuring the AQE video, followed by the al-Rashidi recording.

Fleur sat motionless through it all, soaking up the information like a sponge. When it was over she sat silent for a moment then she said, 'I know you want me to tell you all I know. And I will, but not yet. I want to be sure I know all that you know before I do that. It's the only bargaining tool I have. What I will tell you is that what al-Rashidi told me supports what Joe uncovered in Pakistan. And so does the video sent to the BBC. The clincher seems to be the recording al-Rashidi gave me. It was Costello in that, wasn't it?'

'Yes, but I don't believe that video is genuine,' Wenna said firmly.

'Of course you wouldn't, you have a special relationship with them, don't you.'

'Fleur, we're on your side,' Wenna protested.

'There's a conspiracy at work here,' Fleur said bluntly, 'and I intend to get to the bottom of it. You may not want me to do that but I will. We all have our bosses, Wenna, so I suggest you call yours and tell him or her that there will be some things I want before I make a deal. The first one is, I want to go home.'

'But you're safe here,' Wenna said anxiously, 'and you can access any information you want.'

'You forget, I remember everything now. AQE approached me because they knew I was impartial and now they know the

Americans shot me as well as their man. They may be fanatics but they're not dumb. I'm not in danger from them.'

'Fleur, I beg to differ. You're still in shock. You seem to be calm but...'

'I may be in shock,' Fleur said furiously, 'but I am not calm. I am incandescent with rage; I am angered beyond anything you could even begin to understand. Someone killed my Joe, killed all my tomorrows, and sure as hellfire someone is going to pay the price and if that means destroying everyone in that video, so be it.'

Wenna looked into her eyes and totally believed her.

89

Simone had no idea what the process was for dealing with a dead body; in all her life it was not something she had ever had to consider. There was to be an autopsy and a coroner's enquiry she was told but the implications of that were lost on her. She had likewise been unable to answer when the young PC asked her what arrangements she wanted made thereafter, so took her advice and had the officer call an undertaker from the morgue office.

She took a taxi back to the house, collected her syringe case and then had the driver take her to Genphree Biotics. She had no clear plan in mind; it was simply that habit took over, so she went to work. She was met by an agitated Colin Burcastle.

'My dear Simone, we were worried when you didn't arrive for work and your Ctab was off...'

Simone tried to wave him away and head for her lab but he was having none of it and ushered her into his office. For once Simone lacked the energy to argue and took a seat unbidden as Burcastle closed the door firmly behind them. He was worried by how haggard and weak she looked. When he was about to speak Simone held up a hand to silence him.

'I've just come from the morgue,' she said, annoyed at the slight slurring of her words. 'Auriol died last night.'

Burcastle looked genuinely shocked. 'My dear lady, I had no idea. How, I mean...'

'She killed herself,' Simone said coldly. 'It seems she was less able to deal with my illness than I was. And that is all you need to know.’ It was like being in a play in which she was both author and actor and Burcastle the audience. She felt totally removed from the entire situation, an observer rather than a participant. Yet she was sufficiently self-aware to know she had to concentrate on seeming normal, to hold on to some sense of reality for just a little longer.

Burcastle spluttered out an apology but Simone cut him short. ‘You’ll be glad to hear,’ she said, ‘that I will conclude my work this afternoon. It’s done and I’m finished here. I’ll come in tomorrow for a few hours to finish the protocol report for my successor and then I’ll be gone.’

Burcastle’s relief was transparently obvious. ‘My dear, I cannot tell you how grateful I am that you agreed to stay on to finish the sequence despite your illness...’

‘No tea and chocolate cake, Colin. Tomorrow is just another workday. I want to leave quietly. Please respect my privacy.’

Colin Burcastle spread his hands in acceptance, knowing that was not a request but an order. Her occasionally blurred speech, her intense focus on her diction, her painfully thin body and gaunt features had not escaped him and he noted that as Simone stood she took a second to get her balance before walking stiffly out of the room. Not a day too soon, he thought, not a day too soon.

90

Charles Lovatt watched his visitor as they sat through a re-run of the data button that Salah al-Rashidi had given Fleur. Alex sat in a corner of the room watching them both. Don Costello did not move a muscle until the video was over, then he sat back and nodded as if in agreement.

‘Any comment?’ Charles asked.

‘I look better in profile,’ he said.

‘Then this is real?’ Charles asked without emphasis.

‘Sure is,’ Costello confirmed.

‘Given that I assume you are not admitting to a conspiracy to commit genocide, would you care to let us in on the joke?’

‘No joke, Charlie. All deadly serious I can assure you.’

‘Indeed it is. Fleur Nichols has recovered her memory, she knows about this button and it’s a fair bet al-Rashidi would have told her what’s on it. Who knows what else he passed on?’

‘Ah, I see. You think she may have more...’ he pointed at the monitor, ‘than that, to talk to us about?’

‘Possibly. So we need to convince her that we’re the good guys and she should be sharing with us, not something a journalist would naturally be inclined to do. Immediately after this meeting I’m going to try to debrief her.’

‘Try?’ Costello said, sounding faintly incredulous.

‘She’s just learnt Joe Kendry was blown up in Pakistan and she’s looking for someone to blame. Let’s not make it you or me.’

Costello looked thoughtful. ‘Normally, as you know, we wouldn’t have this conversation, Charlie, and you might want to edit what you’re about to hear, okay? So maybe it was like this. Suppose the enemy had managed to infiltrate one of theirs into our network and suppose we managed to identify and turn him. With his help we mock up that little drama and he feeds it back into their camp. We then convince them we’ve caught and eliminated him. The idea is to get one of their top men to break cover so we can take him out. They go apeshit, convinced they’ve got us by the cojones, and set about deciding how best to use what they’ve got.’

‘How does that get us to Fleur Nichols?’ Charles asked.

Costello shrugged. ‘Suppose they chose her because she was sympathetic and had done business with them previously. Plus she had access to the dear old, trustworthy British Broadcasting Corporation. She takes the bait of a great story and beetles off around the world to meet him. We’ve tracked him out from the Afghan border and finally catch up with him in New Zealand. Boom. End of story.’

‘You could have had him detained in New Zealand, then you could have interrogated him,’ Charles pointed out.

‘You know I don’t usually use bad language, Charlie, but fuck him and fuck them, those Kiwis are a bunch of sad sack lefties, they’d have had civil rights lawyers all over us and tied us up in their courts so we couldn’t get near him for years. Anyway, these bastards all want to be martyrs, all in a hurry for those hundred virgins, so we did him a favour.’

'That's one way of looking at it,' Charles commented.

'This is a war, let's not forget that,' Costello said with an edge in his voice.

'I try not to forget anything,' Charles said firmly. 'Now, what about Joe Kendry?'

'What about him?'

'He was sent to Pakistan by a production house that turns out to be a shell operation. The woman who ran it was an American who disappeared just before Joe was killed. He arrives, uncovers exactly the same alleged plot and is blown up. Co-incidence? I don't think so, do you?'

'Hey, hey, slow down there, Charlie,' Costello protested, 'I'm not on trial here, I'm just trying to help, suggest a possible scenario you could put to the Nichols woman. She probably won't buy it but what the hell.'

'Your people ran a game out of my backyard, Don. Was Joe the backup, in case AQE didn't take the video bait? There has to be a connection. You can bet Fleur Nichols will be asking exactly these questions and she'll expect me to be able to answer them.'

'Since when did we answer to goddamn journalists, Charlie?'

'Since they got shot up, their partner's killed and they've got information we want, that's when. Come on, Don, you've had your win, let's just tidy up the loose ends.'

Costello grunted reluctant acceptance. 'Okay, suppose he was run as a second string. Suppose he was given just enough rope to find out stuff that'd been planted and seemed to support what we were feeding them. He was meant to go public with it. Things go wrong. The local militants blow up the clinic and him with it so we lose out on our support story; she gets sideswiped and loses her memory. Couple of glitches there. So happens it doesn't matter because we nailed the target anyway.'

'And as a bonus, you get to use Fleur to go public with the story,' Alex put in. 'Once we've explained it to her, she'll deliver your story whether she believes it or not. You will neither confirm nor deny, AQE are discredited for buying the genocide fairy-tale and you get to look super-smart.'

Costello turned slightly to look at him, as if surprised to find him there. 'It's called serendipity, son,' he said.

'So Fleur Nichols and Joe Kendry were targeted for this job early on?' Charles asked.

Costello shrugged. 'I wouldn't know but you have to admit they were a likely pair. After all, you had your eye on them yourself, right? Suppose someone semi-official outed her as a terrorist sympathiser on one of the websites we know they monitor. Given her previous background that would've been enough to point the enemy in her direction don't you think?'

'Why bother? The fake video either worked or it didn't and if it did and you could track Salah al-Rashidi from the Afghan border, you didn't need her,' Charles suggested.

'Ah, Charlie, but maybe like me, whoever was running this was a belt and braces man.'

'Whoever was directing this little production, if it wasn't you, certainly cast you in a leading role in the video, Don.'

Costello's look protested his innocence. 'It had to look real didn't it Charlie? They know me; I'm probably as high on their hit list as al-Rashidi was on ours. Bet they were drooling at the thought of discrediting me publicly. It was just a little sweetener.'

Charles nodded. That much he was prepared to believe. 'So let me guess. You had her apartment under AV watch, so you knew when she and AQE had taken the bait. You put a GPS tracker on her. How? Where? Her luggage, handbag, Ctab?'

'That would be jumping to conclusions.'

'All this and you didn't share, Don,' Charles said regretfully.

'Even among the best of friends the need to know rule still applies. Face it, Charlie, you would've done exactly the same.'

'I'm disappointed there wasn't a little more trust,' Charles said.

'Don't be, Charles,' Costello said seriously, 'you're held in the highest regard.'

'What about all the people who're dying before their time in the Muslim world?' Charles asked, changing tack. 'That suggests support for what Joe and al-Rashidi alleged.'

'No. What it suggests is a new strain of Avian Flu that no one's got a vaccine for yet. Talk to the World Health Organisation, put some pressure on and they might admit it.'

'And that's it?' Charles asked.

'That's it, Charlie. All I can guess anyway, it wasn't my game, like I said.'

'No, of course not,' Charles said evenly.

'Okay, well, if that's all, I have half the British SAS plus my own people guarding my President while he has what I'm sure will be a particularly grand lunch at Buck House. Remember, Charles, I've shared beyond the call of duty now, so keep me in the loop with our captive journalist.'

Charles stood up to shake his hand. 'If she were a captive things would be a lot easier,' he said.

'She's a loose cannon, Charlie,' Costello said as they made for the door of Charles's office. 'We really don't want her running round the media spreading anti-US lies, do we? We need her to be guided in the right direction.'

'I may need your help to explain that video, Don.'

'You can do that, surely.'

'It'll come better from the horse's mouth, if you'll forgive the expression.'

Don Costello shrugged. 'Always pleased to help out,' he said.

As he ushered Costello to the door, Charles asked: 'What happened to him?'

'Who?'

'The mole you turned.'

'Ah, sad story that. Auto accident. We looked after the widow of course.'

***

'You could say that it was a neat game well played,' Charles commented when Costello had gone and Alex had re-joined him in his office. 'What do you think?'

'I think he had an answer ready when you asked about the Muslim deaths, as if he was expecting the question, I find the death of the mole very convenient and beyond that I think we've been told what we're expected to pass on to Fleur Nichols now that she's seen it.'

'Certainly we are being used, but how much of it is true, do we think?'

It was probably a rhetorical question but Alex answered it anyway, he was getting used to the way Charles's mind worked. 'I think some of it may be, perhaps quite a lot.'

'But not all.'

Alex shook his head. 'With all due respect to our esteemed colleague,' he said languidly, 'deception is his game and he's been playing it for a long time. I don't think he would know the truth if it leapt up and bit him on the arse.'

For the first time in days Charles allowed himself a slight smile. 'Then let us go and see what Fleur can add to the sum total of our knowledge,' he suggested.

91

'I've an agenda of my own,' Fleur told them when they had been introduced and were seated round the dining table in the safe house, 'and I don't want to waste your time.'

'Our time is yours for the moment,' Charles said urbanely.

Fleur ignored the reply. 'I intend to find out who was responsible for Joe's death,' she said 'and if necessary I will pursue the bastards to the ends of the earth, no matter who they are. There is nothing I won't do and I have no fear for my life. Nobody and nothing will stop me. Have I made myself absolutely clear?' Her tiny face, embellished only by eye makeup and cheeks flushed with anger, was rigid with stress and her body language screamed implacable determination.

Charles flashed a look at Wenna, who was sitting beside Fleur across the table from him and Alex. She nodded slightly, indicating that Fleur meant every word she said. This was what they were up against.

'The best information we have...' Charles began.

'Don't tell me it was an accident or bad luck, don't do that. I'm not an idiot and I will not be patronised. Joe was set up and so was I, and I intend to find out who was responsible. If you get in my way, Mr Lovatt, whether you try to section me in this country or not, I will hang you out to dry very publicly across the world.'

Wenna put her hand briefly on Fleur's arm and felt the tremor of muscles held in rigid control. 'Don't turn your antagonism on us,

Fleur. Nobody is patronising you. We acknowledge your anger but we're on your side. I promised you we would tell you all we can,' she said.

Fleur kept her gaze on Charles, who was looking just a little bemused. 'Does that go for you as well?' she asked him, 'because what I find out may not be something you want made public.'

Charles cleared his throat as he considered what to say. This meeting was not going at all to plan. 'I think perhaps we should begin by assuming that both of us have honest intentions,' he said. 'I can assure you that no one in this room had anything to do with Joe or al-Rashidi's death or what happened to you. I ask you to accept that. So, can we take one step back and start again on a better footing?' He looked enquiringly at her.

Fleur stared back at him as if trying to read his mind. Charles held her gaze. 'I believe Wenna so I might as well believe you.' she replied eventually, 'but belief is not trust, that has to be earned.'

'Good. Trust works both ways, Fleur,' Charles said, aware he was sounding a little pompous. 'So perhaps we can establish some rules that will enable us to both to achieve our aims.'

'There's only one rule,' Fleur said. 'We tell each other the truth. If you lie to me, all bets are off. We work together to find out the truth and in return I tell you all I know, or I go it alone. I'm sure the BBC will back me if necessary.'

Charles considered that uncomfortable alternative and decided honesty was the best policy. 'I won't lie to you,' he said 'but there may be times when, if I think it is in your or the national interest, I will evade the question.'

Fleur considered that for a moment then suddenly stuck out her hand across the table. 'Deal,' she said, 'because I'll know if you do.' Her tiny hand all but disappeared into Charles's paw.

'I take it that there are things al-Rashidi told you that you could put on the table?' Charles asked as the atmosphere relaxed a little.

'Yes, but not until later.'

'May I enquire why?'

'Firstly I want to ensure that you tell me all I want to know and secondly, I don't trust people you may have to share information with.'

The inference was obvious so Charles didn't bother to enquire whom she was talking about. 'This is beginning to sound like a rather one-sided deal,' he said.

'Not at all. I will agree to co-operate in every way except that, for the moment. You can protect me if you feel it's necessary but I intend to return to my apartment. Wenna can stay at my place. She can follow me around and listen in on all my conversations, whatever. I think we can be useful to each other. Now, the beginning would be a very good place to start.'

Charles was very conscious that what he had intended to be a debrief of Fleur Nichols had somehow become Fleur laying out ground rules and putting him to the question. At the root of his problem was that, in return for securing whatever information Fleur had, he would have to reveal some if not all of what Don Costello had suggested might be the true scenario. From what Wenna had told him, Fleur was already part way down the track of making a case against the US. This was going to call for some verbal gymnastics. He began the story.

By the time he had finished a small tic had appeared at the side of Fleur's left eye and Wenna was watching her with a worried look. Charles sat back in his chair and waited. There was a tension-charged silence in the room.

Eventually Fleur said: 'Is that guesswork or are you certain it's the truth?'

'I can't be certain, we're relying on second-hand information.'

'From Don Costello.' It was a statement as much as a question.

'In the main, yes, but it supports what we know for ourselves.'

'So what we have is his version,' Fleur persisted.

'Yes.'

'It sounds plausible so far as it goes, but have you tested its credibility?'

'No time yet, but we will,' Charles assured her.

'Yes,' Fleur repeated, 'we will.' After a moment she added: 'you do realise I may well publish what you've told me.'

'We understand you have to publish your story,' Charles conceded.

Fleur's small fingers were drumming on the table. 'Which has to mean Costello actually wants me to publish or he would never have said a word to you, knowing you'd have to make an explanation to me. That alone makes me suspicious. And what is it he's not saying?'

'Fleur, at the moment we have no logical reason to doubt him.'

'You may not but I do. Between Joe and Costello I know who I believe. So, let's make a start on this co-operation of ours. First up I want to meet Rose Petchek.'

Charles looked apologetic. 'Sorry, I should have said, she and the company that sent Joe to Pakistan have disappeared.'

Fleur nodded slowly. 'Of course,' she said bitterly, 'why did I bother to ask. Right, then we try another avenue, we talk to the biologist Joe interviewed before he left, what's her name, Gofre? He thinks she may be involved somehow. At the very least she has to know if what Joe suspected was possible.'

'Yes I'm sure we can manage that,' Charles agreed. 'But I do urge you not to prejudge the matter. We both want the truth but the truth can often be elusive. Indeed, we may have it already and not recognise it because we're blinded by a need to lay blame.'

'There *is* blame, Charles, and you know that as well as I do. They've already admitted killing al-Rashidi and injuring me.'

'Well, actually no,' Charles corrected her. 'It was put to us only as a possible scenario.'

'Of course.'

'It might help to establish more of the truth,' Charles said hopefully, 'if you could tell us at least some of what you know.'

Fleur stood up and shook her head. 'Sorry, Charles, way too early for that.' She turned to Wenna. 'I intend to go back to my apartment now and get to work. If you're coming with me you'd better get your bag packed.'

92

The house was bleak, cold and silent as Simone let herself in. The only sound was the taxi drawing away from the building. When that had faded into the distance there was nothing to interrupt the deadening silence but her own slow movements. She stopped to take off her raincoat and looked at herself in the antiquated hallstand mirror. For a moment she was disorientated, not recognising the person who looked back at her. It seemed to be the face of a stranger, a face blighted by time and distorted with pain, one that bore no resemblance to the Simone Gofre she was used to confronting in a mirror. Was this really how she appeared to others now?

She wandered into the kitchen with no real intent and, finding herself there, opened the refrigerator. She took out a partly used loaf of sliced bread and a half empty bottle of wine and carried then into the sitting room where she took her usual chair. She chewed on a slice of dry bread and drank the wine from the bottle. What did manners matter now? The sight of herself in the mirror bothered her still. She felt her mind drifting away but forced herself to concentrate. It was vital that she held herself together for one more day, and then she would be free to make her own decisions, unfettered by duty to anyone or anything.

She was due for an injection; she could feel the pain creeping through her again. The syringe she used next would remain empty but would be with her when she went into the office for the last time. Not even Fat Annie would look twice at the syringes, being used to their presence in the unit now, and especially not on Simone's last day. She would take nothing from the lab that was not hers but she had a right, an absolute right, to select from that which she had created.

She stuffed the remnant of bread into her mouth and swilled it down with the last of the wine. Bread and wine and thou, she thought, except that there was no longer any thou. Dear, deluded Auriol, thinking that by killing herself they could be together in heaven. The poor girl had been touched by religion several times in her life, each touch leaving a scar that Simone had sought to heal. She found herself giggling inanely; in the beginning God created biology she thought and for the moment it seemed incredibly funny.

She stopped giggling as she became aware of a warm wet feeling on her upper legs. With a shock she realised she had wet herself. Life had inflicted yet another demeaning indignity upon her. She erupted into sudden violent anger, standing up abruptly and throwing the empty wine bottle across the room where it bounced off the back of Auriol's chair and dropped intact onto the carpeted floor. It seemed even effective dramatic gestures were denied her now. The exertion left her weak and shaking.

When it seemed she might collapse she somehow managed to summon up enough of that old Gofre spirit to replace anger with cold, implacable determination. By sheer effort of will she took herself upstairs to the bedroom and prepared for her injection. Her hand was shaking and the horrifying thought came to her that soon she would not be able to self-inject. She forced the weakening thought aside and completed the operation, laying the empty syringe back in the plastic carry case. It would be contaminated with morphine but that hardly mattered.

Tomorrow she would rise early, spend time on her appearance, go in to work and face the compassionate looks of the workforce. When she returned home there would no longer be any need to keep up a façade. She could put her emotional house in order and go in the time of her own choosing.

In making those plans it did not occur to her that she might already have lost the solid mental balance that she had relied on all her life.

93

Wenna and Fleur arrived at Fleur's apartment in the early evening having endured the frustration of the endemic traffic congestion across the city. Having been empty, the temperature in the apartment had dropped to the ambient outside temperature and the insulation had kept the cold in. It was not a welcoming feel.

They dropped their suitcases in the hallway and Fleur wandered from room to room, hunched up in her jacket, finally returning to the living room where Wenna waited. 'I don't know how long I'll stay here,' she said, and her voice, as cold as the room, summed up her desolation.

Wenna nodded, understanding. There was no reply needed. She switched on the heating and took her suitcase to the spare bedroom whilst Fleur booted up the Hub and settled herself at the console. From the bedroom Wenna could hear one side of the conversation.

'It's me,' Fleur said and, after a beat she added, 'Thanks, not good but I'm coping, I'll be back at work before you know it.'

Another break, then, 'I've got a good part of the story together but I need a few days to make certain of the facts, wouldn't want to go off half-cocked, would we? Can you hold it till then?' A longer break, then: 'That's great, and don't worry about April, I'll talk to her when the time comes. Bye for now. Bye.'

Wenna found herself standing in the bedroom waiting for the call to finish, despite the fact that it was hardly private. With Joe dead Fleur would probably not be having any private conversations for a while. When she re-joined her charge she found her trawling back through Joe's files on his project. Fleur located the number of Genphree Biotics and called it. A male voice answered.

'Hi, this is Fleur Nichols, I'm a BBC journalist,' she said, shading the truth, 'I want to arrange a meeting with Doctor Simone Gofre, preferably tomorrow.'

'I'm sorry, I'm security, most of the staff have gone home but I can tell you that all requests to interview staff members have to be approved by the Director.'

'Who's gone home of course.'

'Yes. And you may be unlucky anyway. Doctor Gofre is coming in tomorrow morning to clear her desk, she's resigned.'

'Why?'

'Health reasons. Now, I'm obliged to tell you this call is being recorded and will be logged under our security protocols.'

'Bit late with that, weren't you?' Fleur said sarcastically and ended the call. She turned to Wenna. 'Health reasons,' she said pointedly.

'I don't think we should jump to any conclusions,' Wenna replied.

'Don't worry,' Fleur replied determinedly, 'before I make a move I'll have all my ducks in a row. Starting with Costello. I want to meet him face to face and hear what he has to say about his 'scenarios' in his own words.'

'We don't issue orders to the likes of Costello,' Wenna pointed out.

'He'll see me and he'll repeat the explanation he gave you,' Fleur said confidently, 'duly sanitised for my ears, no doubt. He wants the information I'm holding back just as much as you do. Why don't you organise it with Charles, and then order us a takeaway. I'm not hungry but I need to keep up my strength.' She turned back to the Hub, naturally assuming Wenna would do her bidding.

There was a lot to do and she intended to keep busy; it kept the memories at bay.

***

They took a meagre breakfast, cobbled together from last night's leftovers and what they found in the fridge. They ate still dressed in their nightclothes and there was little conversation, they had retired late and neither had slept well. Wenna was worried about Fleur; the woman was in a permanent state of barely repressed fury. Her focus was absolute and she had no time for any discussion outside of the scheming that had led to Joe's death. Whilst this obsession was understandable, Wenna was concerned what it was doing to Fleur's mind; at the moment she was certainly not emotionally stable and that did not bode well for the meeting that had been arranged with Costello.

They swapped time in the bathroom without bothering too much to offer each other privacy. Fleur seemed to have accepted Wenna as a part of her life for the time being, an old friend or surrogate sister perhaps, not someone that had to be accorded any particular personal consideration.

They waited for the worst of the morning rush hour to ease before leaving the apartment. Wenna drove them to Thames House and noted that they seemed to be followed at a discreet distance by a nondescript delivery van. Had Charles decided to provide them with extra security? After a while the van turned off and since it was not replaced with another possible tail she assumed she was being super cautious. She said nothing to Fleur and put it out of her mind.

The meeting took place in Charles's office. He had wanted it to take place on his own turf and in what he hoped was the impressive venue of Thames House. Fleur, however, had shown no sign of being impressed, much less overawed. She was introduced to Don Costello, who was at his most urbane.

'I want to offer you my most sincere sympathy for your loss,' he said, holding her tiny hand a second longer than he needed to, 'it was not only a tragic loss for you but, I may say, for America. The

President was made aware of what happened before he left to return home and he expressed his sadness and regret.'

Wenna was on edge. Reading Fleur's body language she knew how near to an emotional explosion she was. But somehow Fleur controlled herself and nodded acceptance. 'Thank you,' she said blandly.

They took seats and Wenna sat between Fleur and Costello, her presence shielding her friend from the man she had been so insistent on meeting.

Charles opened with a warning. 'I have to tell you Fleur that you may soon be privy to information that is subject to the Official Secrets Act. The information is only given to you because we wish to keep our word not to withhold anything relating to Joe's death and your injury.' Fleur stared at him and said nothing. 'Much of what you will hear is conjecture on our part and for that reason alone it would be dangerous to extrapolate from it too freely. I've had to issue a similar verbal warning to the BBC should you discuss anything you hear today with anyone there.'

'You're going to section me?' Fleur asked coldly.

'No, we do not wish to prevent you from telling your story, but we do wish to warn you against telling it in a way that is prejudicial to the security interests of either America or the UK. I'm sure you understand I have to make this clear.'

Fleur nodded. 'To be crude,' she said, 'you're trying to cover your arse.' Wenna hastily covered a grin and coughed into her hand. 'That's fine by me so long as I get to the truth,' Fleur ended.

'We're here to demonstrate what we think the truth is in this matter,' Charles said, 'I'll leave Don to tell you how things may have unfolded. Don...'

Costello went smoothly into his presentation, larding it with sincerity and empathy. 'Fleur, I have to begin by saying that I have not personally had any involvement in the events that impacted on you so severely. I don't know exactly what happened but I can present you with a likely scenario that I suspect will be close to the truth of the matter. Also, nothing I say can be taken as the official position of the US Administration or any part of it, I speak as an individual and I'm here only to render what assistance I can to MI5 and to you. Can you accept that?'

Fleur had her eyes fixed steadily on his face. When she answered her voice was devoid of expression. 'You and Charles, whatever else you are, are experienced bureaucrats and like him you're covering your arse. I accept that, so let's get on with it. What do you have to tell me?'

Don Costello shrugged slightly in polite acceptance of her bluntness and evasion. He went on to give her an airbrushed version of the explanation of al-Rashidi's death he had provided to Charles and Alex. When he finished there was a tense silence as everyone in the room waited for Fleur's response. She stared at him for a few seconds after he had finished speaking, her silence giving voice to her obvious doubts. Wenna watched her closely as the silence grew to the point of embarrassment. She knew exactly what Fleur was doing: she was lining up ducks.

'By appearing in the video your people made you were putting yourself at risk,' she observed eventually.

'I have a high profile job and the risks go with the occupation. I was asked and I said yes. We're fighting a war here, Fleur and I'm very clear about which side I'm on.'

Wenna tensed. It would have been so easy for Fleur to take exception to that comment, yet she did not. She was still staring fixedly at Costello, as if by staring alone she could prise the truth out of him.

'I want the original of that video, the one al-Rashidi gave to me,' she said eventually. 'It's my property and I intend to take it to the BBC and have it analysed before publication. Do you have any objections to that?'

Costello looked at Charles. 'Your call, Charles, you have it, I don't.'

Charles looked distinctly uncomfortable. 'I understand you have a copy on your Ctab...' he began.

Fleur interrupted him. 'I've already copied that to Walter. It's obvious why I want the original button.'

Charles looked grim. 'There hardly seems any point in declining, does there?' he said.

Fleur turned her attention back to Costello. 'So Joe died because you used him as a pawn in the game to target a senior AQE operative,' she said coldly.

Costello bristled, losing some of his composure. 'Joe Kendry died because some terrorist decided to target the UN clinic. If it weren't for that he'd be alive today having done his country a service,' he replied.

'I'm very sorry, Fleur,' Charles put in, sensing an unproductive argument, 'there's not a shred of evidence that Joe's death was anything other than a ghastly misfortune.'

Fleur ignored him. 'How long will you be in this country?' she asked Costello.

'Why?'

'I need a day to think about what you've told me, then I'll tell Charles what I know. You might as well be there.'

Costello stood up to leave. 'In that case I'll do my best to accommodate you,' he said coolly. He nodded to Charles, then Alex led him out to see him to the security capsules and through the security levels to his car in the basement car park.

Once they were well away from Charles's office, Costello took Alex's arm. 'Watch her,' he said, 'she's dangerous and she's busy making up stories in that little head of hers.'

'I thought you confused her with your honesty,' Alex said blandly. 'It put her off her stride.'

Costello shook his head and Alex's arm at the same time. 'Don't try to bullshit me, son, she didn't buy a word of it,' he said. 'And another thing. She's got your Wenna hooked and cooked. Could be a problem, that.'

94

Simone let the doorbell ring, regretting that she had ever agreed to see these people. On the spur of the moment when they had called, the idea of talking to the BBC about her work had appealed to her ego. She had thought that she could say some of the things that would never have been possible whilst she was employed and still concerned for her career.

Now the time had come however, she had forgotten all the vitally important things she wanted to tell them. Besides, she really didn't want to see anyone, she felt woozy, embalmed in distant pain and drained of energy. Increasingly since she had returned home from her last visit to the lab, she had relaxed her iron control over her thoughts and actions. The world had become blurred and indistinct, her thought processes progressively more divorced from the hard edge of reality. Now there were people at the door, something to do with the BBC… She would send them away.

They stared at her for a moment before introducing themselves. Well, she was probably something to be stared at. Wenna and Fleur. Wenna was the tall blonde one and Fleur the shorter one with a plaster on the side of her head. They were both young and beautiful and they made a fine looking couple, like her and Auriol in their prime. Forgetting her earlier resolution she opened the door and stood aside to let them in.

Once in the sitting room she did not know what to do with them but when she waved vaguely in the direction of chairs they sat down as if they had been invited. Had she invited them? She couldn't remember. They were looking at her with the same strained, sympathetic half smiles she had had to endure from her colleagues at the lab that morning. She might share a sisterhood with them but they were beginning to irritate her. Then there was the matter of tea, shouldn't she offer them tea? Was there any tea?

'Tea?' she asked.

'No, thank you,' they answered together.

'Would you mind dreadfully if we asked you some questions?' Wenna asked.

Dreadfully. Would she mind dreadfully? Or come to that would she mind at all. 'I wouldn't mind dreadfully' she answered, slurring her words slightly. She was having difficulty in concentrating on what they were saying.

'Do you remember meeting a film director called Joe Kendry?' the shorter one asked.

What was her name? Yes, Flower, that was it. Simone tried to think through the question. There had been a man, at the lab, with a camera. But that was a long time ago. 'Long time ago,' she said.

'He was my partner,' Flower said.

That made no sense. Surely the other one, Wenna, lovely name, surely she was her partner; you could tell these things seeing them together. Perhaps he was a business partner.

'He was killed. I'm trying to find out why. Will you help me?'

Tumblers fell into place in Simone's confused mind. 'Suicide,' she said.

The two women exchanged looks of incomprehension. Didn't they understand what she said?

'Auriol killed herself,' she told them, articulating individual words with great care.

'I'm sorry,' Wenna said, quickly working out what they were being told about Simone's relationship. 'We had no idea.'

Simone shrugged heavily. 'She's carbon monoxide; I'm terminal invasive carcinoma. CM meet TIC. She was sure we'd meet up in the middle somewhere.' She knew she was falling off her words but there seemed no help for that. Thinking was beginning to give her a headache.

'Look, Doctor Gofre, thanks for your time...' Wenna began but Fleur stopped her with a hand on her arm.

'One last thing,' she said, 'I need to know if it's possible to change Two+One, infect it with a lethal virus that transmits human to human.' She was staring at Simone, looking painfully needy. 'Is it possible?'

Simone found herself wanting to help. 'Possible,' she said, 'everything's possible. World's full of possible.'

'Did you do it? For the Americans?' Flower asked.

Simone found her mind wandering away from the question. 'I knew an American once,' she said, 'didn't last. They own the world you know. Americans.'

'Fleur, I don't think there's any point...' Wenna put in.

Fleur ignored her. 'For humanity's sake, Simone, can you concentrate enough to give me a straight answer?'

Simone heard the urgency in Fleur's voice but she was feeling tired now and really didn't want to answer any more questions. 'Humanity,' she said, latching on to the word and waving a despairing hand, 'think we're special,' she shook her head slowly, 'just bio... logical ent tit tees. Live, breed, die. Live, die.'

Wenna stood up, taking charge. 'Is there anyone who can look after you, Doctor Gofre?' she asked.

Simone smiled up at her concerned face. 'Oh yes,' she said, 'I'm well… Looked after.'

When they had gone Simone closed the front door behind them and walked slowly back to the sitting room. She was glad she had taken trouble with her appearance before she had gone into the lab for the last time that morning. It was always nice to be looking good when visitors came. Such a nice young couple. She was mildly pleased with herself for handling their visit so well.

She went slowly round the room opening one drawer after another, collecting up early love letters, old birthday and Christmas cards with loving messages. She put them in a pile in the grate and, after a few fumbled attempts with the matches, set fire to them.

After tomorrow there would be no memories.

95

'To be frank, Fleur, I don't think Simone Gofre will ever be stable enough to give you the answers you're looking for,' Wenna said on the wet and windy drive back to London.

'It doesn't matter,' Fleur replied tightly, 'she didn't deny the Two+One Project could have been subverted in the way Joe suspected.'

'She told us nothing, Fleur. You can bet the company will deny it and the slurred words of a drugged-up woman whose mind is affected by the death of her partner and the terminal stages of cancer will never stand up as evidence anywhere.'

'Then we'll find someone else,' Fleur said doggedly. 'Somewhere in the world there'll be an honest microbiologist who will do the tests for us.'

'I don't know why you're focusing on the Two+One aspect,' Wenna said.

Fleur flapped a dismissive hand at her. 'The real story isn't about the killing of Salah al-Rashidi; it's about Joe and what he uncovered. It's a time bomb and I'm going to set it off.'

They came to a halt in a line of traffic. Wenna turned the windscreen wipers up as the rain came clattering down, obscuring her view. 'Do be careful,' Wenna said, glancing anxiously at Fleur's grimly determined face. 'You're trying to make a case of genocide against the most powerful nation in the world.'

'Someone has to do it.'

‘Only if it’s true.’

‘Wenna, I haven’t quite figured it out yet, but I will. So why don’t you just drive and leave me to work things out?’

They arrived back at the apartment damp and chilled and bearing with them the results of a visit to a supermarket to stock the larder. They shucked off their coats and Wenna unpacked their purchases while Fleur booted up her Hub and checked for messages. There were calls from Walter Bloom and April Grosse both anxious for her to contact them. She set the Hub on snooze and flopped into a chair as Wenna came in with two glasses of wine and took Joe’s seat opposite her.

‘I was surprised you didn’t ask Don Costello more questions when you had the chance yesterday,’ Wenna commented.

Fleur took a sip of her wine before answering. ‘I just wanted to see him face to face, I never expected him to tell the truth,’ she said. ‘I’ve met men like Costello before, devious, mendacious fanatics who will literally stop at nothing to achieve their aims. Mass murder is entirely acceptable if it’s God’s will or for the greater good as they see it. They may dress well and have civilised manners but look in their eyes and you see no humanity, there’s no soul shining through, they have the eyes of killers. The only difference is, when I’ve seen those men in the past they’ve usually been terrorists, not Western intelligence officials. Al-Rashidi and Costello may wage war on each other but in the end they’re brothers under the skin.’

Wenna recalled what the psychologist had said about the possible emotional and psychological effects if Fleur was shocked into recovering her memory. The most likely event was that Joe’s death was pure chance but there seemed little hope of convincing Fleur of that in her present frame of mind. Perhaps time would dull the edge of her obsession. In the meantime could she divert Fleur from her determination to nail Costello?

‘I don’t like the man,’ she said frankly, ‘but the absolute truth is we have not one shred of evidence to suggest he’s part of some genocidal plot, and neither do you.’

Unexpectedly Fleur stood up, came across to her and gave her a hug and a kiss on the cheek before returning to her chair. ‘You know Wenna, I think you’ve got where you are on the strength of your intellect, your connections, your education and your dedication but you're too trusting. I don't think you should be let out on the street on your own. You're far too nice for the business you're in, you're not devious enough, you don't seem able to think like the bastards of this world. That's the difference between you and me – I can and I don't trust anyone.'

'You can trust me,' Wenna said quickly.

'I know I can,' Fleur replied, 'but don't ask me to trust Costello. Think about it, Wenna, he could have said al-Rashidi faked the video. He could have made up a plausible story around that idea, so why didn't he? I'd have expected that. Instead he wants me to go public on the BBC with his version of the truth, but why? People like him don't deal in the truth. If what he wants is to look good, show how clever he's been, why not do it himself, arrange a leak? And why has he delayed publication, despite the fact that al-Rashidi's death is headline news round the world, what is he waiting for? Something about his story stinks like a dead rat.'

Wenna waved her hands hopelessly. 'Face it Fleur, even if you're right we may never know the answer. He will never be called to account. Dealing with men like Costello is like punching clouds.'

Fleur eyed Wenna over the rim of her glass. 'What haven't you told me?' she asked suddenly.

Wenna shook her head. 'I swear I've told you everything I know. I've never heard of a case where someone outside the service has been told as much as you have. Costello might have been rather more blunt when he was laying out the scenario for us, but essentially what he told you is what he told us.'

'Then he's conning us all.'

'There's no evidence of that,' Wenna repeated.

'Balance of probabilities is enough for me,' Fleur said, 'I've been lied to by experts and he's one.'

'But what do you expect to be able to do?' Wenna asked. 'Without proof no broadcaster could afford to take your story or they'd be sued to high heaven. If you tried to move without evidence you'd be crying wolf and your career would be over, you'd never get to the truth then.'

Fleur was staring at her fixedly, her eyes blazing.

'What?' Wenna asked, taken aback by the ferocity of the look.

'Thank you, Wenna,' Fleur said, 'you've just given me the answer.'

'Now you're worrying me,' Wenna said truthfully.

'I have a duty call to make,' Fleur said standing up abruptly and abandoning her wine glass, *noblesse oblige* kind of thing. Widow of a friend of mine.'

'Who...' Wenna began.

'Alma. You can come if you like but you'll have to stay outside in the car. It's likely to be very emotional and you being there won't help.'

***

Alma Rogers had aged ten years since her beloved Phil had been cremated. As soon as she saw Fleur she burst into tears and wrapped herself round her as a child might take its anguish to its mother, even though Fleur barely came up to her chin.

'Let's go inside, Alma,' Fleur said, detaching herself and closing the front door behind them. 'Don't want to make an exhibition of ourselves in front of the neighbours, do we?'

'No. Sorry. I'll get us some tea.' Alma scrubbed at her eyes with a handkerchief and led the way into the kitchen where she busied herself with the kettle. 'I'll never get over it, I won't,' she said. 'You go into the lounge and I'll bring it through.'

'Alma, did Phil send you any messages while he was in Pakistan, tell you what they were up to?'

'All the time, dear. He was very good like that, was Phil. There's a lot of stuff copied from your Joe as well. I was going to tell you but nobody seemed to know where you were.'

'Can I use your Hub? I'd like to look through what Phil sent.'

'Course you can, love, it's in the lounge, you know where it is, I'll be there in a minute.'

Fleur walked through to the pristine sitting room that Alma insisted was a lounge and booted up the Hub. Joe had copied all the material he had sent to his own Hub at home to Phil and Alma, which suggested he was not absolutely sure about the security of their home Hub. In that he had been absolutely right. Every word he had written and every image had been intercepted by MI5. Well, she wasn't concerned about that now. There were a series of private messages to Alma from Phil and even knowing how blissed out those two were, Fleur had no qualms about reading them.

She knew Phil well; he was a down-to-earth type, pragmatic, ideologically neutral and a good deal cleverer than he let on. He was also uxorious and it seemed he had contacted Alma every day he had been away. She, bless her, had kept all the messages in memory. The last one had been sent on the evening before the two men had made that fateful trip to the UN clinic.

Phil talked about their clandestine plans for that night and it was clear that he did not share Joe's enthusiasm for the conspiracy theory. He simply could not believe anyone could be so evil, especially not someone on 'our' side. Even so, his support for Joe was absolute. If Joe thought there was a story then he was going to be with him all the way. Towards the end he did express a rather surprising doubt. He thought that, if there was a story, it had all been too easy for them to get onto it, given that they were meant to be under such close surveillance. There was no indication as to whether or not he had shared this doubt with Joe and he had signed off with his usual cheery and loving ending.

Fleur closed the Hub down. She had what she had come for, but she sat with Alma through a long cup of tea, sharing thoughts of the men they had lost. Fleur found it emotionally gruelling. All she really wanted to do was to burst into tears and sob her heart out but there was Alma to console and a plan to put into operation. There would be time to mourn later.

'Alma, can I borrow your Ctab?'

'Course, dear, it's on the sideboard there. I'll just clear away.'

A few minutes later Fleur left Alma at the front door with a long hug and a promise to keep in touch, then re-joined Wenna who had been waiting in the car. Wenna looked at her enquiringly. 'Alright?' she asked.

'Am I still under observation?' Fleur asked.

'Only by me,' Wenna replied as she drove away.

'And my Hub is being monitored?'

'Yes. Why do you ask?'

‘Just wondered. Wenna, I want you to arrange a meeting for me with Charles and Costello. Say, ten tomorrow morning at my apartment. I think it’s time we all put our cards on the table.’

‘I’m sure they’ll be very pleased to hear that,’ Wenna said, relief evident in her voice.’

‘And Wenna...’

‘Yes?’

‘Can you cook?’

‘Not really.’

‘Then why did we buy all that stuff at the supermarket?’

96

They had gone to bed early, risen early and breakfasted lightly. Wenna’s repeated attempts to persuade Fleur to tell her what truth she thought she had uncovered or what information al-Rashidi had given her met with polite refusals. Fleur was preoccupied as they waited for Charles and Costello to arrive and spent some time checking back over the material Joe had sent from Pakistan. She was unnaturally calm given the circumstances, whilst Wenna became increasingly anxious as ten o’clock neared.

When they arrived Wenna acted as hostess, bringing the two men through to the sitting room where Fleur was at ease in her usual chair. She did not get up and ignored the offered hands.

‘Gentlemen, let’s get straight to business,’ she said.

‘As you wish, Fleur,’ Charles replied.

Don Costello said nothing but took a chair beside Charles, his face a blank mask. Wenna seated herself to one side halfway between the two parties, where she could see all the faces.

Fleur opened up the dialogue. ‘Let me say first of all that Salah al-Rashidi totally believed the video you managed to infiltrate into his organisation. Why would he not, it came from one of his own people, he thought. When he told me what was on it, I didn’t believe that anyone on either side of this war would go so far as to commit genocide. That was unusually naïve of me, but I didn’t want to believe it of our people and coming from him it simply seemed like propaganda. He wanted to use me, and the BBC, for exactly the same reason you want to, as disinterested and therefore internationally believable sources.' She was looking directly at Costello. 'He didn't get the chance. You killed him, as you had killed his mole. His game came to an end, but yours is still running.'

Costello moved irritably in his chair. 'I didn't come here for a lecture,' he said coldly, 'have you anything to tell us or not?'

'You conned al-Rashidi and his people too well,' Fleur continued. 'In order to convince me your plan was real, he was prepared to give himself up.'

That got the attention of both men. 'Bullshit.' Costello said eventually.

'He agreed to give an interview to the BBC and then hand himself over to MI5. For some reason he didn't trust your people. Can't say I blame him, you do have previous convictions for, what's the euphemism? "Terminating with extreme prejudice"?'

Costello shook his head in disbelief. 'And you swallowed that crap? Like you said, you're naïve.'

'He truly believed you were intent on destroying his people and his faith, there was nothing he wouldn't have done to prevent that.'

'Is that it, is that all?'

'It may interest you to know that I intend to make a documentary. It will be the film Joe would have made if he hadn't been murdered, a film about the way a UN project to ease the population burden in the Third World was subverted by a Western security organisation.'

'So now we have it,' Costello said brutally, 'you've been told what really happened but that's not enough for you. You've been programmed by your terrorist friends to target the US. It's about time you and all the woolly-headed liberals like you understood that these extremists hate the West and all it stands for. They would be quite happy to exterminate us all if they can't convert us. You may be a sympathiser but they would kill you in an instant if it suited their purposes. These bastards want to discredit the Two+One program because it's the UN and the US helping the world's poor in a high profile way. This is a war for hearts and minds and they sure as hell have won yours.'

Fleur fixed him with a glare. 'I'm neutral, Costello, always have been.'

‘You’re a traitor, Nichols. You’re in their pocket. Now, if you’ve nothing else to say I’m going to leave you to your prejudices.’ He started to get out of his chair.

Fleur raised her hand in an imperious gesture that somehow stopped him. ‘Your people might want to try and sue me at some point,’ she said, ‘so better know what I’m going to say. You told your version of the story, now hear mine. I think you’ve been much cleverer than you’ve been prepared to admit. I think virtually all you told us was true, it’s just that it’s not all the truth. Al-Rashidi wasn’t the main target, he was a nice little bonus. Killing him weakened the AQE command structure and strengthened the deception you had planned. That was the real aim, to convince the leadership of AQE that you had a scheme to win the war by viral genocide, by reducing their manpower without risking a single one of your soldiers and that you had the capacity to do it. Not easy to sell such an apparently looney idea to highly intelligent people. But it worked, partly because they hate America so much they’d believe you capable of just about anything, and also because of the existence of a new and deadlier strain of Avian Flu. News of this has been suppressed by the authorities to avoid panic but it’s beginning to kill vulnerable people in large numbers over much of the Muslim world. So AQE bought your story and it cost al-Rashidi his life. And Joe his. And Phil, his cameraman. And the agent you turned. They were all expendable pawns in the great game.’

Costello turned to Charles and shrugged. ‘She’s not on this planet, Charles. Might as well let her loose on the streets to tell her mad stories to whoever will listen.’

‘I think we should hear her out,’ Charles responded.

‘That’s not all,’ Fleur continued implacably. ‘I am quite prepared to believe you didn’t target Joe; he was just in the wrong place at the wrong time. He would actually have been more use to you alive because he totally believed your deception.’

‘Well thank you for that at least,’ Costello said with heavy sarcasm.

‘Joe was both right and wrong. The plot he suspected could have been carried out, the capability is probably sitting in a lab somewhere, but it was deliberately never implemented, the Two+One linctus was never altered, never contaminated, so he would have found nothing. And it was intended that he should find nothing. That was and is essential to the plan '

'And what is this grand plan, do you think?' Charles asked.

'The strategy was to have AQE cry wolf,' Fleur replied. 'Then, when all the publicity has died down and AQE has been well and truly discredited for buying into Costello's scam and losing one of their top operatives into the bargain, the plan can actually be put into operation with no fear that anyone will believe anything the other side says about it until it's too late.'

She turned her attention back to Costello. 'You could even take the moral high ground, persuade yourself that what you were doing was for the greater good, reducing the world population. Of course a vaccine would have, perhaps already has been, prepared in advance ready to be made available to the more privileged parts of the globe. Even so, some Western casualties will have been factored in. Unimportant people like Joe and Phil. Collateral damage. The trouble is, now we all know what the plan really is and if I so much as hint at it in my doco, it can never be brought back to life. Your game is over, Costello, and you can thank one of the men you killed, my Joe, Joe Kendry.'

Don Costello's face was rigid. There was a moment of vicious, hate-filled silence. Wenna shifted slightly in her seat, concerned that he might actually attack Fleur, who was eyeballing him as if daring him to make a move. Costello got slowly to his feet. He wrenched his eyes from Fleur and turned his furious gaze on Charles.

'It's pure fiction, not a word of truth in it,' he said thickly, aiming a stiff finger at her. 'But let's be charitable, let's say she's lost her man and lost her mind... She needs a shrink.'

Fleur shot out of her chair, fists balled, clearly intent on doing physical damage to the big man opposite her. Wenna was only a second slower, grabbing Fleur with both hands, trapping her arms and crushing her onto her chest.

'Glad she's yours, Charles,' Costello said harshly. 'Wouldn't want a dangerous traitor like that in our camp.' He turned and walked out in stiff-legged fury, slamming the door behind him.

When he had gone Wenna slowly released Fleur who was shaking from the confrontation and led her back to her chair.

'You've made a bad enemy there,' Charles said.

'No. He's the one that's made a bad enemy. He may not have planted the bomb, but he's responsible for Joe's death and I intend to finish him.'

***

Too angry to wait for the lift, Costello stormed down the stairs of the apartment block and out onto the street in a blind rage. For once in his life he had no idea what his next move would be but whatever it was, it was going to impact heavily on Fleur Nichols. What a pity the Brits had to be involved. If this had been contained in the US he'd have long since dealt with Nichols once and for all. He was not a man who took kindly to losing.

He rounded the corner of the block and strode up to where his chauffeur/bodyguard was waiting in the car with the darkened windows. He wrenched open the passenger door and was half in the car before he realised something was wrong. His driver had not moved, he was leaning back against his seat and his head lolled at an unlikely angle. It took a couple of seconds for Costello to register the neat hole in his neck and the trickle of blood that was staining his shirt collar. Despite his age his reaction was remarkably quick but his knees were bent and he was already half in the car, which cost him vital seconds.

On a distant corner a clean-shaven and smartly dressed young man with a briefcase had stopped to consult his Ctab. Mohammed Asami pressed a single digit as his target tried to escape the vehicle. The explosion blew the car apart, taking out the front of a ground floor apartment, shattering nearby windows, killing Costello and fatally wounding an elderly man passing by. Asami watched it happen but felt nothing for the old man, nothing but elation at the success of his mission.

He was several blocks away, walking at a steady, innocent pace when the first police car passed him.

***

In Fleur's apartment the blast hit like an earthquake, shaking the building and threatening to blow the windows out. Charles reacted quickest, bypassing the usual emergency number and calling the crisis number at Scotland Yard's Anti-Terrorist Squad.

Fleur was sitting on the edge of her seat, eyes wide and mouth slightly open, a stunned look on her face. Charles called Don Costello's number but there was an unobtainable signal. He pocketed his Ctab and looked hard at Wenna. 'Have you been with Fleur every minute?' he asked.

'Yes, of course,' Wenna said, seeing which way Charles's thinking was going and not liking it. If the blast was aimed at Costello there would obviously be questions for Fleur to answer but this was hardly the moment, Fleur looked shocked out of her mind.

'Stay with her,' Charles ordered as he headed for the door. 'Don't let her out of your sight.'

Left alone with Fleur, who seemed to have been struck dumb, Wenna could think of nothing better to do than to make tea for them both. What a very English reaction to what was certainly going to be a disaster, she found herself thinking. When she returned with a cup in each hand it did not look as if Fleur had moved but she looked up as Wenna placed the cups on the coffee table.

'It was him, wasn't it?' she asked.

'It seems likely,' Wenna agreed.

'I'm not sorry,' Fleur said quietly, 'I'm not sorry at all.'

97

Simone looked slowly around the crowded concourse at Heathrow, not at all displeased by the crush of people. No one wants to die alone. She did not, and never had, feared death itself, only the manner of her going and now she had resolved that problem. She was in pain but it was dull and distant and she was feeling oddly pleased with herself as she made her slow way to the International Departure lounge. She had no ticket and no luggage and had no need of either.

Most people simply exist, and then pass on leaving no trace of their being. Not her, she had made her mark on the world, people would know of her work and what she had achieved after she had gone.

The constant cacophony of loud conversation in many different tongues and the chatter of information announcements was unceasing and it jarred her nerves. When she could stand it no longer she made her uncertain way to the female toilets, passing two patrolling police officers armed to the teeth and wearing bulletproof jackets. They glanced at her, assessed her as nil risk, and moved on.

Secure in a cubicle Simone took the syringe case from her jacket pocket. She had no second thoughts, indeed no thoughts at all as she removed the syringe and bared her arm. The vein came up at last and she made the injection with a hand shaking from incapacity, not fear.

When she left the cubicle she abandoned the syringe in a sharps bin. Out in the concourse a flight to Hong Kong was being called. Simone made no calculation as to how long she had as she mingled with the travellers but she was sure it would be long enough.

98

By the time Charles returned to Fleur's apartment the bombing had been on breaking news. Charles had brought Alex with him. He no longer sees me as a completely independent witness, Wenna thought. Or was she getting paranoid over this whole mess? Fleur had composed herself and this time greeted the two men in a more polite fashion.

'I have some difficult questions to put to you,' Charles began.

'I know,' Fleur replied. 'Such as did I set Costello up and incidentally cause the deaths of two other innocent people.'

'And did you?' Charles asked quietly. 'Wenna tells me that when you called on Alma Rogers you went in alone.'

'I thought about it,' Fleur admitted. 'But perhaps, unlike Costello and al-Rashidi, I lack the killer instinct.'

'How can we be sure of that?' Charles asked.

'You can't. And it wasn't Wenna's fault, I ordered her to stay in the car.'

Charles raised his eyebrows at that. 'We have to wonder then how the enemy located him. His movements are known to precious few people and of course you were one of them.'

'You of all people shouldn't underestimate AQE, Charles. You think they don't have their own kill list? You think they didn't want to revenge their man's death? You think they aren't capable of locating Costello the same way he traced al-Rashidi? They would have known he was here with the President and he was the star of the video. I'd have a small bet they've had a watch on your office and the US embassy and that somewhere in the block opposite this flat there's an apartment that's empty right now, don't you think?'

Charles looked at her thoughtfully. 'You knew that was a possibility before you insisted on having Costello and me meet with you here.'

'Yes.'

'Then you knew you were deliberately putting his life at risk, and others.'

Fleur flushed in annoyance. 'I can't be responsible for the actions of every madman in the world,' she retorted, 'and I wanted him on my territory when I brought him down to earth.'

'If Alma or you made a call from her house it will be possible to trace it,' Charles pointed out.

Fleur shrugged. 'If you think that has any value go ahead. Afterwards I'll accept your apology. So far as I'm concerned, Al-Rashidi and Costello were casualties of war, they had a quick death without the indignity of being collateral and that's more than either of them deserve.'

'There will be a thorough police investigation of course and you can be sure Scotland Yard will not be as easy to convince as I might be,' Charles said pointedly.

'If I'm ever arrested it would be great publicity and it might give my life some meaning. Now, if there's nothing else, I have a film to prep.'

***

She didn't set to work on her film of course; she went to her bedroom as soon as Charles and Alex had left. At first she cried silently, then she broke into loud weeping and finally wracking, anguished sobs that shook her entire body and left her emotionally exhausted. It was two hours before she reappeared.

It had given Wenna time to prepare what she wanted to say. She gave Fleur a hug and led her to her chair, kneeling in front of her to talk to her at face level.

'I don't believe you made that call, Fleur, and I don't want you to give up,' she said. 'I know you don't want to hear this but there is life after Joe. I'm sure he'd want you to make the film but I'm also sure he'd want you to hold him in your heart and move on.'

'I won't give up but there'll never be anyone else,' Fleur said dully.

'Perhaps not but there can be a worthwhile life. I know you want to sell this apartment, so do that. Come and stay with me until you find another place.' There, it was said. Wenna held her breath.

Fleur shook her head in incomprehension. 'Why would you do that? What's in it for you?' she asked.

'There doesn't have to be anything. Friendship, if you like.'

'That may not go down well with your bosses.'

'The work you do and I do are two sides of the same coin. Besides, it's not their affair. I want to see you your old self again and back at work putting the world right.'

'Ah, if only I could. What have we achieved? At least six people dead and we'll probably never know the truth.'

'But your scenario made sense. And you seemed so certain.'

'Yes, but would Costello really have gone through with it and released a lethal virus on the world? Was he really that insane? Or was he simply going to threaten AQE into submission? I don't know. And now he's dead we'll never know.'

'Perhaps not but look at the positives. Either way there'll be no genocide. You did that, Fleur, no one else,' Wenna said.

Fleur smiled wanly at her. 'Dear Wenna,' she said, 'thank goodness for you.'

99

Simone had reserved a small amount of the virus she had injected herself with and emptied it onto her hands before disposing of the syringe. It was a thing of her own creation, hers to do with as she willed. She rubbed her hands together and sniffed the innocent-seeming liquid. It didn't have a name and was known simply by the batch number she had given it: AF/G5.

Out in the concourse she mingled unsteadily with the milling crowds of travellers from all over the world, frequently touching handrails and drifting fingers across stationary luggage. In the densest parts of the throng she took in breaths as deep as she could and breathed out, moving her head from side to side, spreading a lethal contagion.

She lasted almost twenty minutes before a final mental and physical paralysis overtook her and she slumped to the ground. As her world shrank to the area of concerned strangers around her, her last thoughts were of a job well done.

A compassionate young Indian girl knelt beside her and cradled her head in her arms.

Simone Gofre died at peace, convinced she had saved humanity from itself.

****

The Ladies' Game

The second book in the *Evolution's Path* series

They all want feisty British journalist Fleur Nichols dead.

The CIA think she is a Jihadist sympathiser.

The Jihadists think she is a CIA informant.

She is on the hit list of a renegade professional assassin.

If that wasn't enough her partner has been killed by a suicide bomber in Pakistan and the whistleblowing documentary they were working on has been suppressed by the government.

Now it seems that Wenna Cavendish, deputy head of MI5 and once her friend has turned against her.

But the biggest threat of all is the deadly virus that has been let loose on the world, leading to the closure of international borders and the imposition of martial law.

As the death toll rises and the killers close in, Fleur discovers she is pregnant.

The seemingly impossible fight is on to protect herself and her unborn child from her adversaries and to preserve the kind of democratic society she has always fought for.

A gripping, fast-moving thriller set in an ominously believable near future.

The third book in this series:

Procreation

Whoever controls these men controls the future of the world.

After the virus, men are rare.

Fertile males are even rarer.

They have to be protected and milked of their semen if humankind is to survive.

In this female-dominated world all but a handful of the viable males are in England.

With the threat of functional extinction looming, where women have ascended to political supremacy, England's possession of these valuable males is increasingly in jeopardy as resentment stirs up the rivalry of old enemies America and Russia.

They both have the military might to simply take what they want. All that stops them is a nerve-jangling nuclear stand-off.

England's weak defences start to buckle, society fragments and its leaders begin to lose control.

In this dangerously fractured world can Fleur Nichols, thrust into an unwanted leadership role, put aside the agony of her son's abduction and save her country from annexation as the major powers jostle for dominance?

Or has everything gone beyond the point of no return?

A mother's love is a ferocious weapon but the odds are stacked heavily against her.

Get these exciting techno-thrillers to discover what the future may hold for mankind.

Other books by Peter Hill

The Staunton and Wyndsor Series

The Hunters
The Liars
The Enthusiast
The Savages

The Commander Allan Dice Books

The Fanatics
The Washermen

These are all British Detective police thrillers published worldwide by major publishing houses in both hard and paperback versions and now available as eBooks and new independently published paperbacks

These are all stand-alone stories, set in different locations in Britain, but with the same major protagonists.

Writing as **John Eyers** and based on famous British TV series

Survivors: Genesis of a Hero

Amongst the first of the post-apocalyptic novels, written in the 1970s, and just as relevant today.

And

Special Branch: In at the Kill

Featuring Detective Chief Inspector Alan Craven and Detective Inspector Tom Haggerty.

Find out more about all these books by visiting Peter's website.

peterjohneyershill.com

PRESS COMMENT ON PETER HILL'S PREVIOUS BOOKS

The New York Times
'This is a taut, handsome job, beautifully written, full of real characters and acute observations.'

The Times
'Bizarre murder and a full, meaty, thoroughly absorbing account of the investigation.'

The Bookseller
'…an acute professionalism. What is even better, it has the holding qualities of a rock-loving limpet.'

Publisher's Weekly (US)
'Peter Hill does a fine job with character, plot, atmosphere and suspense.'

Columbus Sunday Dispatch
'Exceptionally well told, with satisfying outcome.'

The Daily Telegraph
'A really good thriller writer. Very clever at the way he measures out clues… Written in staccato sentences, each a drum tap tautening the tension.'

Essex Chronicle
'A really first-class who-dunnit'

Pittsburgh Press
'…two of Scotland Yard's finest in this entertaining mystery with an extra twist or two… or three.'

London Evening News

'To follow… the brilliantly inspired tracking of Hill's two detectives is a joy, apart from the brain-teasing pleasure of accepting the author's challenge to identify the murderer.'

Coventry Evening Telegraph

'Peter Hill has done it again—a fast-moving, action-packed thriller involving the secret service, the police, and underworld criminals.'

Author's Note

If you have enjoyed *Killing Tomorrow* I'd love it if you would be kind enough to spend a few moments posting a review on the site where you bought it. Independent authors rely very much on word of mouth to bring their books to the attention of readers and reviews are an excellent way to do this.

Thank you.

Peter.

Printed in Great Britain
by Amazon

37274870R00165